BIRTHRIGHT

VOLUME NINE
WAR OF THE WORLDS

SKYBOUND

Robert Kirkman *Chairman*
David Alpert *CEO*
Sean Mackiewicz *SVP, Editor-in-Chief*
Shawn Kirkham *SVP, Business Development*
Brian Huntington *VP, Online Content*
Shauna Wynne *Publicity Director*
Andres Juarez *Art Director*
Alex Antone *Senior Editor*
Jon Moisan *Editor*
Arielle Basich *Associate Editor*
Carina Taylor *Graphic Designer*
Paul Shin *Business Development Manager*
Johnny O'Dell *Social Media Manager*
Dan Petersen *Sr. Director of Operations & Events*

International inquiries: *ag@sequentialrights.com*
Licensing inquiries: *contact@skybound.com*
SKYBOUND.COM

IMAGE COMICS, INC.
Robert Kirkman *Chief Operating Officer*
Erik Larsen *Chief Financial Officer*
Todd McFarlane *President*
Marc Silvestri *Chief Executive Officer*
Jim Valentino *Vice President*

Eric Stephenson *Publisher*
Jeff Boison *Director of Sales &Publishing Planning*
Jeff Stang *Director of Direct Market Sales*
Kat Salazar *Director of PR & Marketing*
Drew Gill *Cover Editor*
Heather Doornink *Production Director*
Nicole Lapalme *Controller*
www.imagecomics.com

BIRTHRIGHT VOLUME 9: WAR OF THE WORLDS. ISBN: 978-1-5343-1601-0. First Printing. Published by Image Comics, Inc. Office of publication: 2701 NW Vaughn St., Ste. 780, Portland, OR 97210. Copyright © 2020 Skybound, LLC. All rights reserved. Originally published in single magazine format as BIRTHRIGHT #41-45. BIRTHRIGHT™ (including all prominent characters featured herein), its logo and all character likenesses are trademarks of Skybound, LLC, unless otherwise noted. Image Comics® and its logos are registered trademarks and copyrights of Image Comics, Inc. All rights reserved. No part of this publication may be reproduced or transmitted in any form or by any means (except for short excerpts for review purposes) without the express written permission of Image Comics, Inc. All names, characters, events and locales in this publication are entirely fictional. Any resemblance to actual persons (living or dead), events or places, without satiric intent, is coincidental. Printed in the U.S.A.

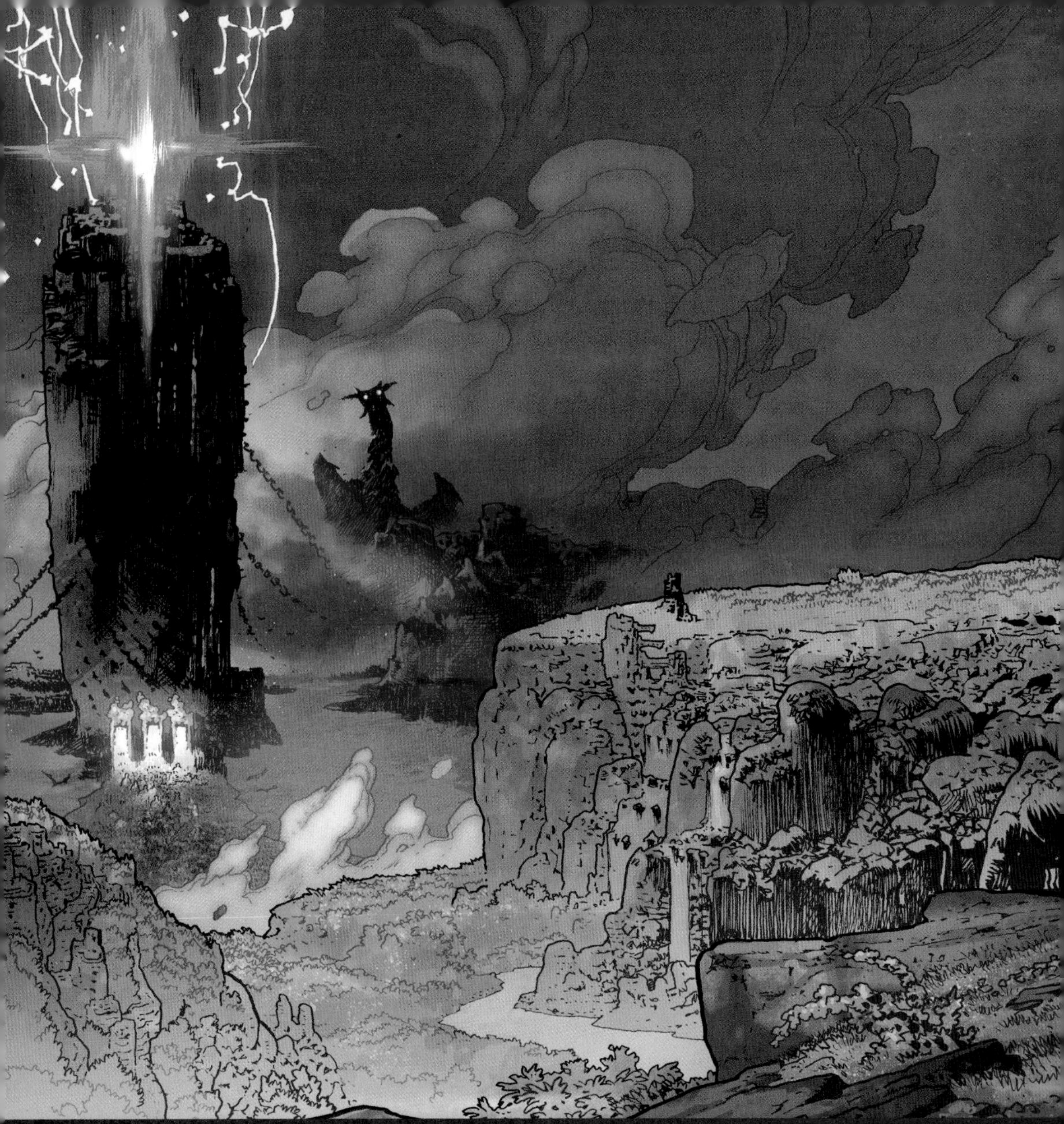

Joshua Williamson
creator, writer

Andrei Bressan
creator, artist

Adriano Lucas
colorist

Pat Brosseau
letterer

Sean Mackiewicz
editor

cover by **Andrei Bressan** *and* **Adriano Lucas**

logo design by **Rian Hughes**

production design by **Robbie Biederman** *and production by* **Carina Taylor**

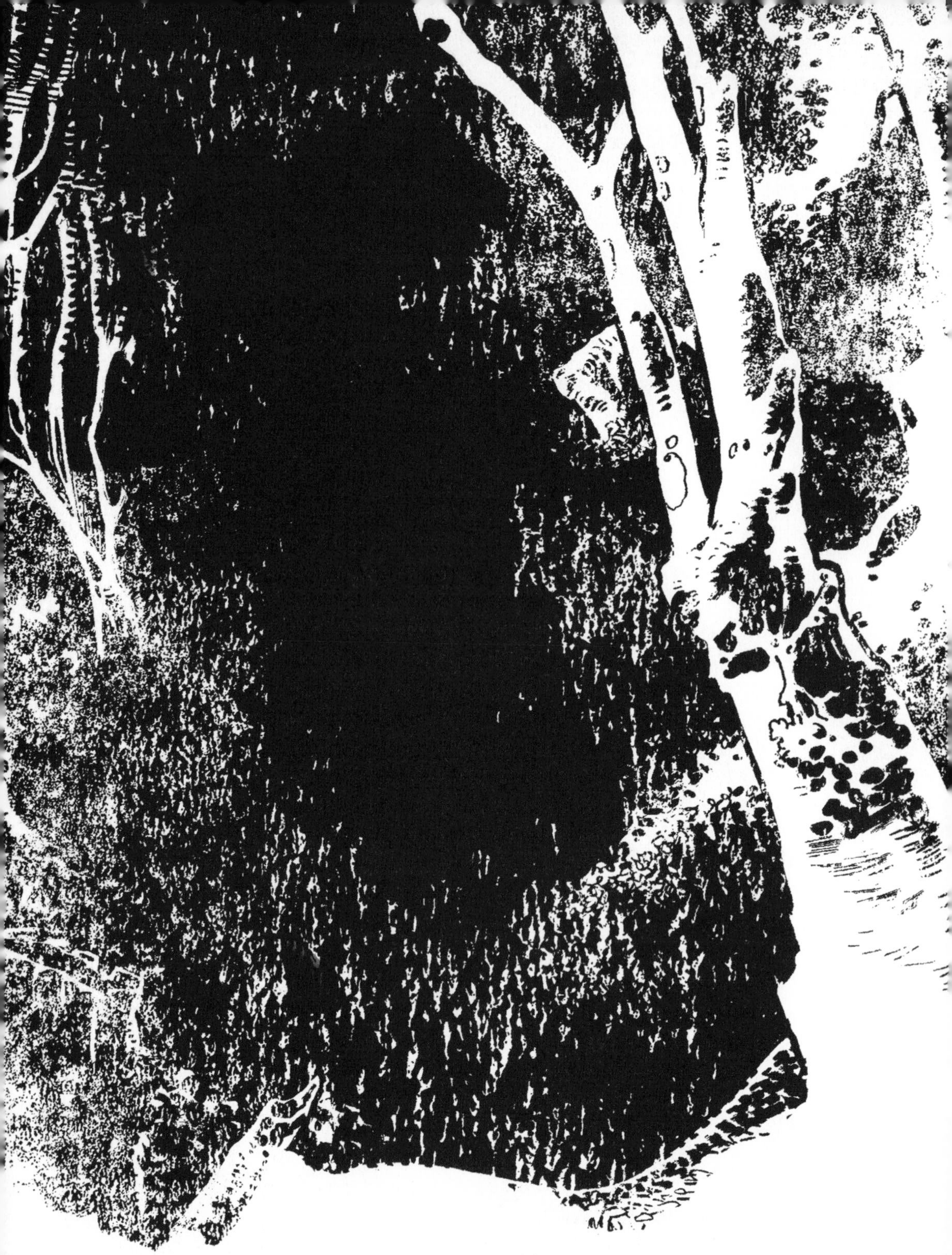

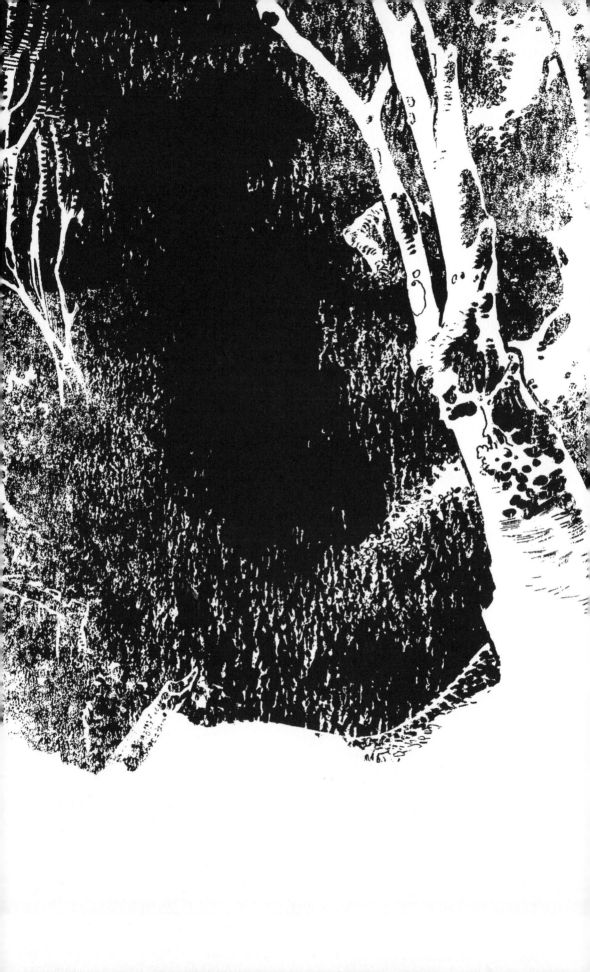

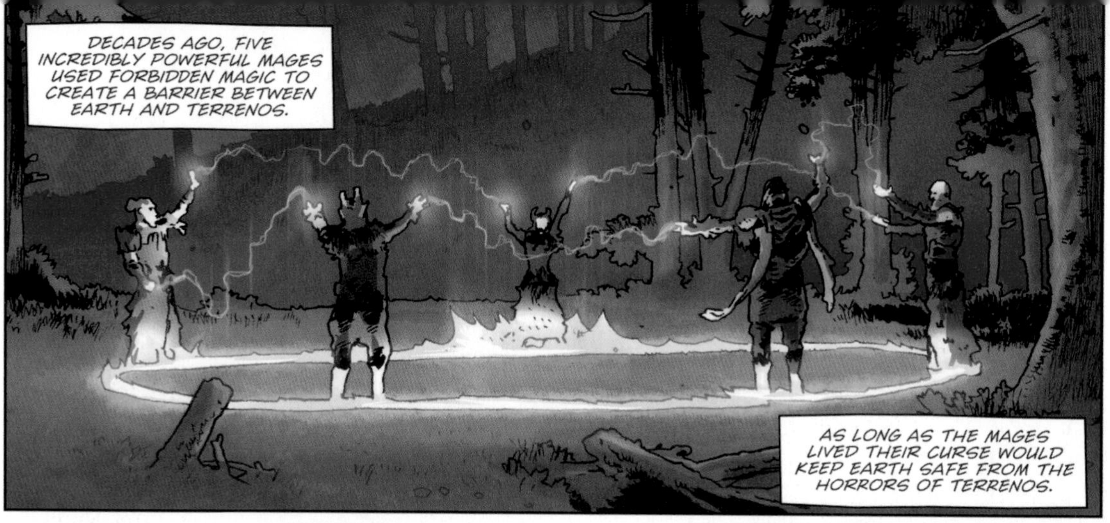
DECADES AGO, FIVE INCREDIBLY POWERFUL MAGES USED FORBIDDEN MAGIC TO CREATE A BARRIER BETWEEN EARTH AND TERRENOS.
AS LONG AS THE MAGES LIVED THEIR CURSE WOULD KEEP EARTH SAFE FROM THE HORRORS OF TERRENOS.

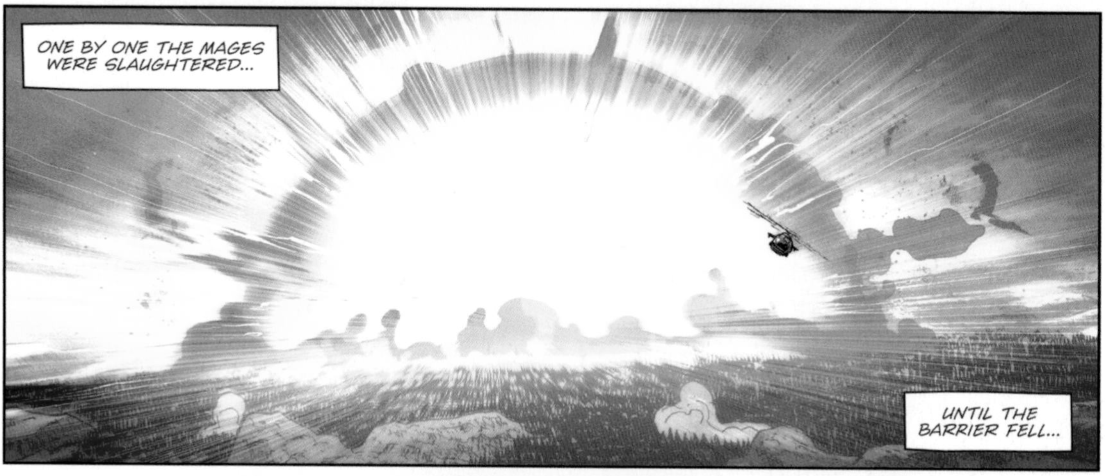
ONE BY ONE THE MAGES WERE SLAUGHTERED...
UNTIL THE BARRIER FELL...

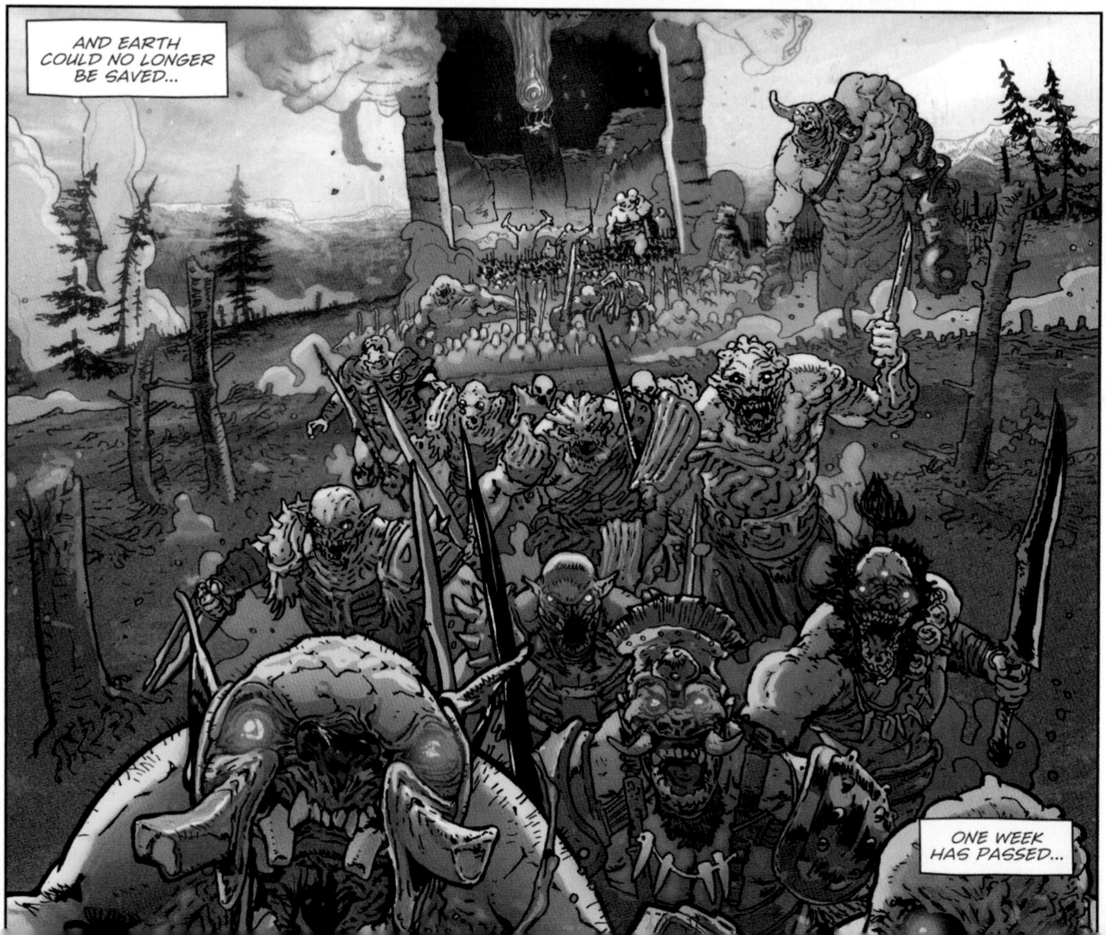
AND EARTH COULD NO LONGER BE SAVED...
ONE WEEK HAS PASSED...

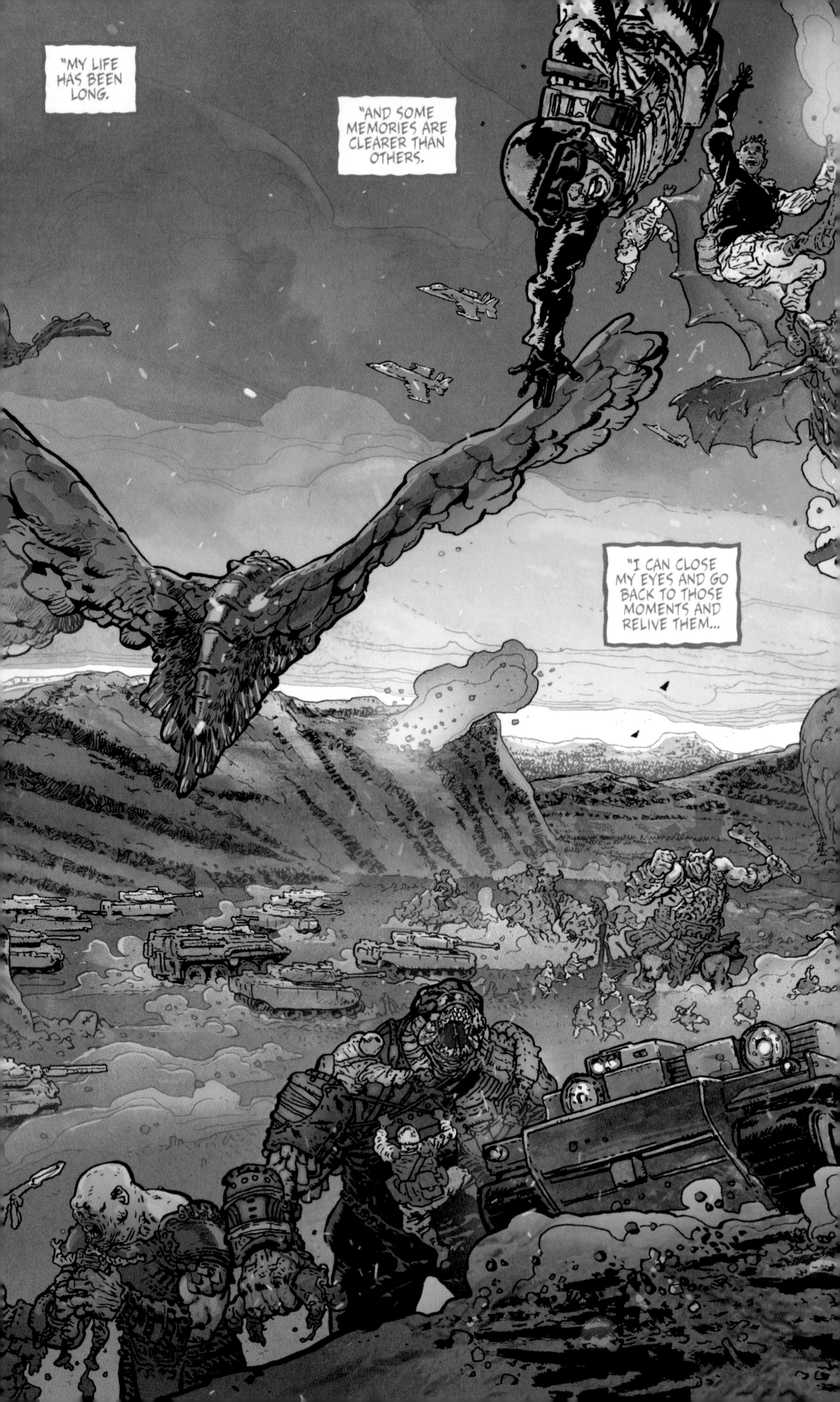
"MY LIFE HAS BEEN LONG.
"AND SOME MEMORIES ARE CLEARER THAN OTHERS.
"I CAN CLOSE MY EYES AND GO BACK TO THOSE MOMENTS AND RELIVE THEM...

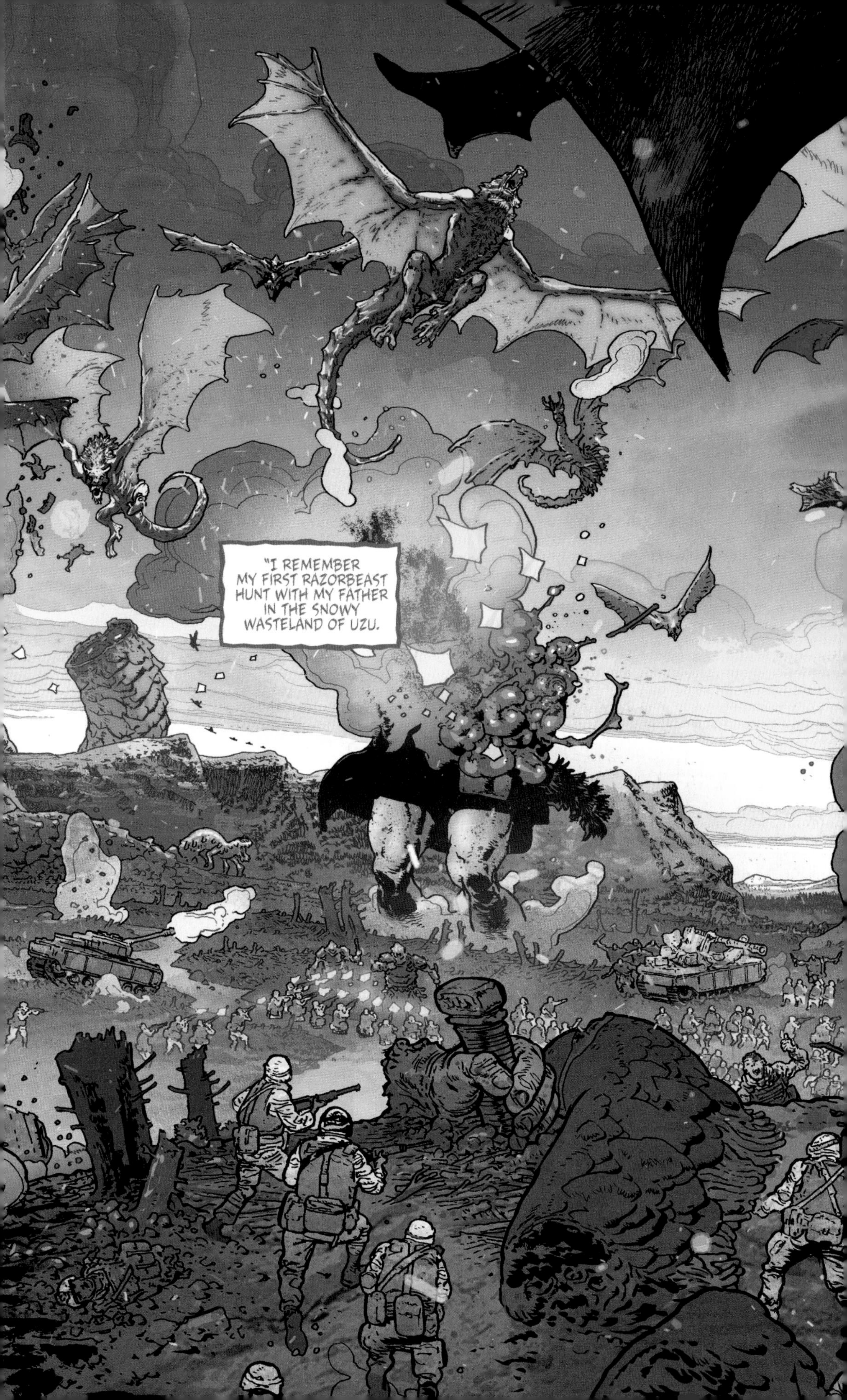
"I REMEMBER MY FIRST RAZORBEAST HUNT WITH MY FATHER IN THE SNOWY WASTELAND OF UZU.

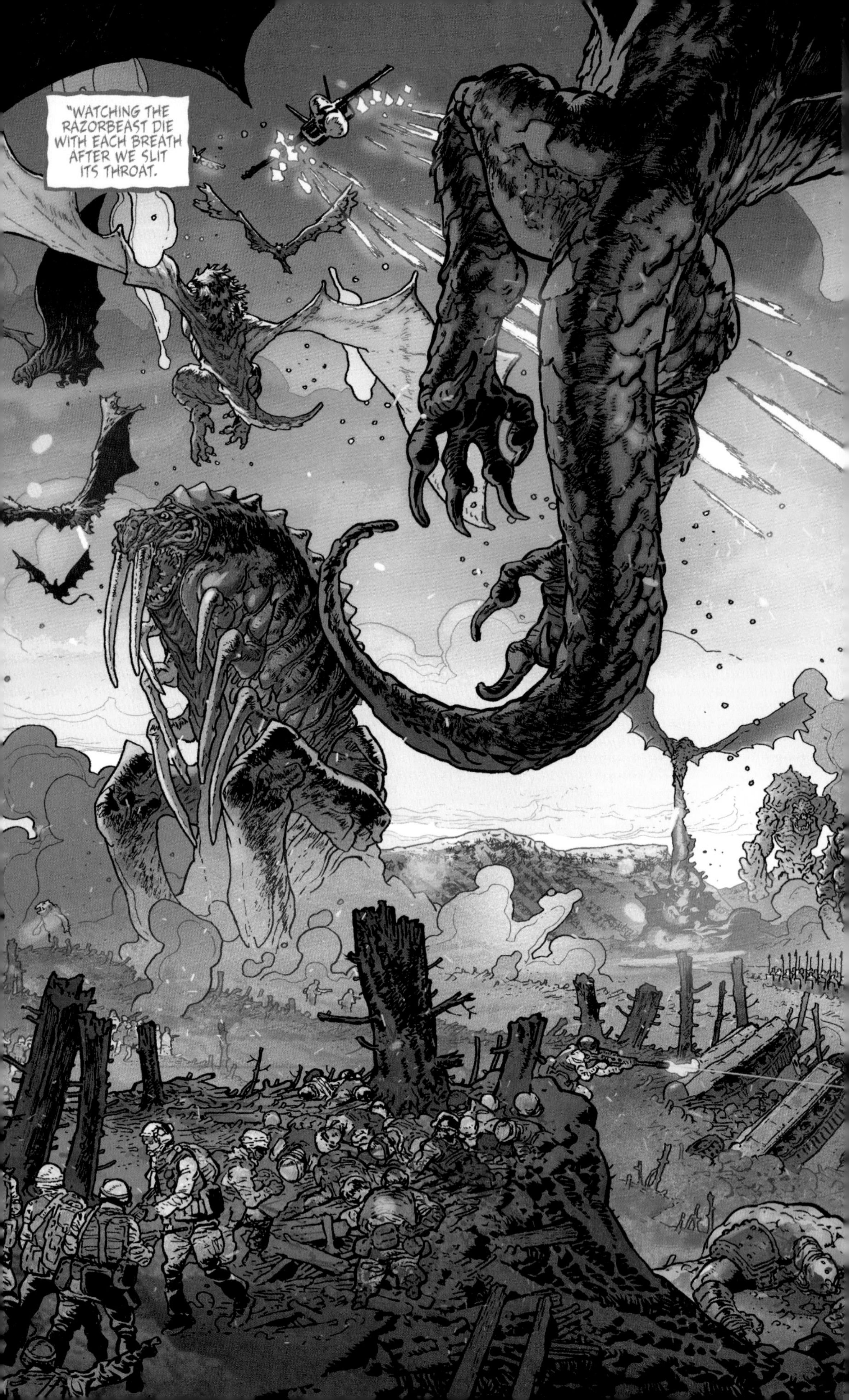
"WATCHING THE RAZORBEAST DIE WITH EACH BREATH AFTER WE SLIT ITS THROAT.

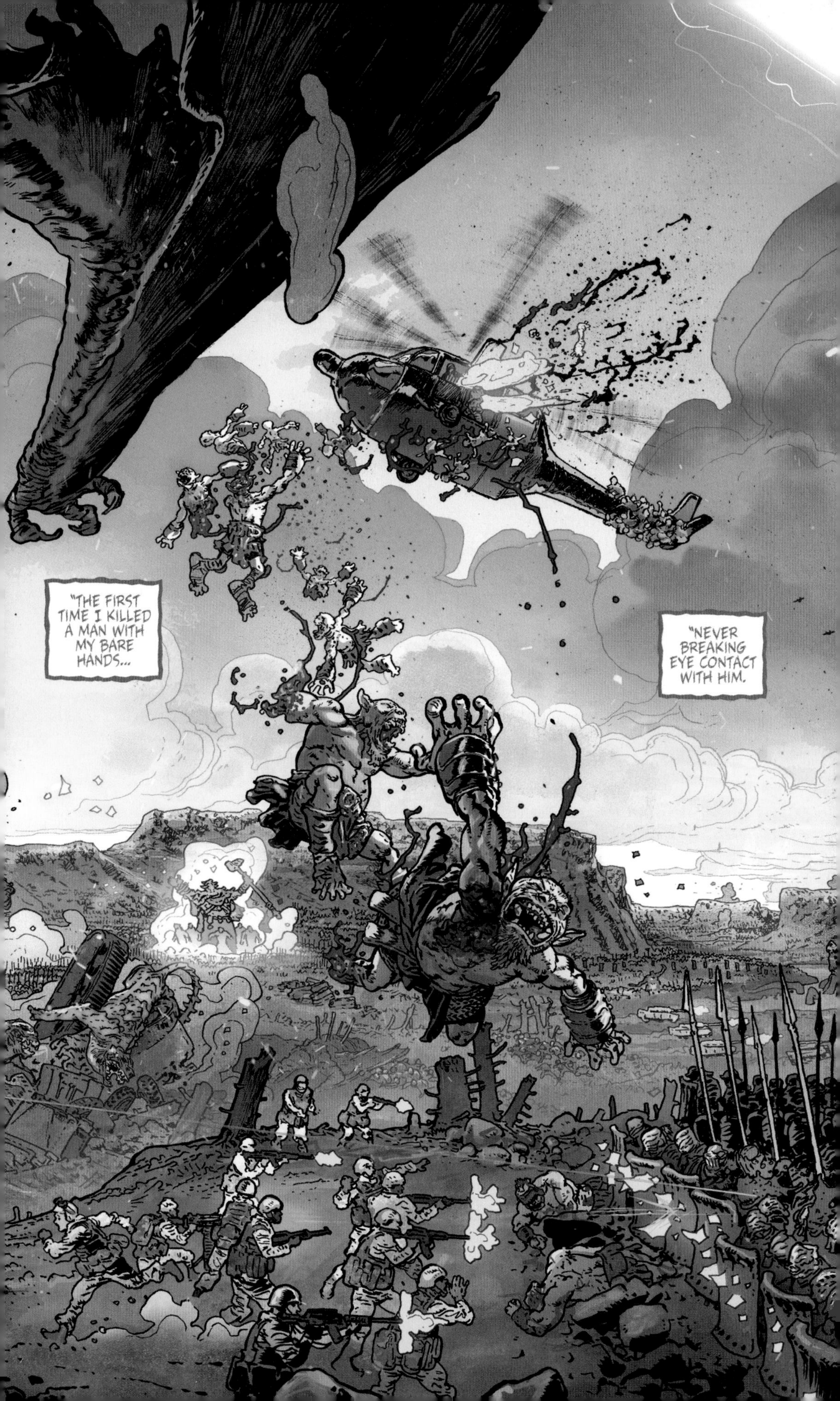
"THE FIRST TIME I KILLED A MAN WITH MY BARE HANDS...
"NEVER BREAKING EYE CONTACT WITH HIM.

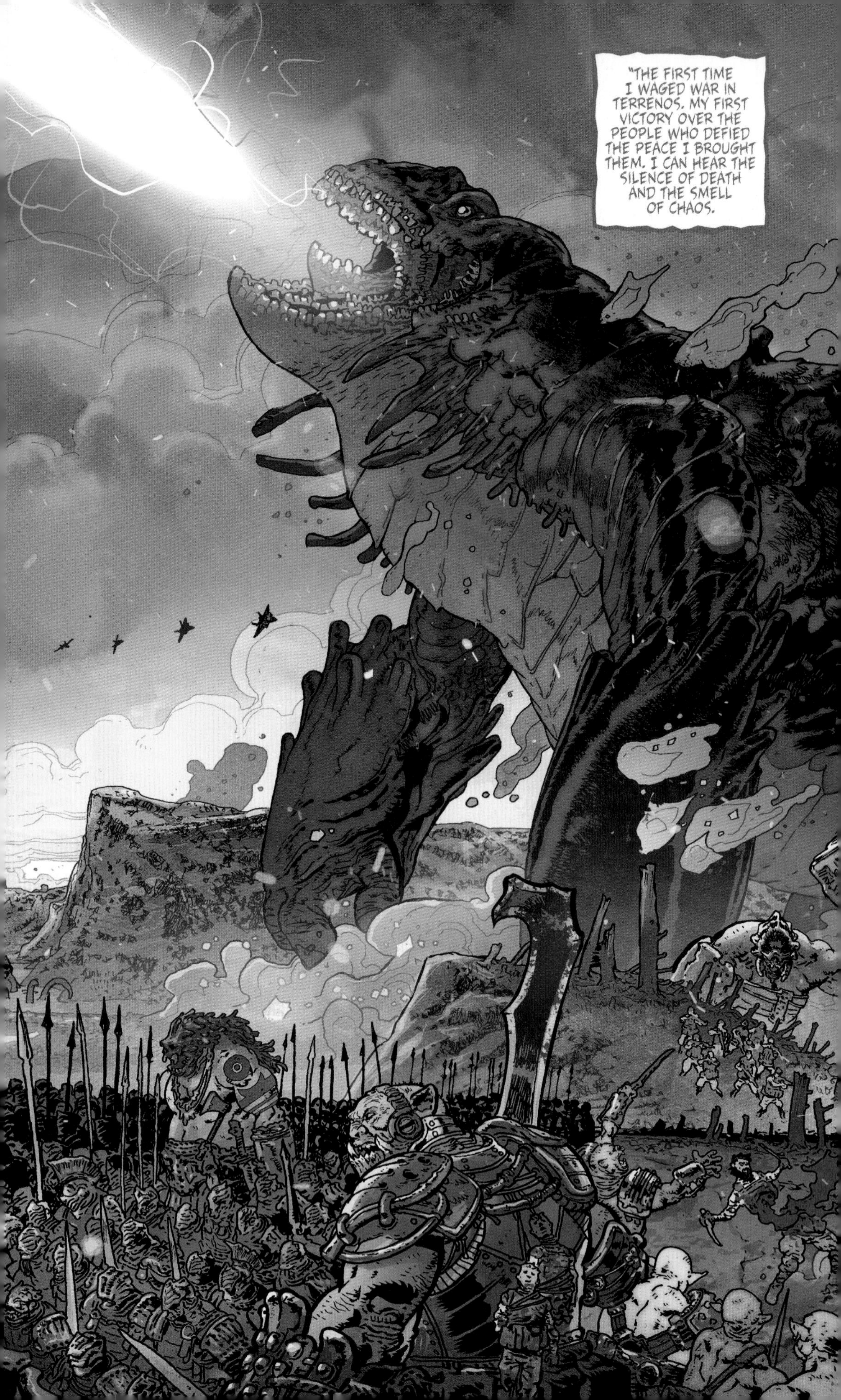
"THE FIRST TIME I WAGED WAR IN TERRENOS. MY FIRST VICTORY OVER THE PEOPLE WHO DEFIED THE PEACE I BROUGHT THEM. I CAN HEAR THE SILENCE OF DEATH AND THE SMELL OF CHAOS.

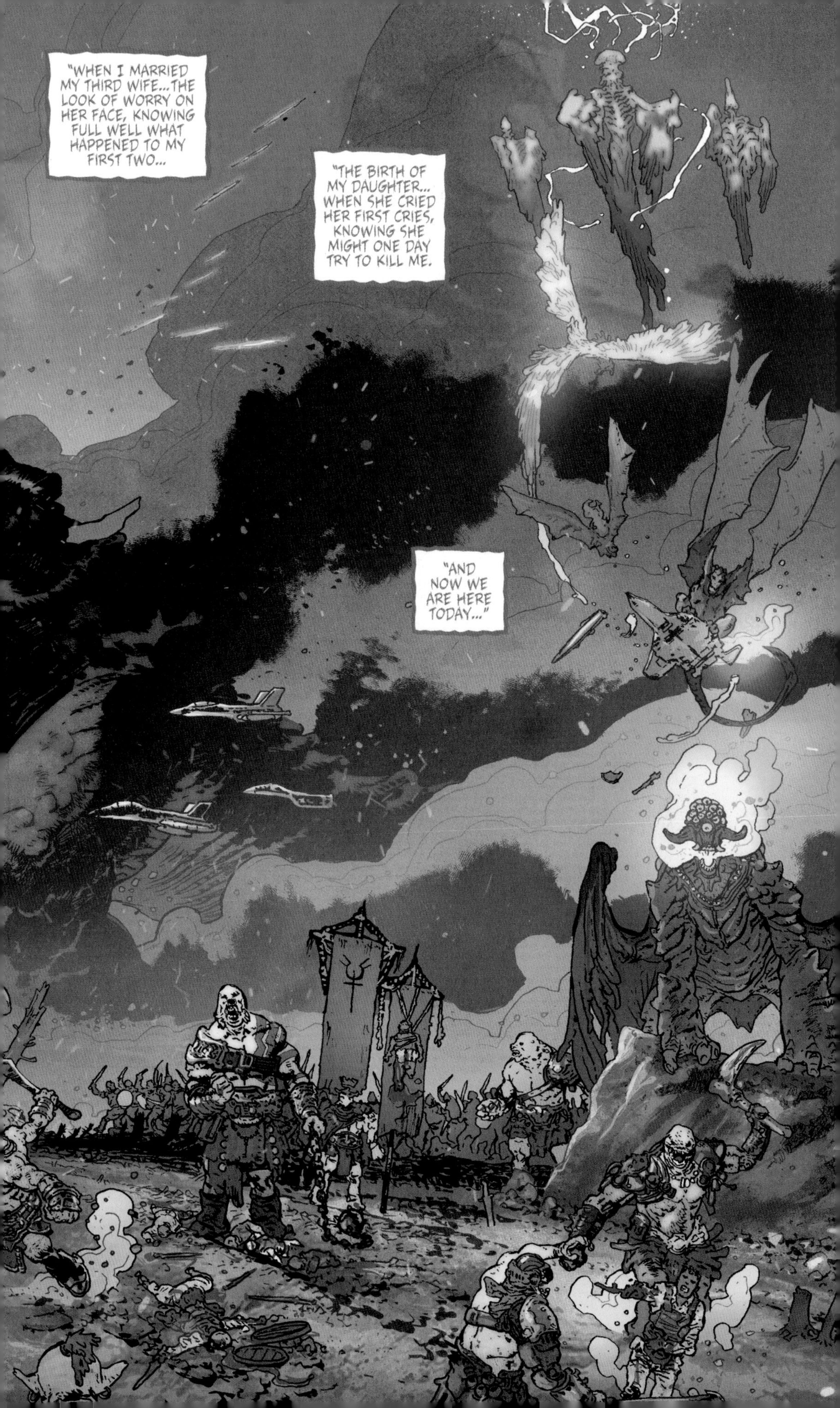
"WHEN I MARRIED MY THIRD WIFE...THE LOOK OF WORRY ON HER FACE, KNOWING FULL WELL WHAT HAPPENED TO MY FIRST TWO...
"THE BIRTH OF MY DAUGHTER... WHEN SHE CRIED HER FIRST CRIES, KNOWING SHE MIGHT ONE DAY TRY TO KILL ME.
"AND NOW WE ARE HERE TODAY..."

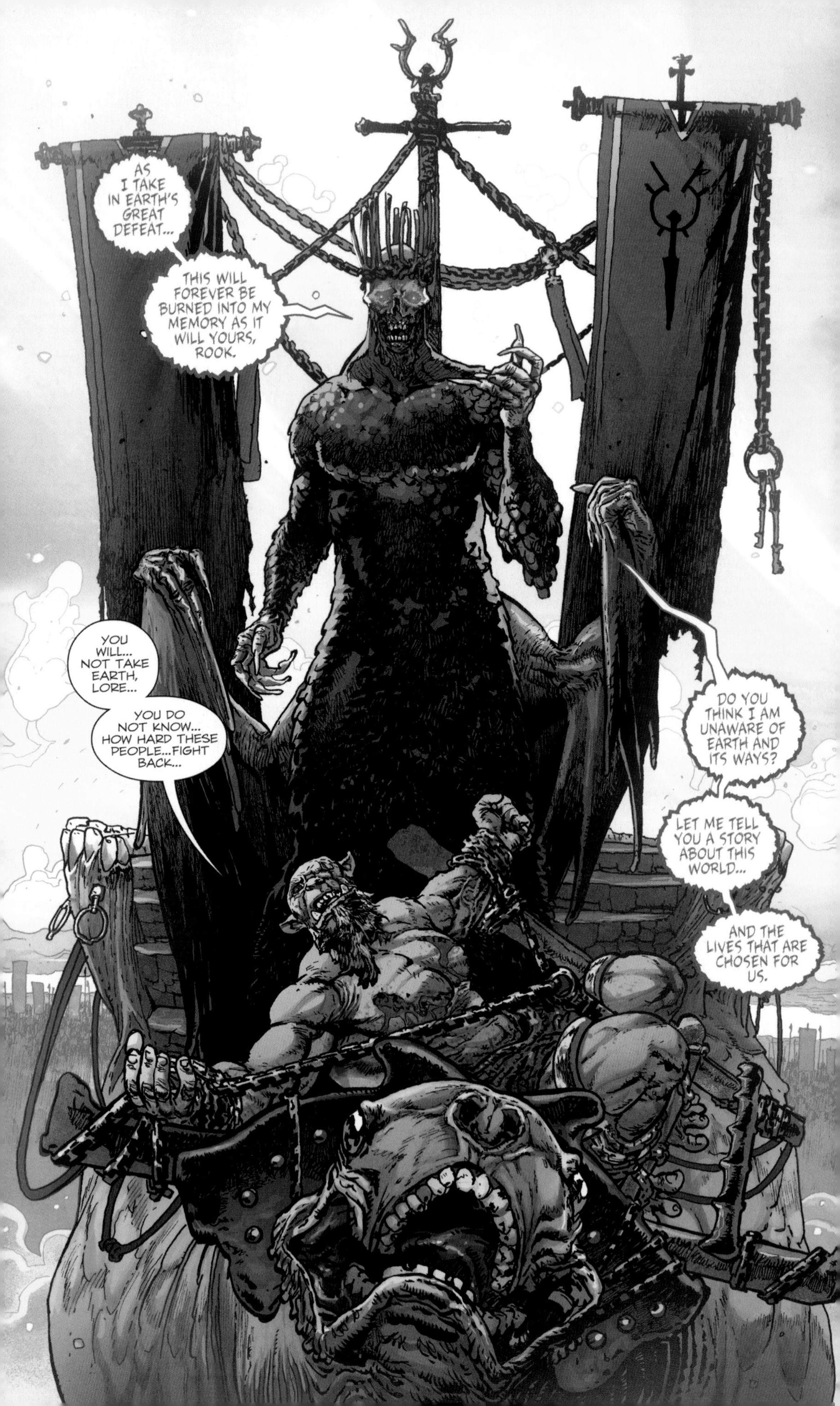
AS I TAKE IN EARTH'S GREAT DEFEAT...
THIS WILL FOREVER BE BURNED INTO MY MEMORY AS IT WILL YOURS, ROOK.
YOU WILL... NOT TAKE EARTH, LORE...
YOU DO NOT KNOW... HOW HARD THESE PEOPLE...FIGHT BACK...
DO YOU THINK I AM UNAWARE OF EARTH AND ITS WAYS?
LET ME TELL YOU A STORY ABOUT THIS WORLD...
AND THE LIVES THAT ARE CHOSEN FOR US.

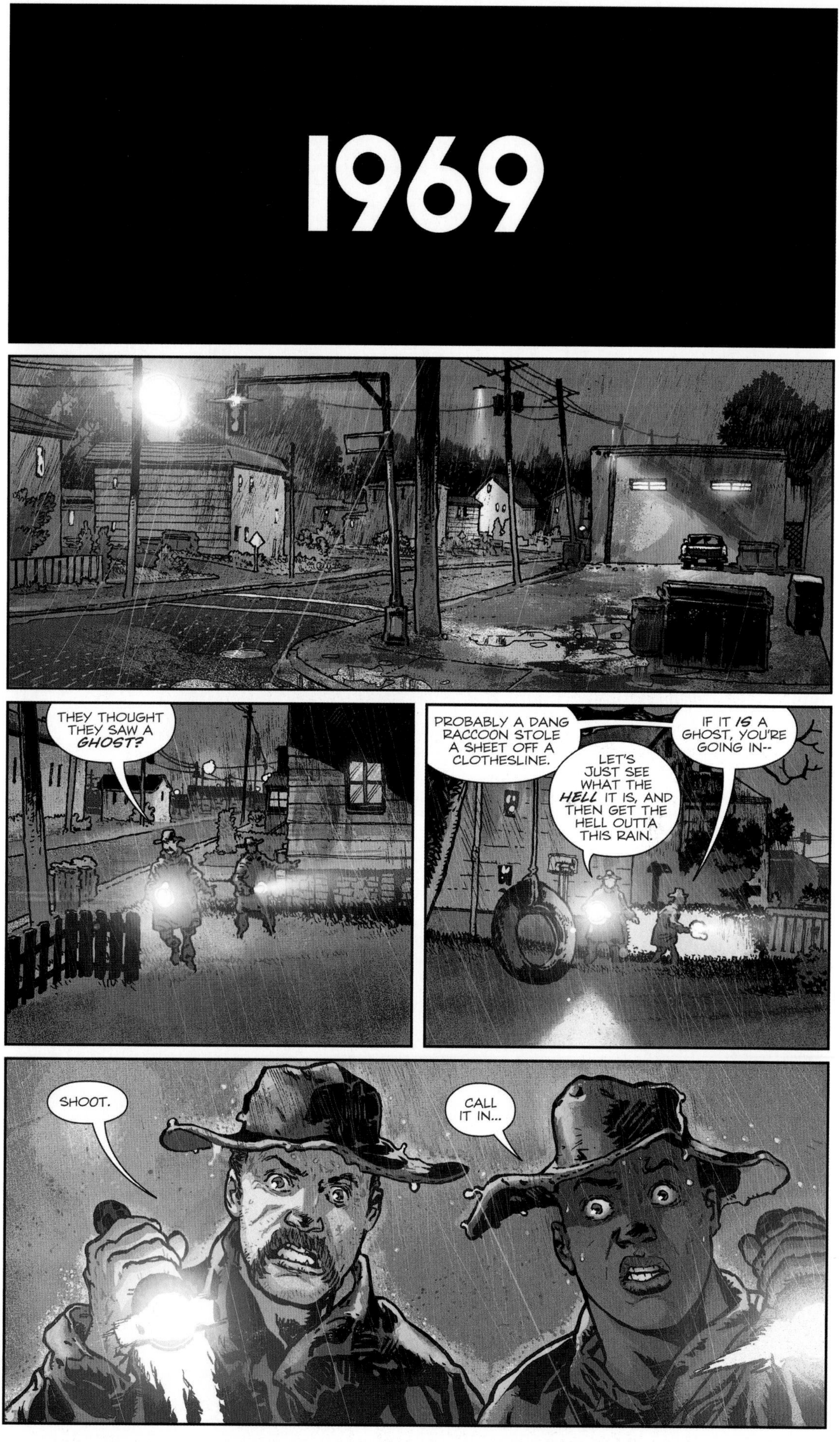
1969
THEY THOUGHT THEY SAW A *GHOST?*
PROBABLY A DANG RACCOON STOLE A SHEET OFF A CLOTHESLINE.
IF IT *IS* A GHOST, YOU'RE GOING IN--
LET'S JUST SEE WHAT THE *HELL* IT IS, AND THEN GET THE HELL OUTTA THIS RAIN.
SHOOT.
CALL IT IN...

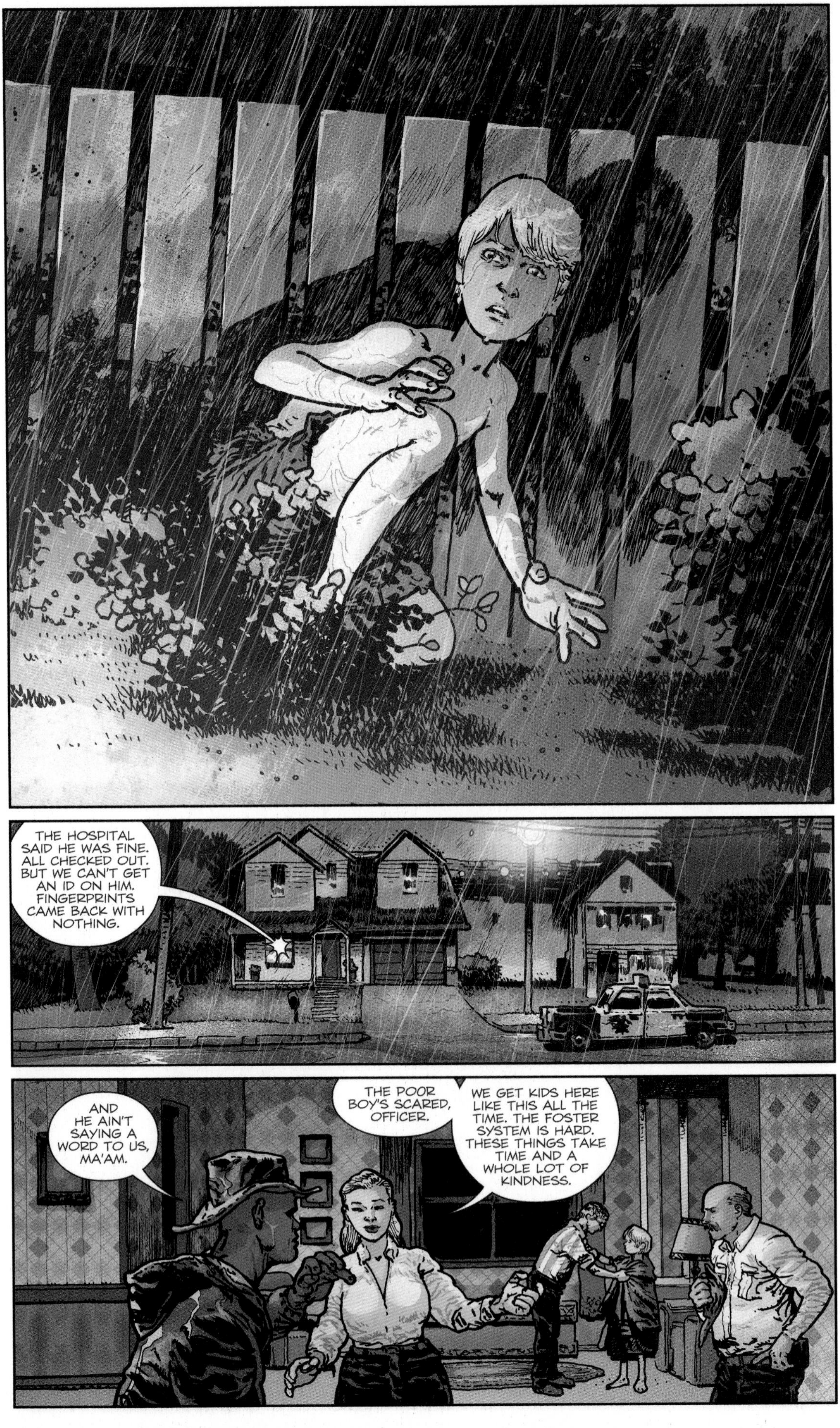
THE HOSPITAL SAID HE WAS FINE. ALL CHECKED OUT. BUT WE CAN'T GET AN ID ON HIM. FINGERPRINTS CAME BACK WITH NOTHING.
AND HE AIN'T SAYING A WORD TO US, MA'AM.
THE POOR BOY'S SCARED, OFFICER.
WE GET KIDS HERE LIKE THIS ALL THE TIME. THE FOSTER SYSTEM IS HARD. THESE THINGS TAKE TIME AND A WHOLE LOT OF KINDNESS.

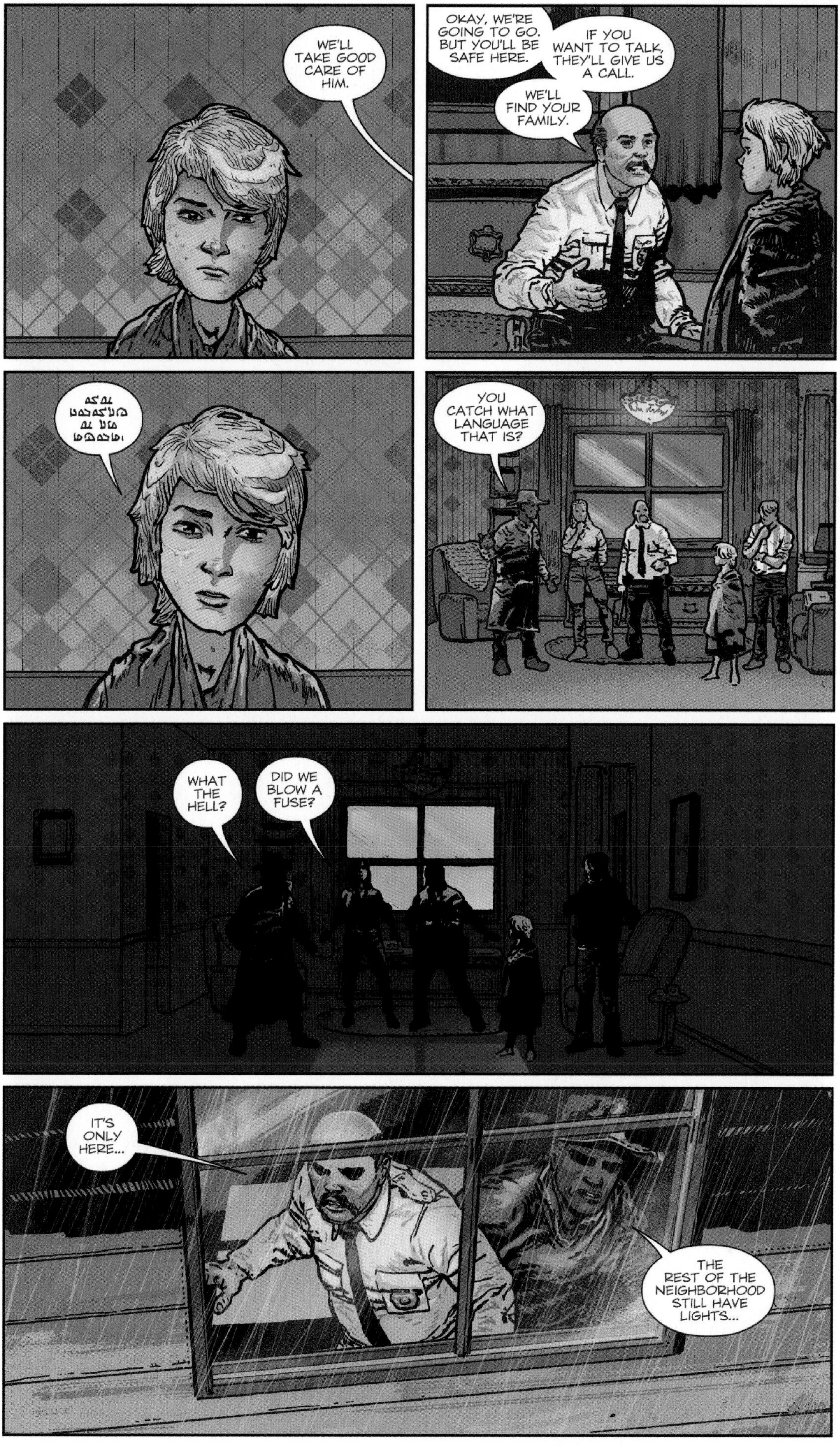

WE'LL TAKE GOOD CARE OF HIM.
OKAY, WE'RE GOING TO GO. BUT YOU'LL BE SAFE HERE.
IF YOU WANT TO TALK, THEY'LL GIVE US A CALL.
WE'LL FIND YOUR FAMILY.
YOU CATCH WHAT LANGUAGE THAT IS?
WHAT THE HELL?
DID WE BLOW A FUSE?
IT'S ONLY HERE...
THE REST OF THE NEIGHBORHOOD STILL HAVE LIGHTS...

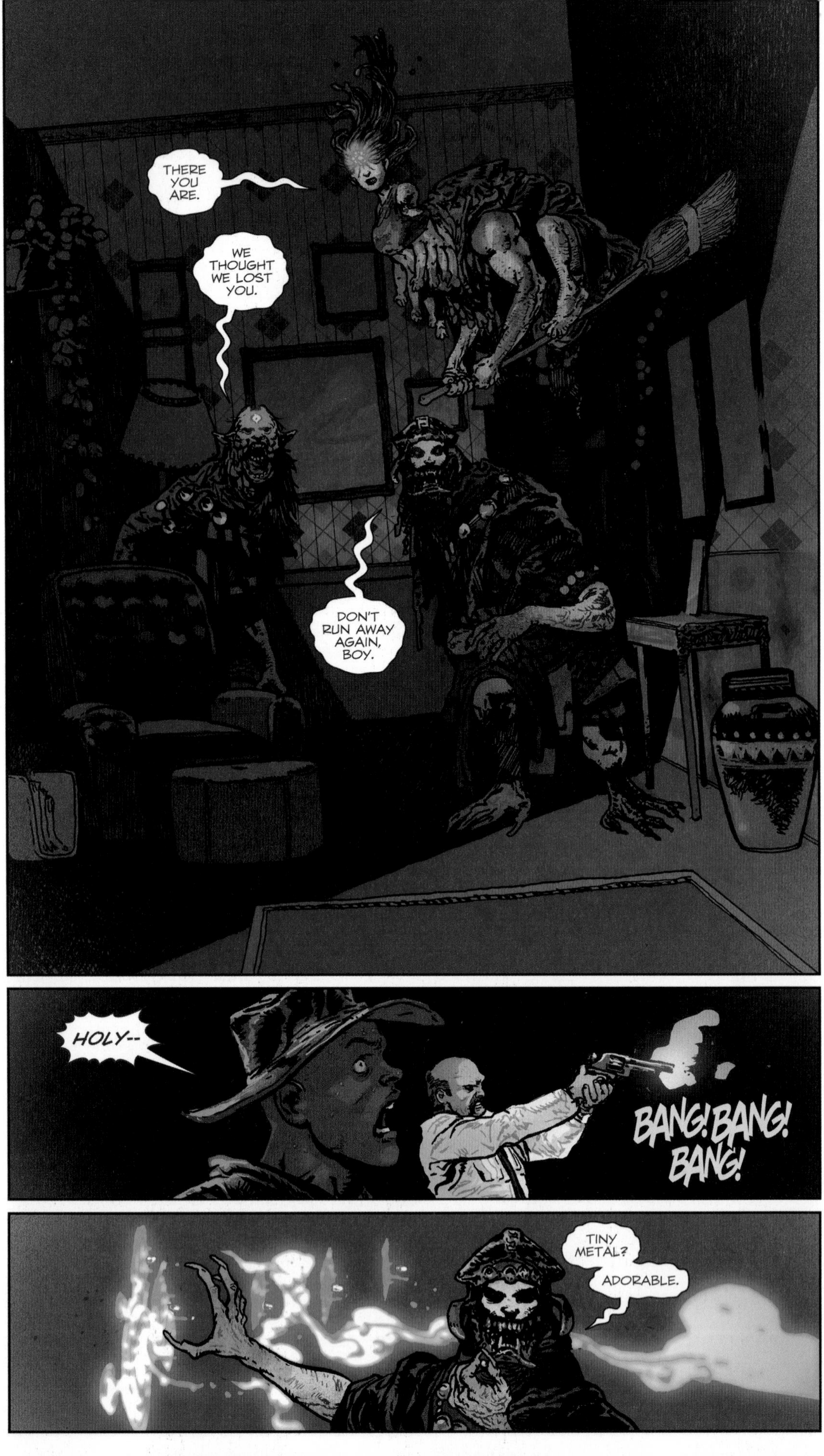

THERE YOU ARE.
WE THOUGHT WE LOST YOU.
DON'T RUN AWAY AGAIN, BOY.
HOLY--
BANG! BANG! BANG!
TINY METAL?
ADORABLE.

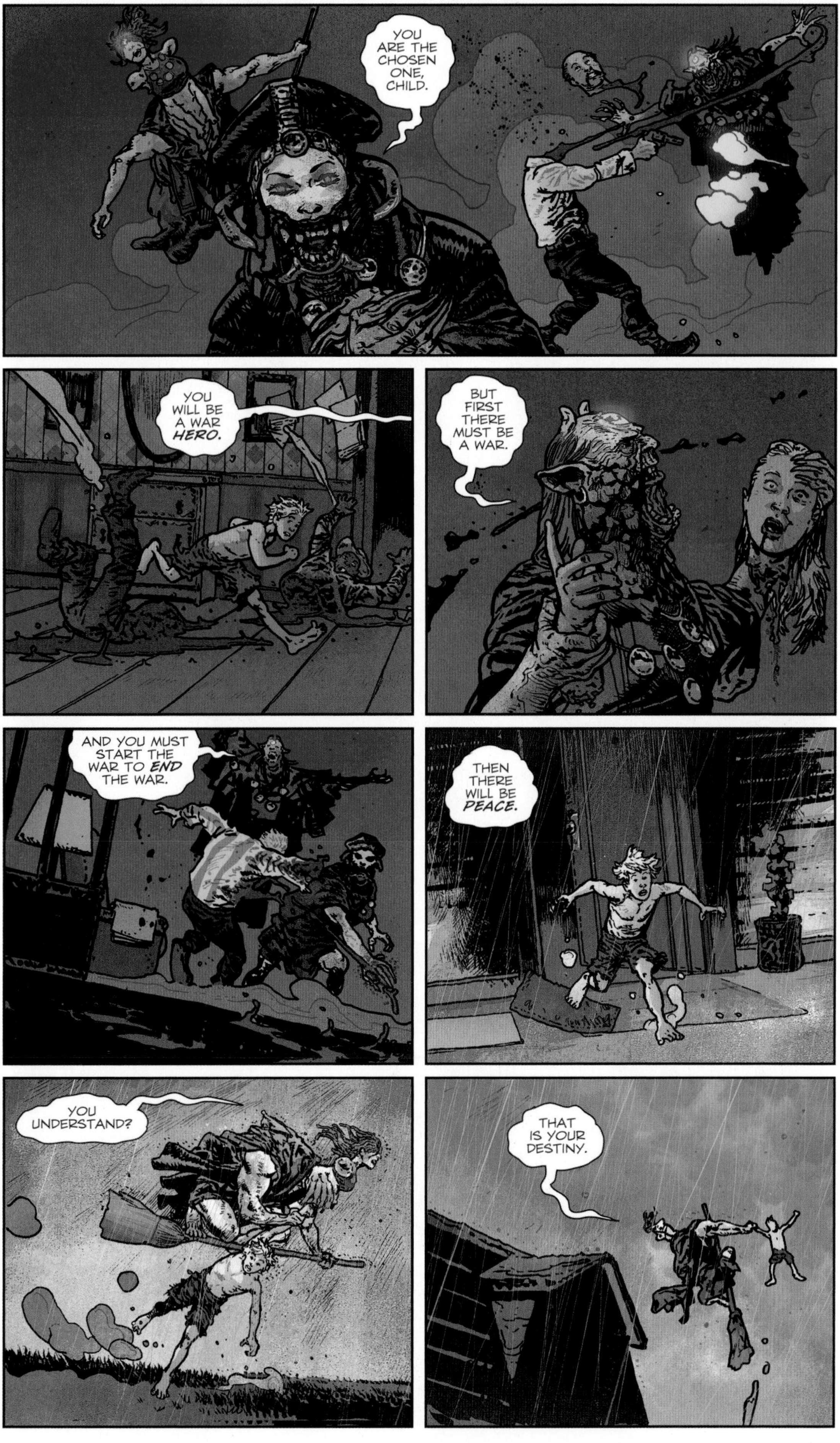
YOU ARE THE CHOSEN ONE, CHILD.
YOU WILL BE A WAR HERO.
BUT FIRST THERE MUST BE A WAR.
AND YOU MUST START THE WAR TO END THE WAR.
THEN THERE WILL BE PEACE.
YOU UNDERSTAND?
THAT IS YOUR DESTINY.

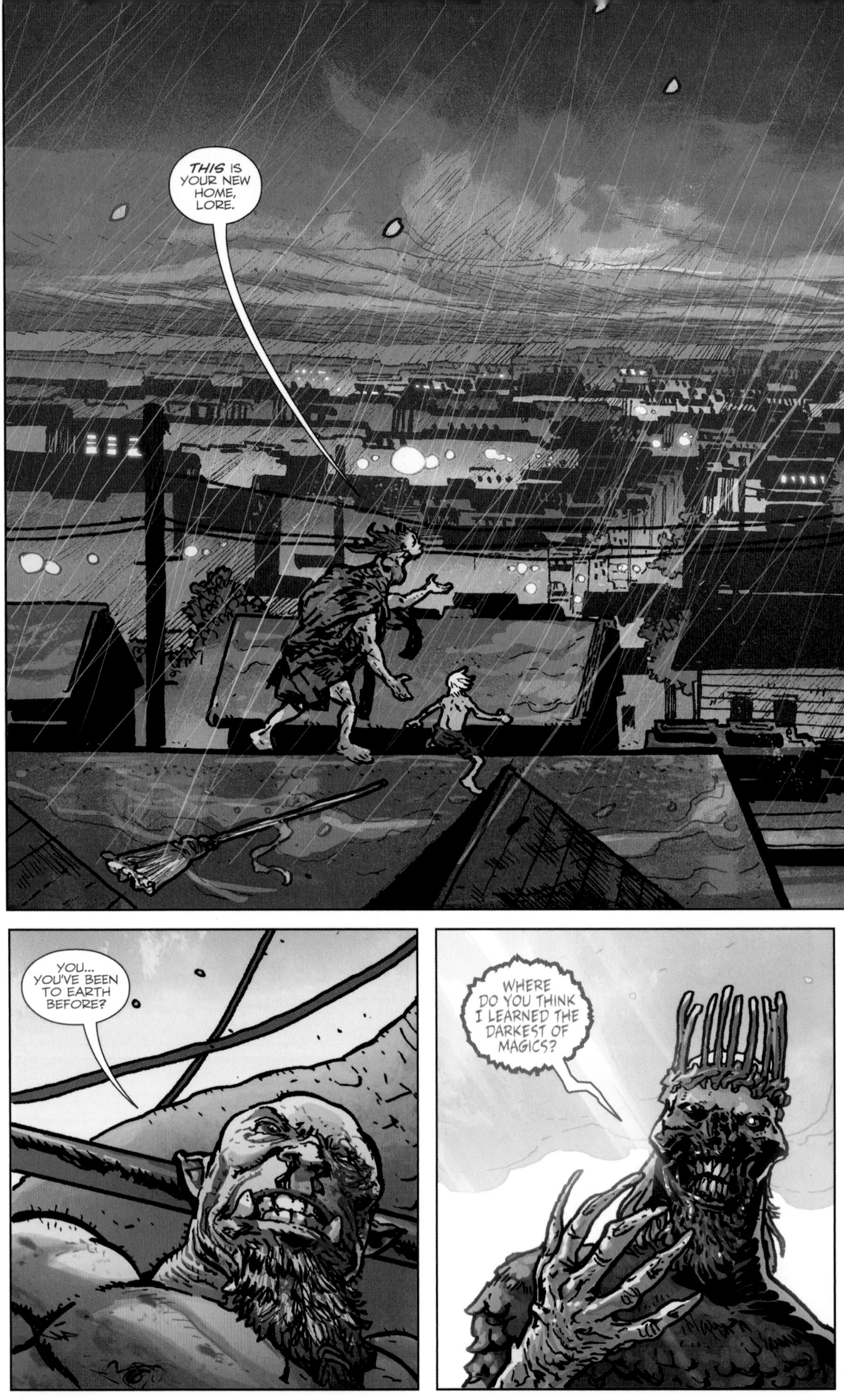
THIS IS YOUR NEW HOME, LORE.
YOU... YOU'VE BEEN TO EARTH BEFORE?
WHERE DO YOU THINK I LEARNED THE DARKEST OF MAGICS?

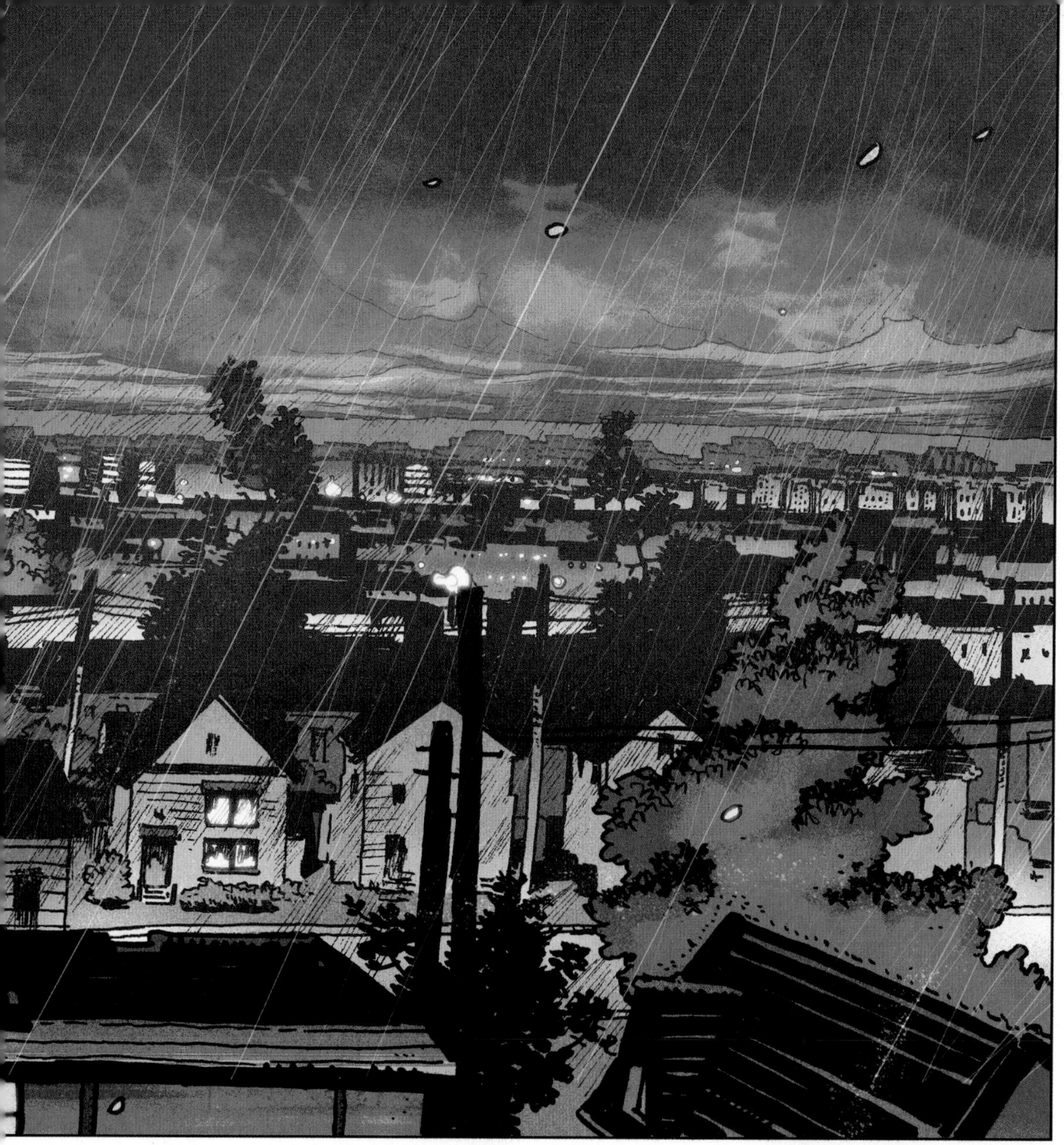

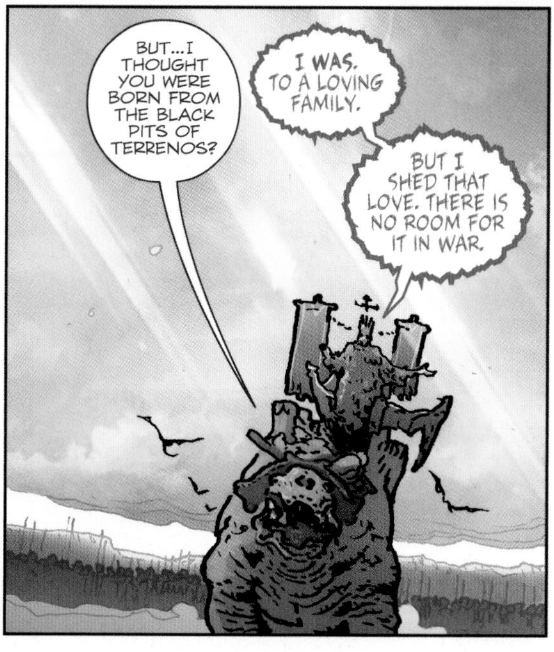
BUT...I THOUGHT YOU WERE BORN FROM THE BLACK PITS OF TERRENOS?
I WAS. TO A LOVING FAMILY.
BUT I SHED THAT LOVE. THERE IS NO ROOM FOR IT IN WAR.

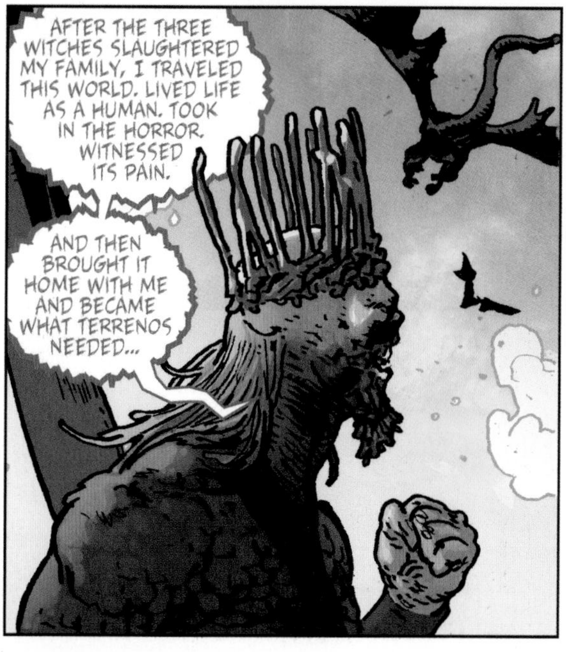
AFTER THE THREE WITCHES SLAUGHTERED MY FAMILY, I TRAVELED THIS WORLD. LIVED LIFE AS A HUMAN. TOOK IN THE HORROR. WITNESSED ITS PAIN.
AND THEN BROUGHT IT HOME WITH ME AND BECAME WHAT TERRENOS NEEDED...

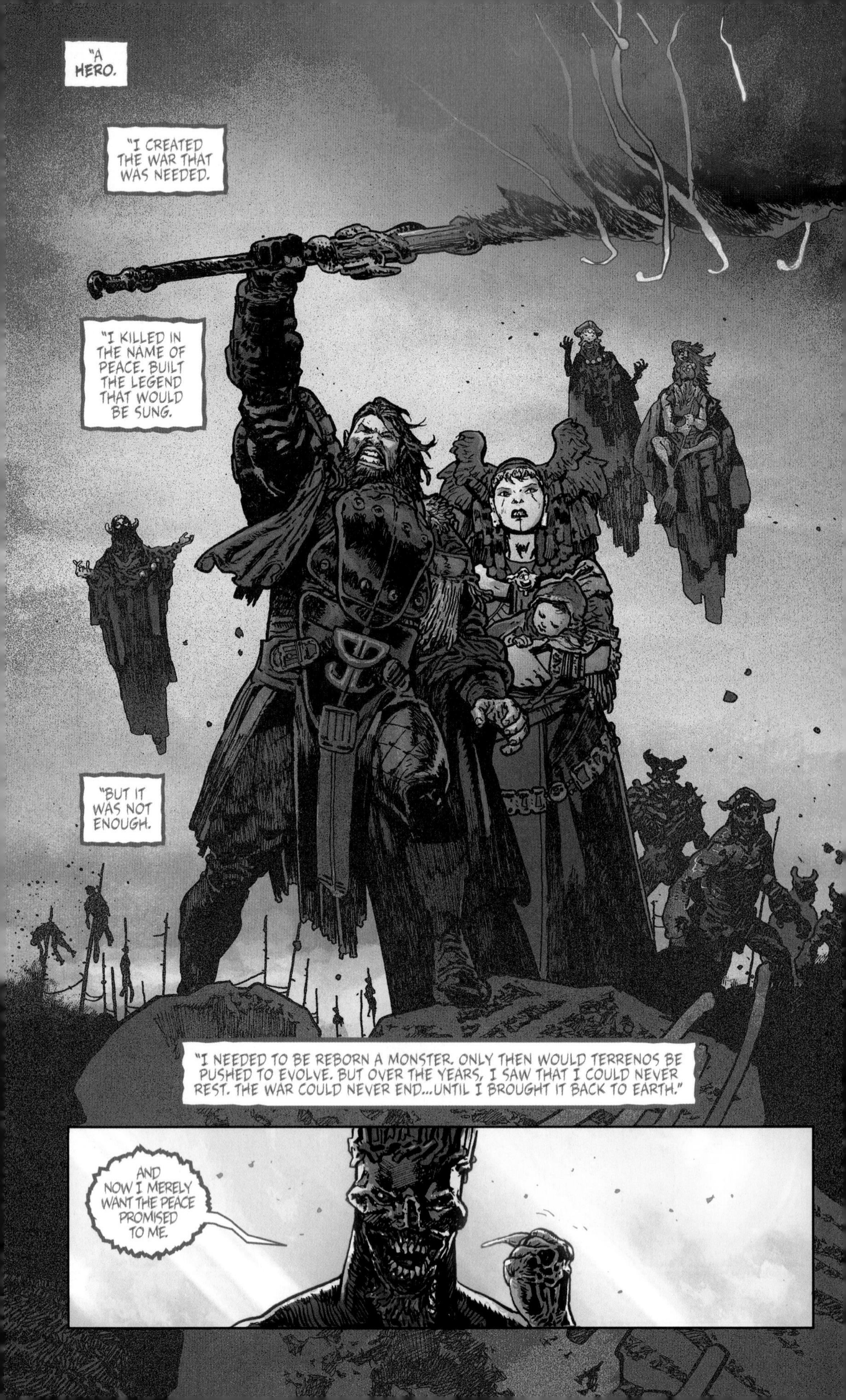
"A HERO.
"I CREATED THE WAR THAT WAS NEEDED.
"I KILLED IN THE NAME OF PEACE. BUILT THE LEGEND THAT WOULD BE SUNG.
"BUT IT WAS NOT ENOUGH.
"I NEEDED TO BE REBORN A MONSTER. ONLY THEN WOULD TERRENOS BE PUSHED TO EVOLVE. BUT OVER THE YEARS, I SAW THAT I COULD NEVER REST. THE WAR COULD NEVER END...UNTIL I BROUGHT IT BACK TO EARTH."
AND NOW I MERELY WANT THE PEACE PROMISED TO ME.

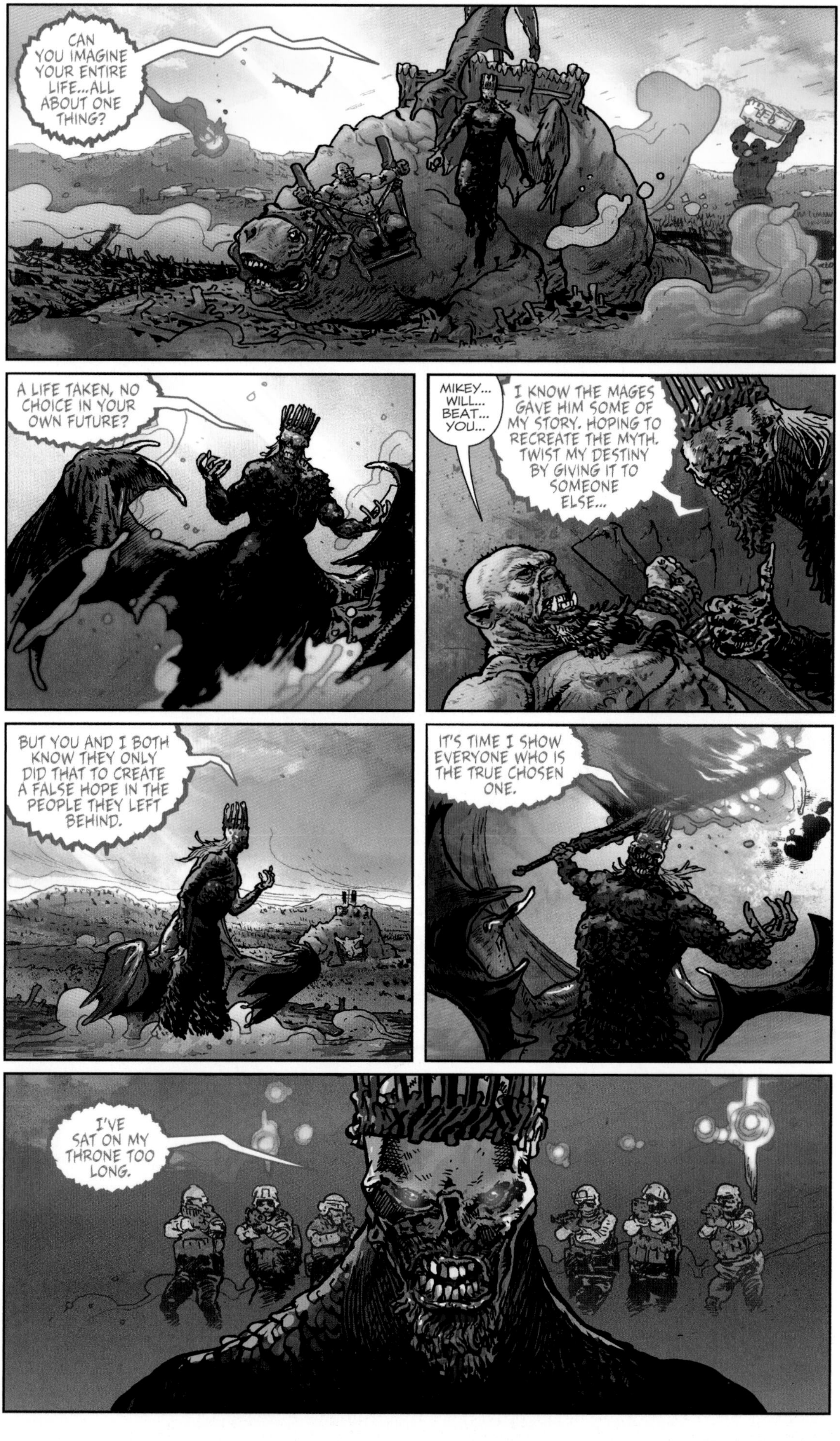
CAN YOU IMAGINE YOUR ENTIRE LIFE...ALL ABOUT ONE THING?
A LIFE TAKEN, NO CHOICE IN YOUR OWN FUTURE?
MIKEY... WILL... BEAT... YOU...
I KNOW THE MAGES GAVE HIM SOME OF MY STORY. HOPING TO RECREATE THE MYTH. TWIST MY DESTINY BY GIVING IT TO SOMEONE ELSE...
BUT YOU AND I BOTH KNOW THEY ONLY DID THAT TO CREATE A FALSE HOPE IN THE PEOPLE THEY LEFT BEHIND.
IT'S TIME I SHOW EVERYONE WHO IS THE TRUE CHOSEN ONE.
I'VE SAT ON MY THRONE TOO LONG.

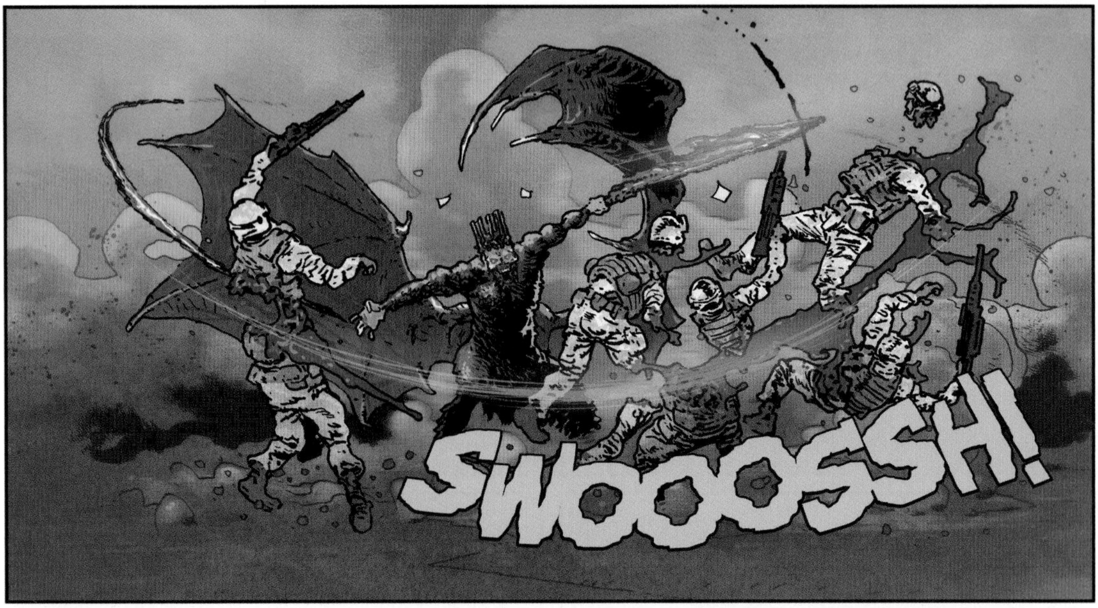
SWOOOSSH!

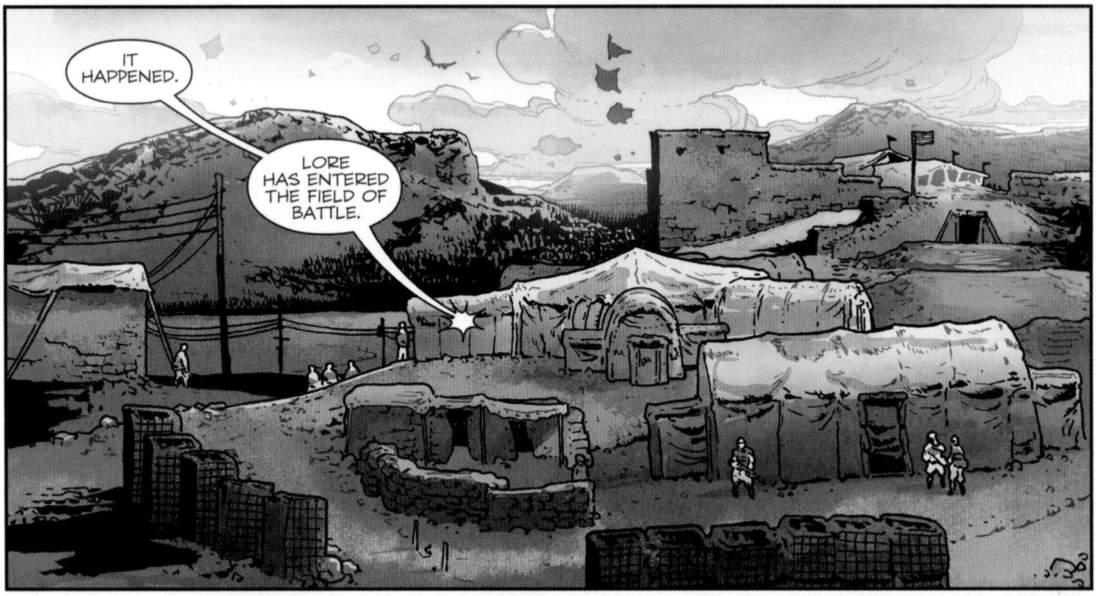
IT HAPPENED.
LORE HAS ENTERED THE FIELD OF BATTLE.

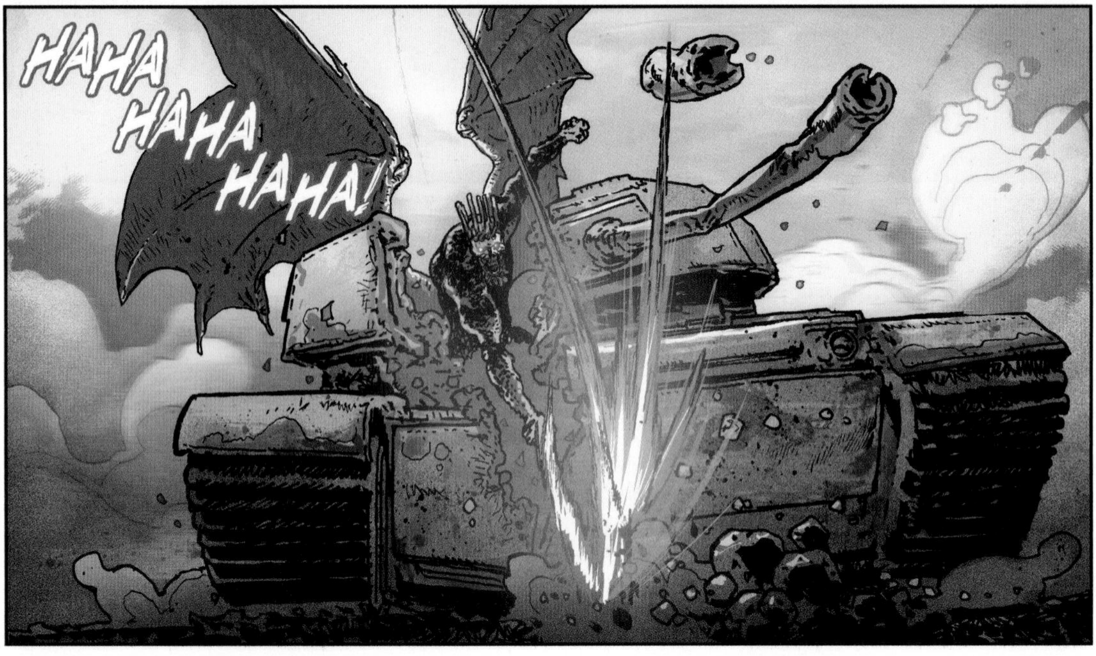
HAHA HAHA HAHA!

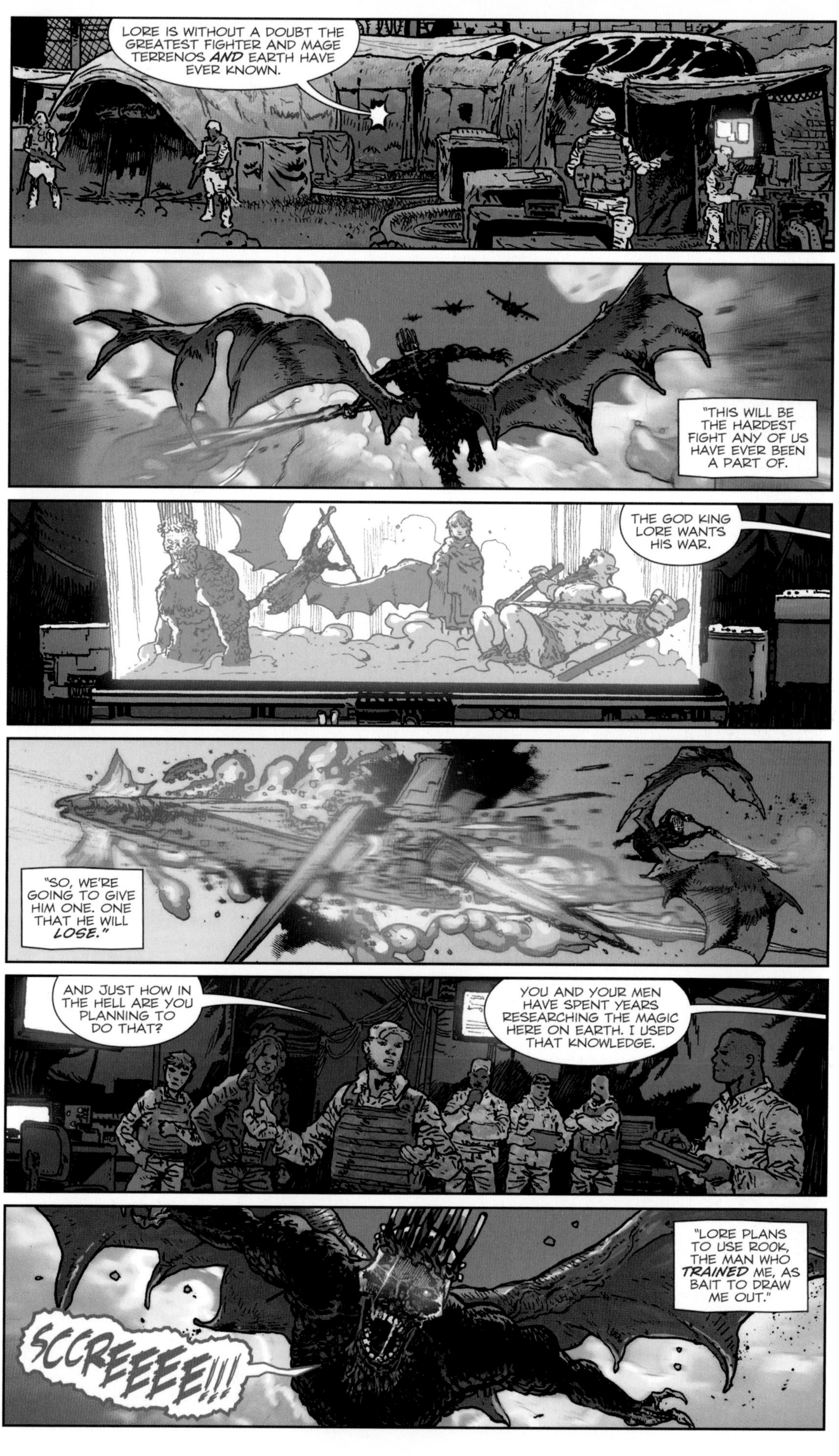
LORE IS WITHOUT A DOUBT THE GREATEST FIGHTER AND MAGE TERRENOS AND EARTH HAVE EVER KNOWN.
"THIS WILL BE THE HARDEST FIGHT ANY OF US HAVE EVER BEEN A PART OF.
THE GOD KING LORE WANTS HIS WAR.
"SO, WE'RE GOING TO GIVE HIM ONE. ONE THAT HE WILL LOSE."
AND JUST HOW IN THE HELL ARE YOU PLANNING TO DO THAT?
YOU AND YOUR MEN HAVE SPENT YEARS RESEARCHING THE MAGIC HERE ON EARTH. I USED THAT KNOWLEDGE.
"LORE PLANS TO USE ROOK, THE MAN WHO TRAINED ME, AS BAIT TO DRAW ME OUT."
SCCREEEEE!!!

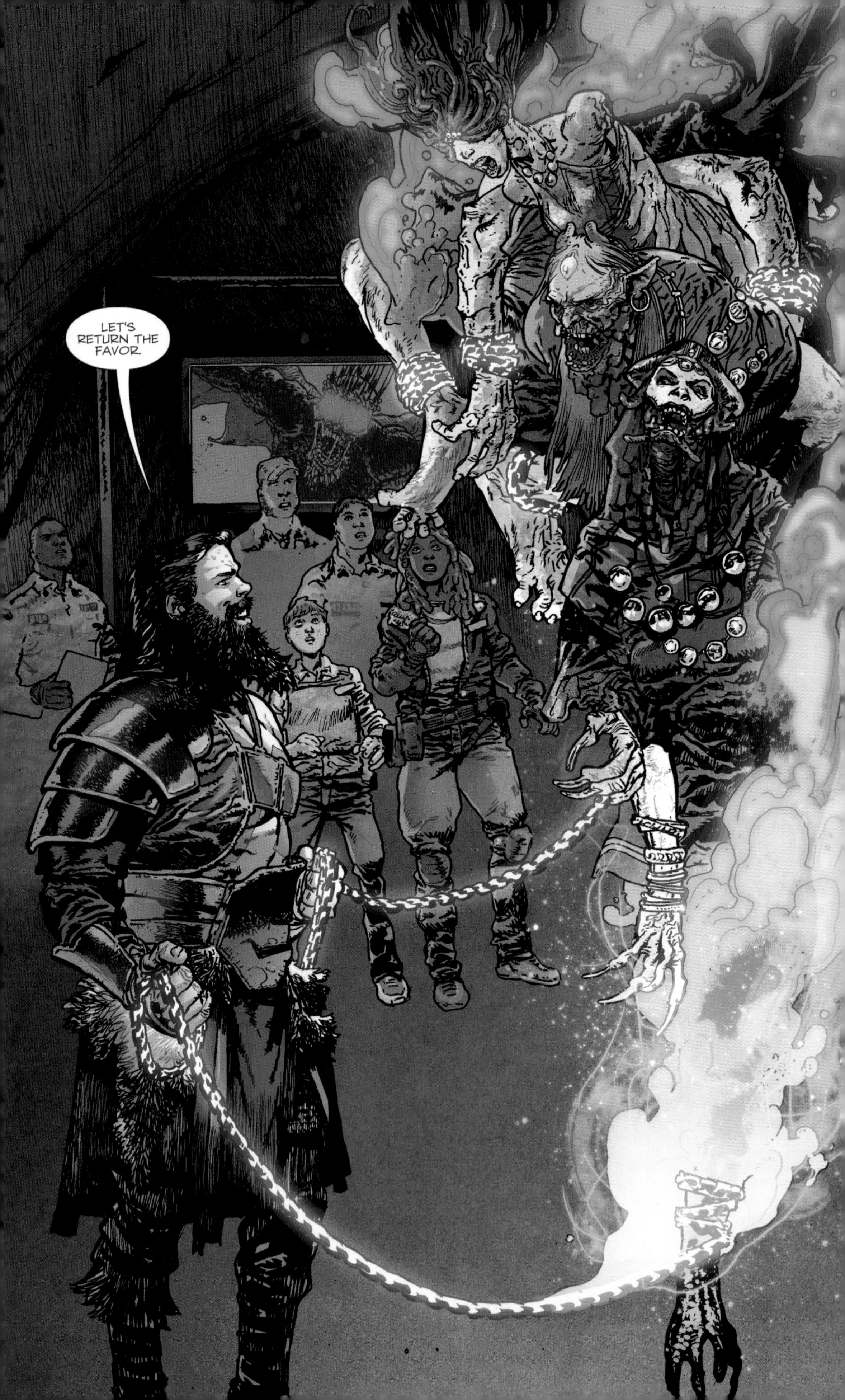
LET'S RETURN THE FAVOR.

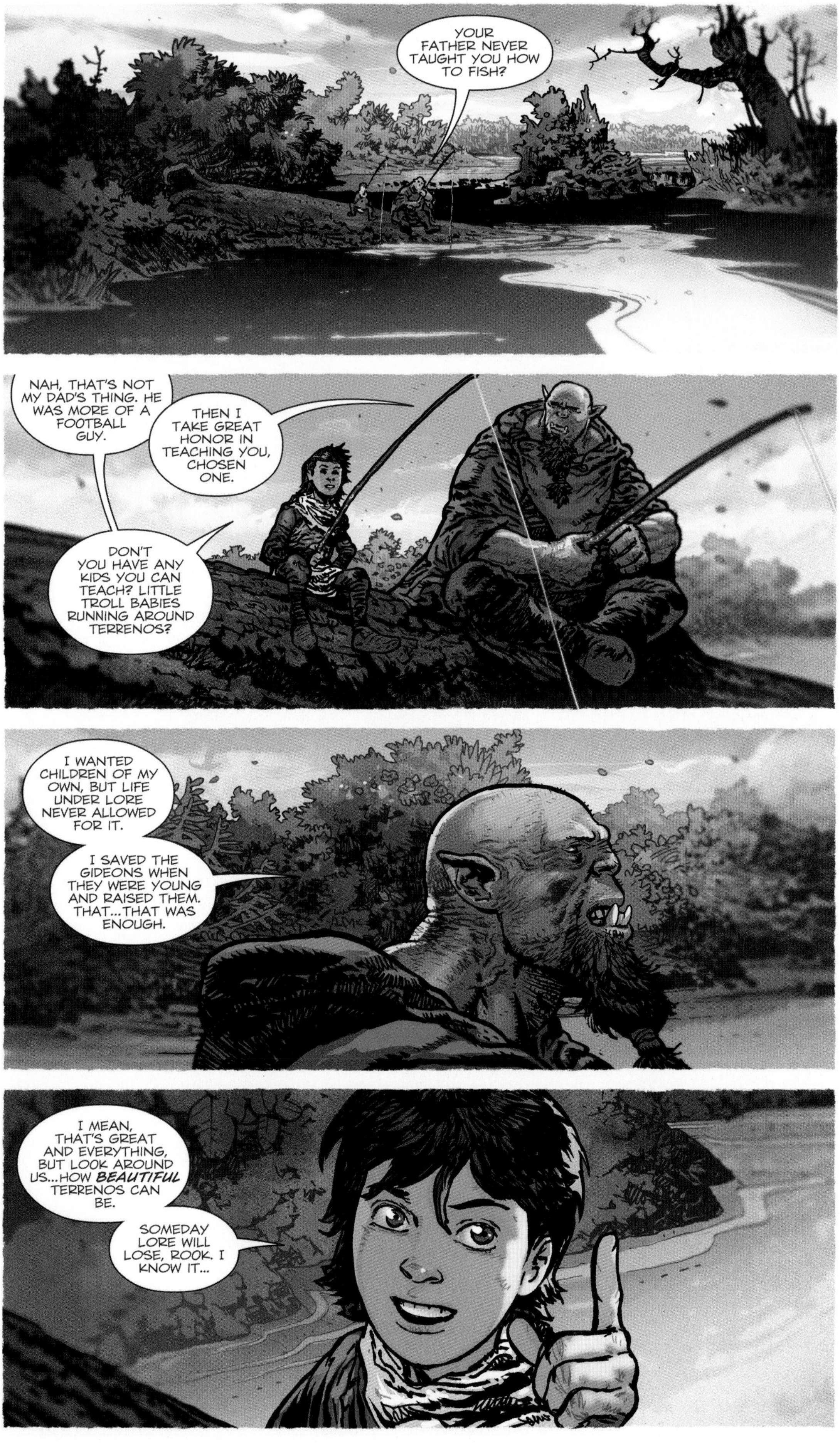
YOUR FATHER NEVER TAUGHT YOU HOW TO FISH?
NAH, THAT'S NOT MY DAD'S THING. HE WAS MORE OF A FOOTBALL GUY.
THEN I TAKE GREAT HONOR IN TEACHING YOU, CHOSEN ONE.
DON'T YOU HAVE ANY KIDS YOU CAN TEACH? LITTLE TROLL BABIES RUNNING AROUND TERRENOS?
I WANTED CHILDREN OF MY OWN, BUT LIFE UNDER LORE NEVER ALLOWED FOR IT.
I SAVED THE GIDEONS WHEN THEY WERE YOUNG AND RAISED THEM. THAT...THAT WAS ENOUGH.
I MEAN, THAT'S GREAT AND EVERYTHING, BUT LOOK AROUND US...HOW ***BEAUTIFUL*** TERRENOS CAN BE.
SOMEDAY LORE WILL LOSE, ROOK. I KNOW IT...

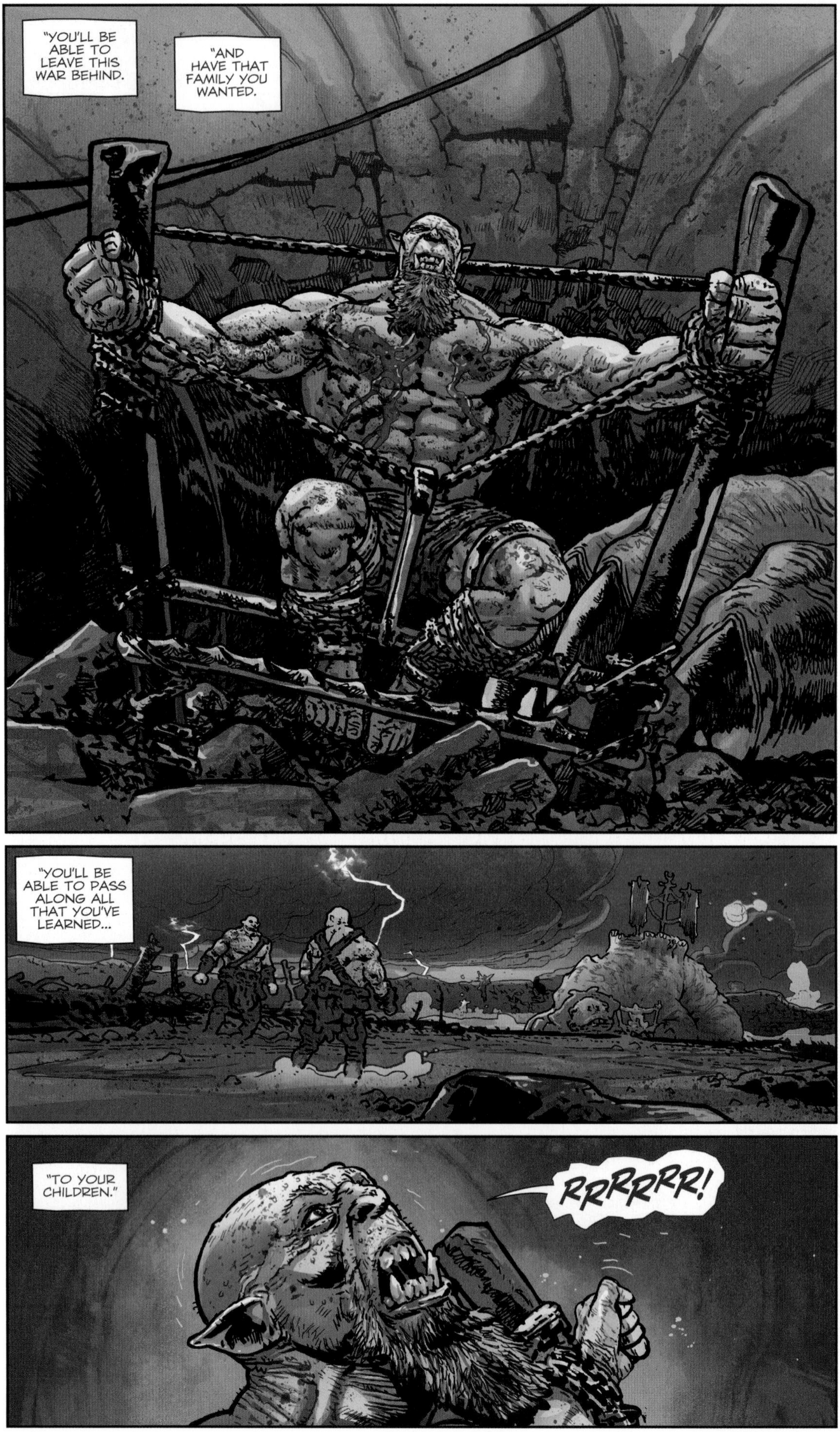
"YOU'LL BE ABLE TO LEAVE THIS WAR BEHIND.
"AND HAVE THAT FAMILY YOU WANTED.
"YOU'LL BE ABLE TO PASS ALONG ALL THAT YOU'VE LEARNED...
"TO YOUR CHILDREN."
RRRRRR!

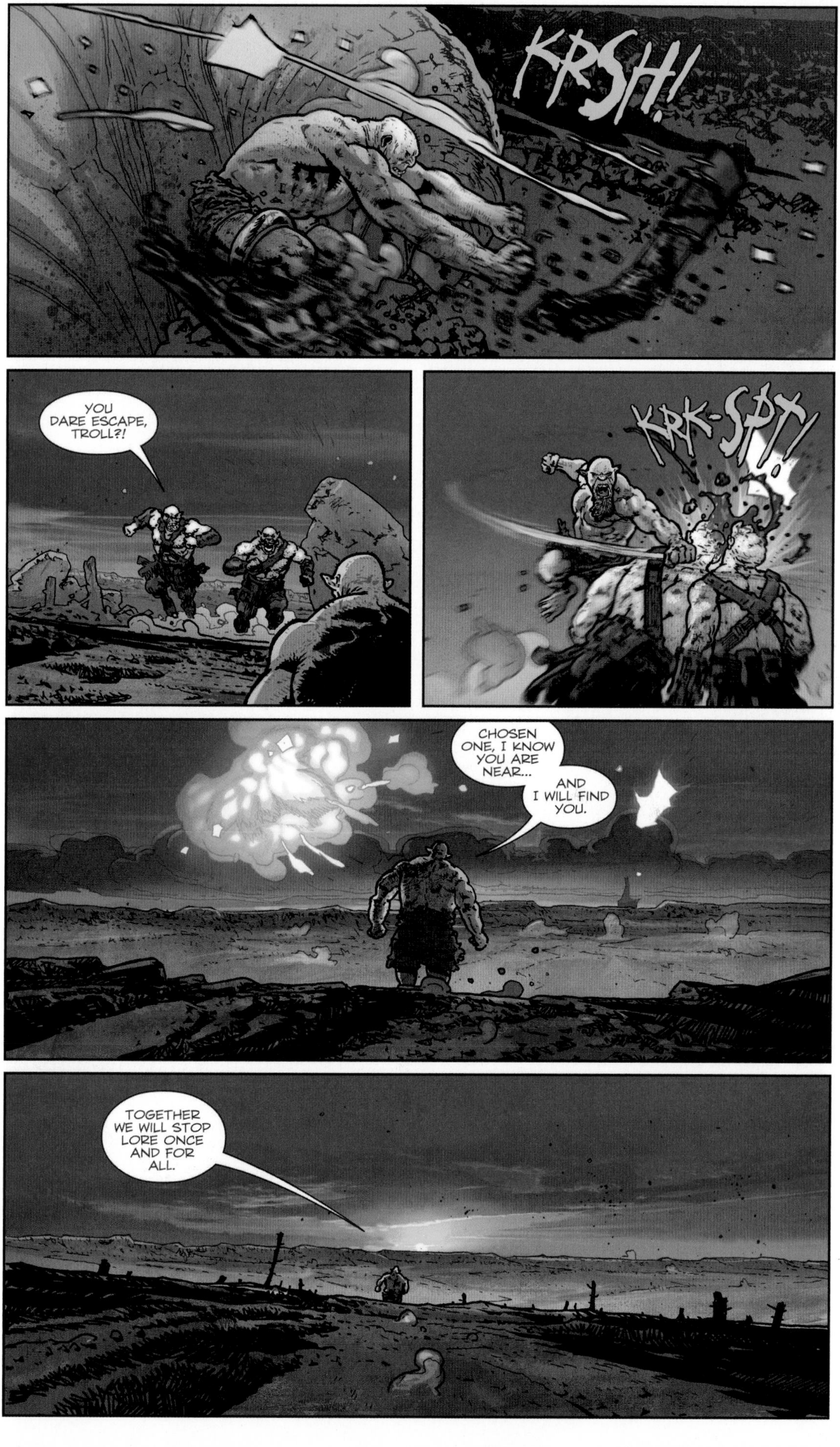
KRSH!
YOU DARE ESCAPE, TROLL?!
KRK-SPT!
CHOSEN ONE, I KNOW YOU ARE NEAR...
AND I WILL FIND YOU.
TOGETHER WE WILL STOP LORE ONCE AND FOR ALL.

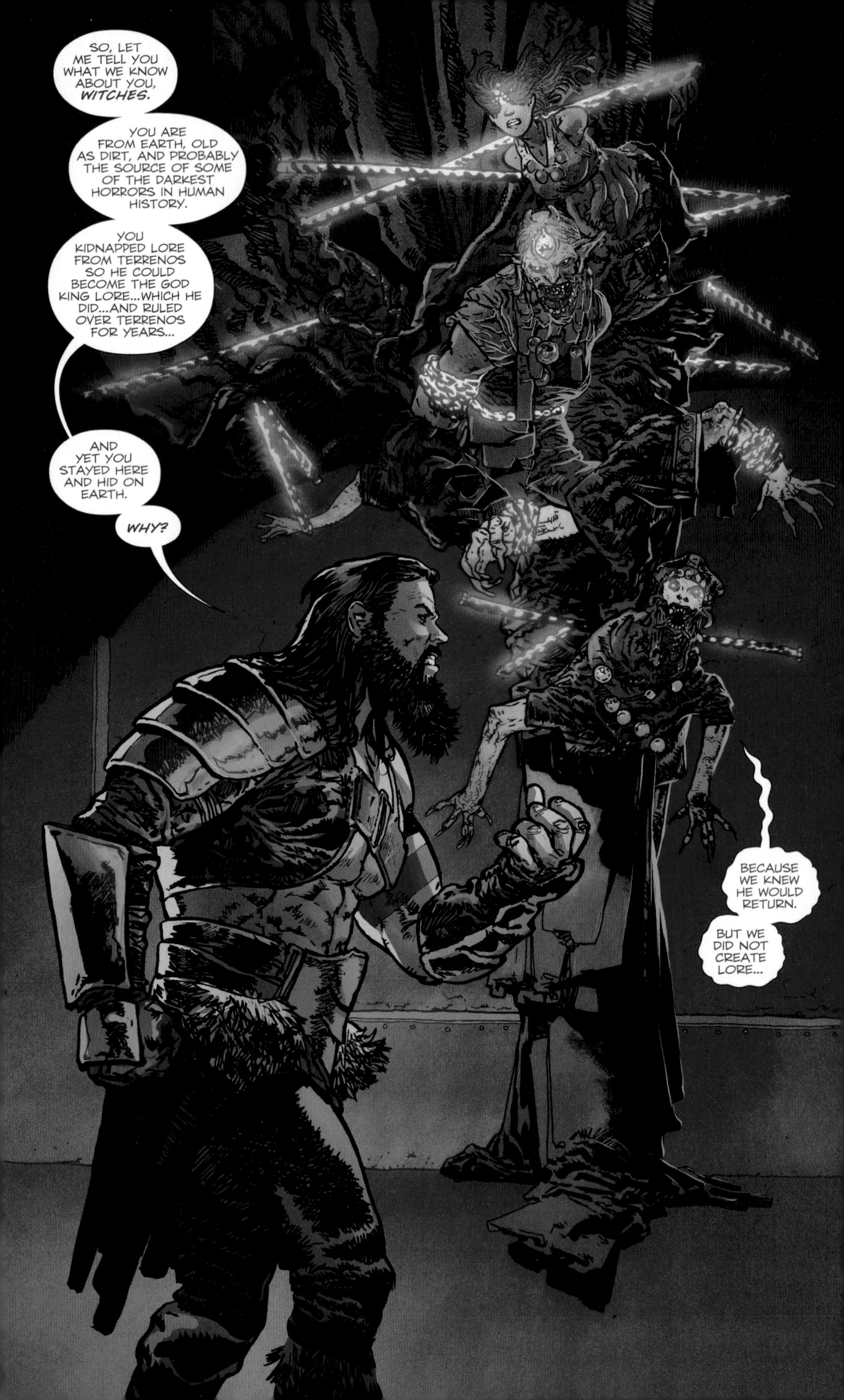
SO, LET ME TELL YOU WHAT WE KNOW ABOUT YOU, *WITCHES.*
YOU ARE FROM EARTH, OLD AS DIRT, AND PROBABLY THE SOURCE OF SOME OF THE DARKEST HORRORS IN HUMAN HISTORY.
YOU KIDNAPPED LORE FROM TERRENOS SO HE COULD BECOME THE GOD KING LORE...WHICH HE DID...AND RULED OVER TERRENOS FOR YEARS...
AND YET YOU STAYED HERE AND HID ON EARTH.
WHY?
BECAUSE WE KNEW HE WOULD RETURN.
BUT WE DID NOT CREATE LORE...

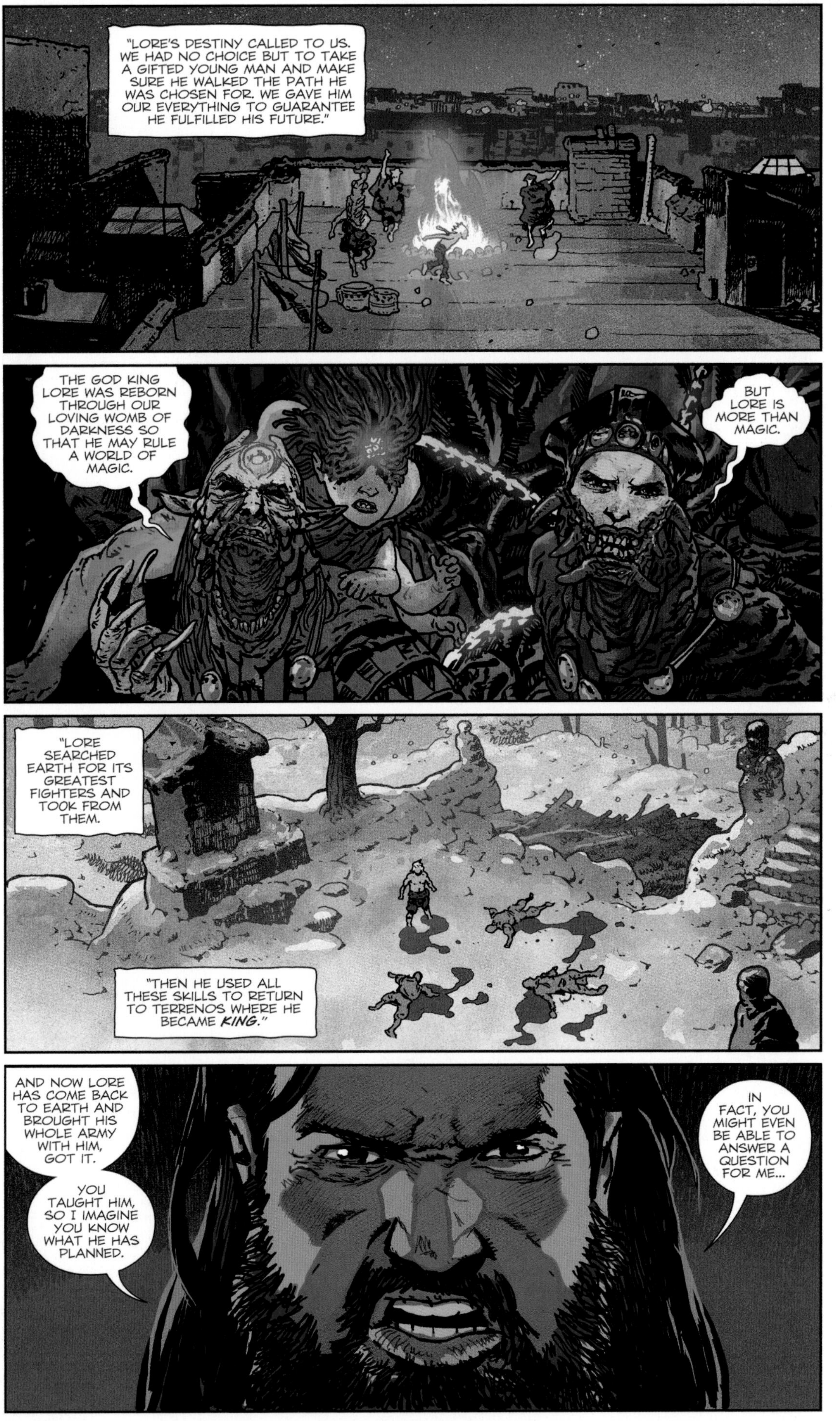
"LORE'S DESTINY CALLED TO US. WE HAD NO CHOICE BUT TO TAKE A GIFTED YOUNG MAN AND MAKE SURE HE WALKED THE PATH HE WAS CHOSEN FOR. WE GAVE HIM OUR EVERYTHING TO GUARANTEE HE FULFILLED HIS FUTURE."
THE GOD KING LORE WAS REBORN THROUGH OUR LOVING WOMB OF DARKNESS SO THAT HE MAY RULE A WORLD OF MAGIC.
BUT LORE IS MORE THAN MAGIC.
"LORE SEARCHED EARTH FOR ITS GREATEST FIGHTERS AND TOOK FROM THEM.
"THEN HE USED ALL THESE SKILLS TO RETURN TO TERRENOS WHERE HE BECAME *KING*."
AND NOW LORE HAS COME BACK TO EARTH AND BROUGHT HIS WHOLE ARMY WITH HIM, GOT IT.
YOU TAUGHT HIM, SO I IMAGINE YOU KNOW WHAT HE HAS PLANNED.
IN FACT, YOU MIGHT EVEN BE ABLE TO ANSWER A QUESTION FOR ME...

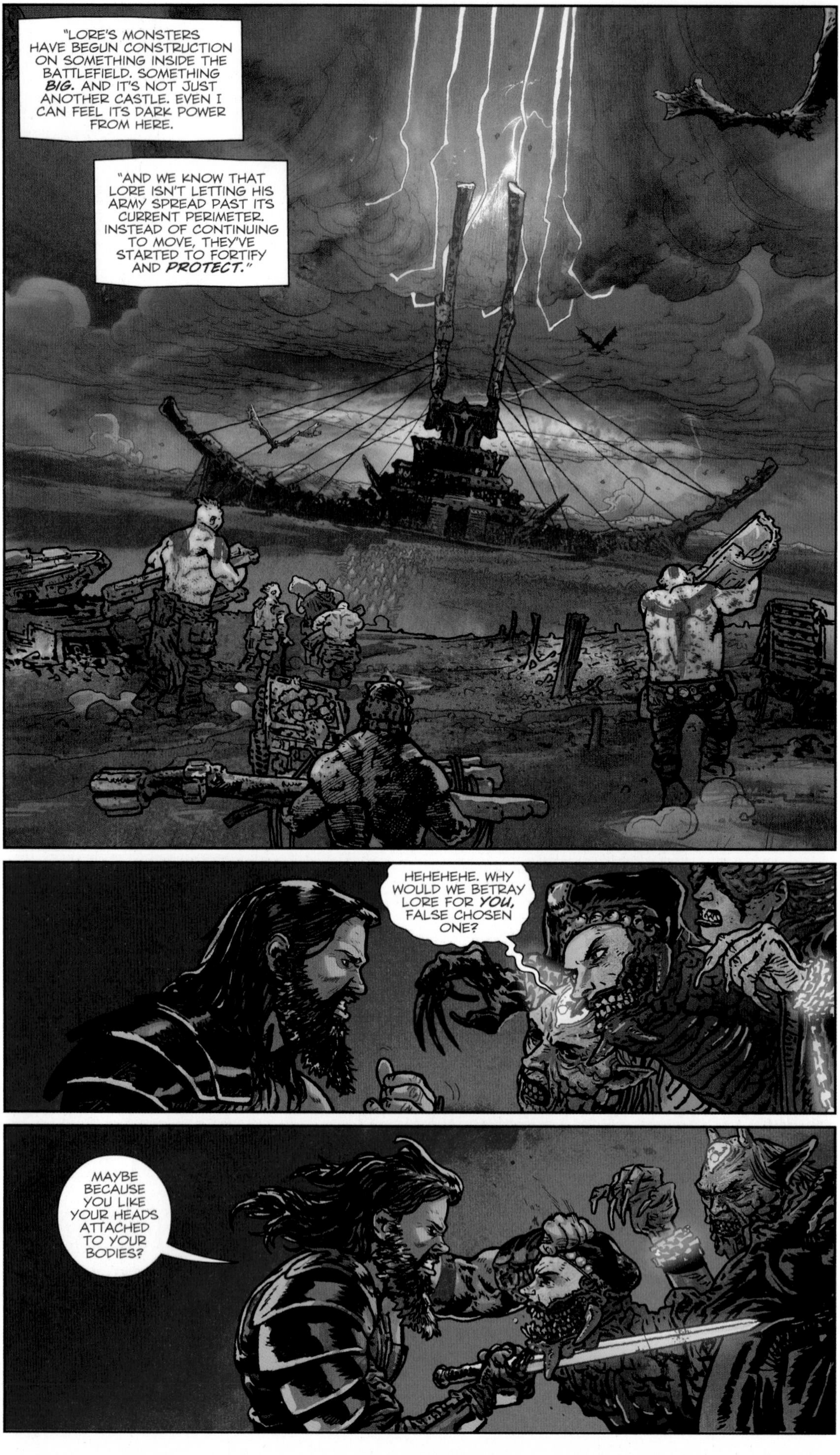
"LORE'S MONSTERS HAVE BEGUN CONSTRUCTION ON SOMETHING INSIDE THE BATTLEFIELD. SOMETHING BIG. AND IT'S NOT JUST ANOTHER CASTLE. EVEN I CAN FEEL ITS DARK POWER FROM HERE.
"AND WE KNOW THAT LORE ISN'T LETTING HIS ARMY SPREAD PAST ITS CURRENT PERIMETER. INSTEAD OF CONTINUING TO MOVE, THEY'VE STARTED TO FORTIFY AND PROTECT."
HEHEHEHE. WHY WOULD WE BETRAY LORE FOR YOU, FALSE CHOSEN ONE?
MAYBE BECAUSE YOU LIKE YOUR HEADS ATTACHED TO YOUR BODIES?

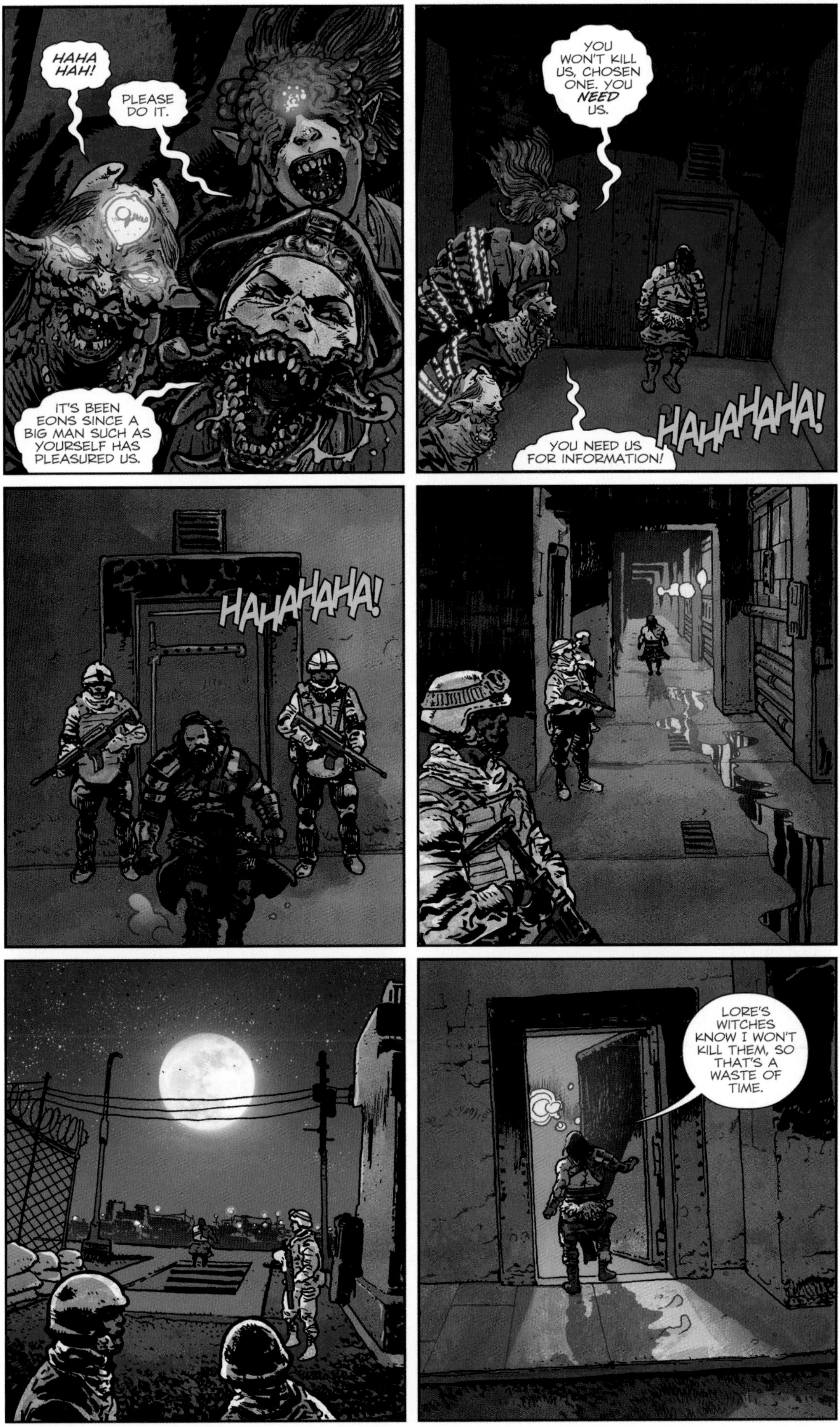
HAHA HAH!
PLEASE DO IT.
IT'S BEEN EONS SINCE A BIG MAN SUCH AS YOURSELF HAS PLEASURED US.
YOU WON'T KILL US, CHOSEN ONE. YOU NEED US.
YOU NEED US FOR INFORMATION!
HAHAHAHA!
HAHAHAHA!
LORE'S WITCHES KNOW I WON'T KILL THEM, SO THAT'S A WASTE OF TIME.

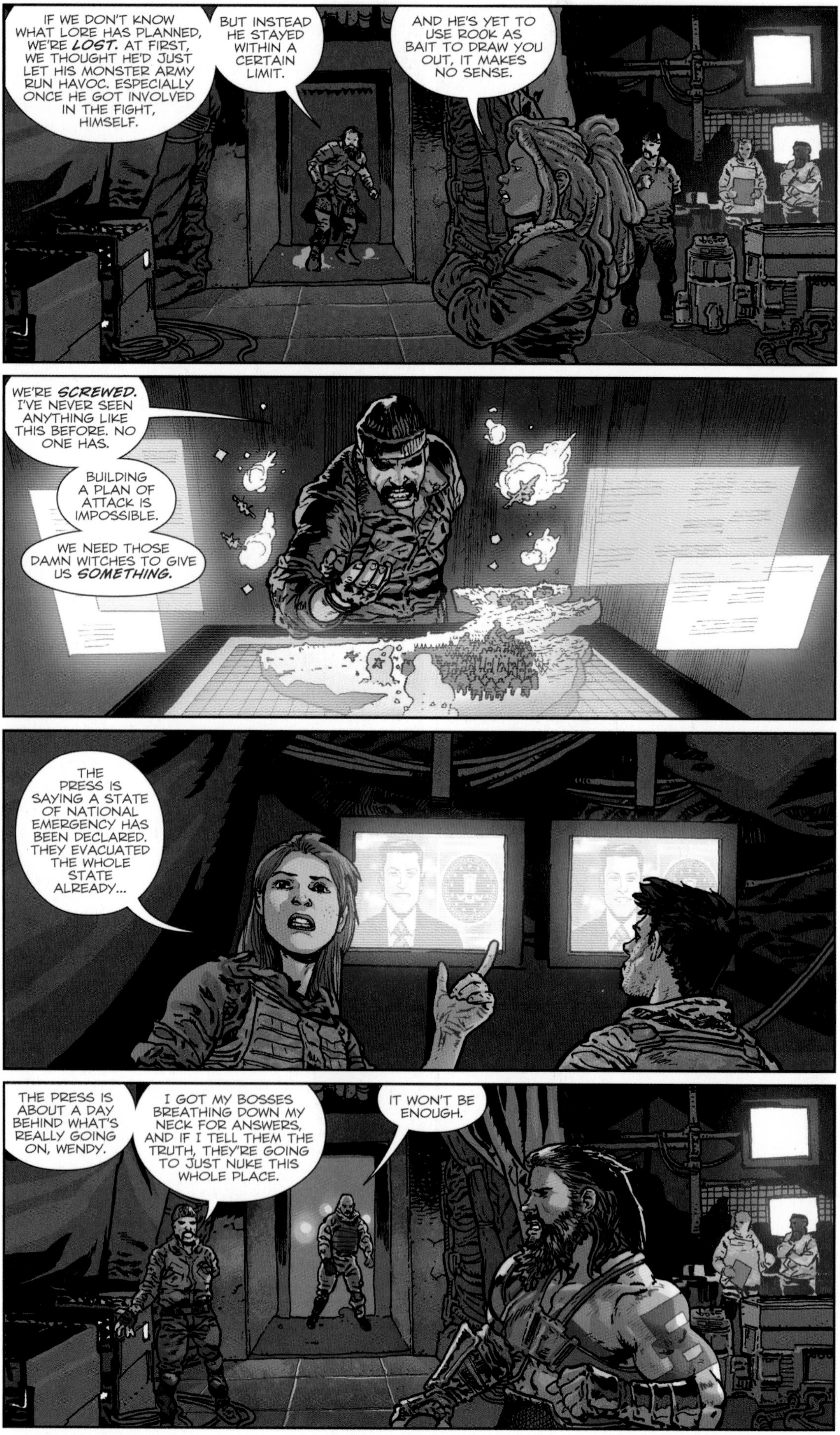
IF WE DON'T KNOW WHAT LORE HAS PLANNED, WE'RE LOST. AT FIRST, WE THOUGHT HE'D JUST LET HIS MONSTER ARMY RUN HAVOC. ESPECIALLY ONCE HE GOT INVOLVED IN THE FIGHT, HIMSELF.
BUT INSTEAD HE STAYED WITHIN A CERTAIN LIMIT.
AND HE'S YET TO USE ROOK AS BAIT TO DRAW YOU OUT, IT MAKES NO SENSE.
WE'RE SCREWED. I'VE NEVER SEEN ANYTHING LIKE THIS BEFORE. NO ONE HAS.
BUILDING A PLAN OF ATTACK IS IMPOSSIBLE.
WE NEED THOSE DAMN WITCHES TO GIVE US SOMETHING.
THE PRESS IS SAYING A STATE OF NATIONAL EMERGENCY HAS BEEN DECLARED. THEY EVACUATED THE WHOLE STATE ALREADY...
THE PRESS IS ABOUT A DAY BEHIND WHAT'S REALLY GOING ON, WENDY.
I GOT MY BOSSES BREATHING DOWN MY NECK FOR ANSWERS, AND IF I TELL THEM THE TRUTH, THEY'RE GOING TO JUST NUKE THIS WHOLE PLACE.
IT WON'T BE ENOUGH.

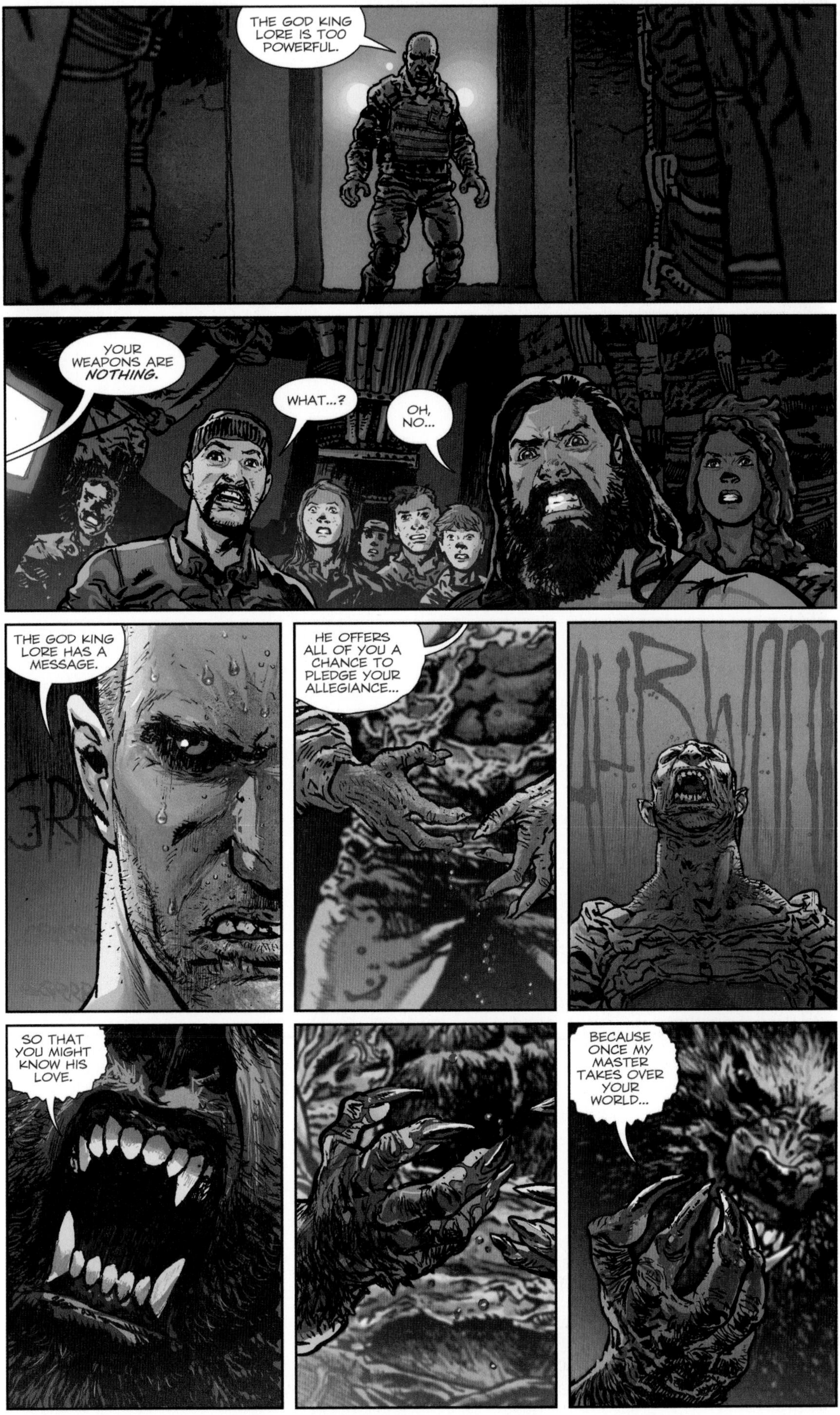
THE GOD KING LORE IS TOO POWERFUL.
YOUR WEAPONS ARE *NOTHING.*
WHAT...?
OH, NO...
THE GOD KING LORE HAS A MESSAGE.
HE OFFERS ALL OF YOU A CHANCE TO PLEDGE YOUR ALLEGIANCE...
SO THAT YOU MIGHT KNOW HIS LOVE.
BECAUSE ONCE MY MASTER TAKES OVER YOUR WORLD...

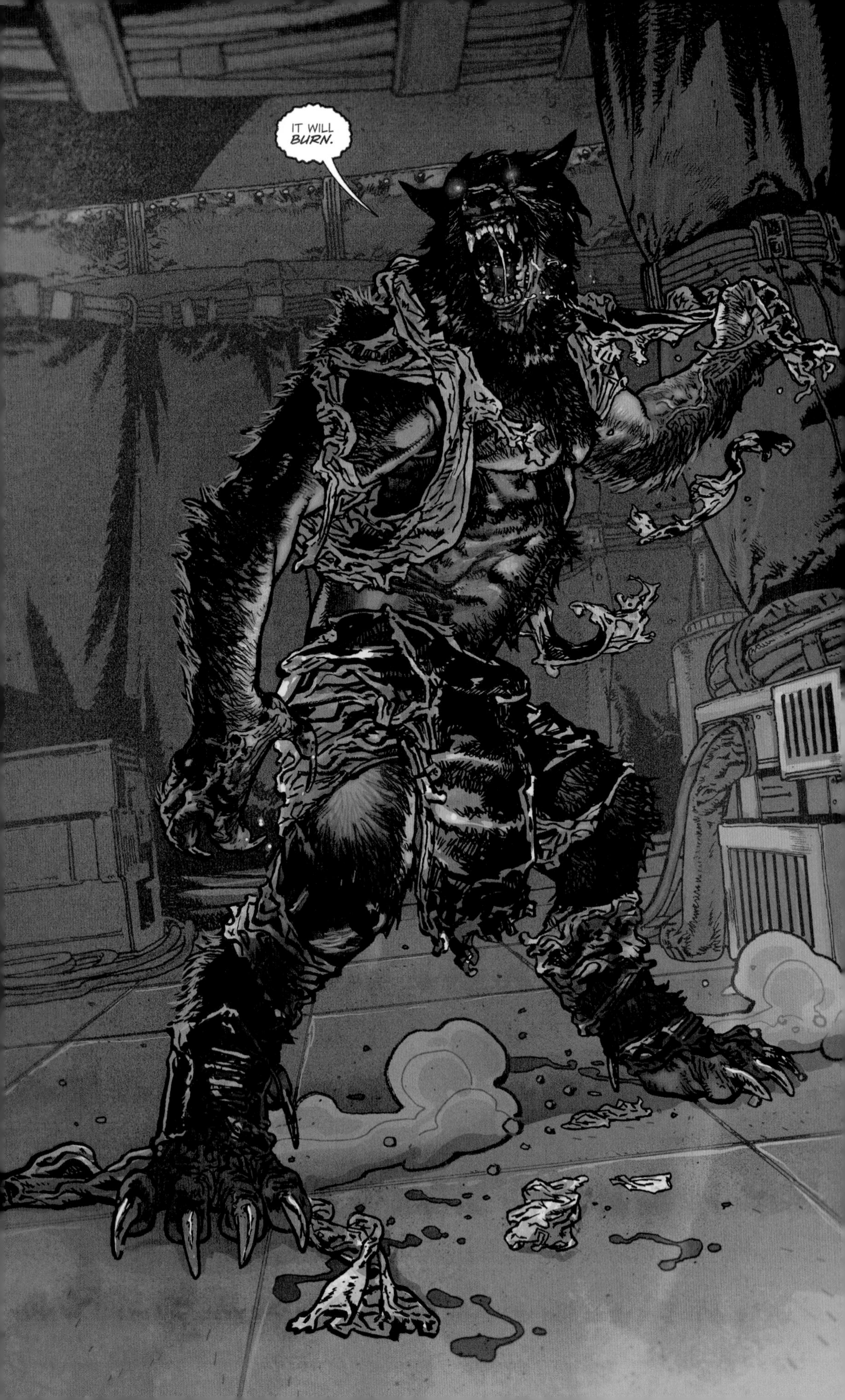
IT WILL BURN.

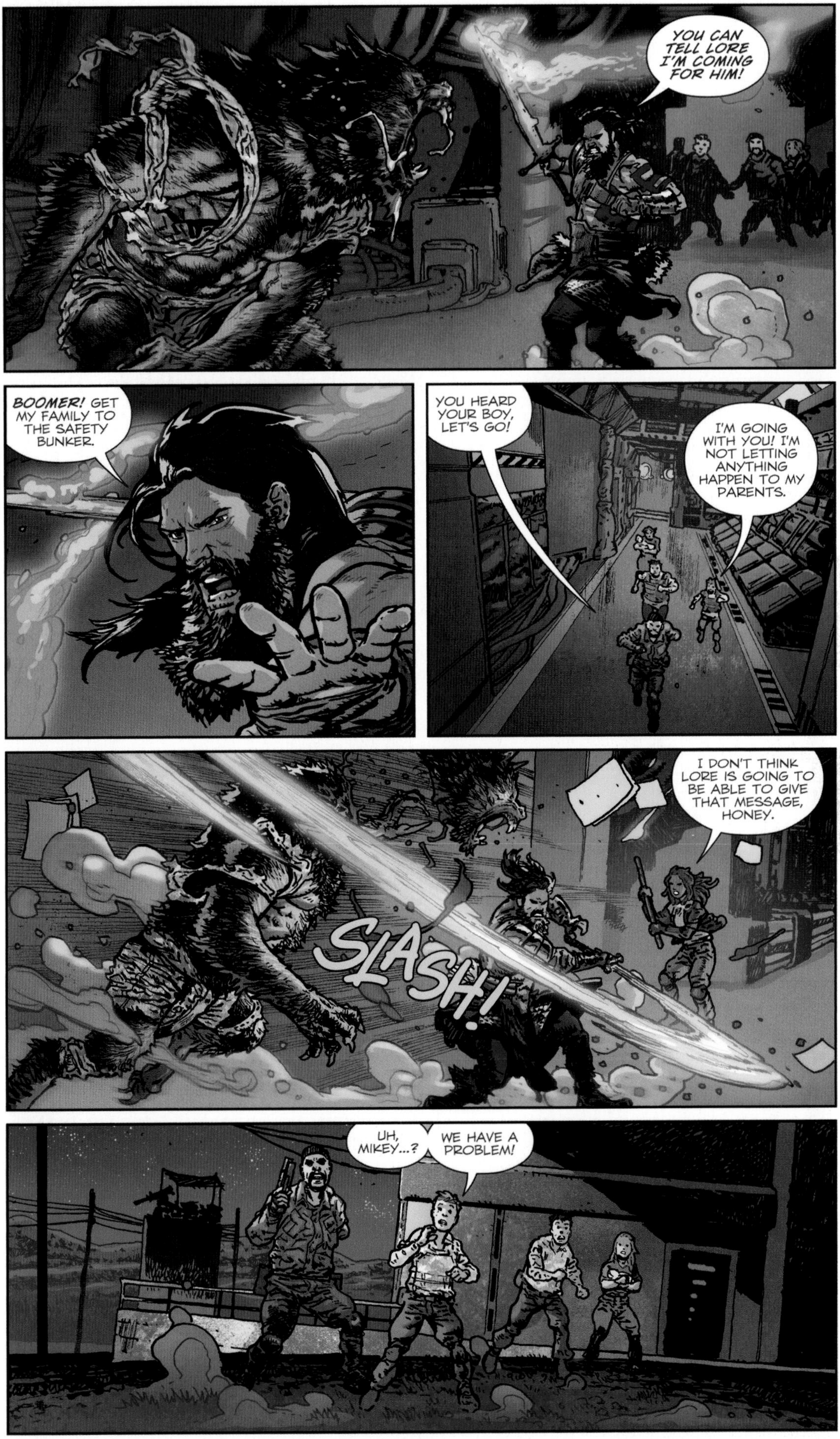
YOU CAN TELL LORE I'M COMING FOR HIM!
BOOMER! GET MY FAMILY TO THE SAFETY BUNKER.
YOU HEARD YOUR BOY, LET'S GO!
I'M GOING WITH YOU! I'M NOT LETTING ANYTHING HAPPEN TO MY PARENTS.
I DON'T THINK LORE IS GOING TO BE ABLE TO GIVE THAT MESSAGE, HONEY.
SLASH!
UH, MIKEY...?
WE HAVE A PROBLEM!

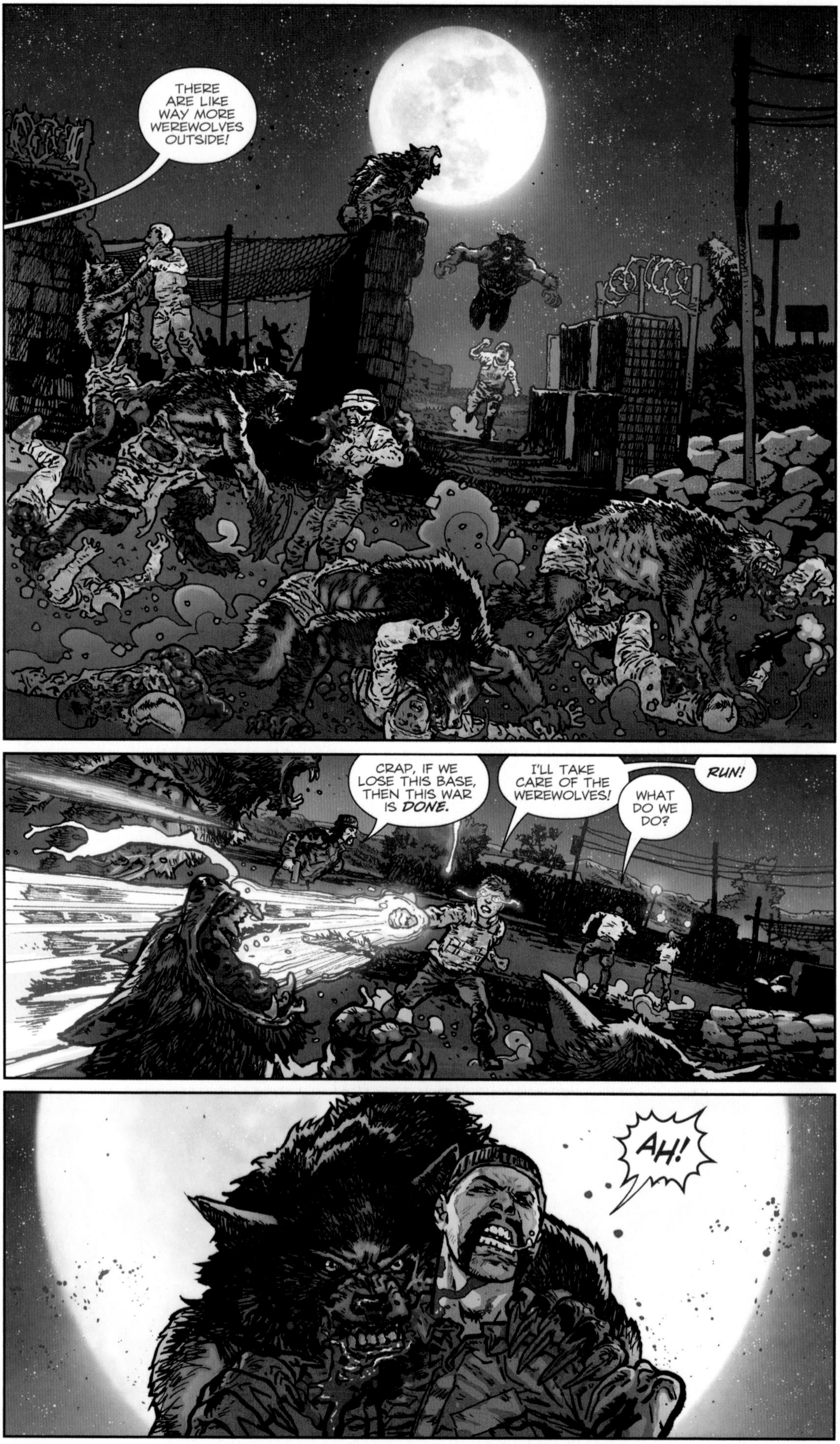
THERE ARE LIKE WAY MORE WEREWOLVES OUTSIDE!
CRAP, IF WE LOSE THIS BASE, THEN THIS WAR IS *DONE.*
I'LL TAKE CARE OF THE WEREWOLVES!
RUN!
WHAT DO WE DO?
AH!

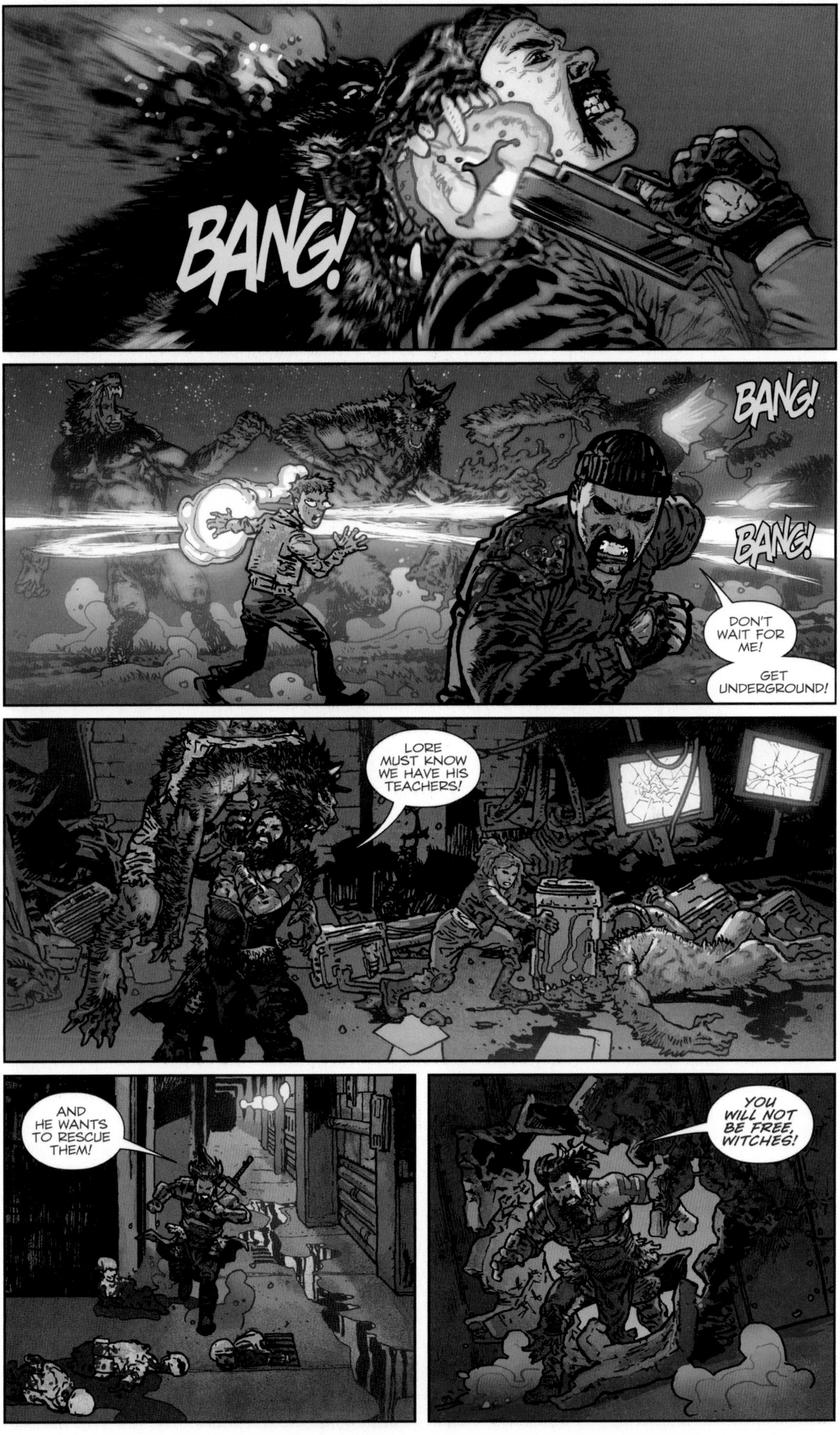
BANG!
BANG!
BANG!
DON'T WAIT FOR ME!
GET UNDERGROUND!
LORE MUST KNOW WE HAVE HIS TEACHERS!
AND HE WANTS TO RESCUE THEM!
YOU WILL NOT BE FREE, WITCHES!

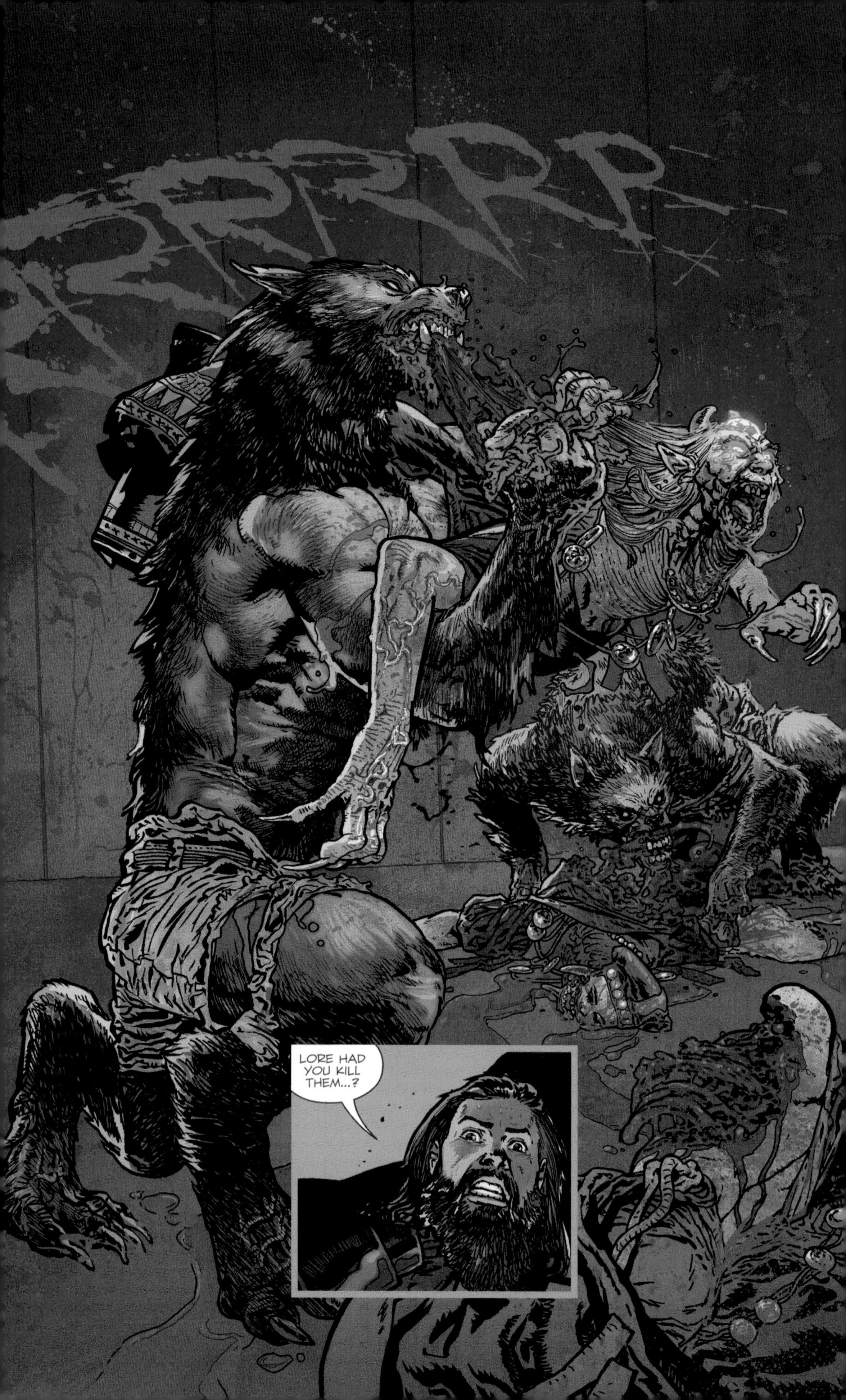
LORE HAD YOU KILL THEM...?

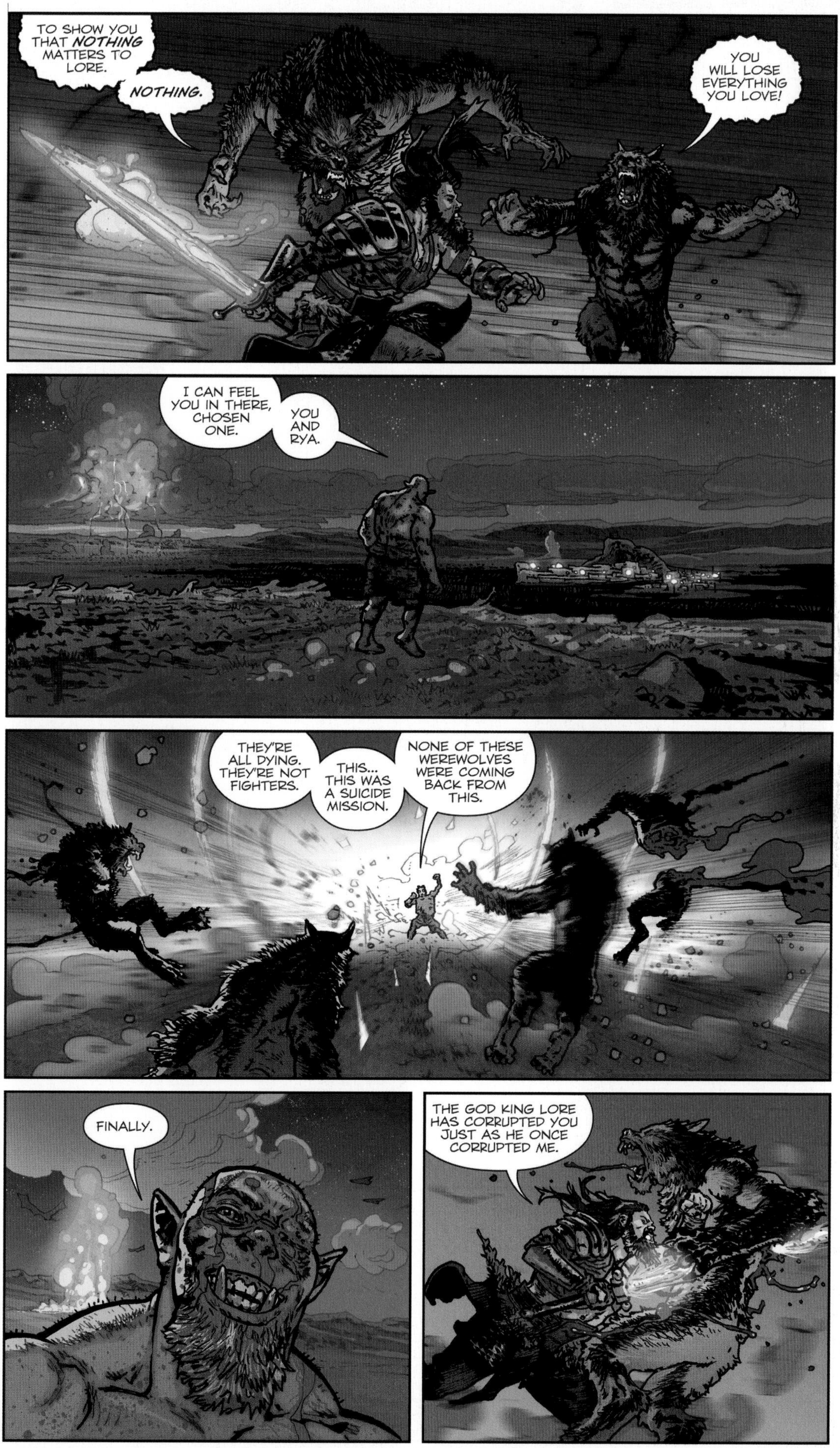
TO SHOW YOU THAT NOTHING MATTERS TO LORE.
NOTHING.
YOU WILL LOSE EVERYTHING YOU LOVE!
I CAN FEEL YOU IN THERE, CHOSEN ONE.
YOU AND RYA.
THEY'RE ALL DYING. THEY'RE NOT FIGHTERS.
THIS... THIS WAS A SUICIDE MISSION.
NONE OF THESE WEREWOLVES WERE COMING BACK FROM THIS.
FINALLY.
THE GOD KING LORE HAS CORRUPTED YOU JUST AS HE ONCE CORRUPTED ME.

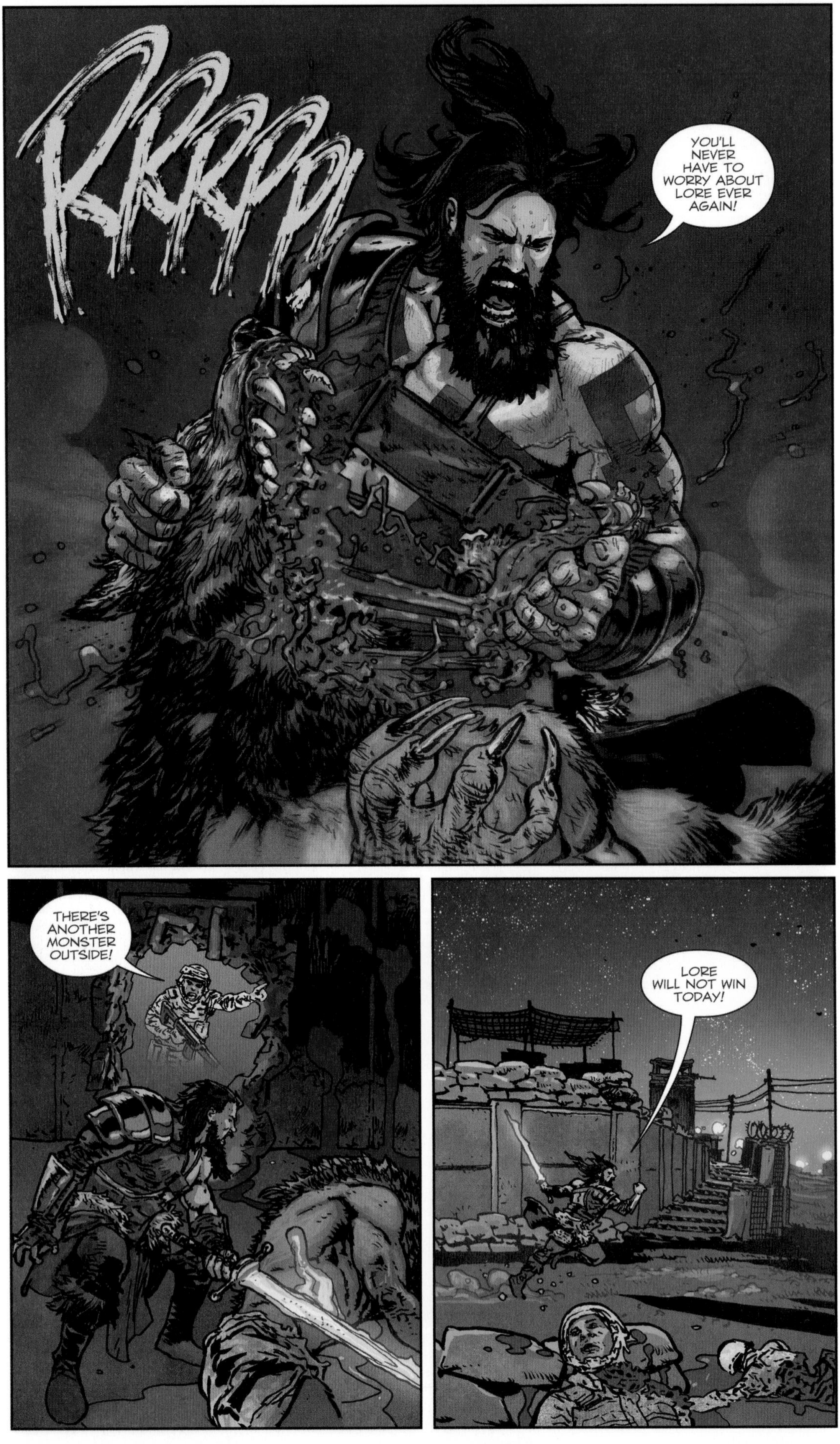
RRRRP!
YOU'LL NEVER HAVE TO WORRY ABOUT LORE EVER AGAIN!
THERE'S ANOTHER MONSTER OUTSIDE!
LORE WILL NOT WIN TODAY!

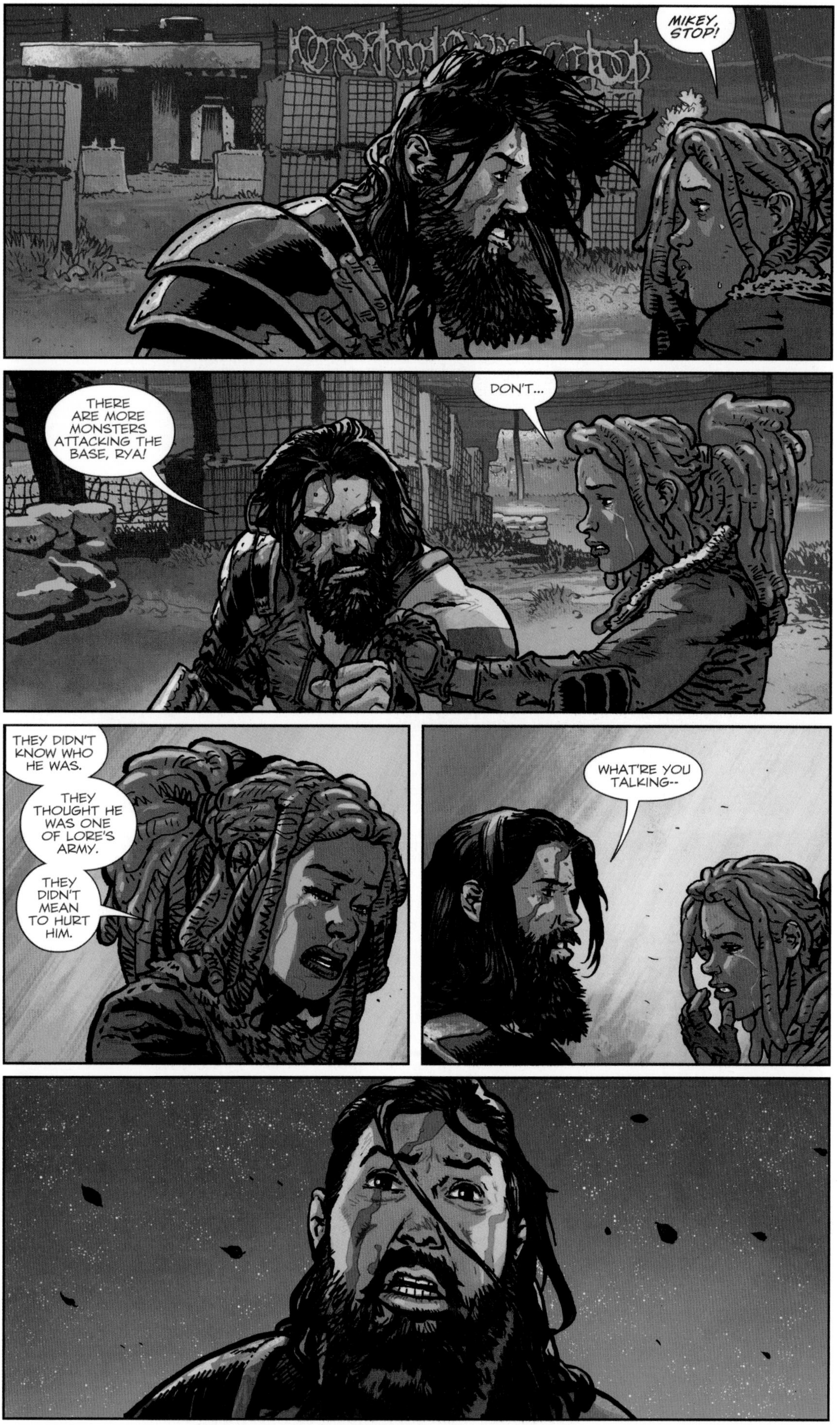
MIKEY, STOP!
THERE ARE MORE MONSTERS ATTACKING THE BASE, RYA!
DON'T...
THEY DIDN'T KNOW WHO HE WAS.
THEY THOUGHT HE WAS ONE OF LORE'S ARMY.
THEY DIDN'T MEAN TO HURT HIM.
WHAT'RE YOU TALKING--

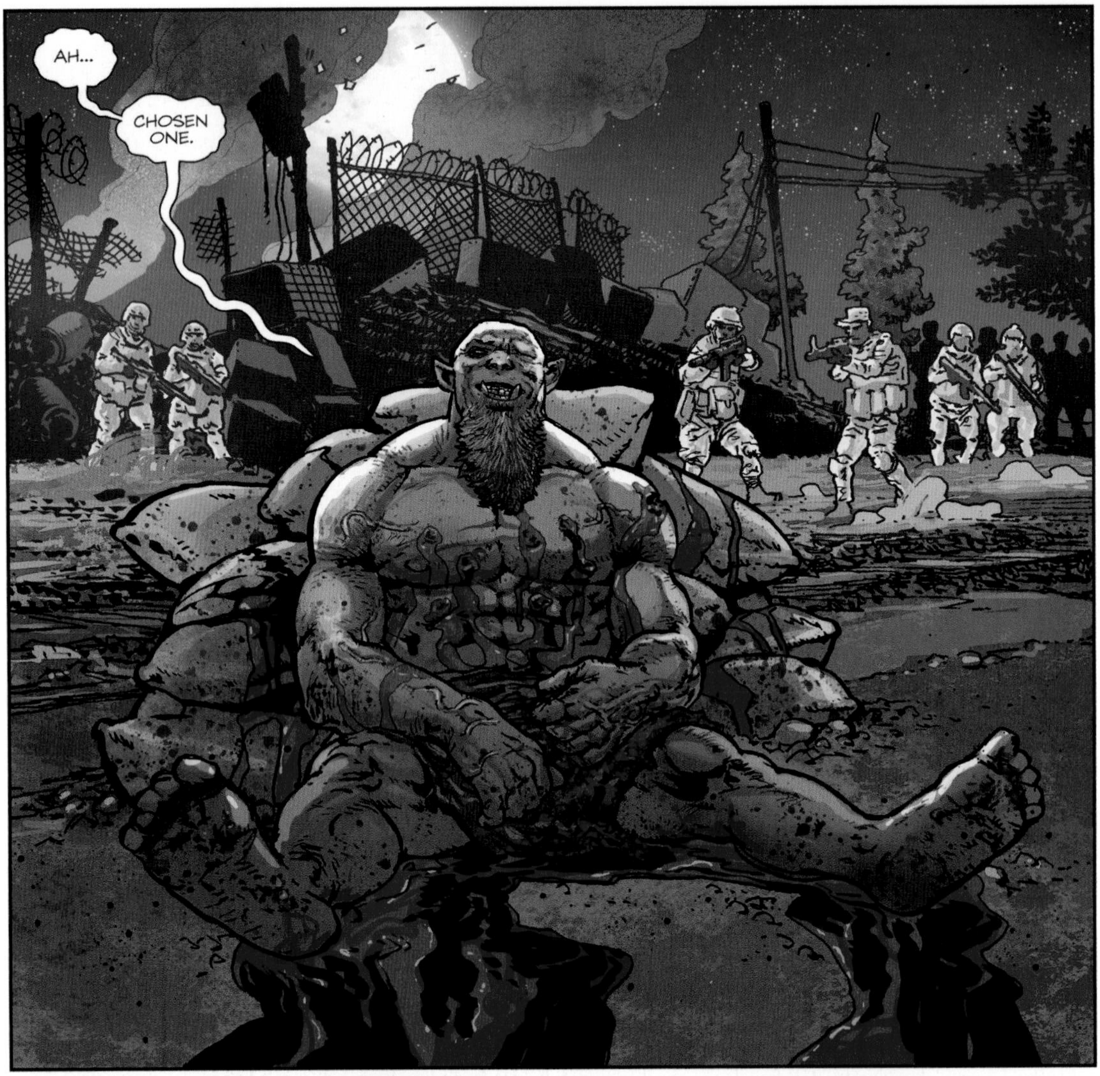
AH...
CHOSEN ONE.

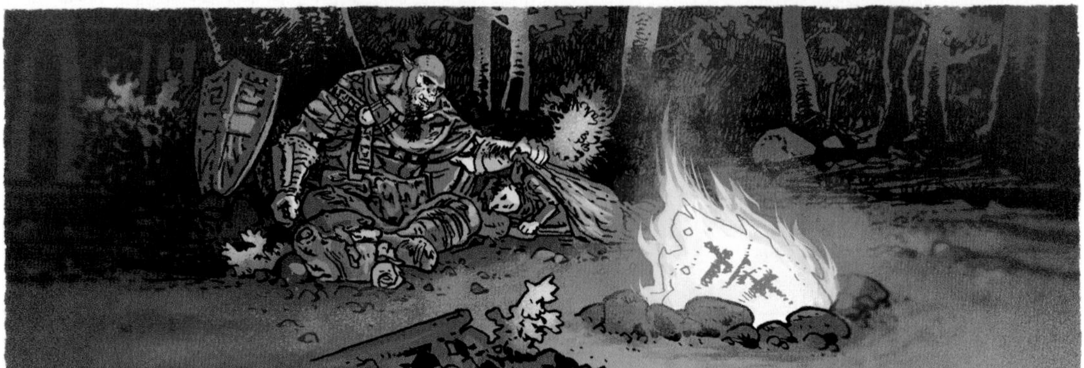

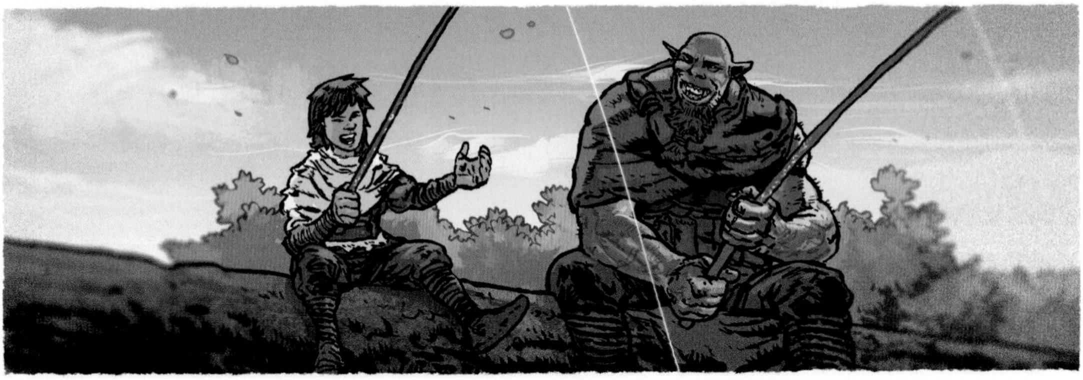

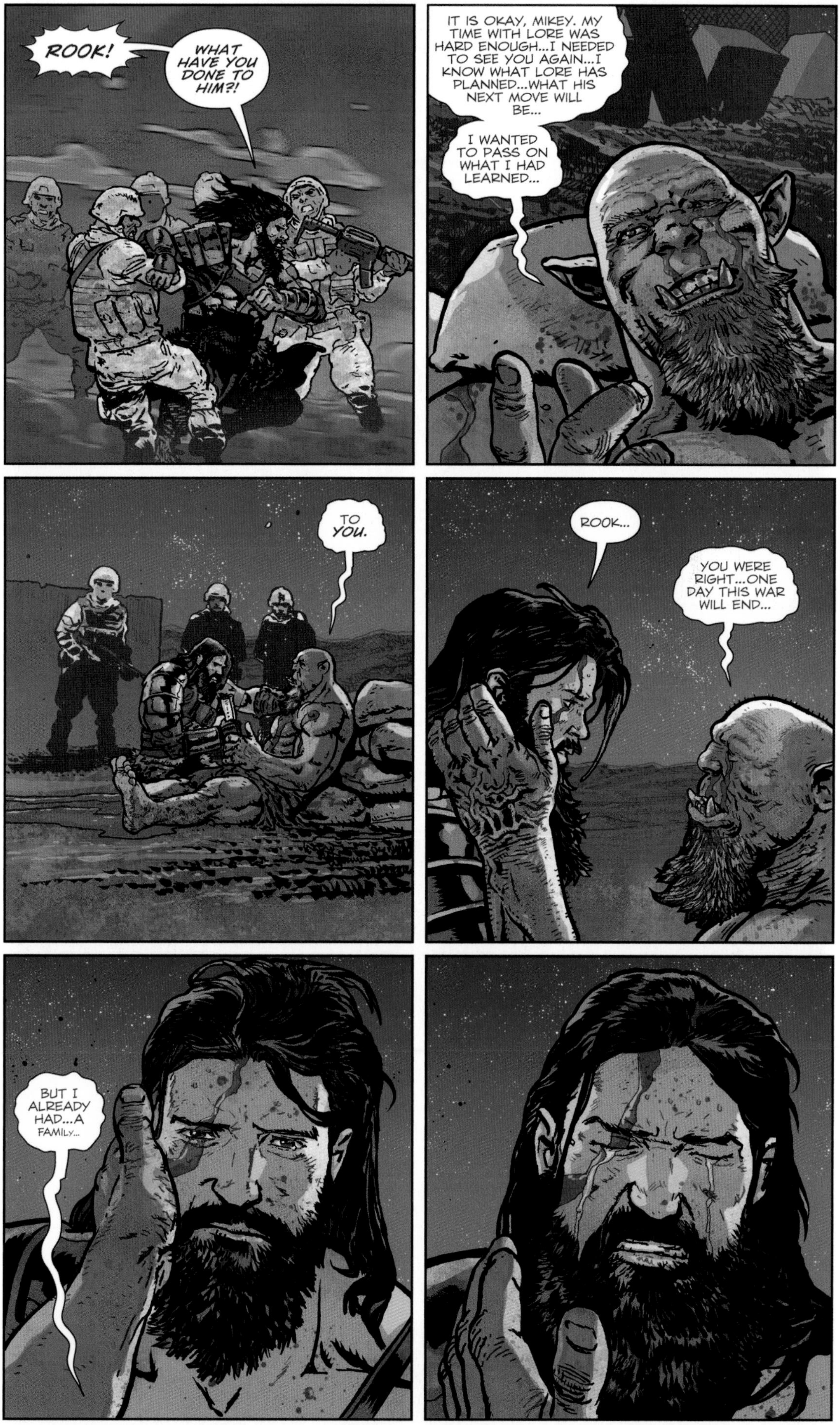
ROOK!
WHAT HAVE YOU DONE TO HIM?!
IT IS OKAY, MIKEY. MY TIME WITH LORE WAS HARD ENOUGH...I NEEDED TO SEE YOU AGAIN...I KNOW WHAT LORE HAS PLANNED...WHAT HIS NEXT MOVE WILL BE...
I WANTED TO PASS ON WHAT I HAD LEARNED...
TO YOU.
ROOK...
YOU WERE RIGHT...ONE DAY THIS WAR WILL END...
BUT I ALREADY HAD...A FAMILY...

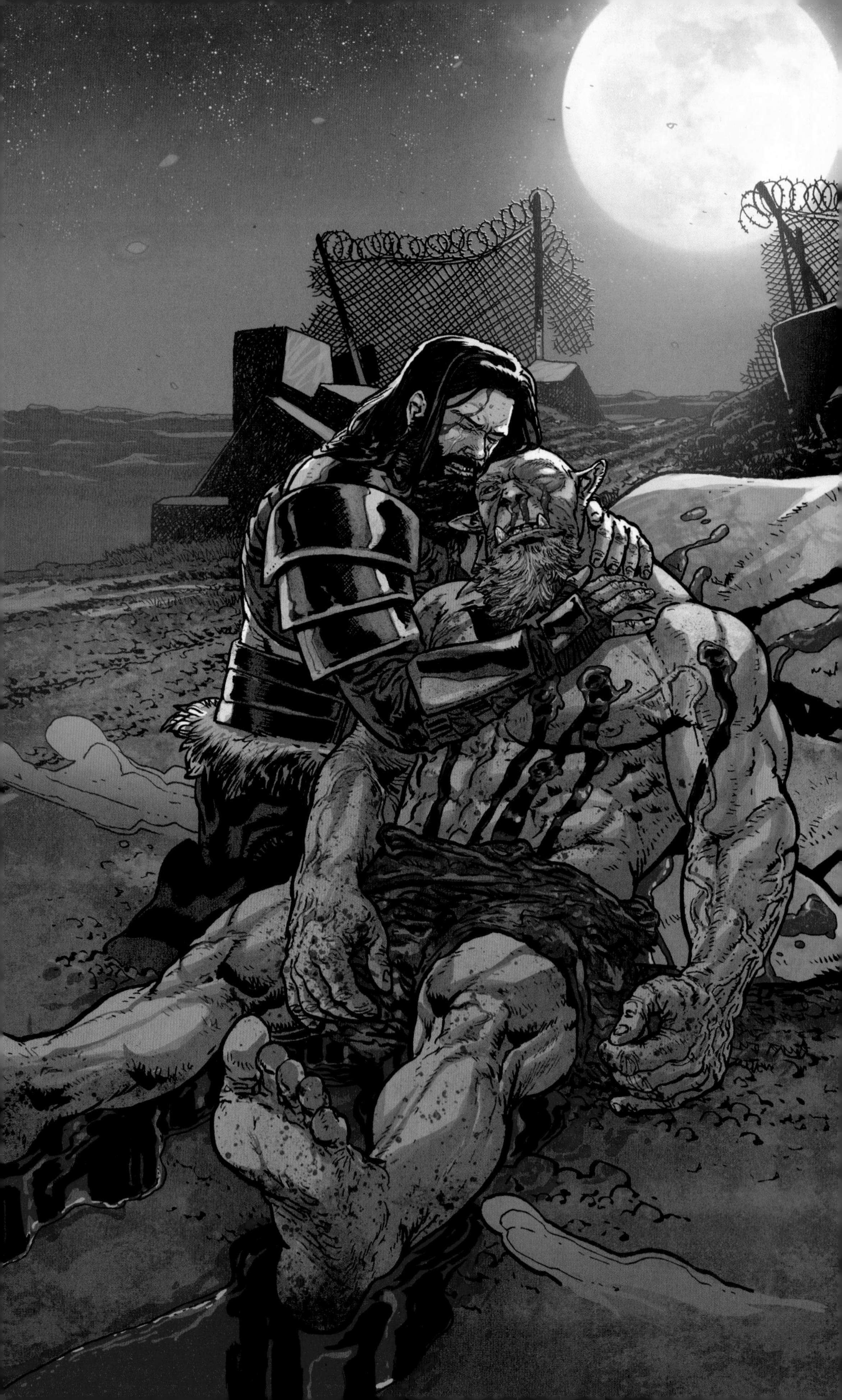

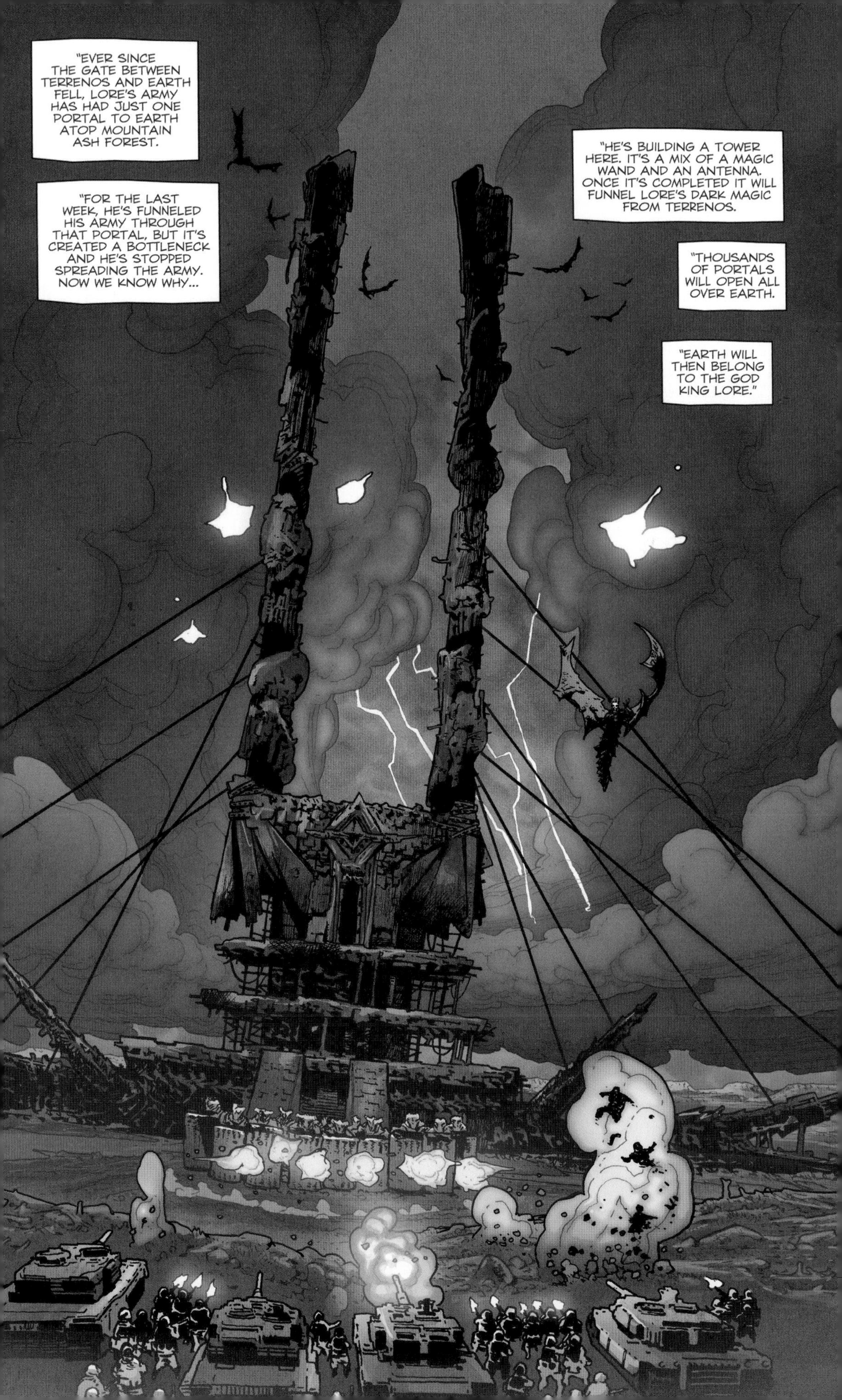
"EVER SINCE THE GATE BETWEEN TERRENOS AND EARTH FELL, LORE'S ARMY HAS HAD JUST ONE PORTAL TO EARTH ATOP MOUNTAIN ASH FOREST.
"FOR THE LAST WEEK, HE'S FUNNELED HIS ARMY THROUGH THAT PORTAL, BUT IT'S CREATED A BOTTLENECK AND HE'S STOPPED SPREADING THE ARMY. NOW WE KNOW WHY...
"HE'S BUILDING A TOWER HERE. IT'S A MIX OF A MAGIC WAND AND AN ANTENNA. ONCE IT'S COMPLETED IT WILL FUNNEL LORE'S DARK MAGIC FROM TERRENOS.
"THOUSANDS OF PORTALS WILL OPEN ALL OVER EARTH.
"EARTH WILL THEN BELONG TO THE GOD KING LORE."

THIS IS WHAT ROOK SACRIFICED HIMSELF TO GET TO US.

ROOK DIED SO THAT WE'D KNOW LORE'S PLANS. AND I'LL BE DAMNED IF I'LL LET ROOK DIE IN VAIN.

SO, I'M GOING TO GO *KILL* LORE.

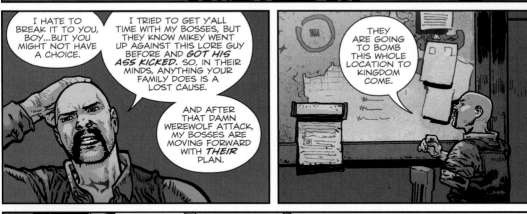

I HATE TO BREAK IT TO YOU, BOY...BUT YOU MIGHT NOT HAVE A CHOICE.

I TRIED TO GET Y'ALL TIME WITH MY BOSSES, BUT THEY KNOW MIKEY WENT UP AGAINST THIS LORE GUY BEFORE AND *GOT HIS ASS KICKED.* SO, IN THEIR MINDS, ANYTHING YOUR FAMILY DOES IS A LOST CAUSE.

AND AFTER THAT DAMN WEREWOLF ATTACK, MY BOSSES ARE MOVING FORWARD WITH *THEIR* PLAN.

THEY ARE GOING TO BOMB THIS WHOLE LOCATION TO KINGDOM COME.

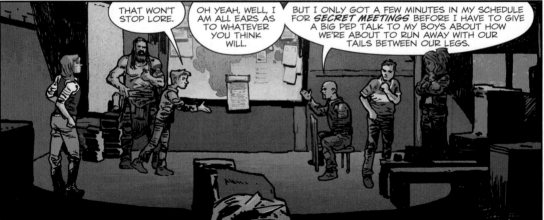

THAT WON'T STOP LORE.

OH YEAH, WELL, I AM ALL EARS AS TO WHATEVER YOU THINK WILL.

BUT I ONLY GOT A FEW MINUTES IN MY SCHEDULE FOR *SECRET MEETINGS* BEFORE I HAVE TO GIVE A BIG PEP TALK TO MY BOYS ABOUT HOW WE'RE ABOUT TO RUN AWAY WITH OUR TAILS BETWEEN OUR LEGS.

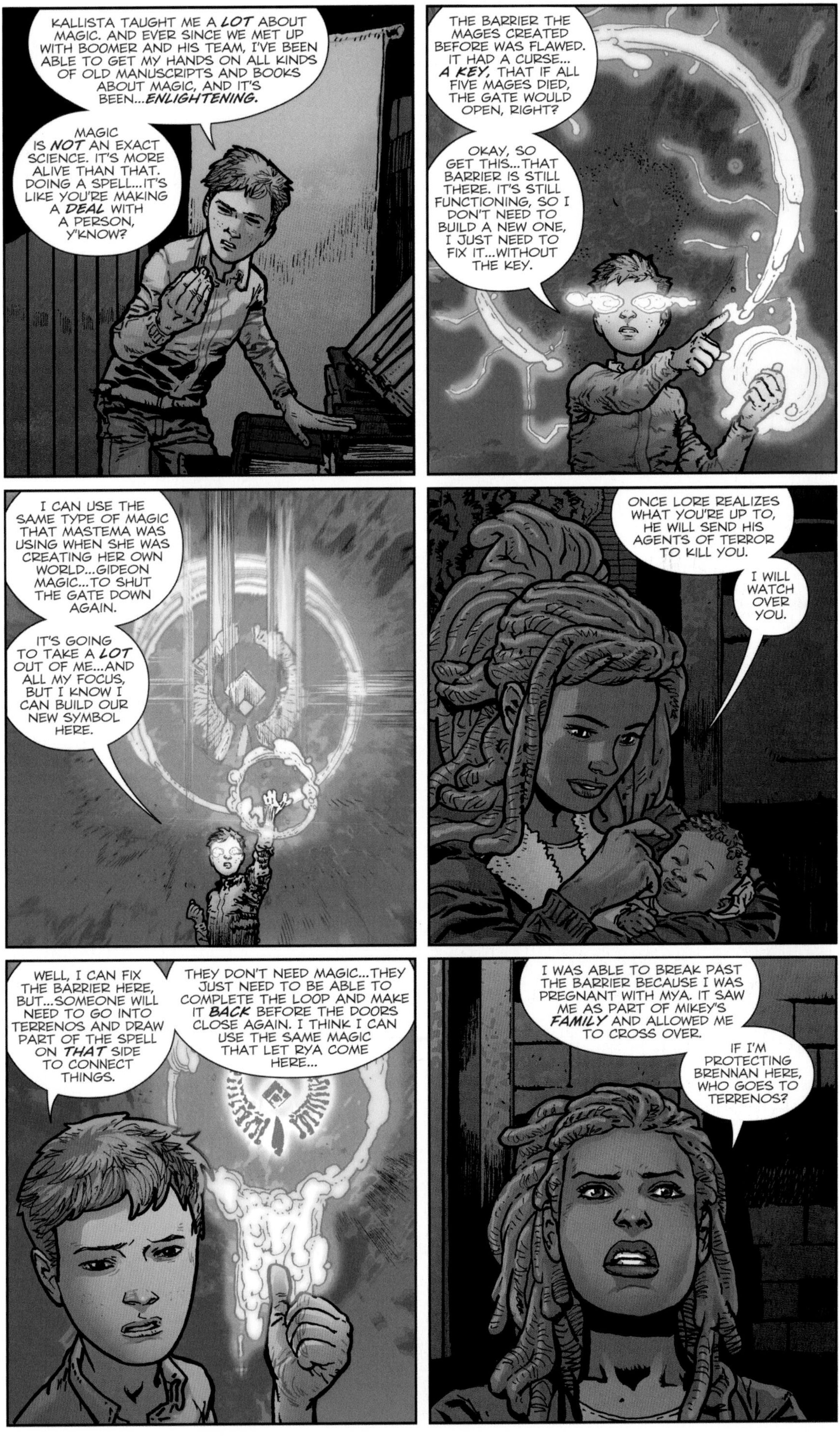
KALLISTA TAUGHT ME A LOT ABOUT MAGIC. AND EVER SINCE WE MET UP WITH BOOMER AND HIS TEAM, I'VE BEEN ABLE TO GET MY HANDS ON ALL KINDS OF OLD MANUSCRIPTS AND BOOKS ABOUT MAGIC, AND IT'S BEEN...ENLIGHTENING.
MAGIC IS NOT AN EXACT SCIENCE. IT'S MORE ALIVE THAN THAT. DOING A SPELL...IT'S LIKE YOU'RE MAKING A DEAL WITH A PERSON, Y'KNOW?
THE BARRIER THE MAGES CREATED BEFORE WAS FLAWED. IT HAD A CURSE... A KEY, THAT IF ALL FIVE MAGES DIED, THE GATE WOULD OPEN, RIGHT?
OKAY, SO GET THIS...THAT BARRIER IS STILL THERE. IT'S STILL FUNCTIONING, SO I DON'T NEED TO BUILD A NEW ONE, I JUST NEED TO FIX IT...WITHOUT THE KEY.
I CAN USE THE SAME TYPE OF MAGIC THAT MASTEMA WAS USING WHEN SHE WAS CREATING HER OWN WORLD...GIDEON MAGIC...TO SHUT THE GATE DOWN AGAIN.
IT'S GOING TO TAKE A LOT OUT OF ME...AND ALL MY FOCUS, BUT I KNOW I CAN BUILD OUR NEW SYMBOL HERE.
ONCE LORE REALIZES WHAT YOU'RE UP TO, HE WILL SEND HIS AGENTS OF TERROR TO KILL YOU.
I WILL WATCH OVER YOU.
WELL, I CAN FIX THE BARRIER HERE, BUT...SOMEONE WILL NEED TO GO INTO TERRENOS AND DRAW PART OF THE SPELL ON THAT SIDE TO CONNECT THINGS.
THEY DON'T NEED MAGIC...THEY JUST NEED TO BE ABLE TO COMPLETE THE LOOP AND MAKE IT BACK BEFORE THE DOORS CLOSE AGAIN. I THINK I CAN USE THE SAME MAGIC THAT LET RYA COME HERE...
I WAS ABLE TO BREAK PAST THE BARRIER BECAUSE I WAS PREGNANT WITH MYA. IT SAW ME AS PART OF MIKEY'S FAMILY AND ALLOWED ME TO CROSS OVER.
IF I'M PROTECTING BRENNAN HERE, WHO GOES TO TERRENOS?

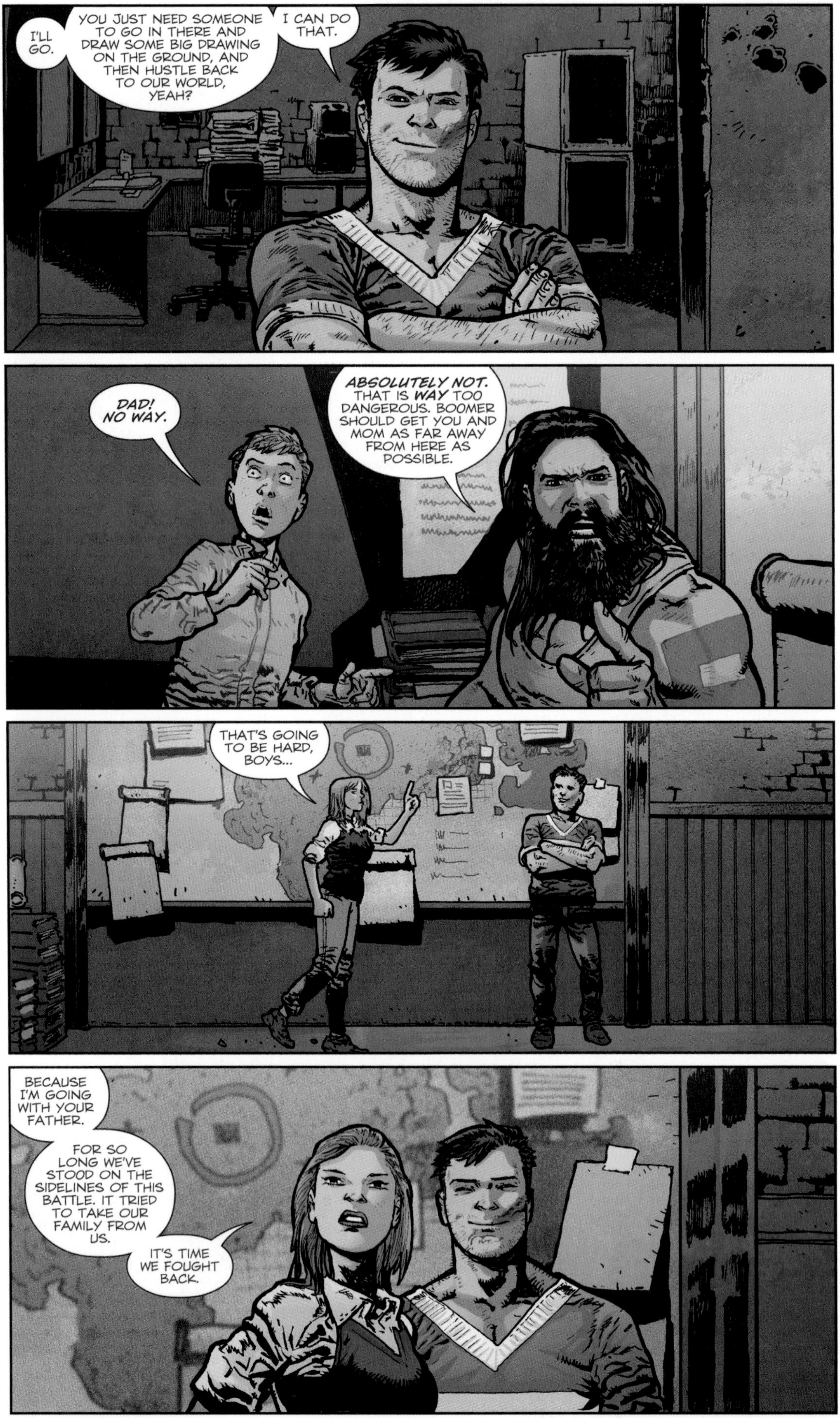
I'LL GO.
YOU JUST NEED SOMEONE TO GO IN THERE AND DRAW SOME BIG DRAWING ON THE GROUND, AND THEN HUSTLE BACK TO OUR WORLD, YEAH?
I CAN DO THAT.
DAD! NO WAY.
ABSOLUTELY NOT. THAT IS WAY TOO DANGEROUS. BOOMER SHOULD GET YOU AND MOM AS FAR AWAY FROM HERE AS POSSIBLE.
THAT'S GOING TO BE HARD, BOYS...
BECAUSE I'M GOING WITH YOUR FATHER.
FOR SO LONG WE'VE STOOD ON THE SIDELINES OF THIS BATTLE. IT TRIED TO TAKE OUR FAMILY FROM US.
IT'S TIME WE FOUGHT BACK.

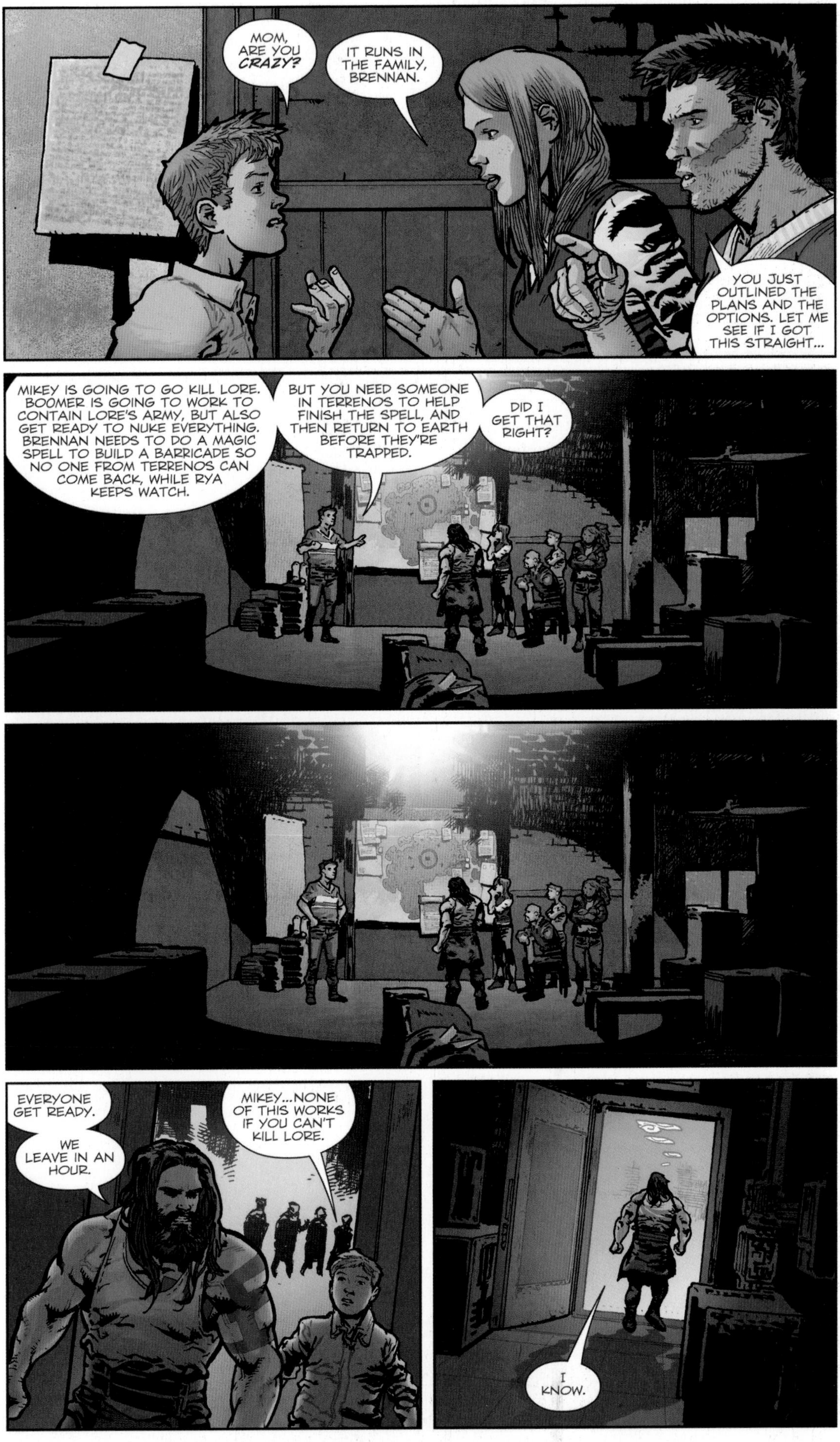
MOM, ARE YOU CRAZY?
IT RUNS IN THE FAMILY, BRENNAN.
YOU JUST OUTLINED THE PLANS AND THE OPTIONS. LET ME SEE IF I GOT THIS STRAIGHT...
MIKEY IS GOING TO GO KILL LORE. BOOMER IS GOING TO WORK TO CONTAIN LORE'S ARMY, BUT ALSO GET READY TO NUKE EVERYTHING. BRENNAN NEEDS TO DO A MAGIC SPELL TO BUILD A BARRICADE SO NO ONE FROM TERRENOS CAN COME BACK, WHILE RYA KEEPS WATCH.
BUT YOU NEED SOMEONE IN TERRENOS TO HELP FINISH THE SPELL, AND THEN RETURN TO EARTH BEFORE THEY'RE TRAPPED.
DID I GET THAT RIGHT?
EVERYONE GET READY.
WE LEAVE IN AN HOUR.
MIKEY...NONE OF THIS WORKS IF YOU CAN'T KILL LORE.
I KNOW.

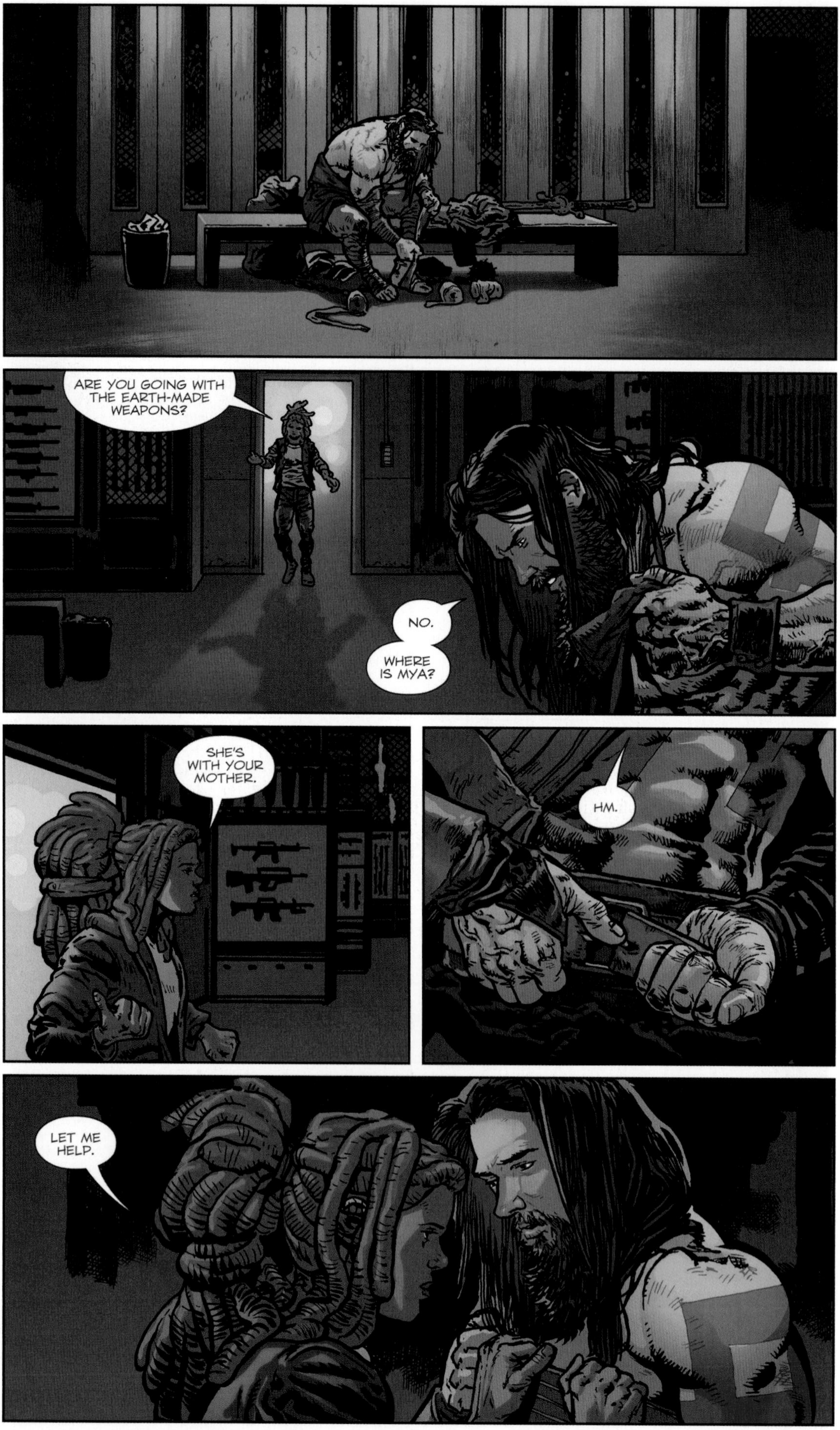

ARE YOU GOING WITH THE EARTH-MADE WEAPONS?
NO.
WHERE IS MYA?
SHE'S WITH YOUR MOTHER.
HM.
LET ME HELP.

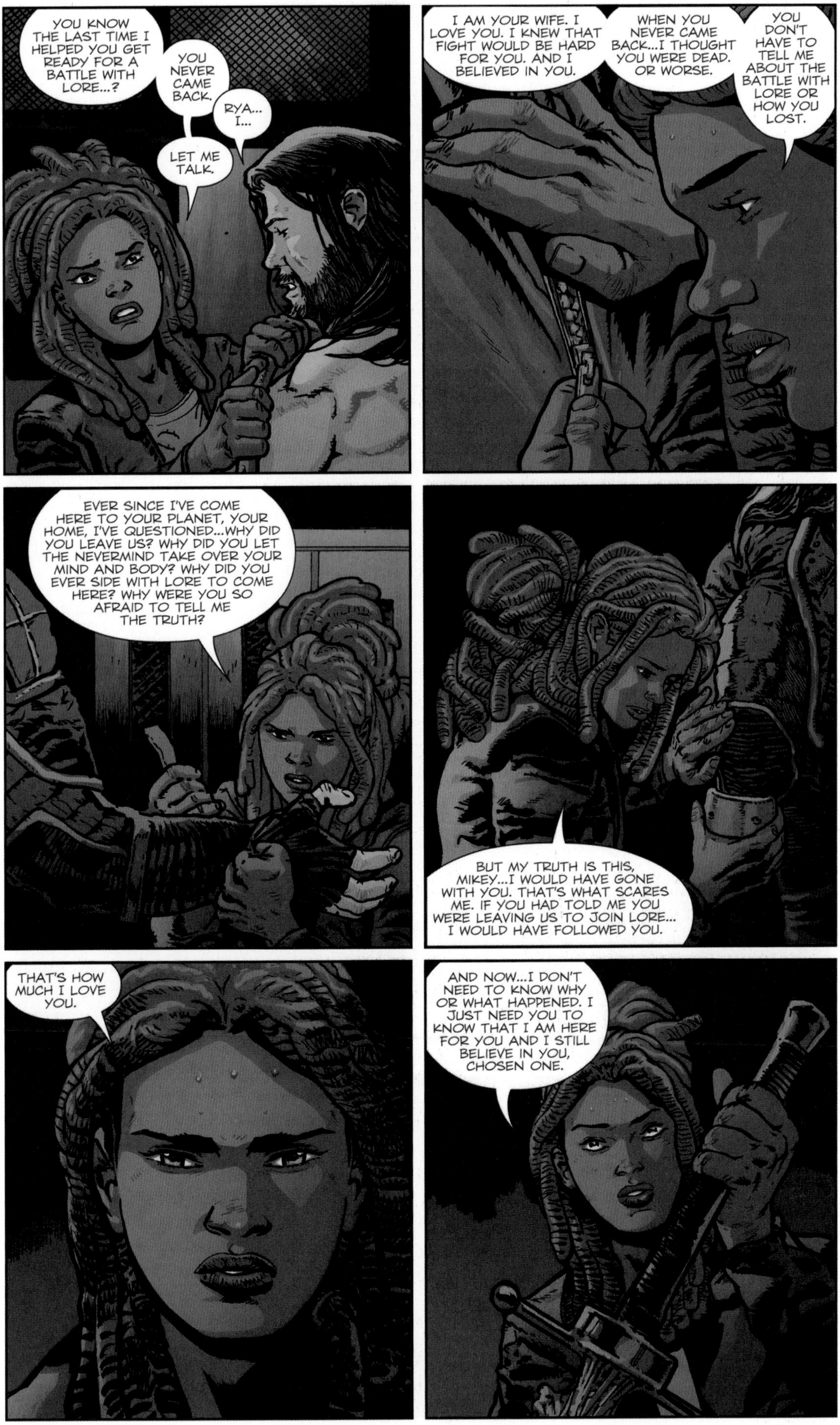
YOU KNOW THE LAST TIME I HELPED YOU GET READY FOR A BATTLE WITH LORE...?
YOU NEVER CAME BACK.
RYA... I...
LET ME TALK.
I AM YOUR WIFE. I LOVE YOU. I KNEW THAT FIGHT WOULD BE HARD FOR YOU. AND I BELIEVED IN YOU.
WHEN YOU NEVER CAME BACK...I THOUGHT YOU WERE DEAD. OR WORSE.
YOU DON'T HAVE TO TELL ME ABOUT THE BATTLE WITH LORE OR HOW YOU LOST.
EVER SINCE I'VE COME HERE TO YOUR PLANET, YOUR HOME, I'VE QUESTIONED...WHY DID YOU LEAVE US? WHY DID YOU LET THE NEVERMIND TAKE OVER YOUR MIND AND BODY? WHY DID YOU EVER SIDE WITH LORE TO COME HERE? WHY WERE YOU SO AFRAID TO TELL ME THE TRUTH?
BUT MY TRUTH IS THIS, MIKEY...I WOULD HAVE GONE WITH YOU. THAT'S WHAT SCARES ME. IF YOU HAD TOLD ME YOU WERE LEAVING US TO JOIN LORE... I WOULD HAVE FOLLOWED YOU.
THAT'S HOW MUCH I LOVE YOU.
AND NOW...I DON'T NEED TO KNOW WHY OR WHAT HAPPENED. I JUST NEED YOU TO KNOW THAT I AM HERE FOR YOU AND I STILL BELIEVE IN YOU, CHOSEN ONE.

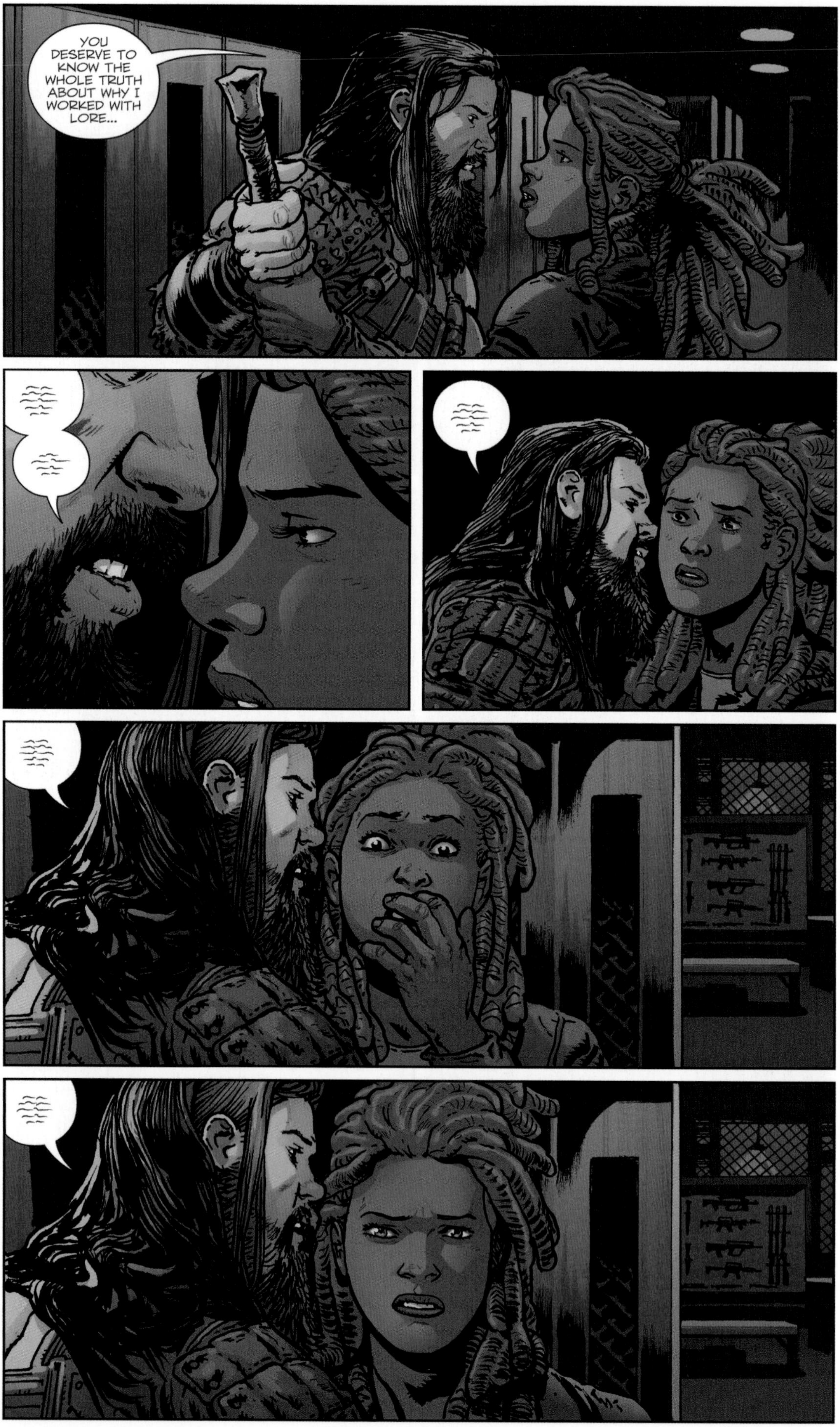
YOU DESERVE TO KNOW THE WHOLE TRUTH ABOUT WHY I WORKED WITH LORE...

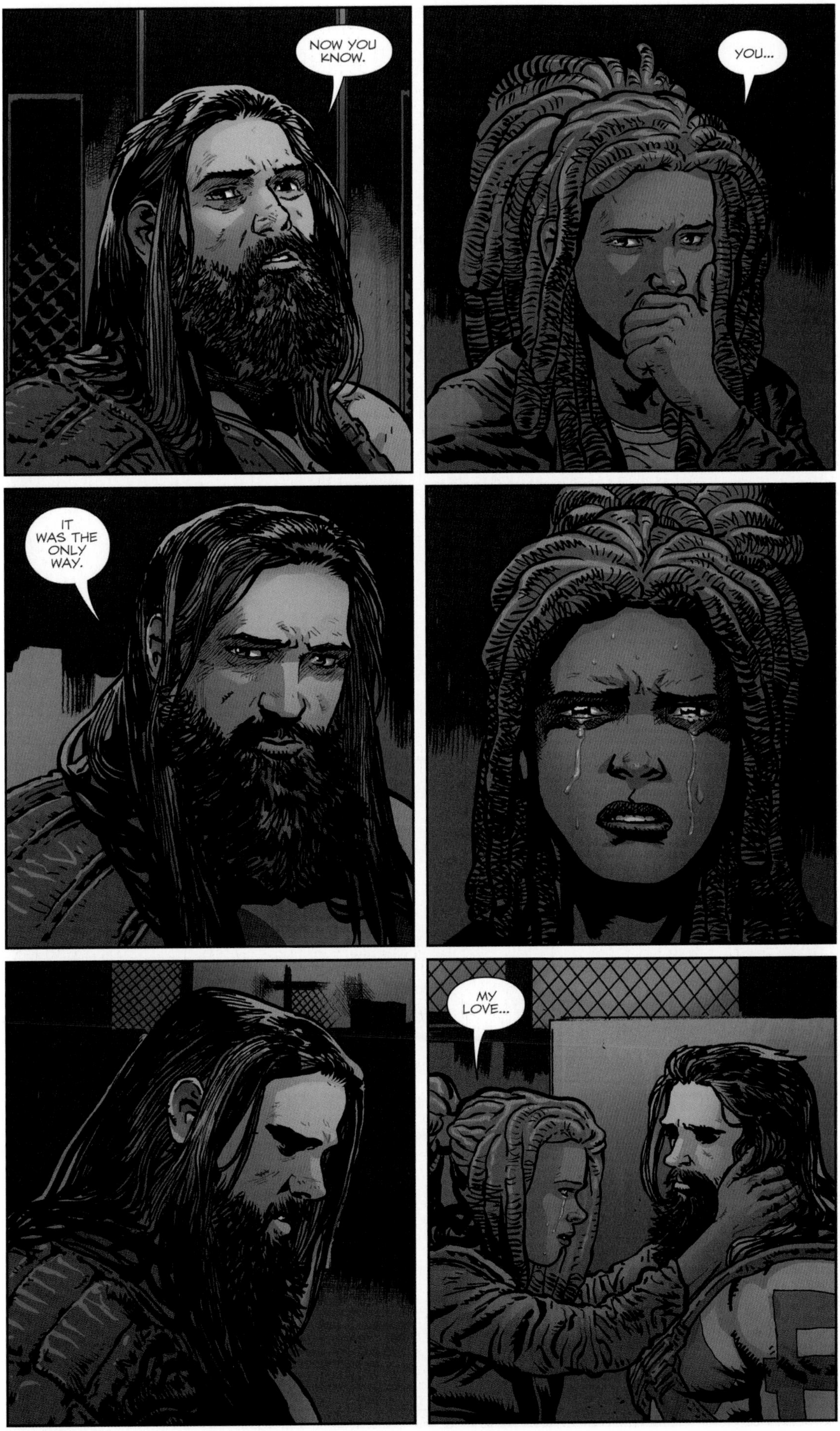
NOW YOU KNOW.
YOU...
IT WAS THE ONLY WAY.
MY LOVE...

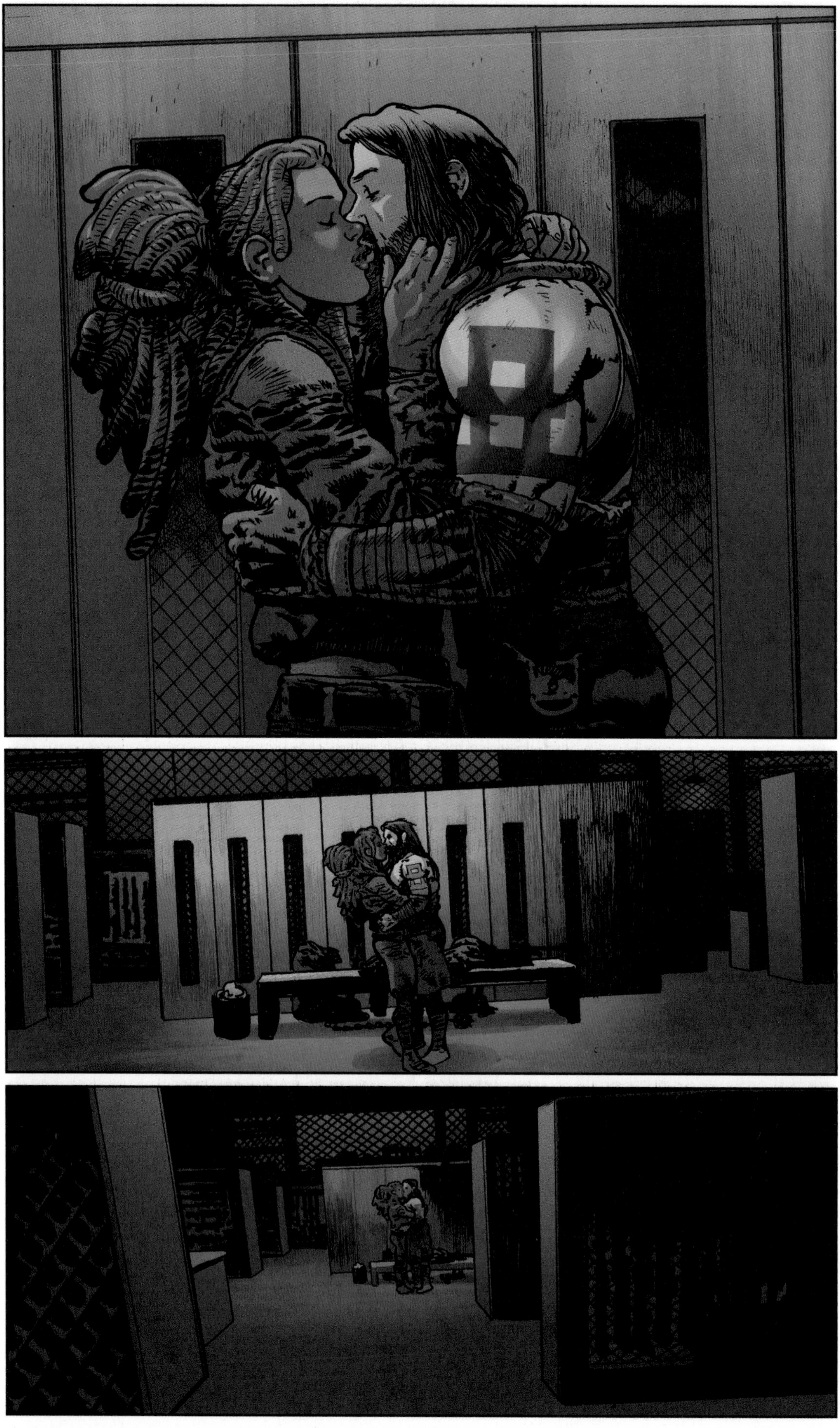

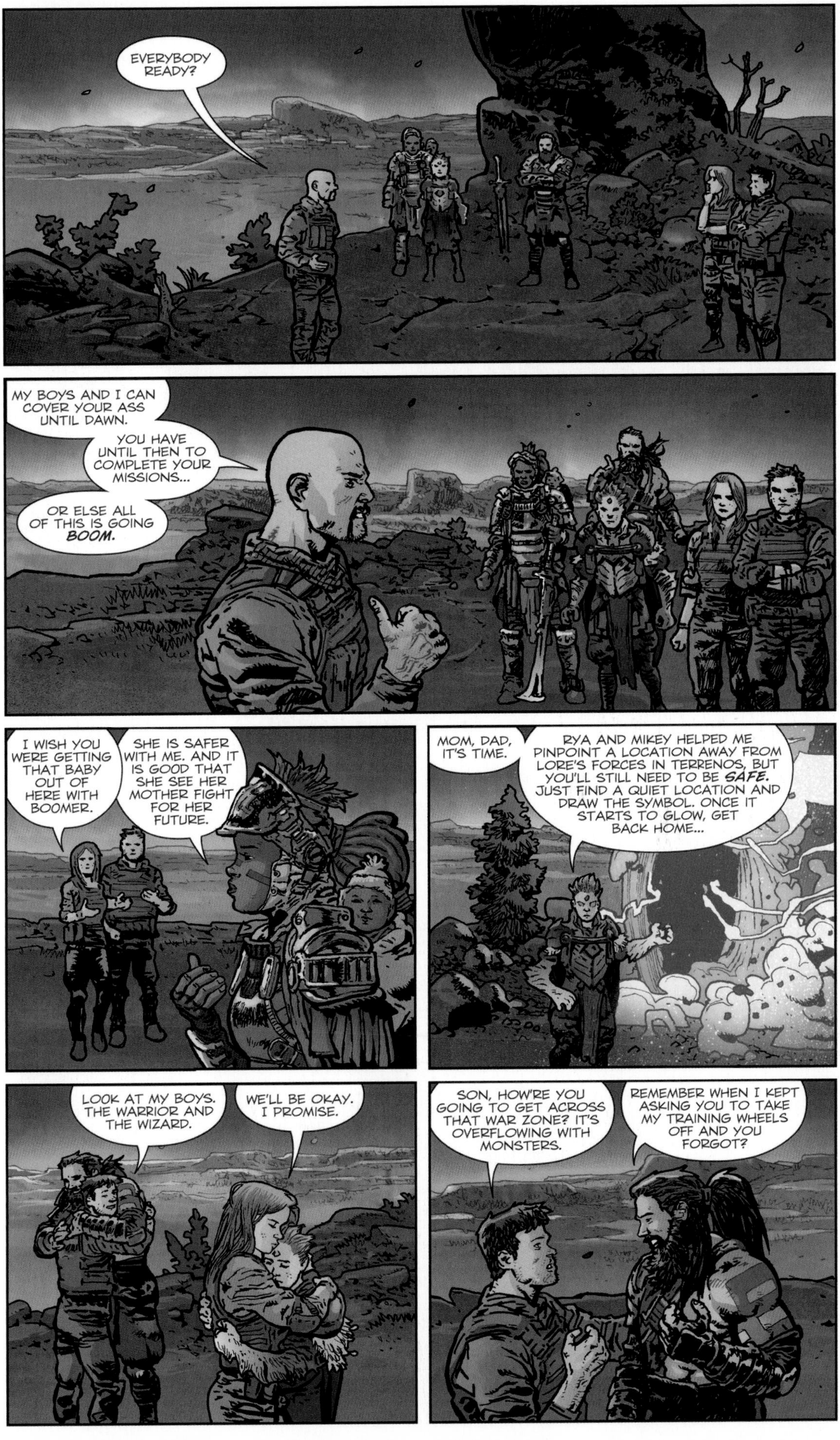
EVERYBODY READY?
MY BOYS AND I CAN COVER YOUR ASS UNTIL DAWN.
YOU HAVE UNTIL THEN TO COMPLETE YOUR MISSIONS...
OR ELSE ALL OF THIS IS GOING *BOOM.*
I WISH YOU WERE GETTING THAT BABY OUT OF HERE WITH BOOMER.
SHE IS SAFER WITH ME. AND IT IS GOOD THAT SHE SEE HER MOTHER FIGHT FOR HER FUTURE.
MOM, DAD, IT'S TIME.
RYA AND MIKEY HELPED ME PINPOINT A LOCATION AWAY FROM LORE'S FORCES IN TERRENOS, BUT YOU'LL STILL NEED TO BE *SAFE.* JUST FIND A QUIET LOCATION AND DRAW THE SYMBOL. ONCE IT STARTS TO GLOW, GET BACK HOME...
LOOK AT MY BOYS. THE WARRIOR AND THE WIZARD.
WE'LL BE OKAY. I PROMISE.
SON, HOW'RE YOU GOING TO GET ACROSS THAT WAR ZONE? IT'S OVERFLOWING WITH MONSTERS.
REMEMBER WHEN I KEPT ASKING YOU TO TAKE MY TRAINING WHEELS OFF AND YOU FORGOT?

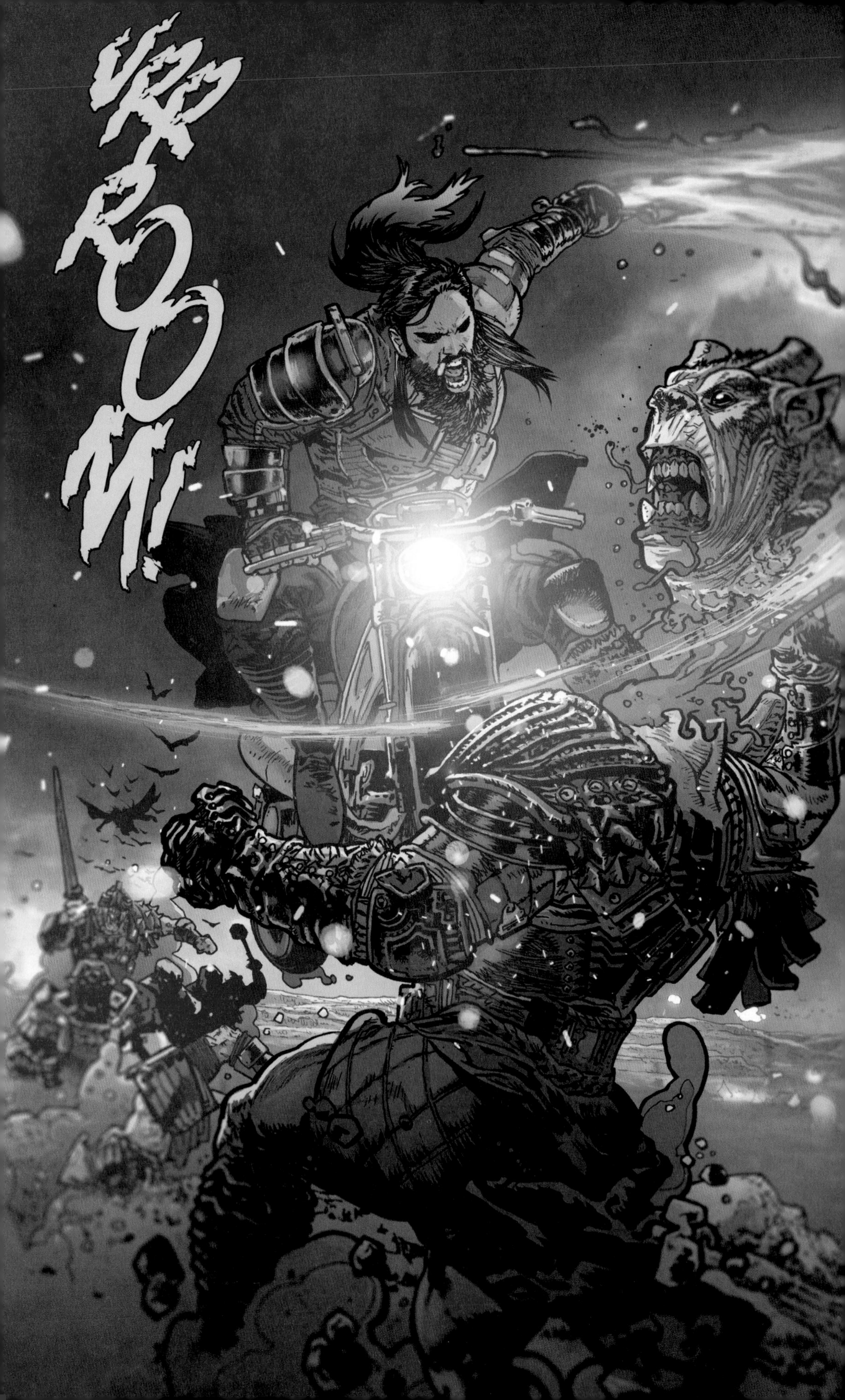
VRROOM!

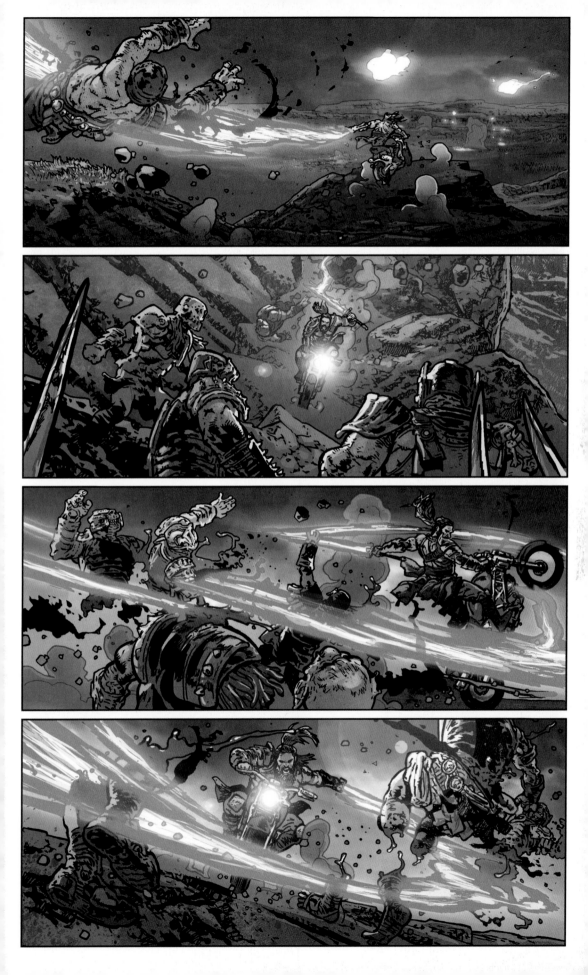

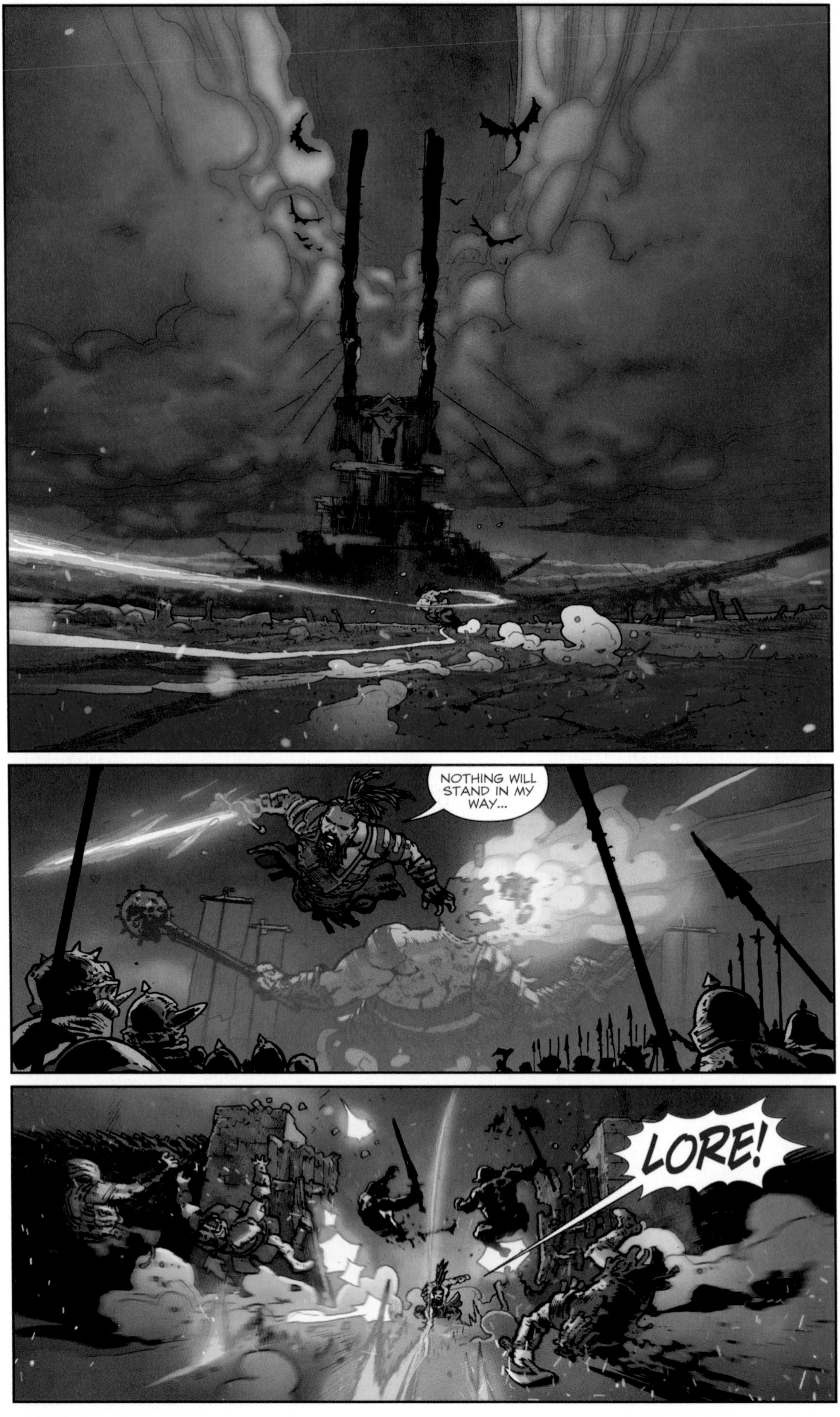
NOTHING WILL STAND IN MY WAY...
LORE!

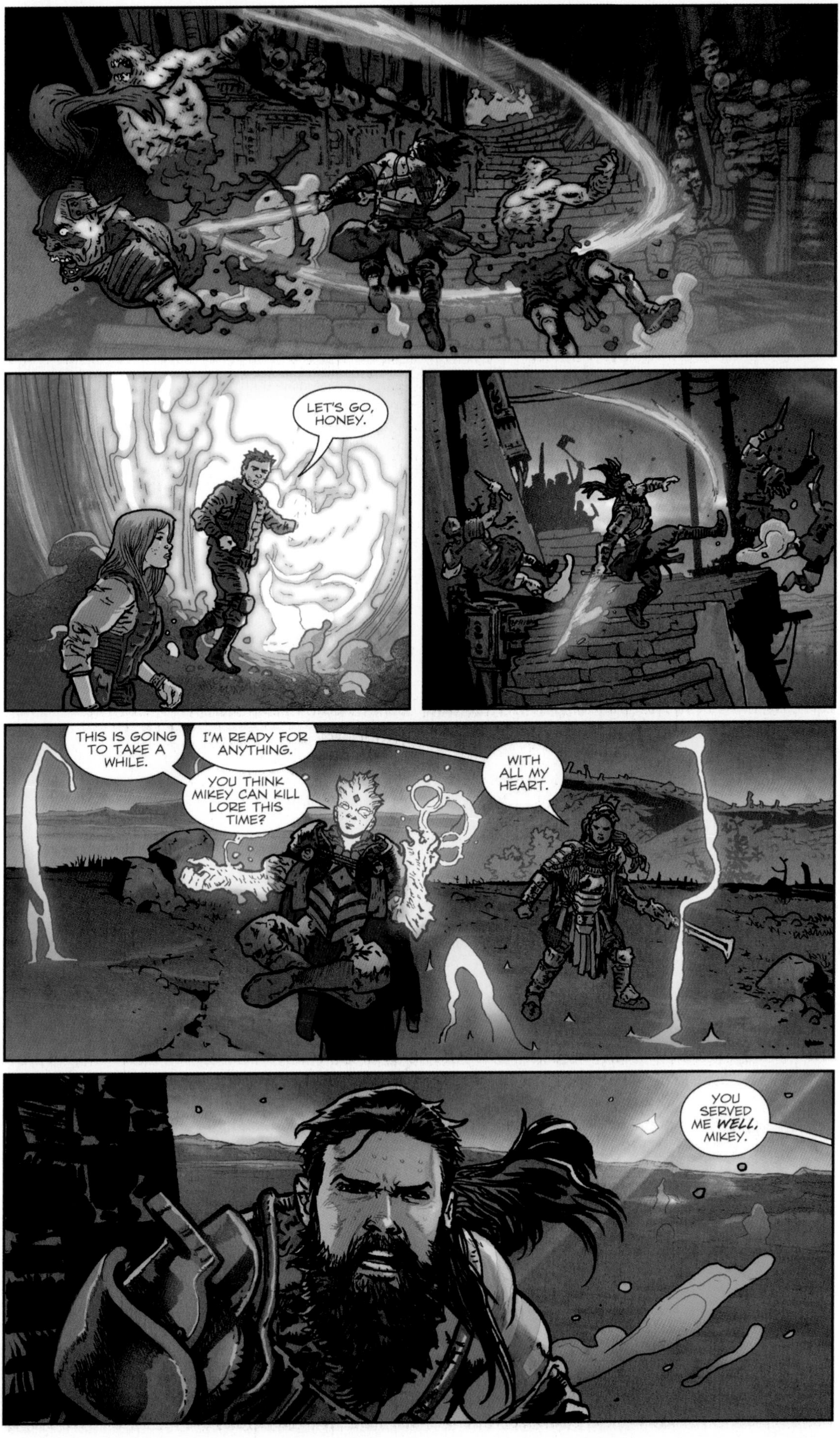
LET'S GO, HONEY.
THIS IS GOING TO TAKE A WHILE.
I'M READY FOR ANYTHING.
YOU THINK MIKEY CAN KILL LORE THIS TIME?
WITH ALL MY HEART.
YOU SERVED ME WELL, MIKEY.

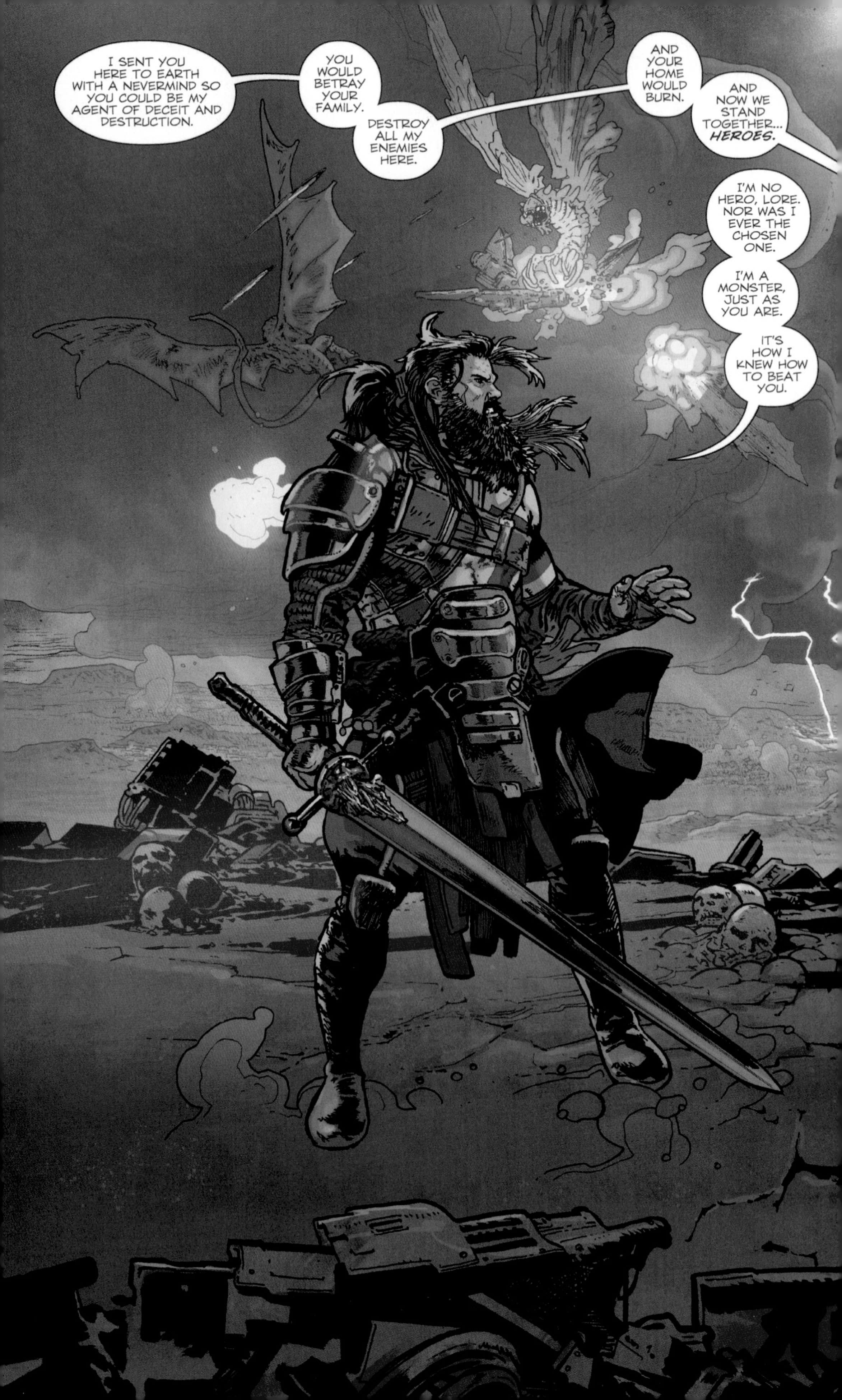
I SENT YOU HERE TO EARTH WITH A NEVERMIND SO YOU COULD BE MY AGENT OF DECEIT AND DESTRUCTION.
YOU WOULD BETRAY YOUR FAMILY.
DESTROY ALL MY ENEMIES HERE.
AND YOUR HOME WOULD BURN.
AND NOW WE STAND TOGETHER... *HEROES.*
I'M NO HERO, LORE. NOR WAS I EVER THE CHOSEN ONE.
I'M A MONSTER, JUST AS YOU ARE.
IT'S HOW I KNEW HOW TO BEAT YOU.

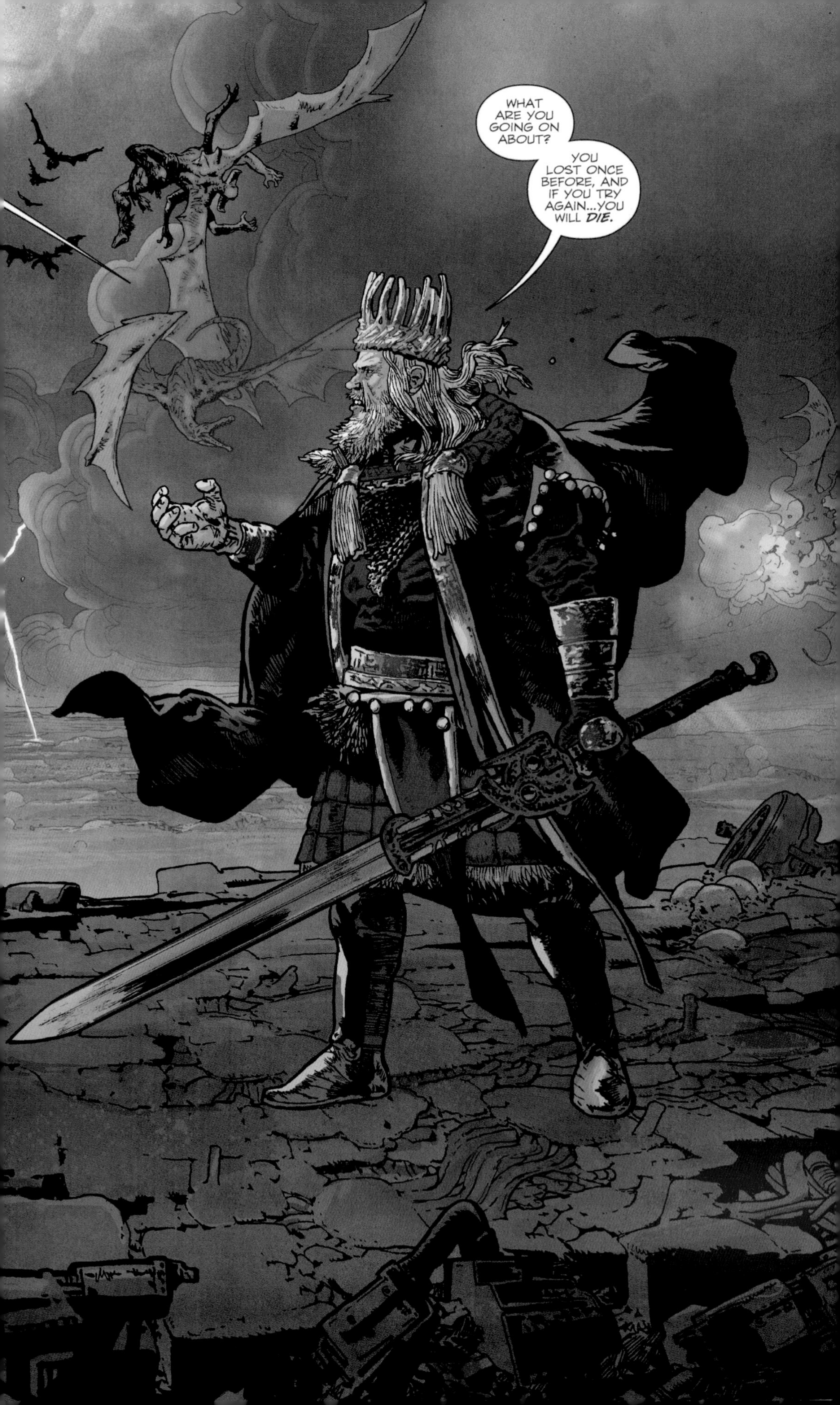
WHAT ARE YOU GOING ON ABOUT?
YOU LOST ONCE BEFORE, AND IF YOU TRY AGAIN...YOU WILL *DIE.*

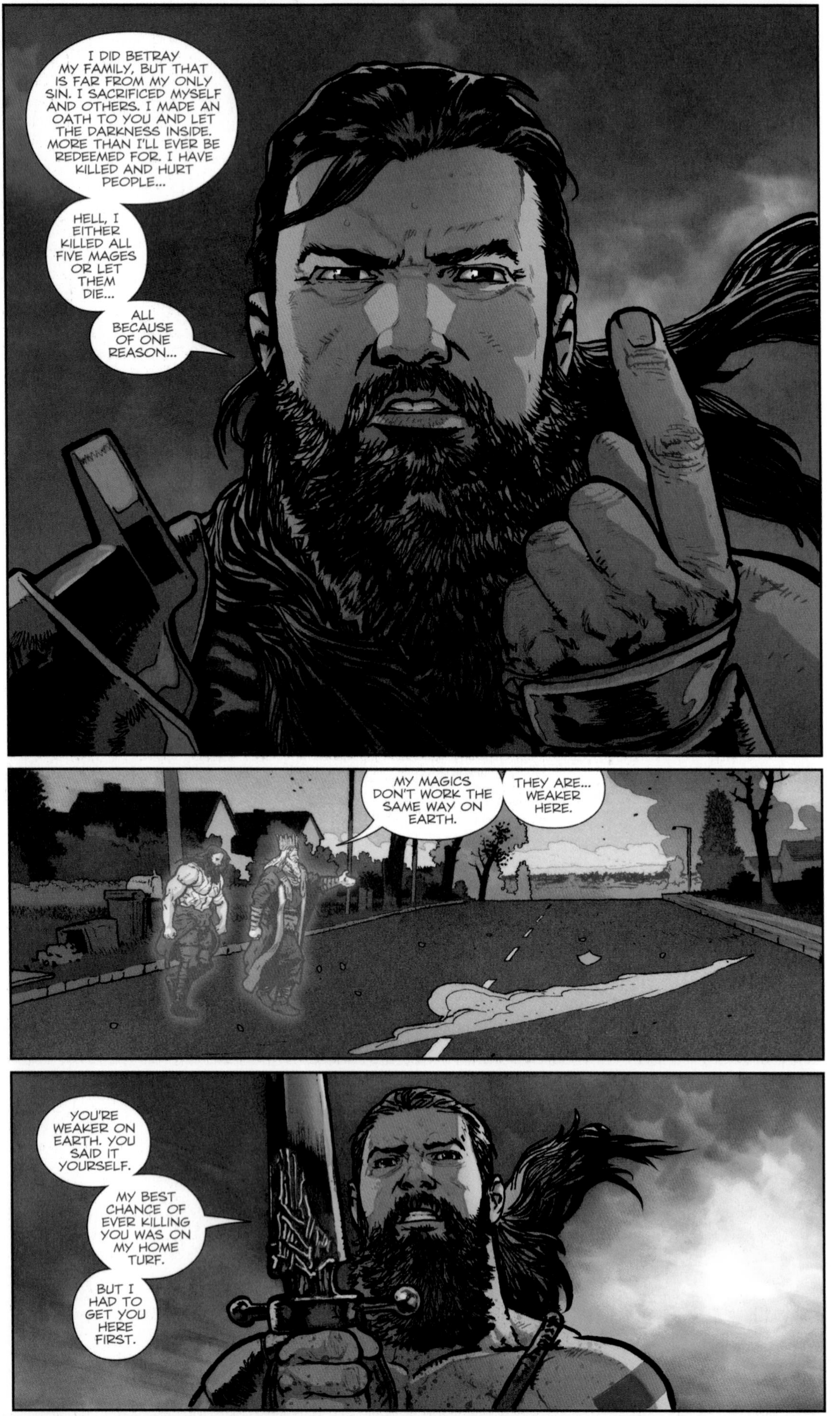
I DID BETRAY MY FAMILY, BUT THAT IS FAR FROM MY ONLY SIN. I SACRIFICED MYSELF AND OTHERS. I MADE AN OATH TO YOU AND LET THE DARKNESS INSIDE. MORE THAN I'LL EVER BE REDEEMED FOR. I HAVE KILLED AND HURT PEOPLE...
HELL, I EITHER KILLED ALL FIVE MAGES OR LET THEM DIE...
ALL BECAUSE OF ONE REASON...
MY MAGICS DON'T WORK THE SAME WAY ON EARTH.
THEY ARE... WEAKER HERE.
YOU'RE WEAKER ON EARTH. YOU SAID IT YOURSELF.
MY BEST CHANCE OF EVER KILLING YOU WAS ON MY HOME TURF.
BUT I HAD TO GET YOU HERE FIRST.

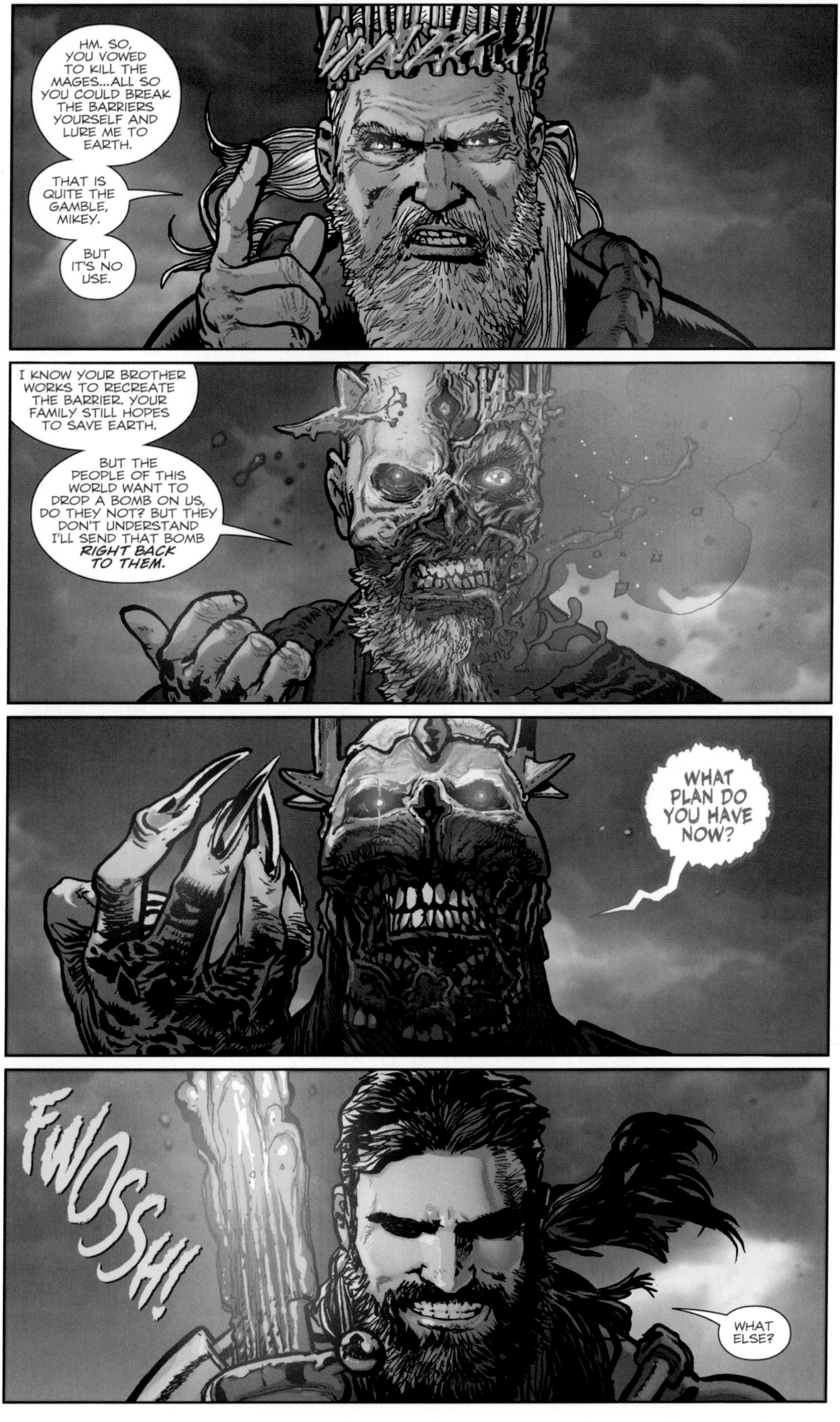
HM. SO, YOU VOWED TO KILL THE MAGES...ALL SO YOU COULD BREAK THE BARRIERS YOURSELF AND LURE ME TO EARTH.
THAT IS QUITE THE GAMBLE, MIKEY.
BUT IT'S NO USE.
I KNOW YOUR BROTHER WORKS TO RECREATE THE BARRIER. YOUR FAMILY STILL HOPES TO SAVE EARTH.
BUT THE PEOPLE OF THIS WORLD WANT TO DROP A BOMB ON US, DO THEY NOT? BUT THEY DON'T UNDERSTAND I'LL SEND THAT BOMB *RIGHT BACK TO THEM.*
WHAT PLAN DO YOU HAVE NOW?
FWOSSH!
WHAT ELSE?

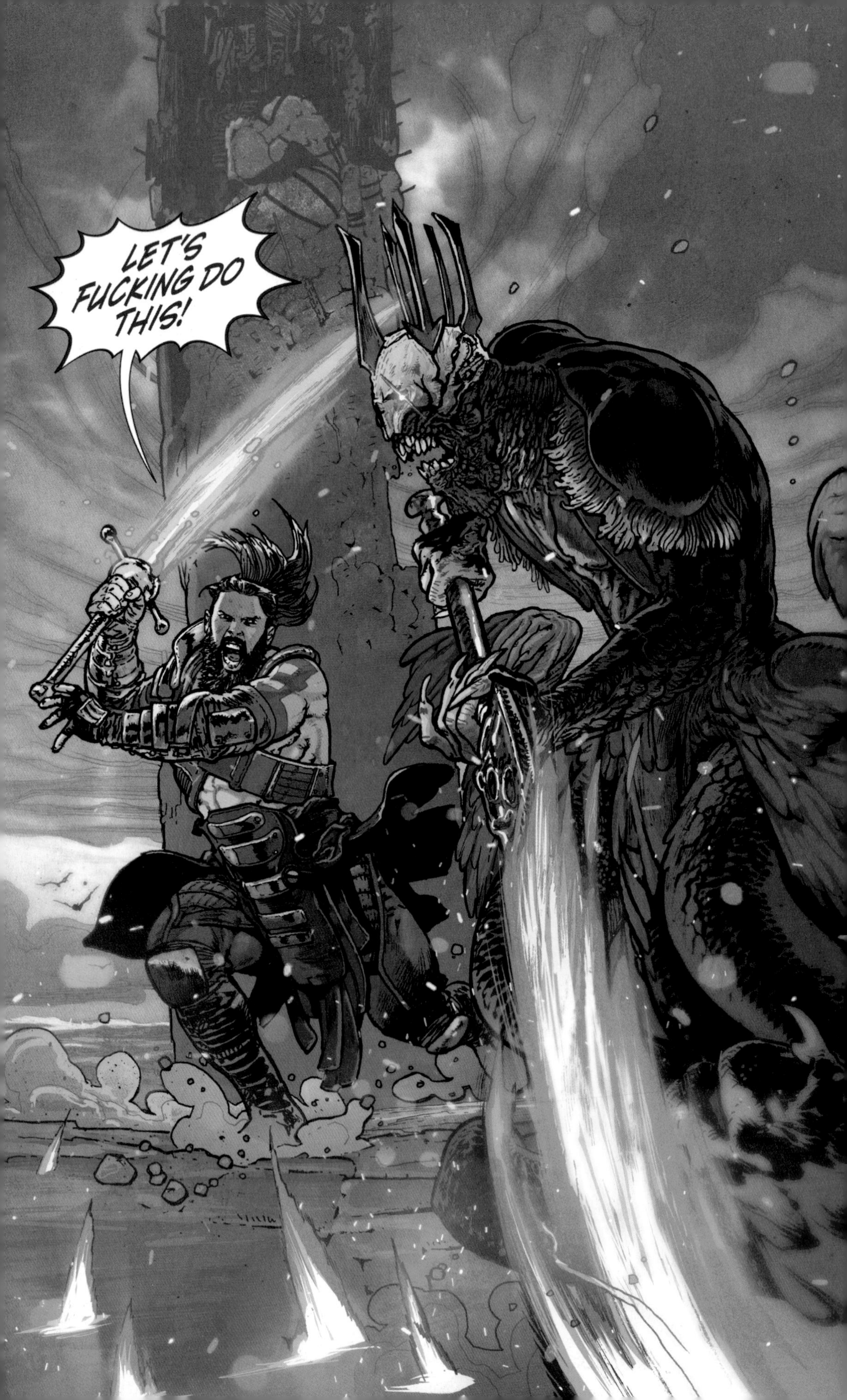
LET'S FUCKING DO THIS!

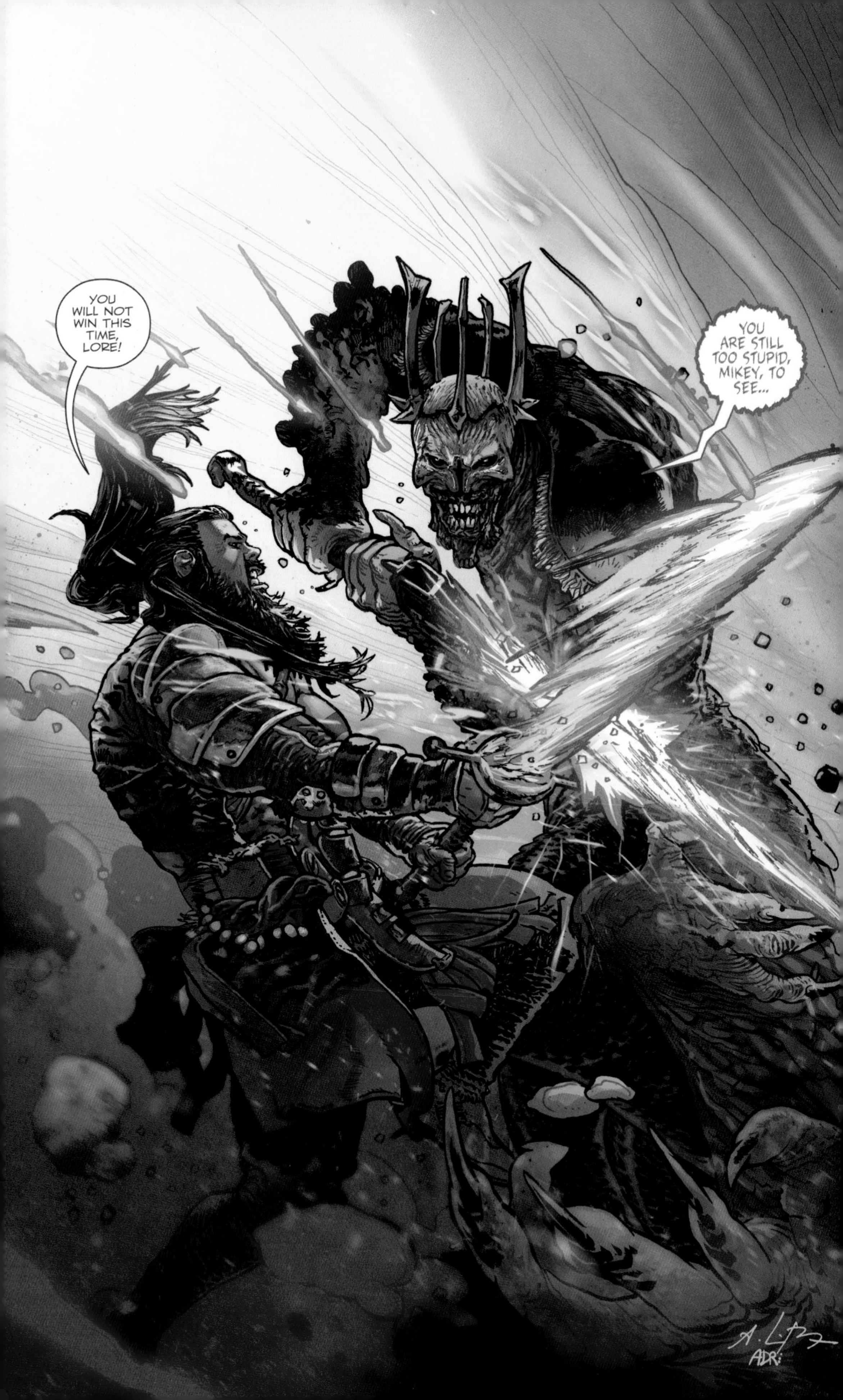
YOU WILL NOT WIN THIS TIME, LORE!
YOU ARE STILL TOO STUPID, MIKEY, TO SEE...

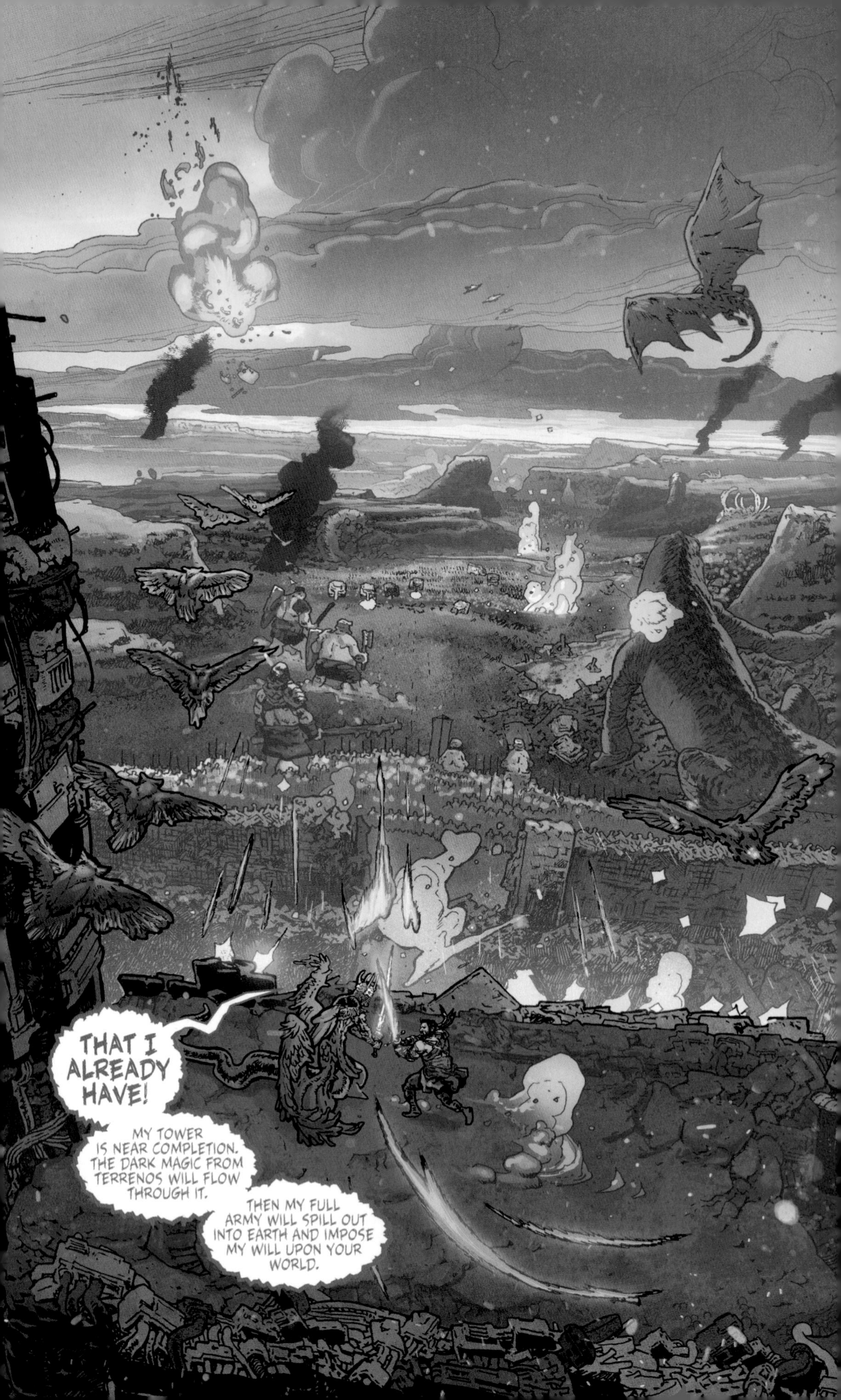
THAT I ALREADY HAVE!
MY TOWER IS NEAR COMPLETION. THE DARK MAGIC FROM TERRENOS WILL FLOW THROUGH IT.
THEN MY FULL ARMY WILL SPILL OUT INTO EARTH AND IMPOSE MY WILL UPON YOUR WORLD.

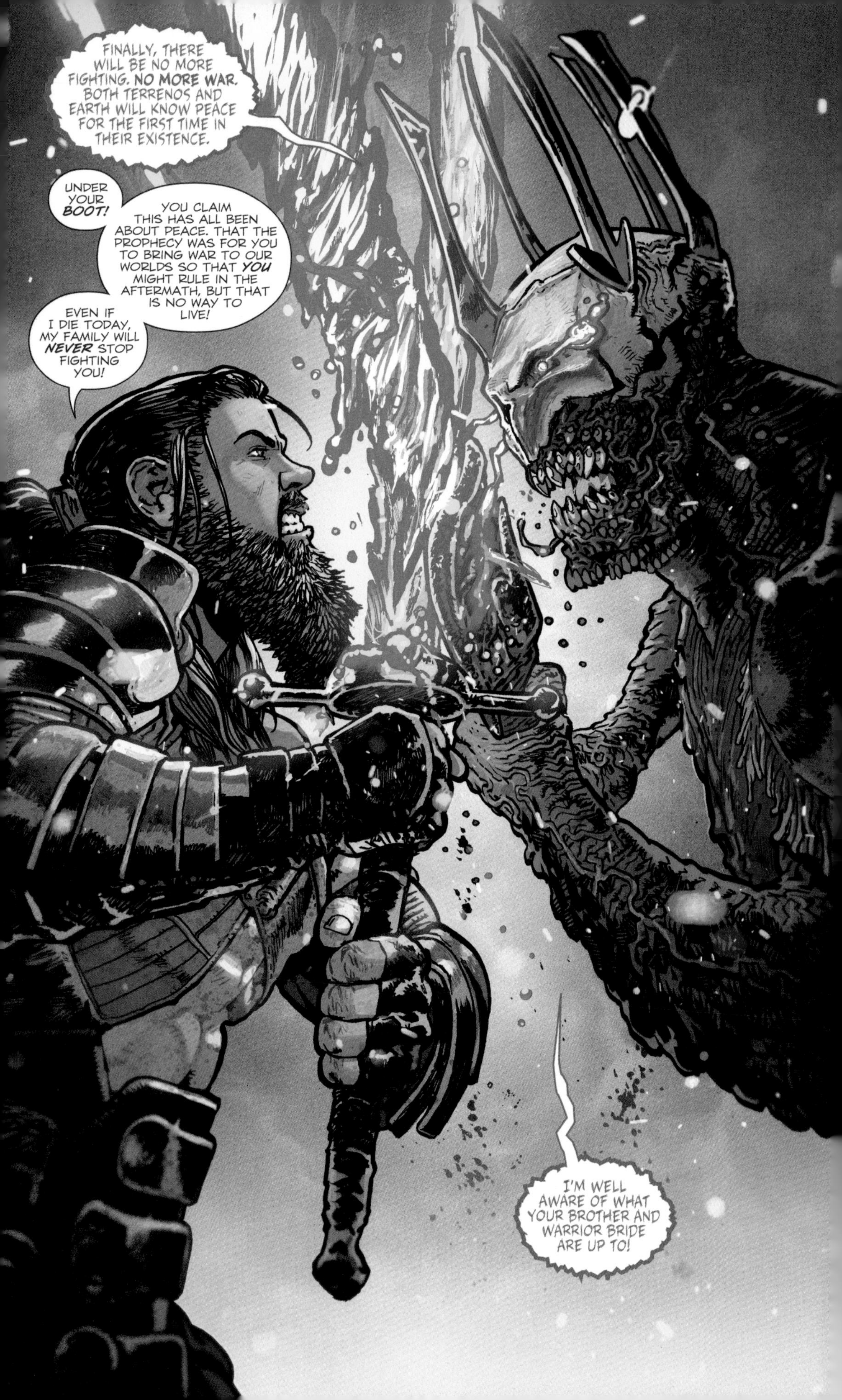

FINALLY, THERE WILL BE NO MORE FIGHTING. NO MORE WAR. BOTH TERRENOS AND EARTH WILL KNOW PEACE FOR THE FIRST TIME IN THEIR EXISTENCE.
UNDER YOUR BOOT!
YOU CLAIM THIS HAS ALL BEEN ABOUT PEACE. THAT THE PROPHECY WAS FOR YOU TO BRING WAR TO OUR WORLDS SO THAT YOU MIGHT RULE IN THE AFTERMATH, BUT THAT IS NO WAY TO LIVE!
EVEN IF I DIE TODAY, MY FAMILY WILL NEVER STOP FIGHTING YOU!
I'M WELL AWARE OF WHAT YOUR BROTHER AND WARRIOR BRIDE ARE UP TO!

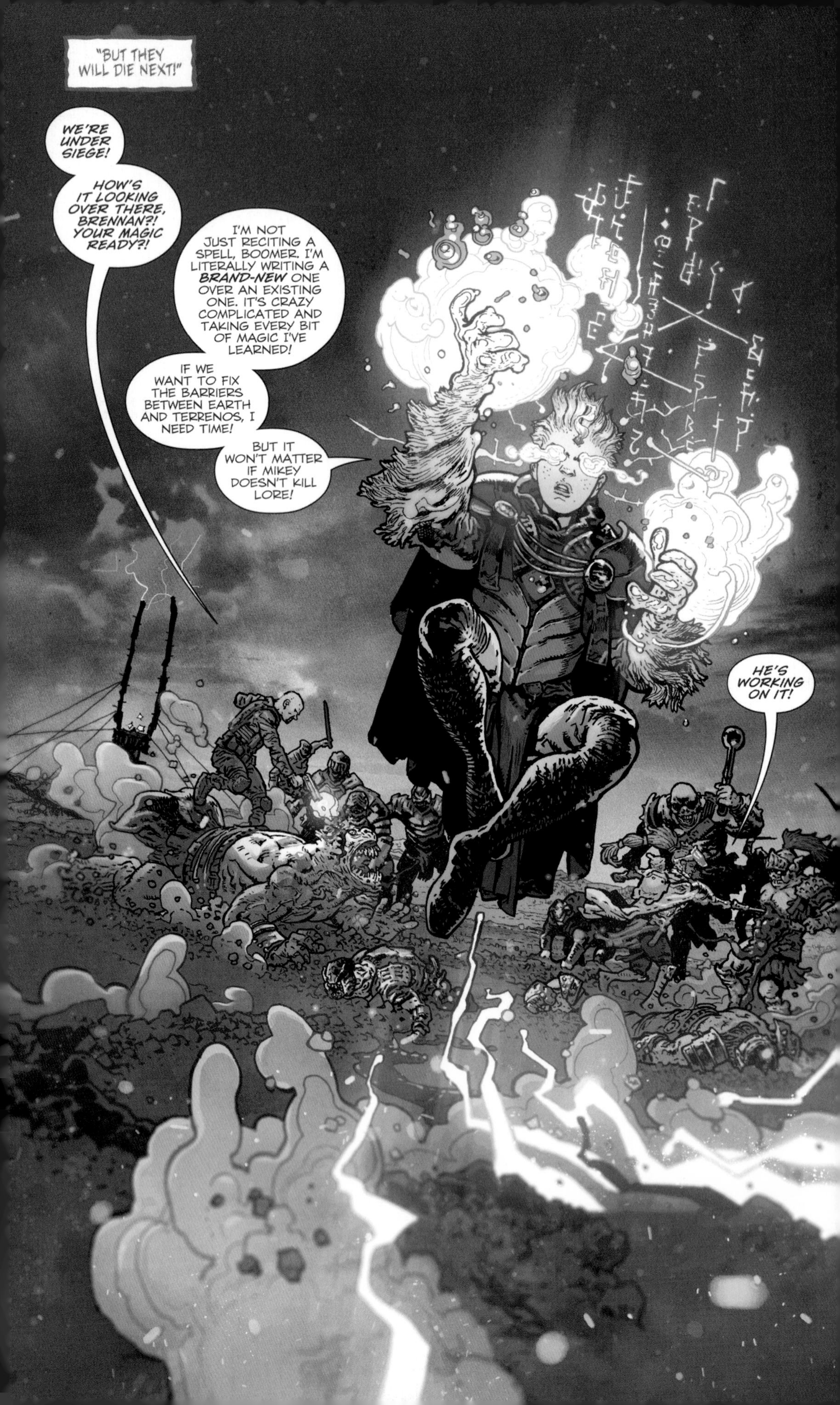
"BUT THEY WILL DIE NEXT!"
WE'RE UNDER SIEGE!
HOW'S IT LOOKING OVER THERE, BRENNAN?! YOUR MAGIC READY?!
I'M NOT JUST RECITING A SPELL, BOOMER. I'M LITERALLY WRITING A BRAND-NEW ONE OVER AN EXISTING ONE. IT'S CRAZY COMPLICATED AND TAKING EVERY BIT OF MAGIC I'VE LEARNED!
IF WE WANT TO FIX THE BARRIERS BETWEEN EARTH AND TERRENOS, I NEED TIME!
BUT IT WON'T MATTER IF MIKEY DOESN'T KILL LORE!
HE'S WORKING ON IT!

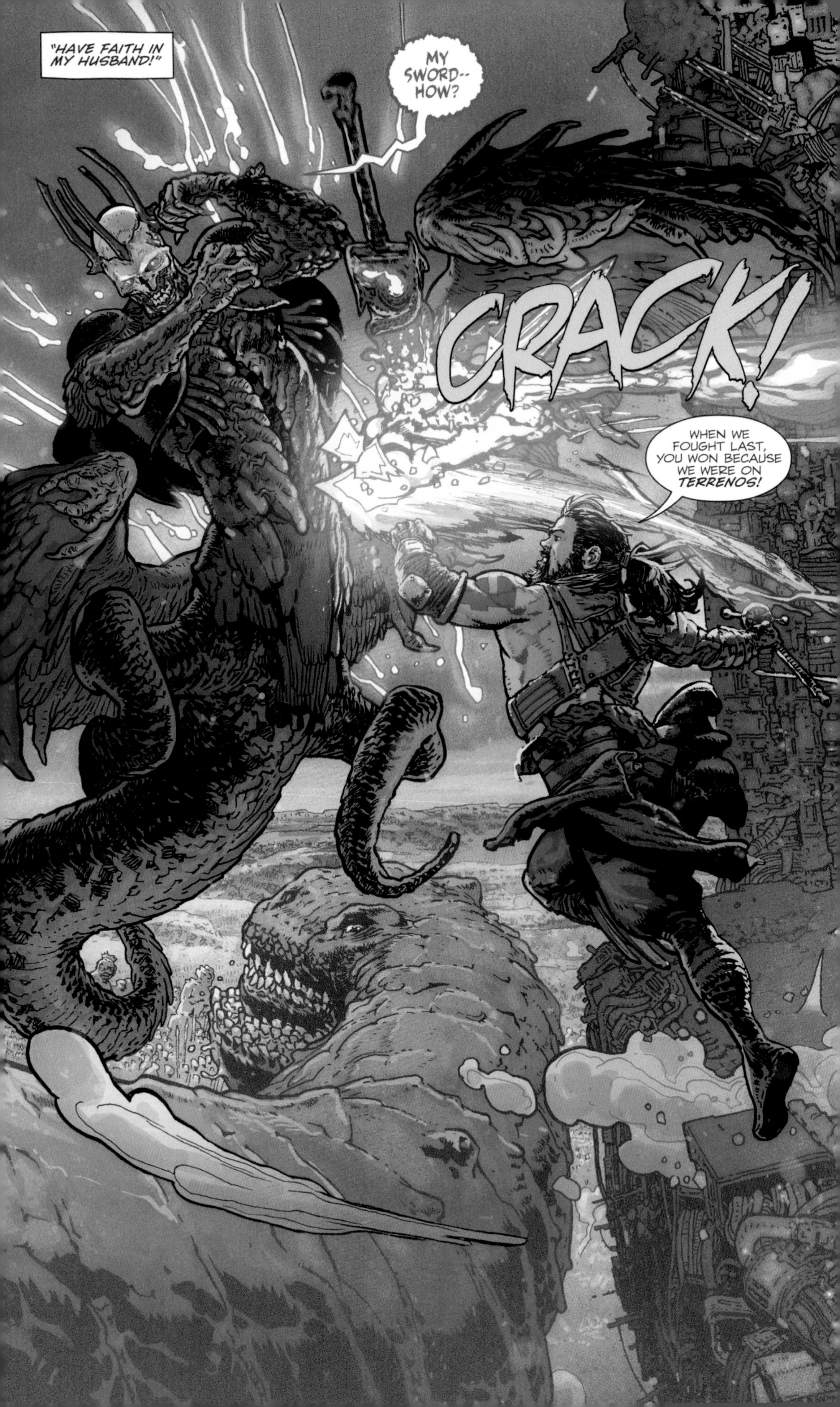
"HAVE FAITH IN MY HUSBAND!"
MY SWORD-- HOW?
CRACK!
WHEN WE FOUGHT LAST, YOU WON BECAUSE WE WERE ON TERRENOS!

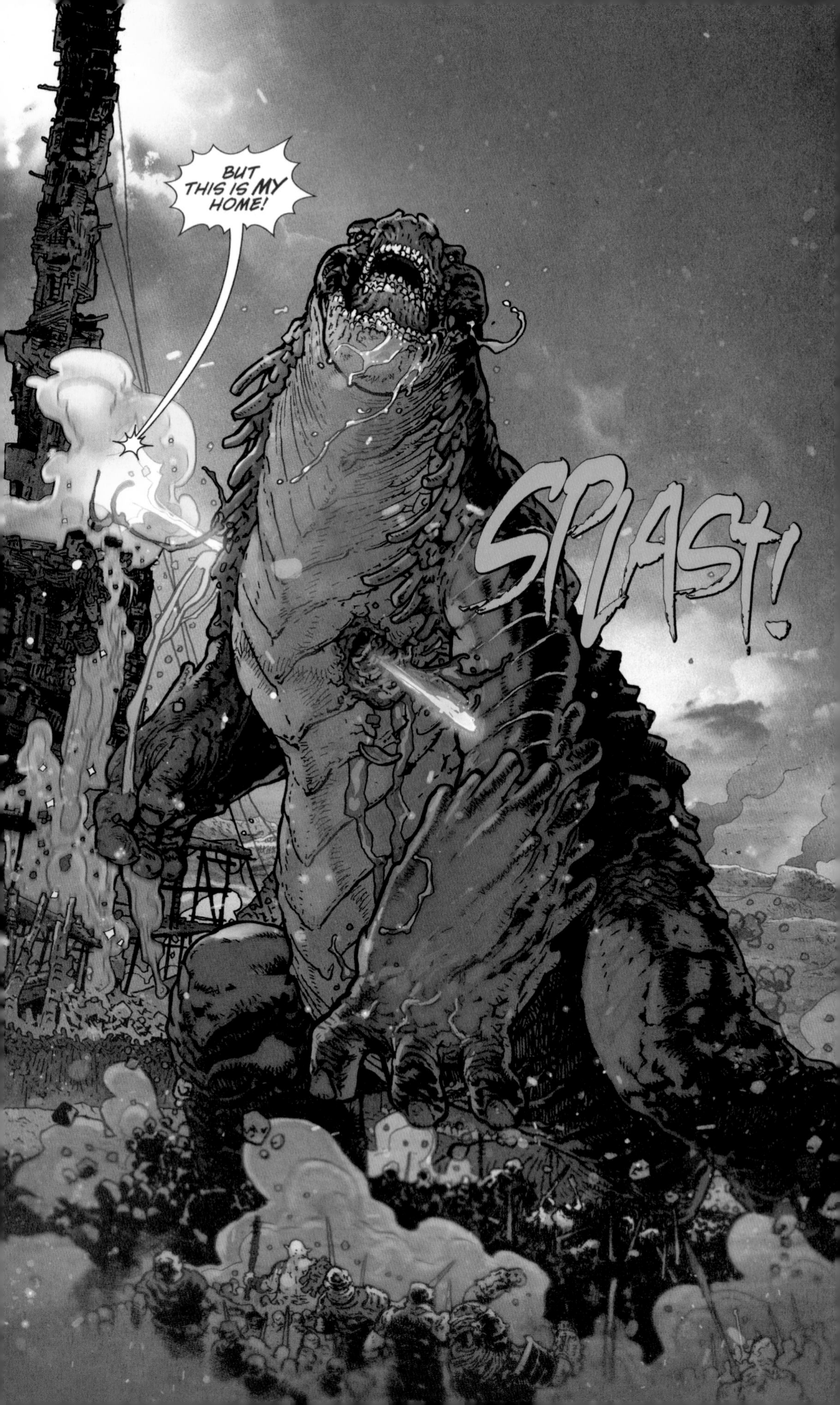

BUT THIS IS MY HOME!
SPLASH!

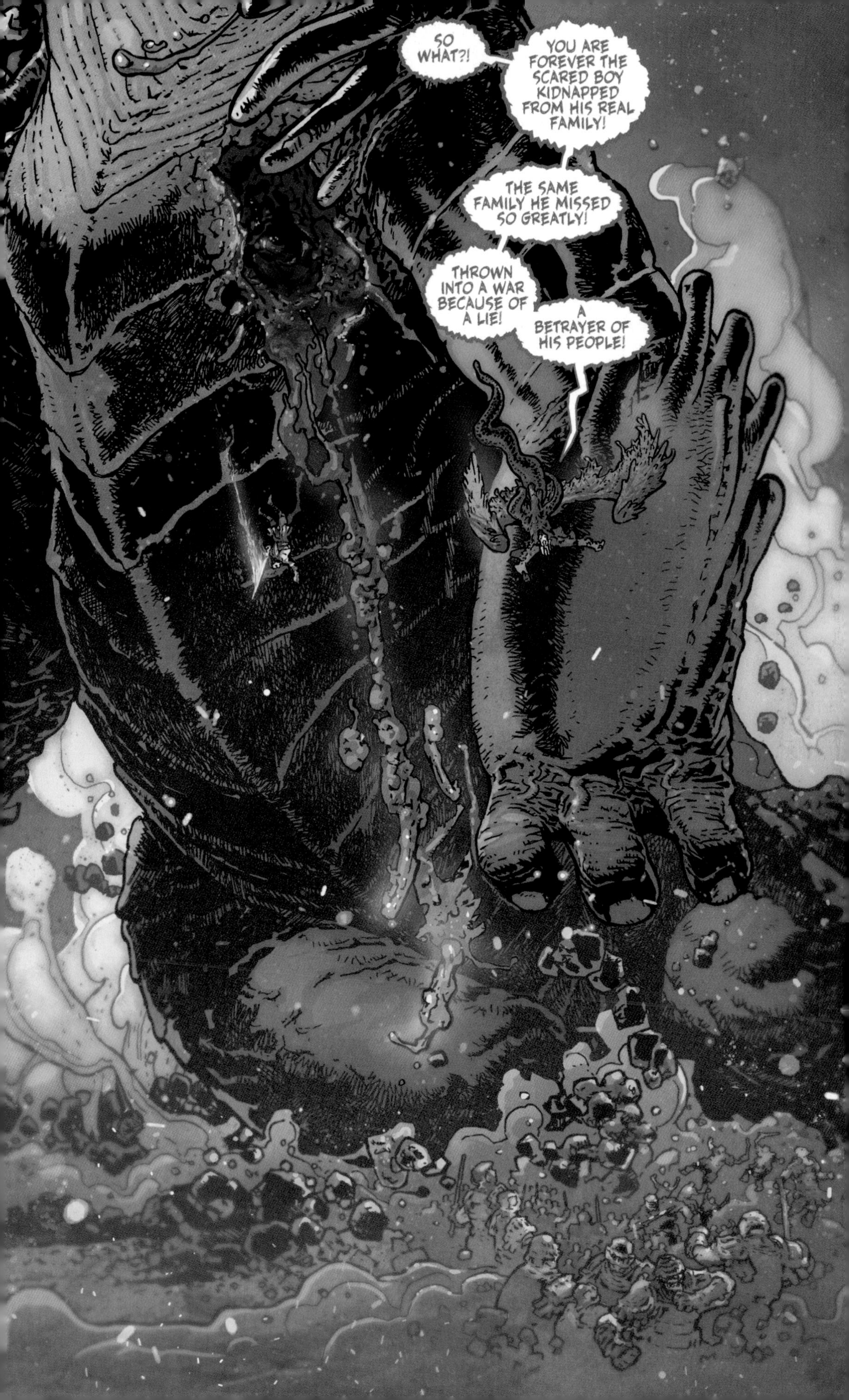
SO WHAT?!
YOU ARE FOREVER THE SCARED BOY KIDNAPPED FROM HIS REAL FAMILY!
THE SAME FAMILY HE MISSED SO GREATLY!
THROWN INTO A WAR BECAUSE OF A LIE!
A BETRAYER OF HIS PEOPLE!

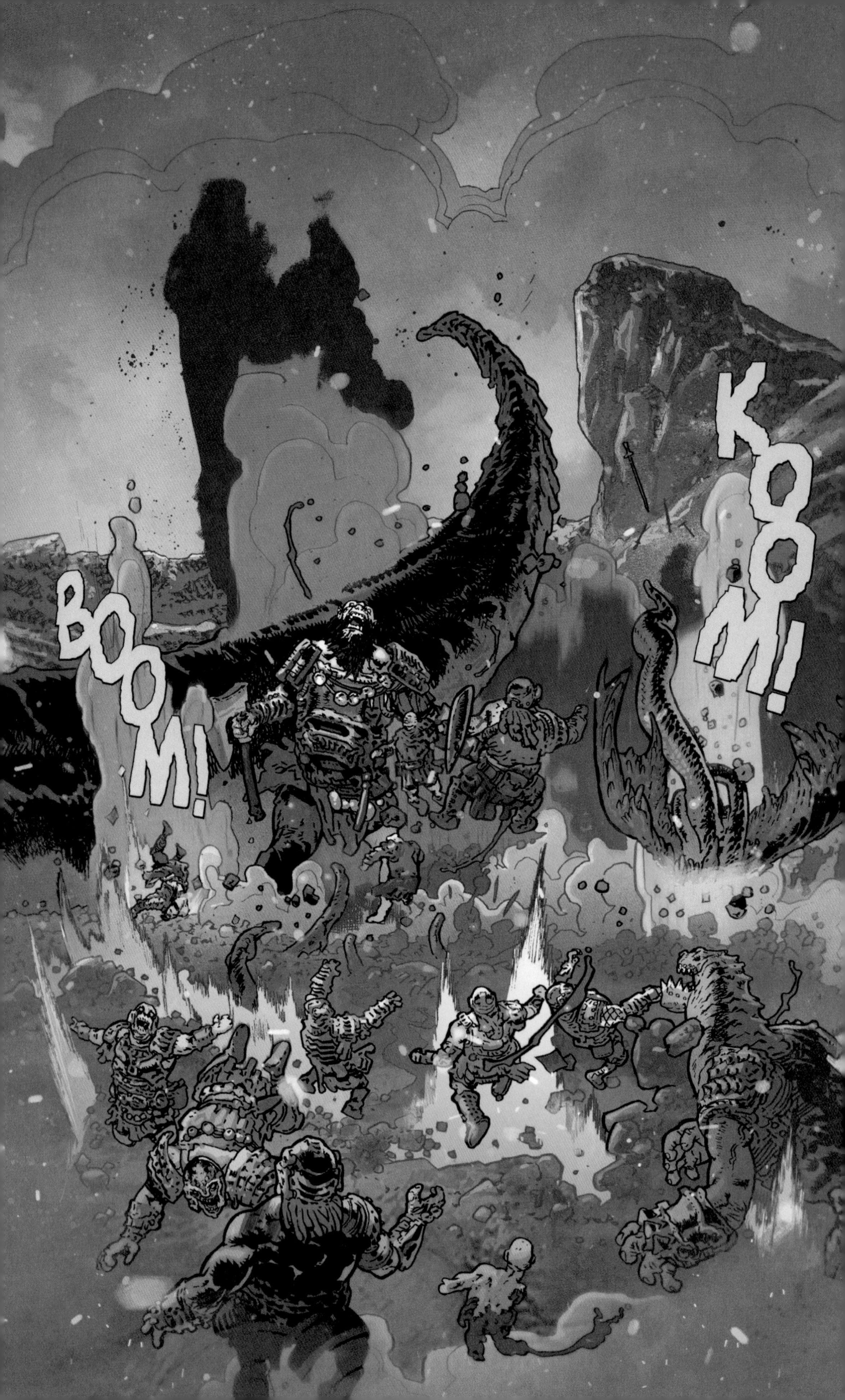
BOOM!
KOOM!

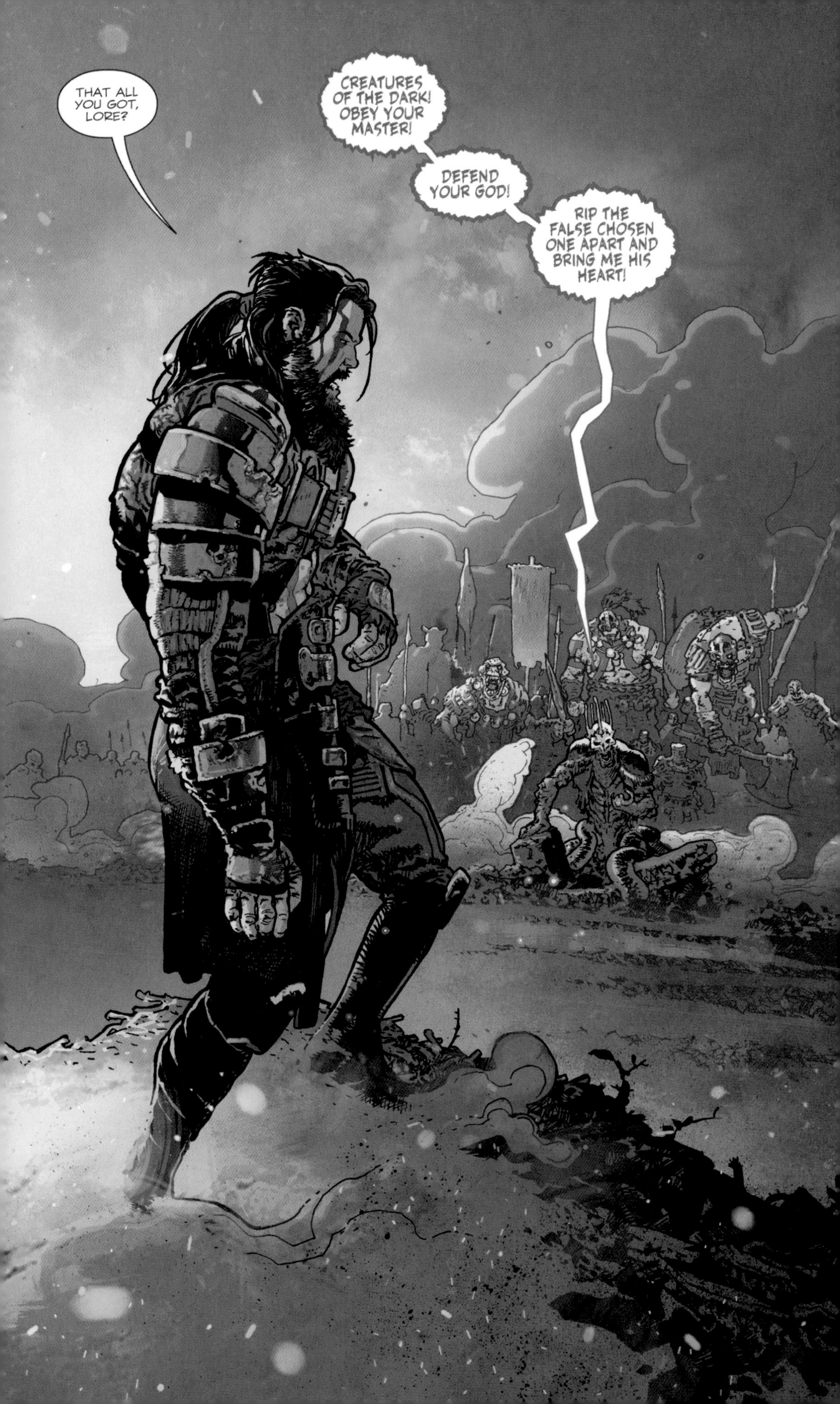
THAT ALL YOU GOT, LORE?
CREATURES OF THE DARK! OBEY YOUR MASTER!
DEFEND YOUR GOD!
RIP THE FALSE CHOSEN ONE APART AND BRING ME HIS HEART!

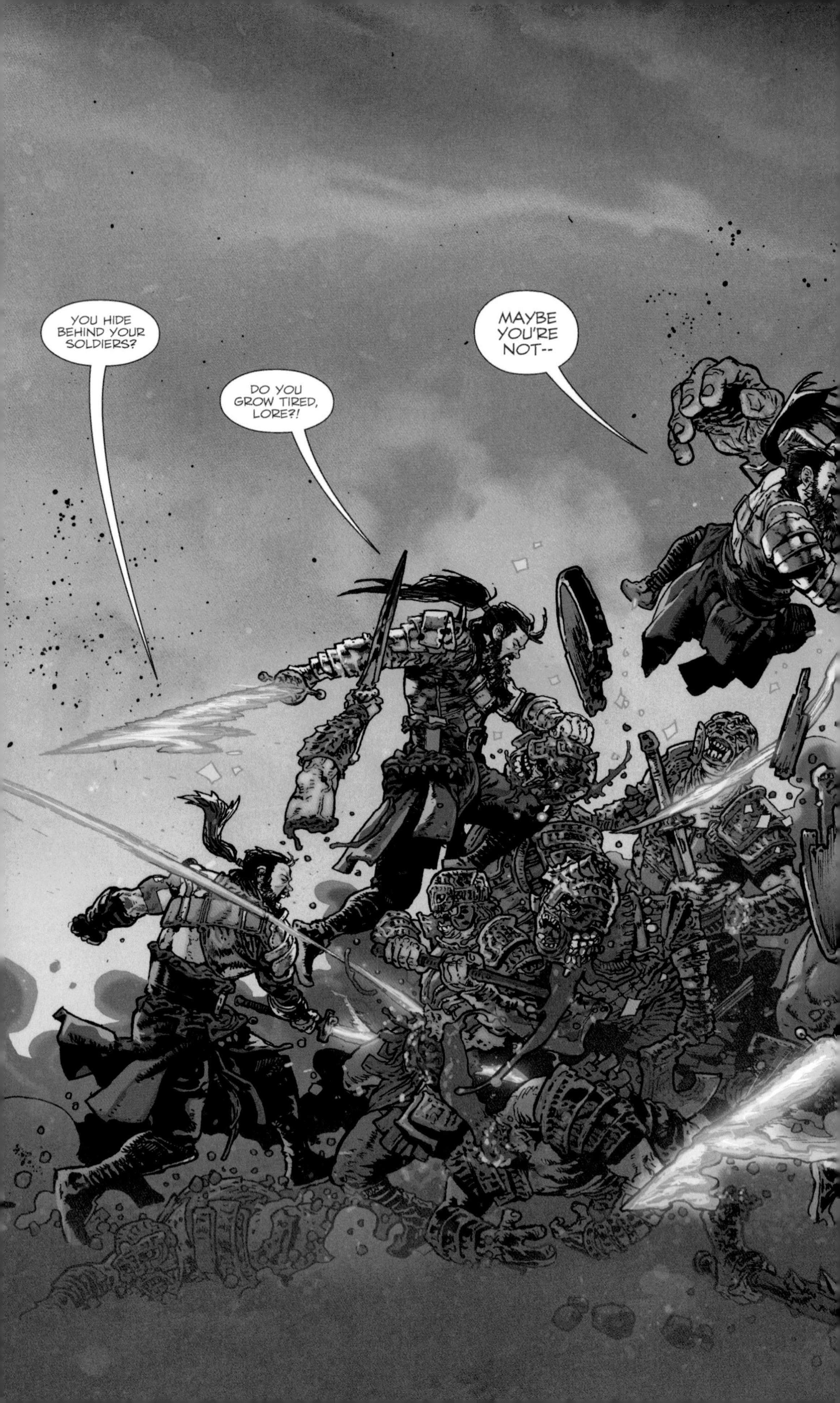
YOU HIDE BEHIND YOUR SOLDIERS?
DO YOU GROW TIRED, LORE?!
MAYBE YOU'RE NOT--

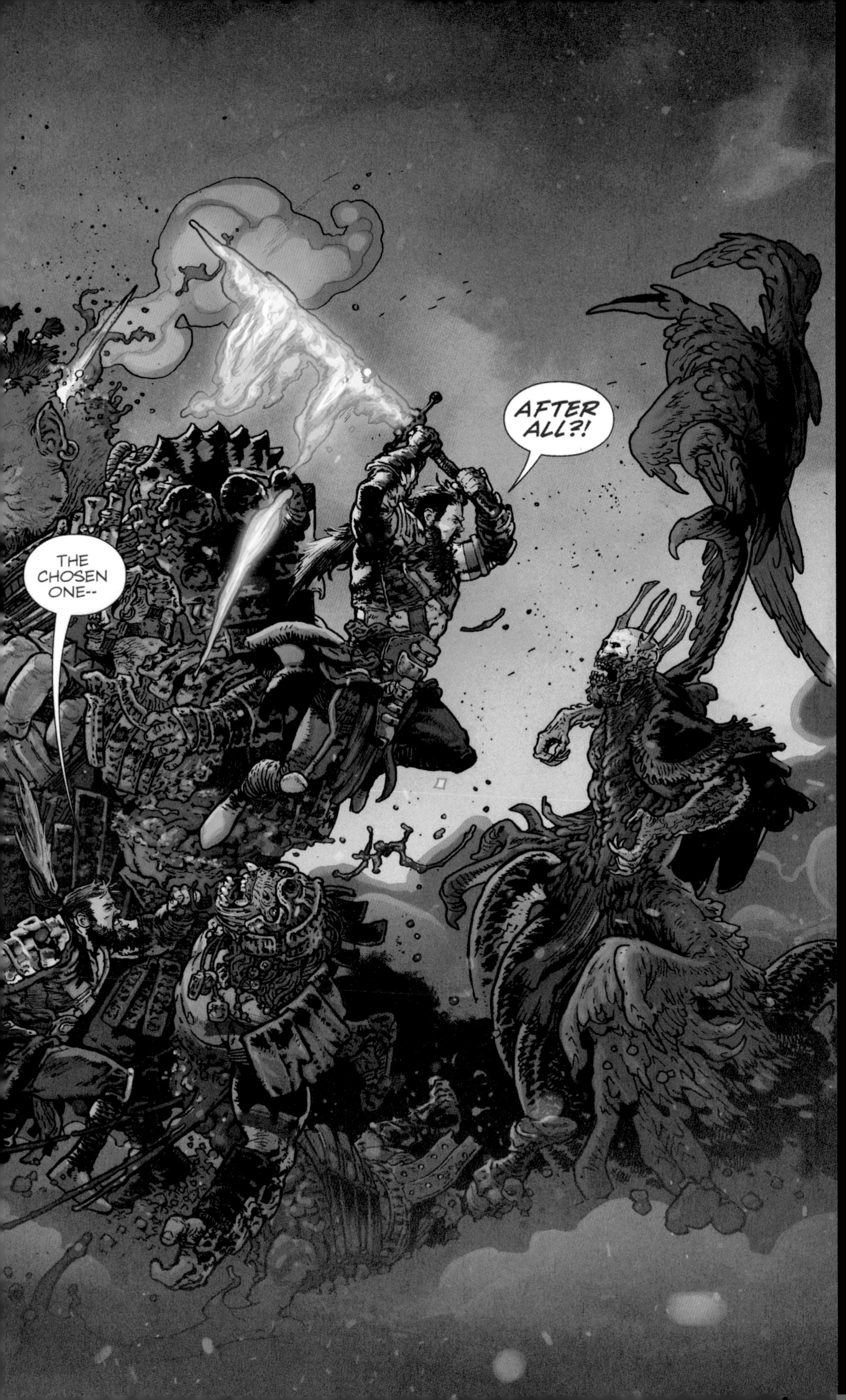
THE CHOSEN ONE--
AFTER ALL?!

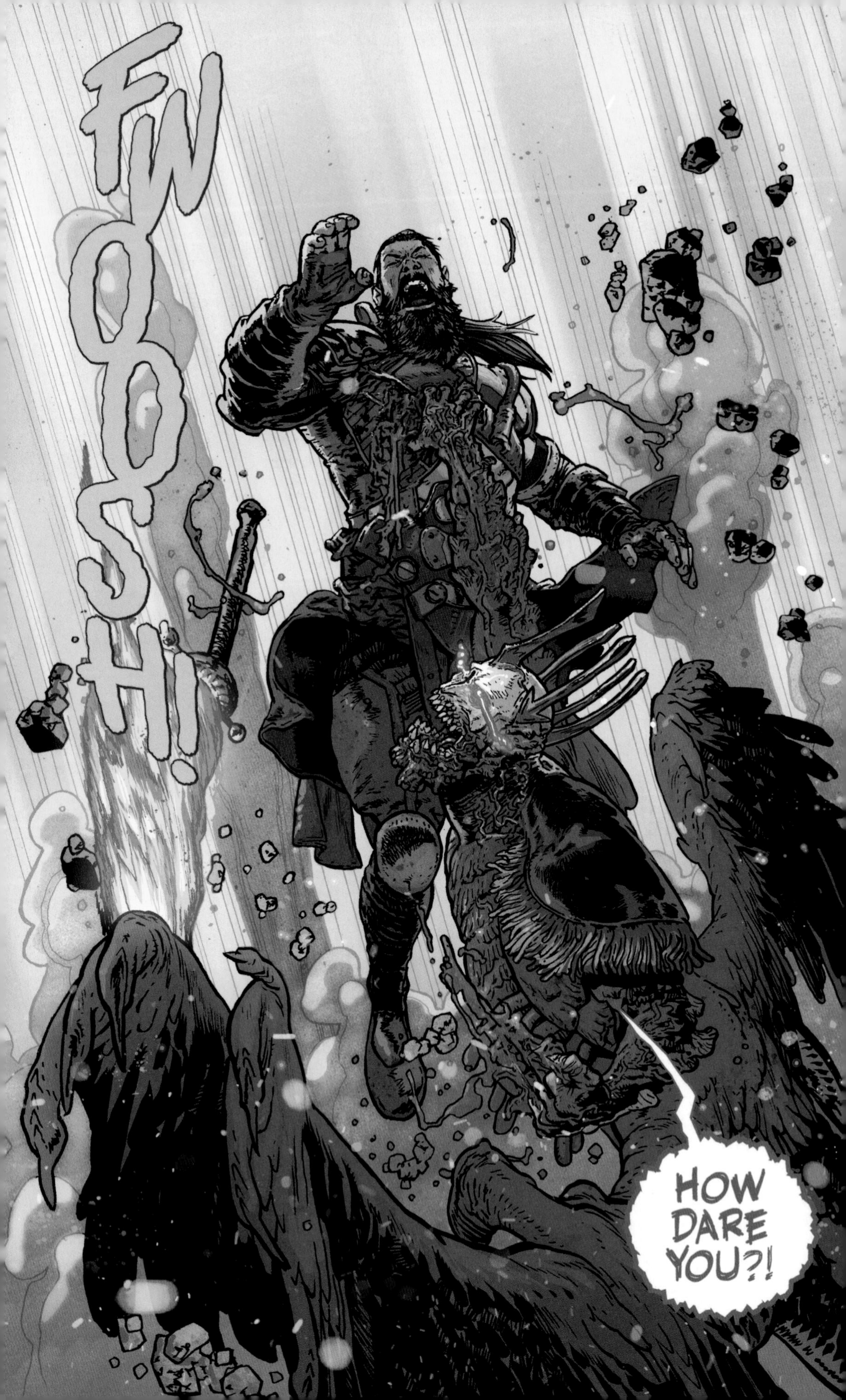
FWOOSH!
HOW DARE YOU?!

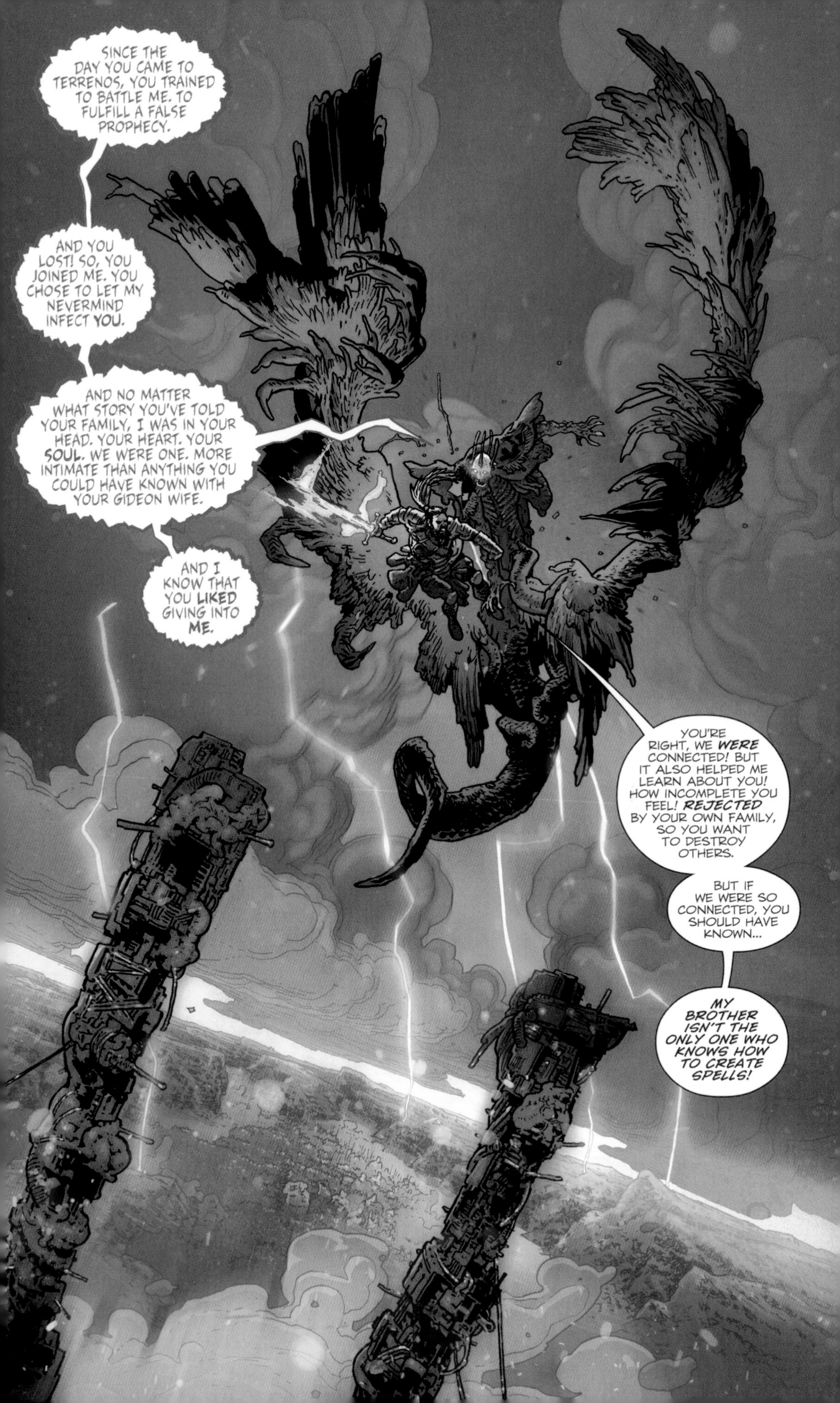
SINCE THE DAY YOU CAME TO TERRENOS, YOU TRAINED TO BATTLE ME. TO FULFILL A FALSE PROPHECY.
AND YOU LOST! SO, YOU JOINED ME. YOU CHOSE TO LET MY NEVERMIND INFECT **YOU.**
AND NO MATTER WHAT STORY YOU'VE TOLD YOUR FAMILY, I WAS IN YOUR HEAD. YOUR HEART. YOUR **SOUL.** WE WERE ONE. MORE INTIMATE THAN ANYTHING YOU COULD HAVE KNOWN WITH YOUR GIDEON WIFE.
AND I KNOW THAT YOU **LIKED** GIVING INTO **ME.**
YOU'RE RIGHT, WE ***WERE*** CONNECTED! BUT IT ALSO HELPED ME LEARN ABOUT YOU! HOW INCOMPLETE YOU FEEL! ***REJECTED*** BY YOUR OWN FAMILY, SO YOU WANT TO DESTROY OTHERS.
BUT IF WE WERE SO CONNECTED, YOU SHOULD HAVE KNOWN...
MY BROTHER ISN'T THE ONLY ONE WHO KNOWS HOW TO CREATE SPELLS!

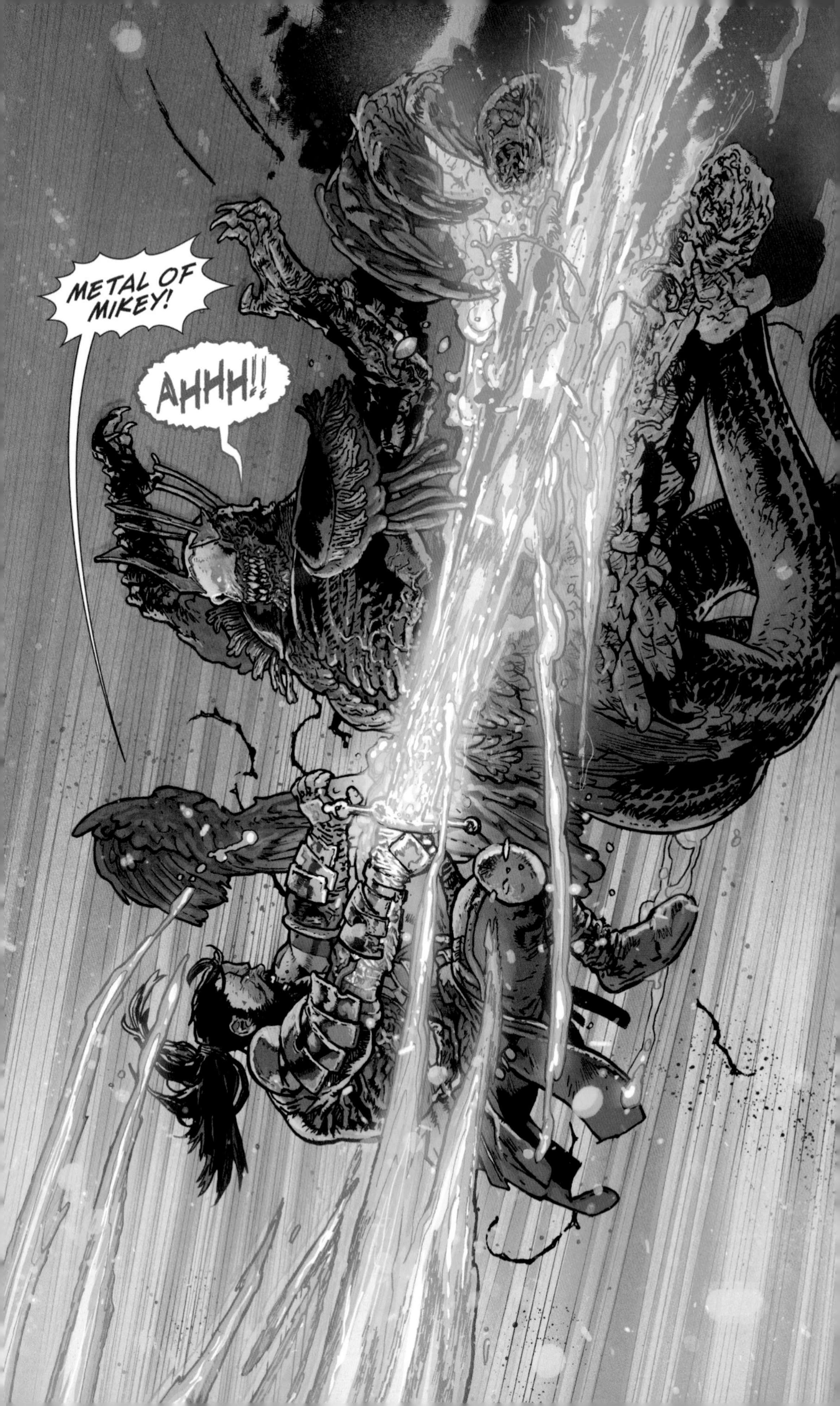
METAL OF MIKEY!
AHHH!!

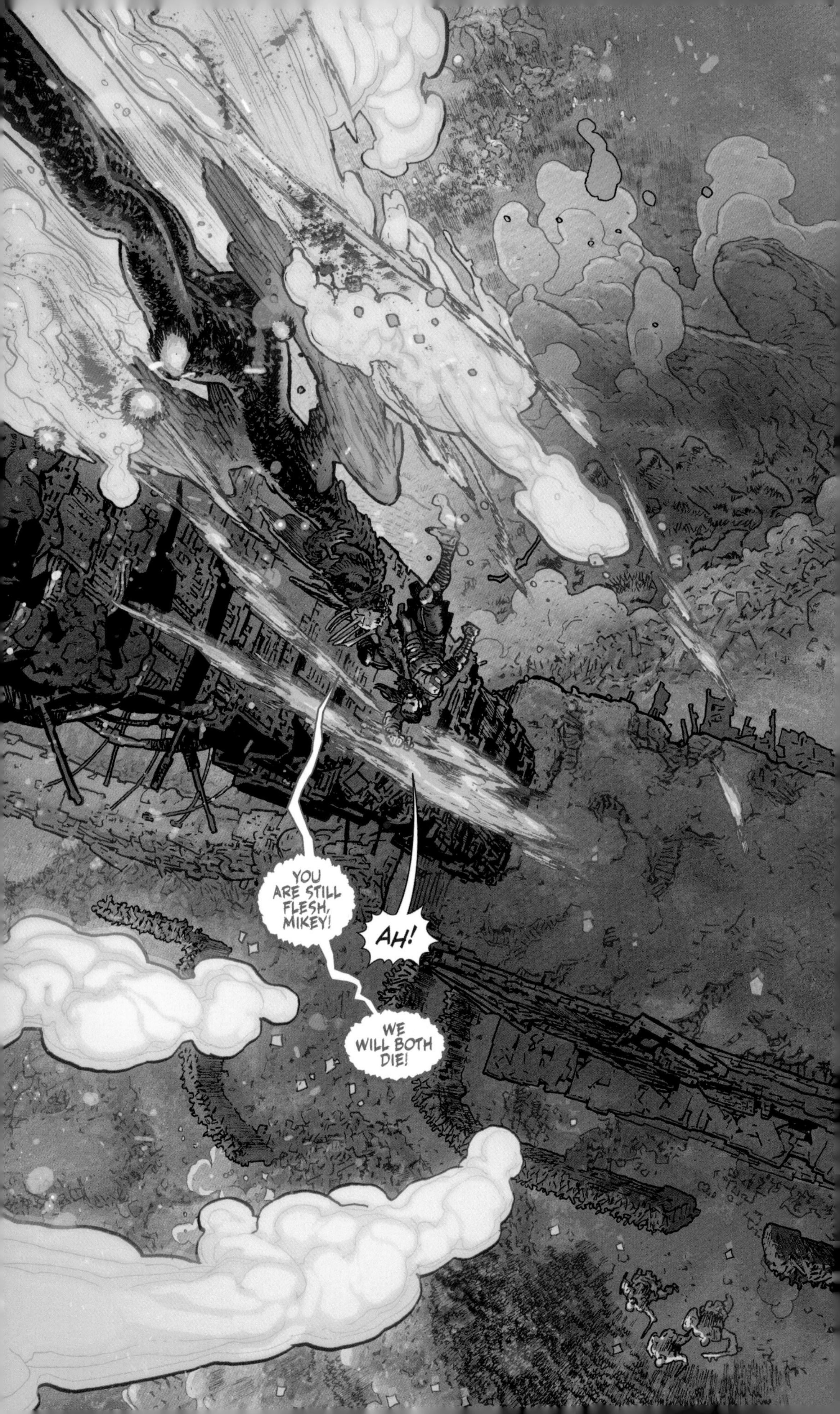
YOU ARE STILL FLESH, MIKEY!
AH!
WE WILL BOTH DIE!

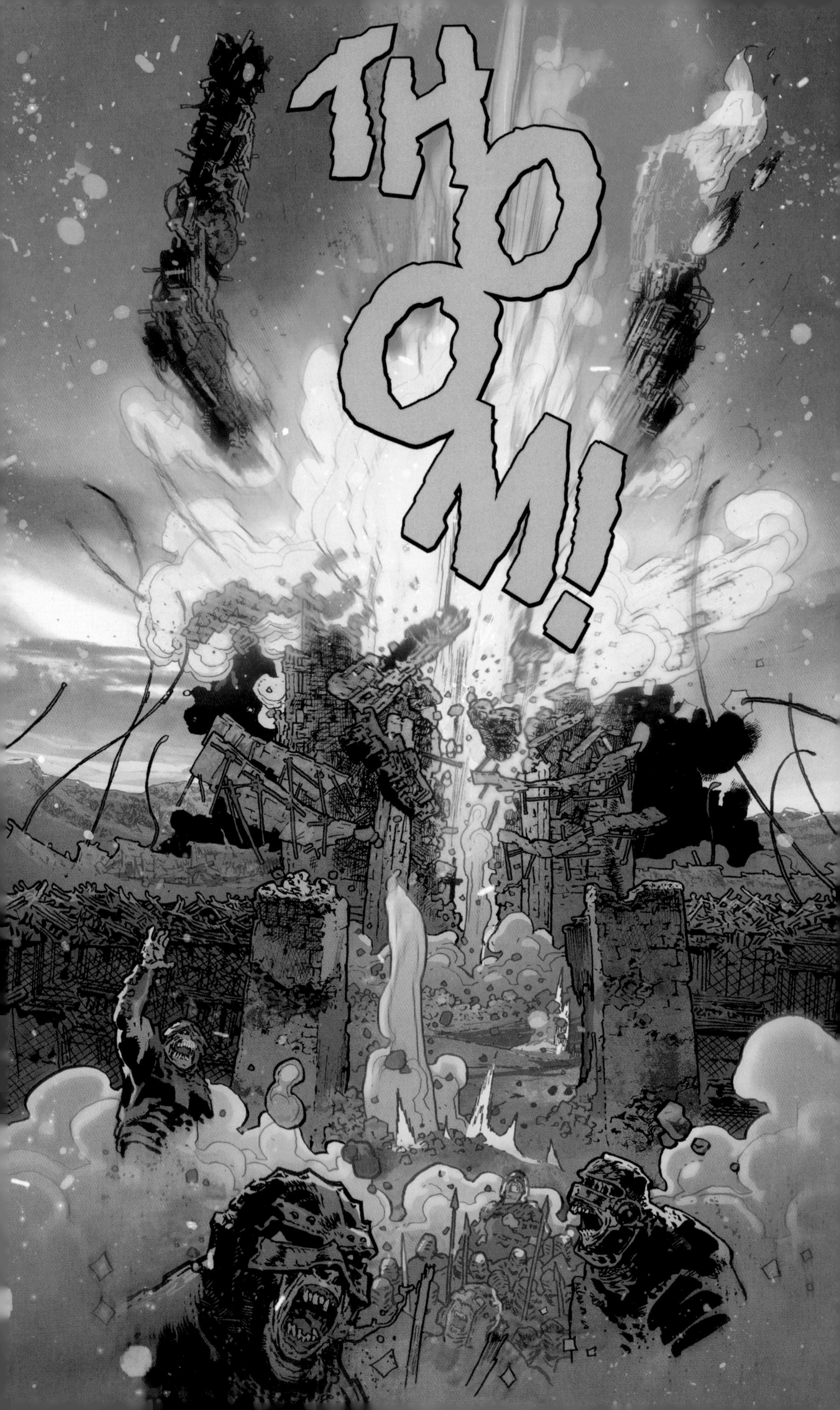
THOOM!

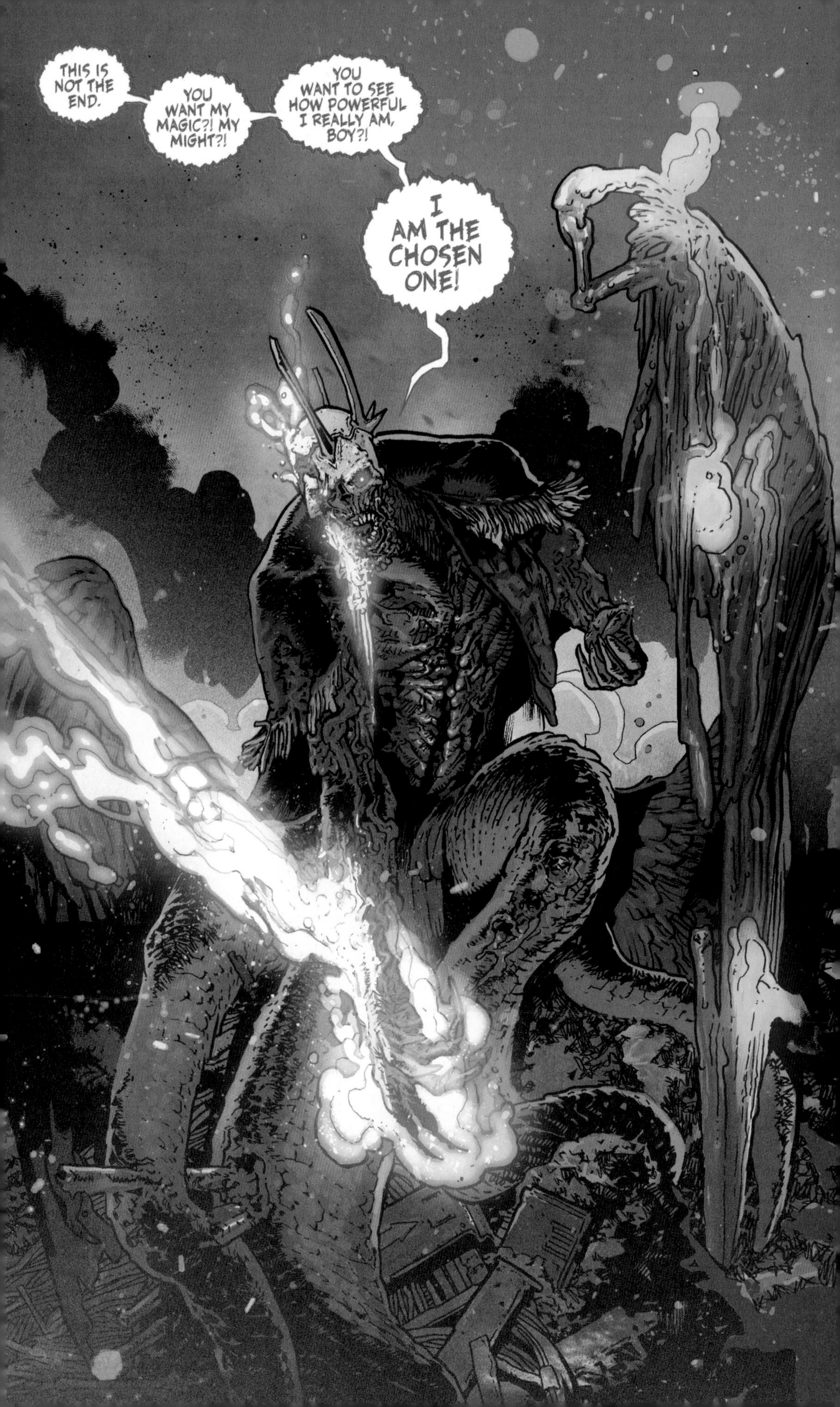
THIS IS NOT THE END.
YOU WANT MY MAGIC?! MY MIGHT?!
YOU WANT TO SEE HOW POWERFUL I REALLY AM, BOY?!
I AM THE CHOSEN ONE!

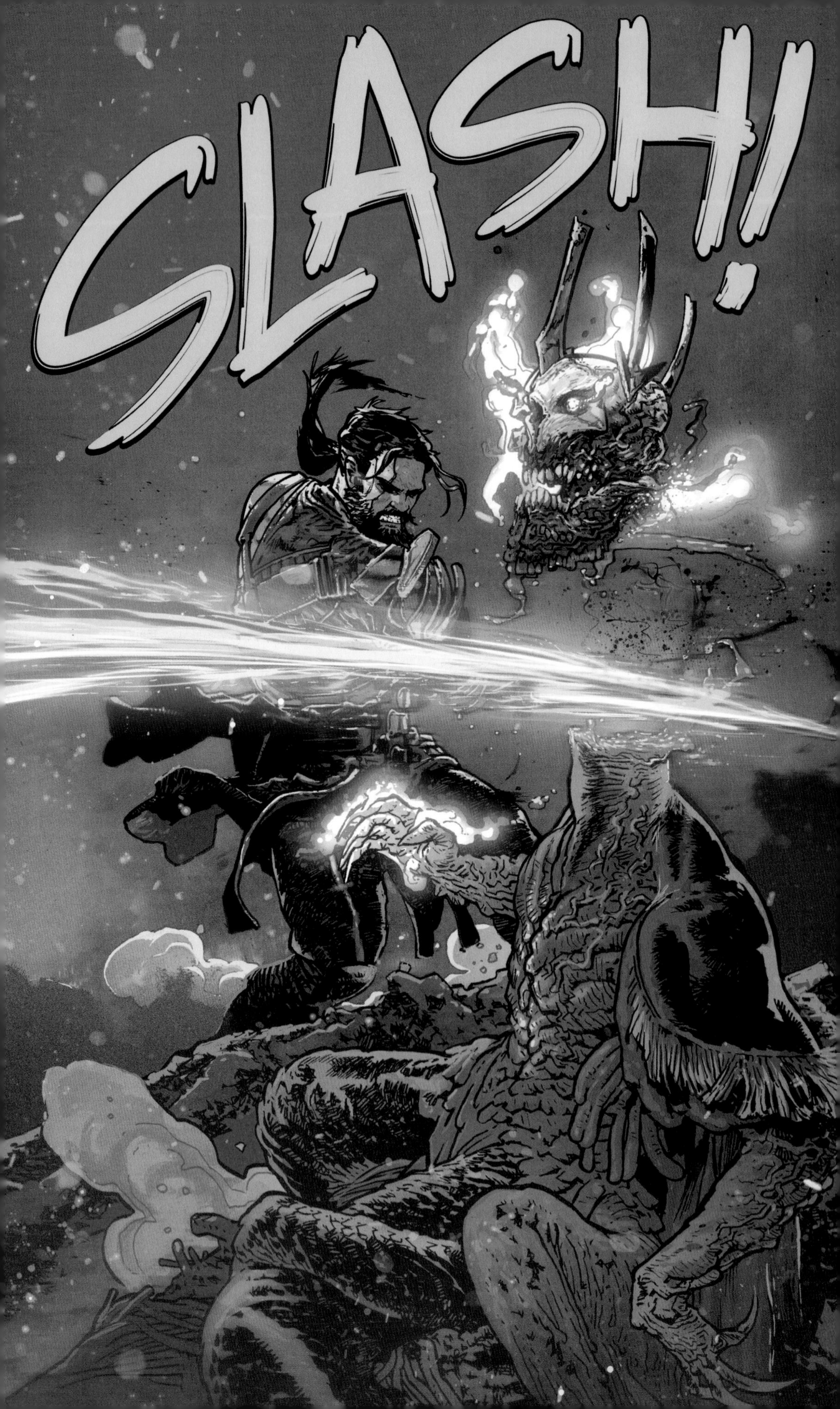
SLASH!!

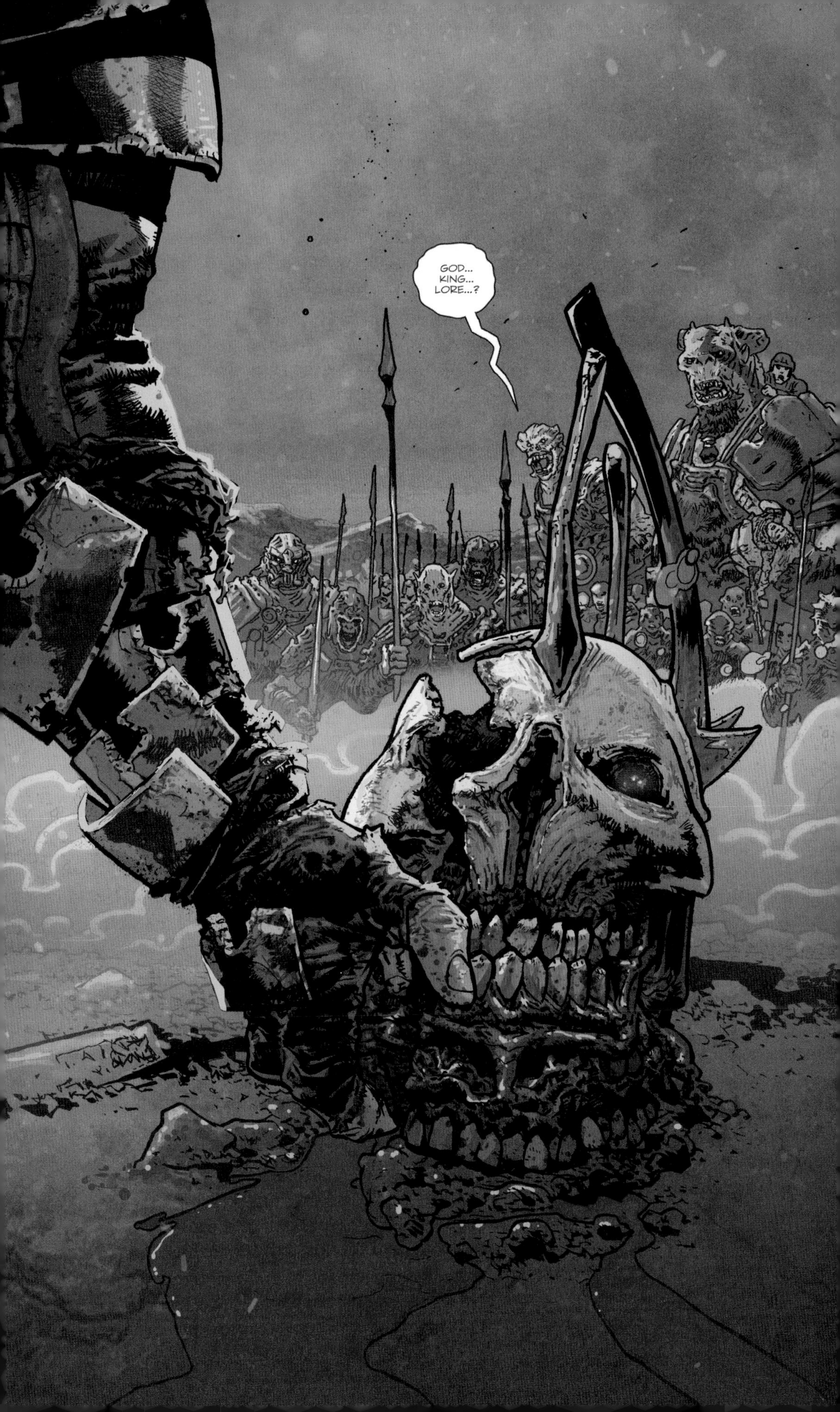
GOD... KING... LORE...?

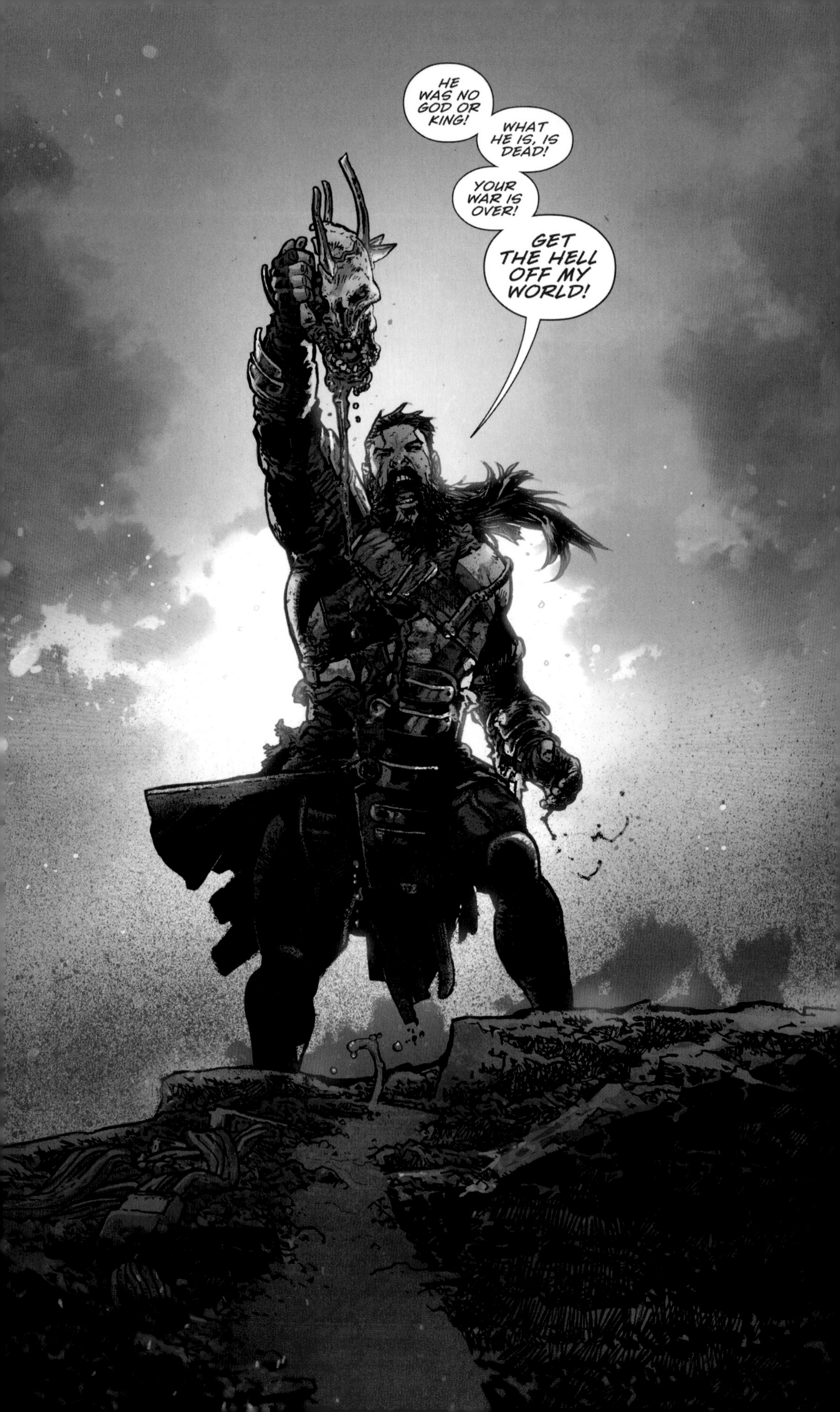
HE WAS NO GOD OR KING!
WHAT HE IS, IS DEAD!
YOUR WAR IS OVER!
GET THE HELL OFF MY WORLD!

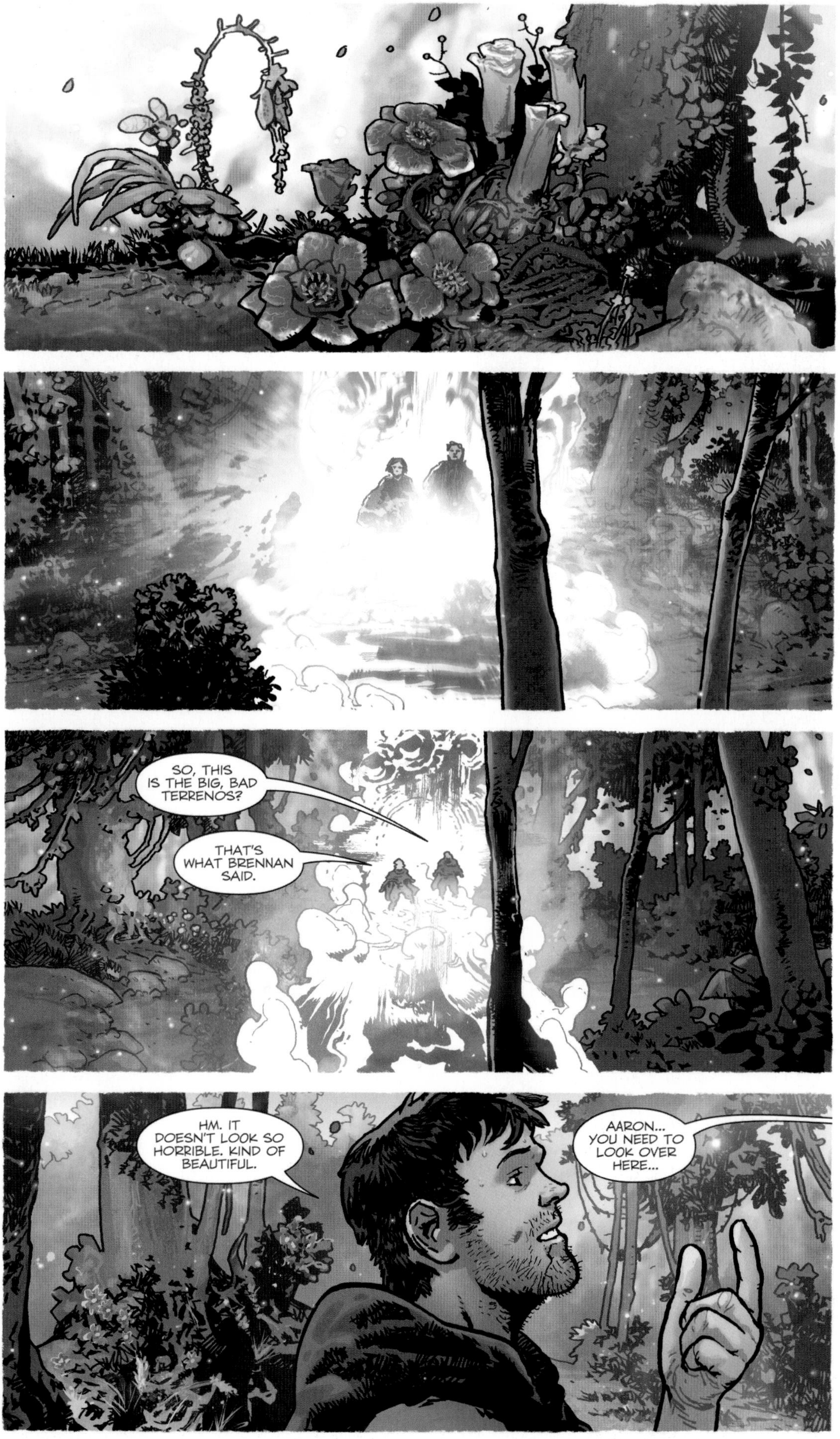
SO, THIS IS THE BIG, BAD TERRENOS?
THAT'S WHAT BRENNAN SAID.
HM. IT DOESN'T LOOK SO HORRIBLE. KIND OF BEAUTIFUL.
AARON... YOU NEED TO LOOK OVER HERE...

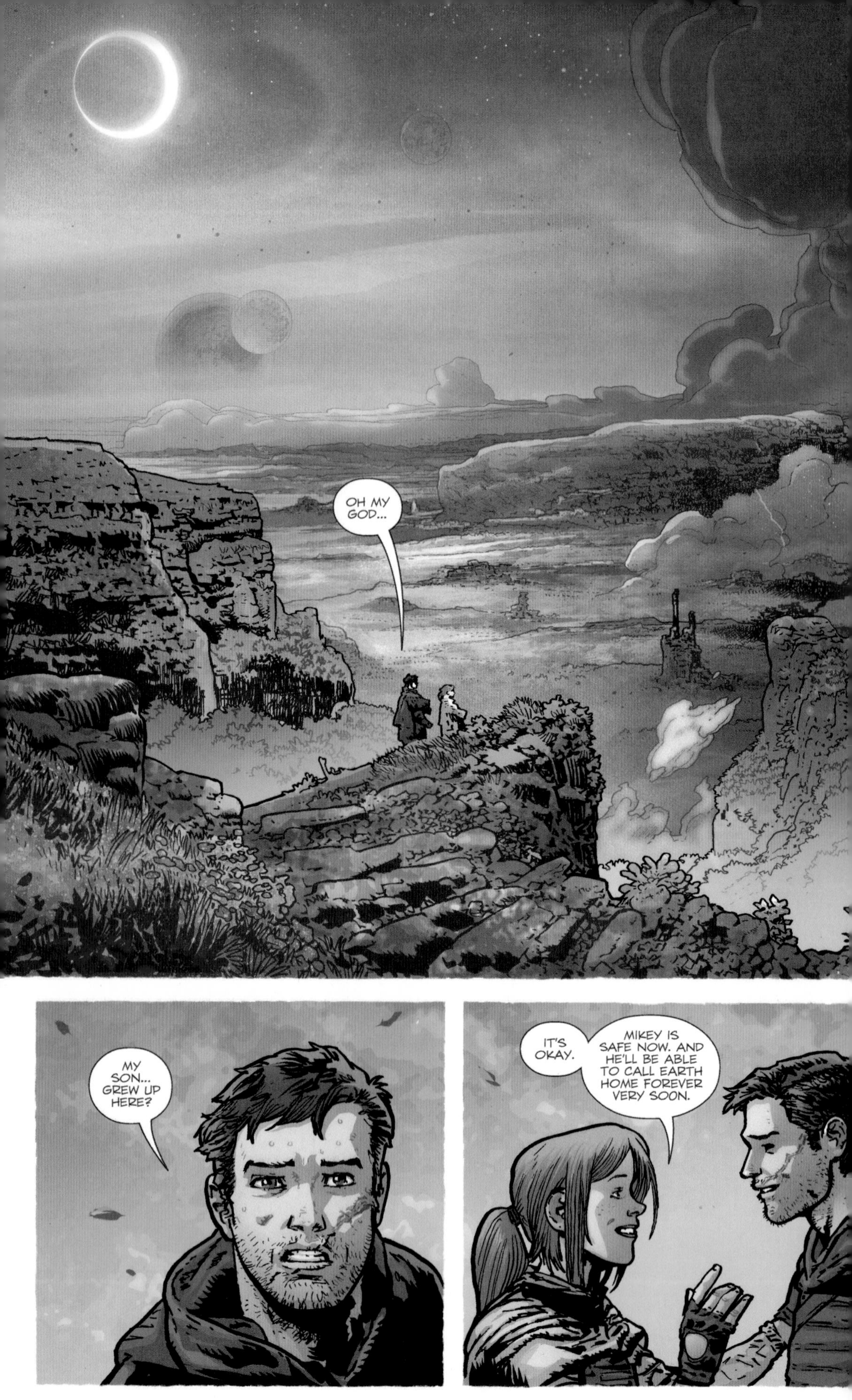
OH MY GOD...
MY SON... GREW UP HERE?
IT'S OKAY.
MIKEY IS SAFE NOW. AND HE'LL BE ABLE TO CALL EARTH HOME FOREVER VERY SOON.

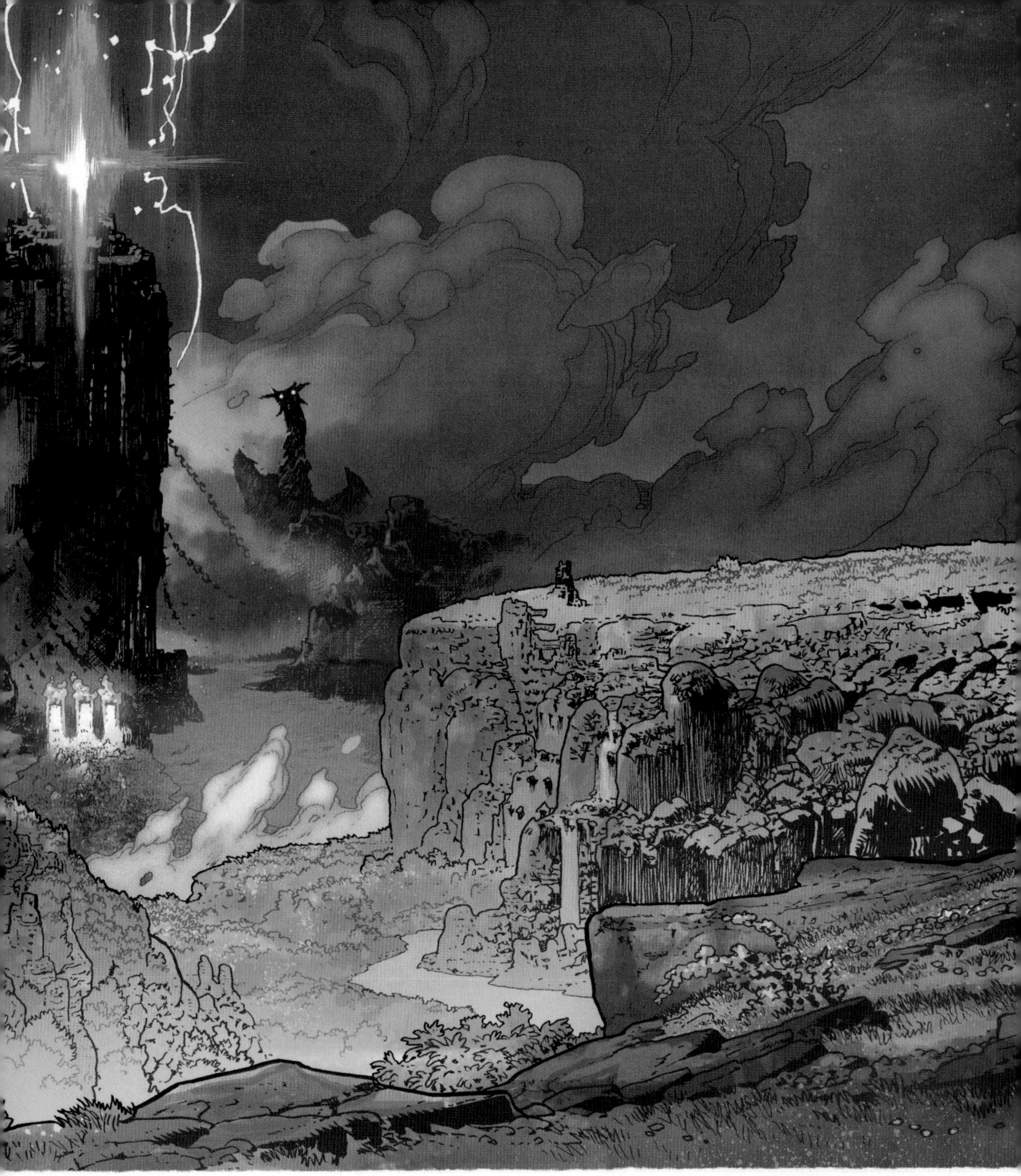

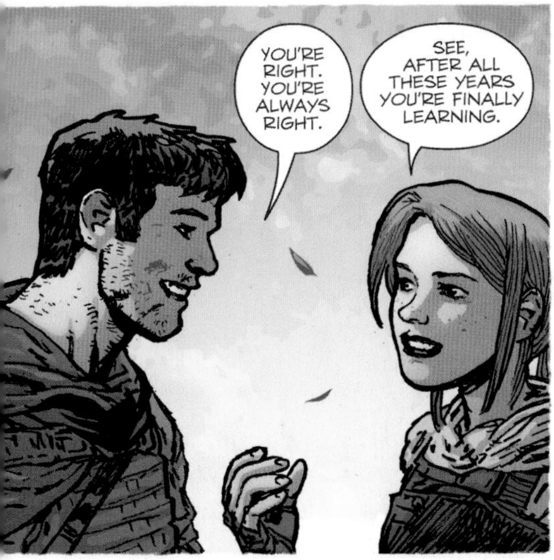
YOU'RE RIGHT. YOU'RE ALWAYS RIGHT.
SEE, AFTER ALL THESE YEARS YOU'RE FINALLY LEARNING.

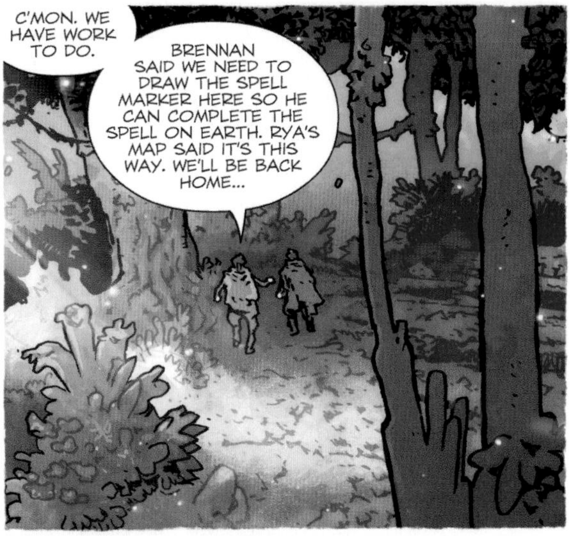
C'MON. WE HAVE WORK TO DO.
BRENNAN SAID WE NEED TO DRAW THE SPELL MARKER HERE SO HE CAN COMPLETE THE SPELL ON EARTH. RYA'S MAP SAID IT'S THIS WAY. WE'LL BE BACK HOME...

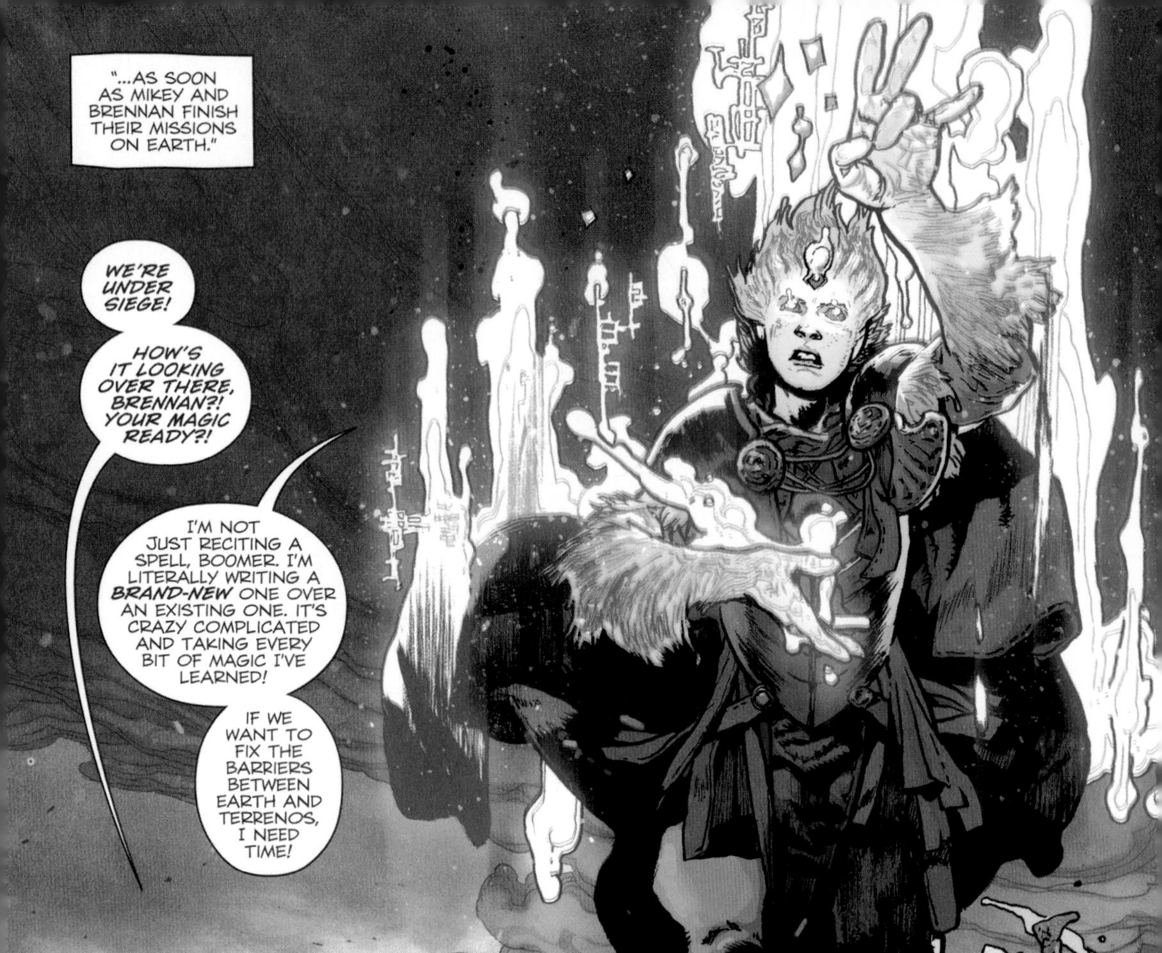
"...AS SOON AS MIKEY AND BRENNAN FINISH THEIR MISSIONS ON EARTH."
WE'RE UNDER SIEGE!
HOW'S IT LOOKING OVER THERE, BRENNAN?! YOUR MAGIC READY?!
I'M NOT JUST RECITING A SPELL, BOOMER. I'M LITERALLY WRITING A BRAND-NEW ONE OVER AN EXISTING ONE. IT'S CRAZY COMPLICATED AND TAKING EVERY BIT OF MAGIC I'VE LEARNED!
IF WE WANT TO FIX THE BARRIERS BETWEEN EARTH AND TERRENOS, I NEED TIME!

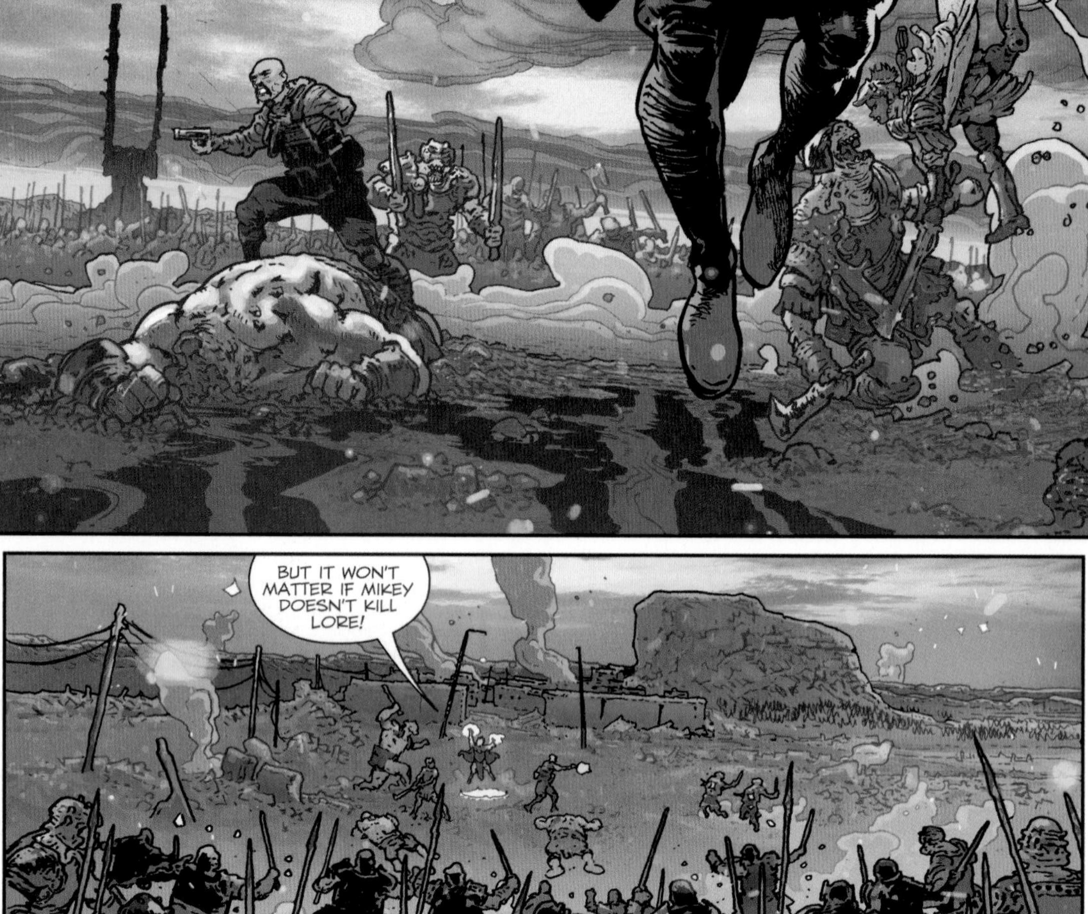
BUT IT WON'T MATTER IF MIKEY DOESN'T KILL LORE!

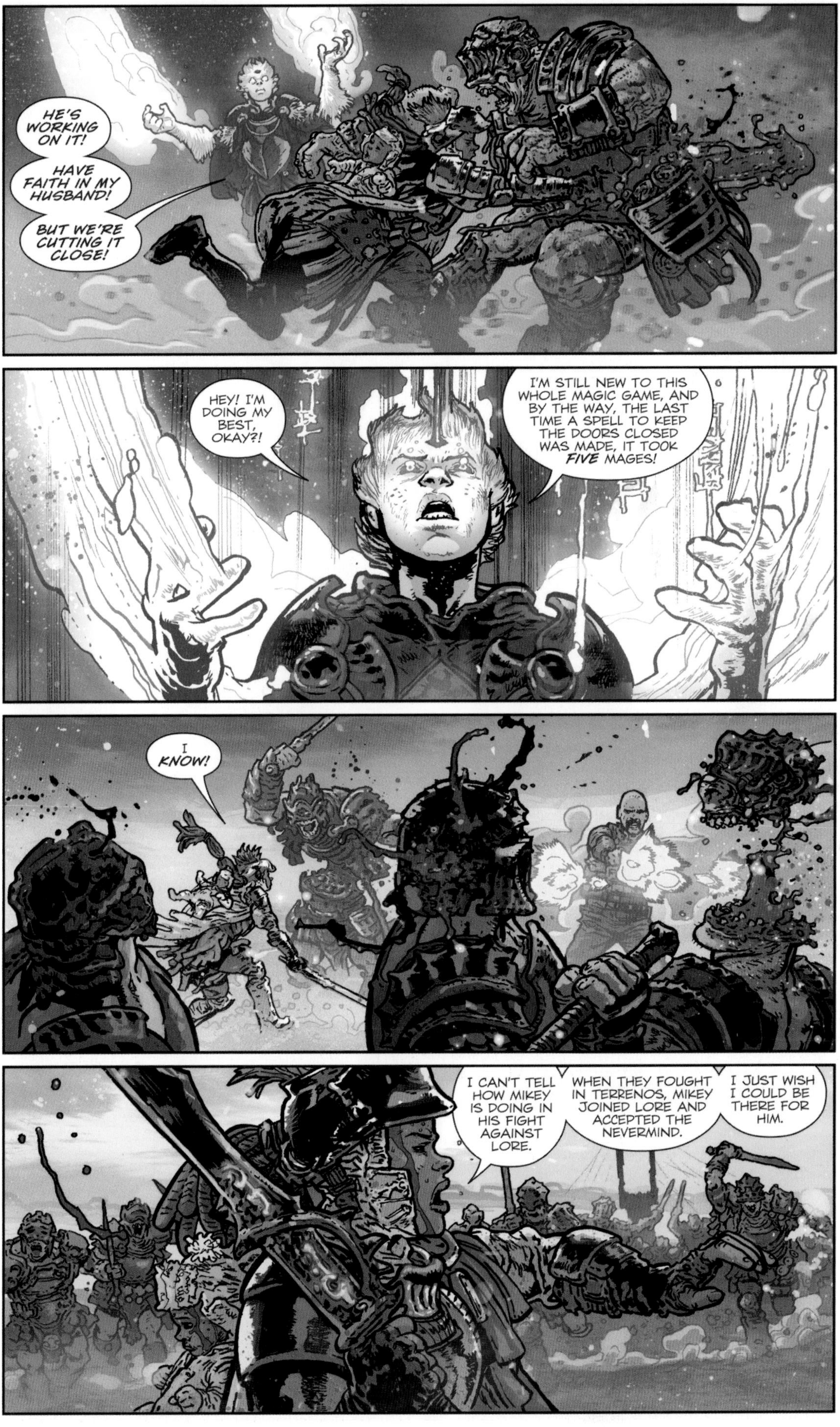

HE'S WORKING ON IT!
HAVE FAITH IN MY HUSBAND!
BUT WE'RE CUTTING IT CLOSE!
HEY! I'M DOING MY BEST, OKAY?!
I'M STILL NEW TO THIS WHOLE MAGIC GAME, AND BY THE WAY, THE LAST TIME A SPELL TO KEEP THE DOORS CLOSED WAS MADE, IT TOOK *FIVE* MAGES!
I *KNOW*!
I CAN'T TELL HOW MIKEY IS DOING IN HIS FIGHT AGAINST LORE.
WHEN THEY FOUGHT IN TERRENOS, MIKEY JOINED LORE AND ACCEPTED THE NEVERMIND.
I JUST WISH I COULD BE THERE FOR HIM.

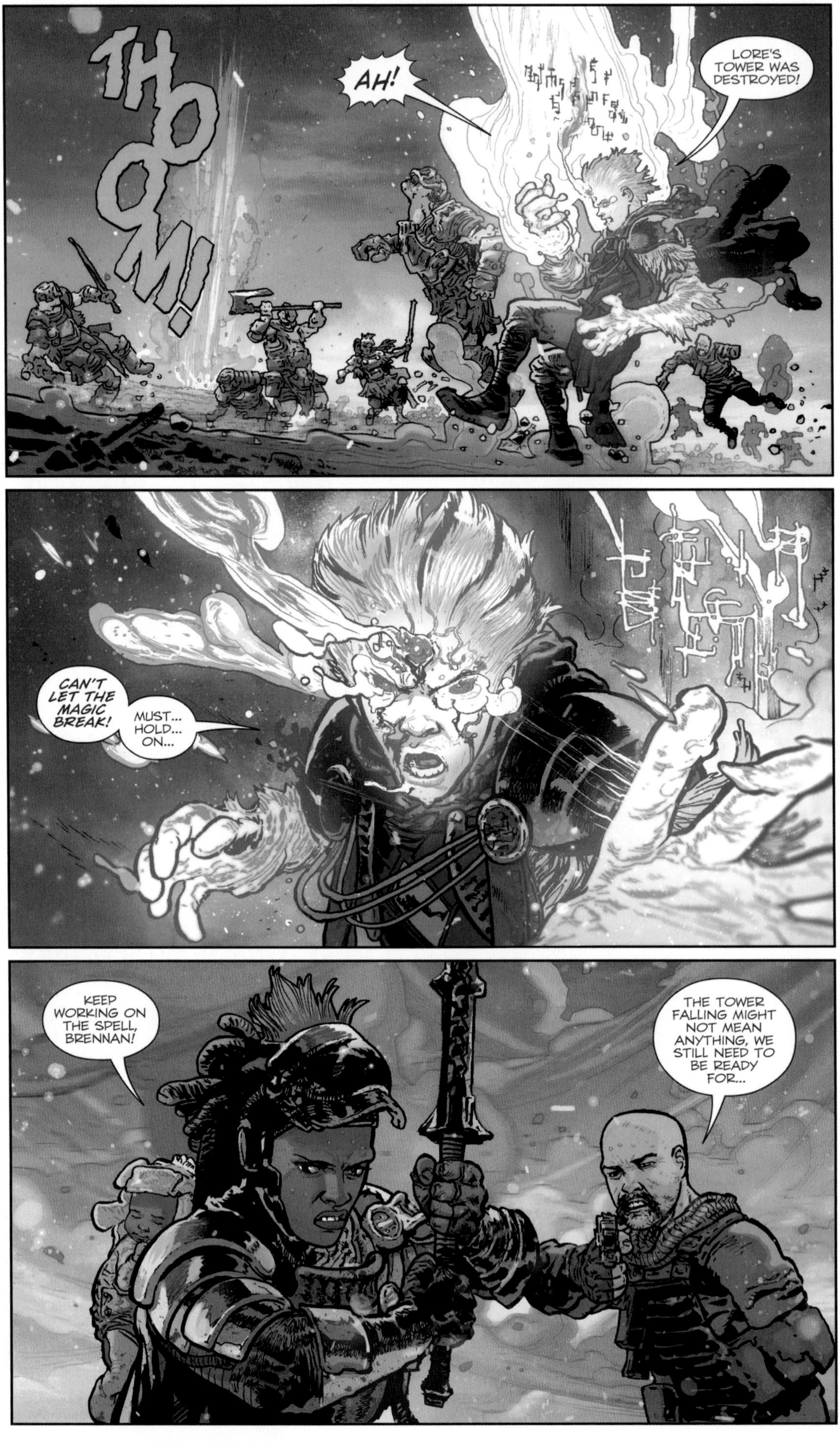
THOOM!
AH!
LORE'S TOWER WAS DESTROYED!
CAN'T LET THE MAGIC BREAK!
MUST... HOLD... ON...
KEEP WORKING ON THE SPELL, BRENNAN!
THE TOWER FALLING MIGHT NOT MEAN ANYTHING, WE STILL NEED TO BE READY FOR...

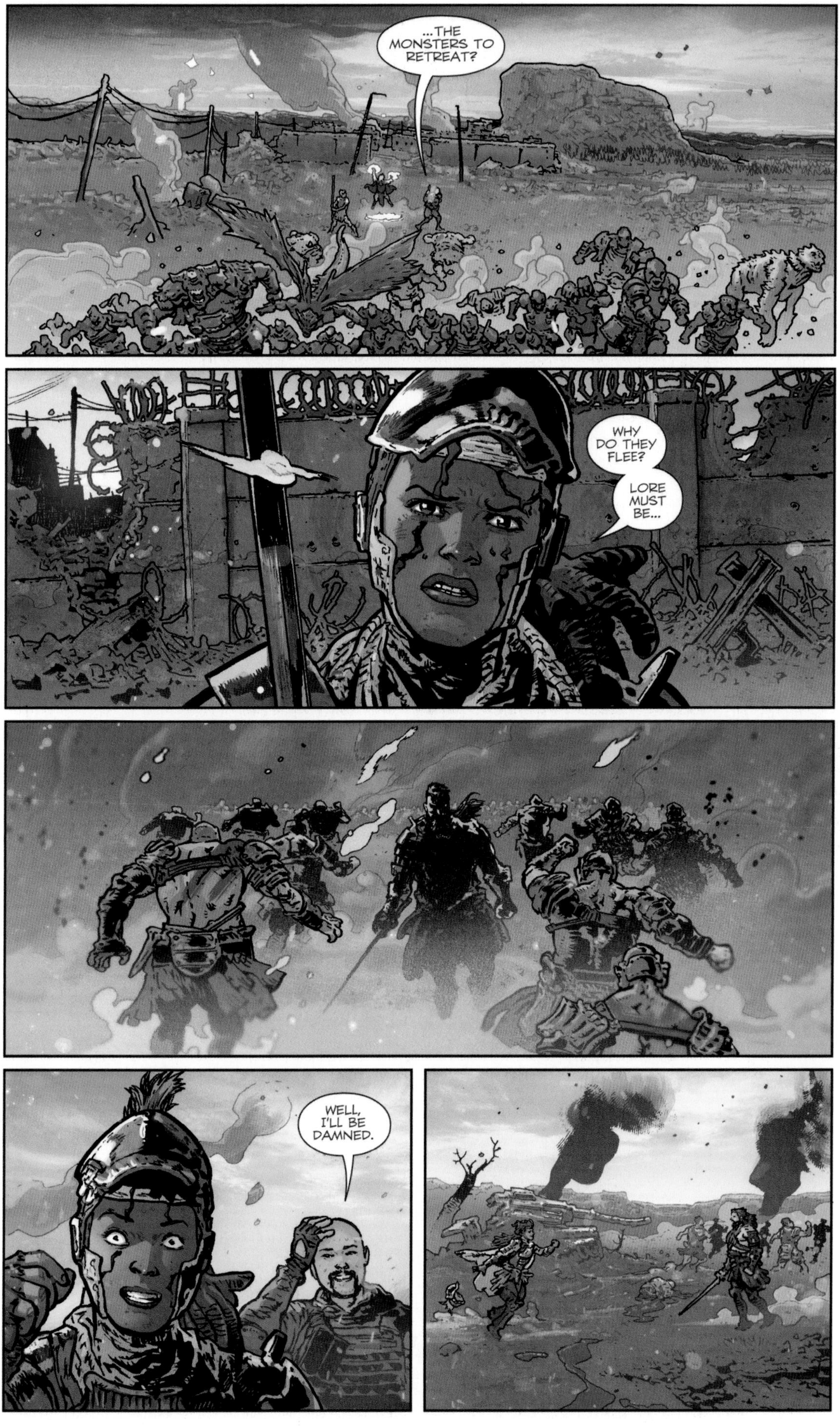
...THE MONSTERS TO RETREAT?
WHY DO THEY FLEE?
LORE MUST BE...
WELL, I'LL BE DAMNED.

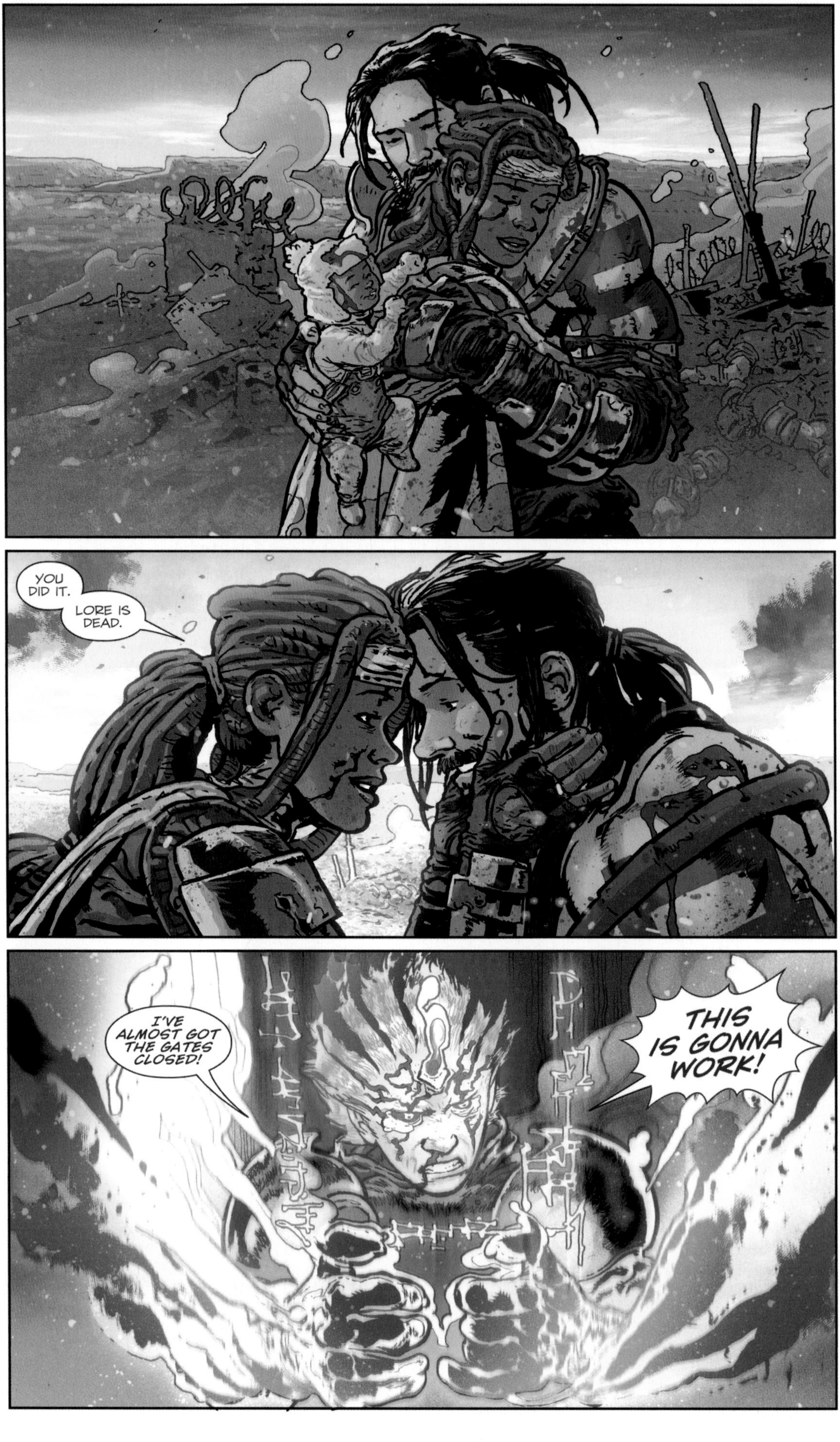
YOU DID IT.
LORE IS DEAD.
I'VE ALMOST GOT THE GATES CLOSED!
THIS IS GONNA WORK!

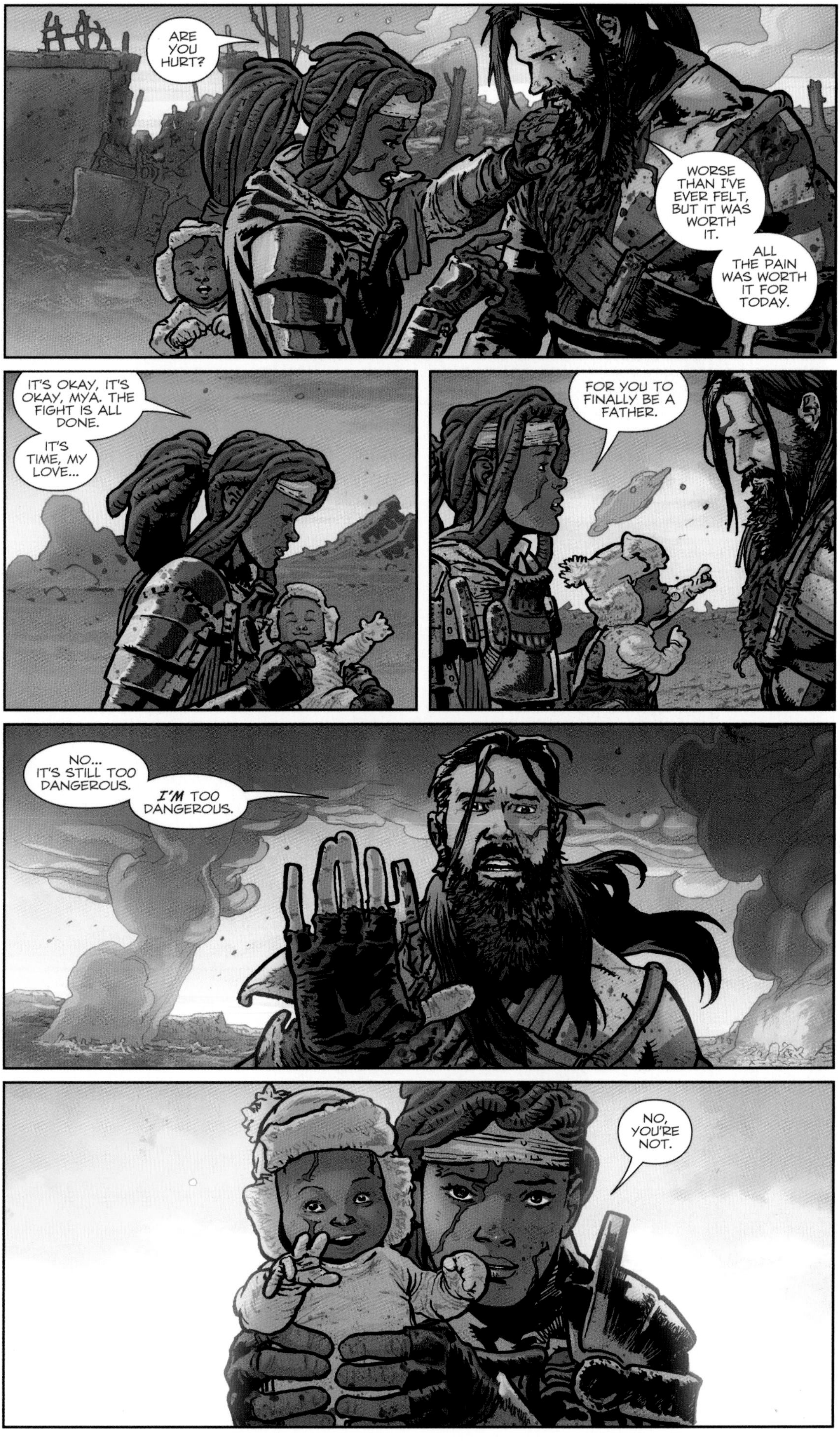
ARE YOU HURT?
WORSE THAN I'VE EVER FELT, BUT IT WAS WORTH IT.
ALL THE PAIN WAS WORTH IT FOR TODAY.
IT'S OKAY, IT'S OKAY, MYA. THE FIGHT IS ALL DONE.
IT'S TIME, MY LOVE...
FOR YOU TO FINALLY BE A FATHER.
NO... IT'S STILL TOO DANGEROUS.
I'M TOO DANGEROUS.
NO, YOU'RE NOT.

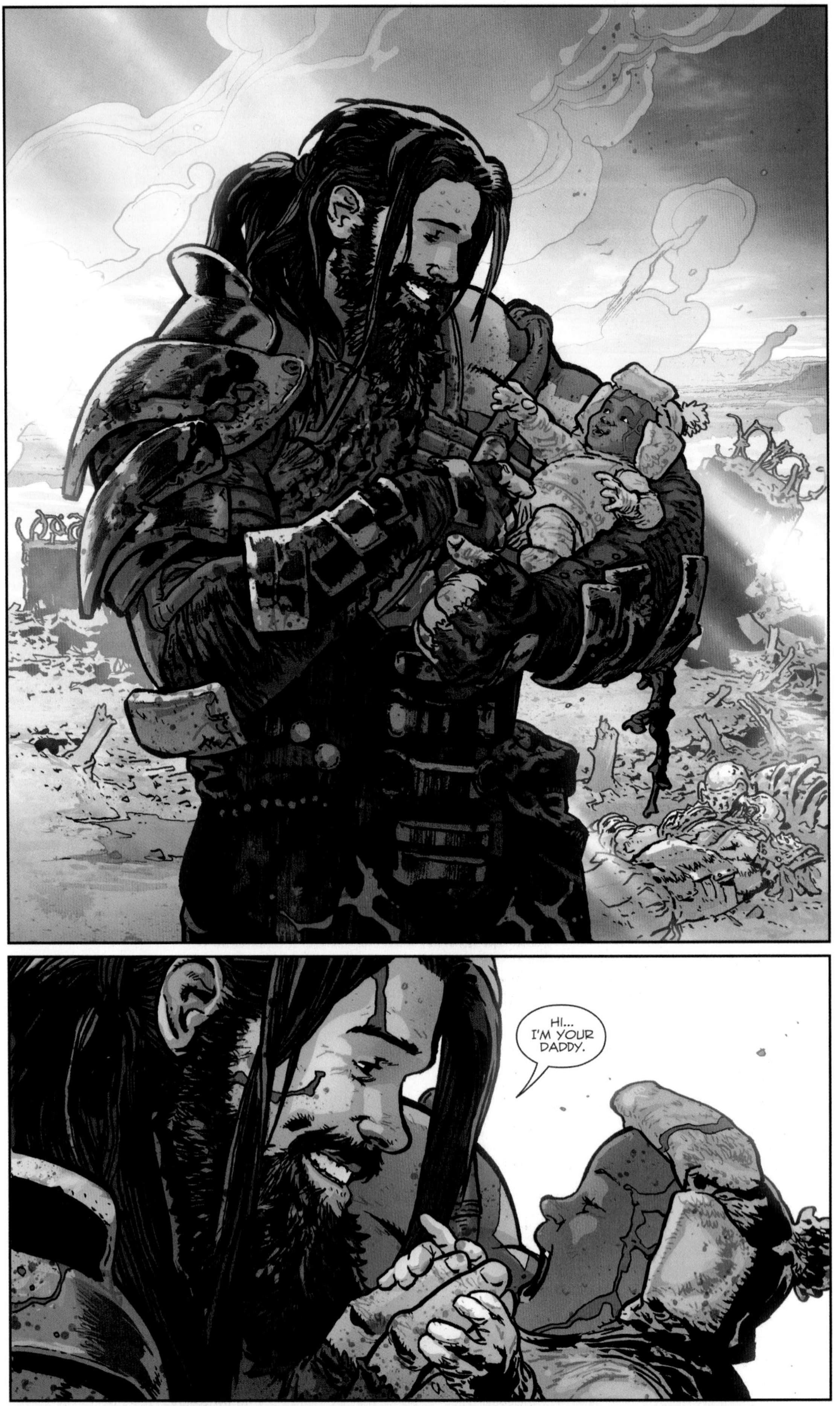
HI... I'M YOUR DADDY.

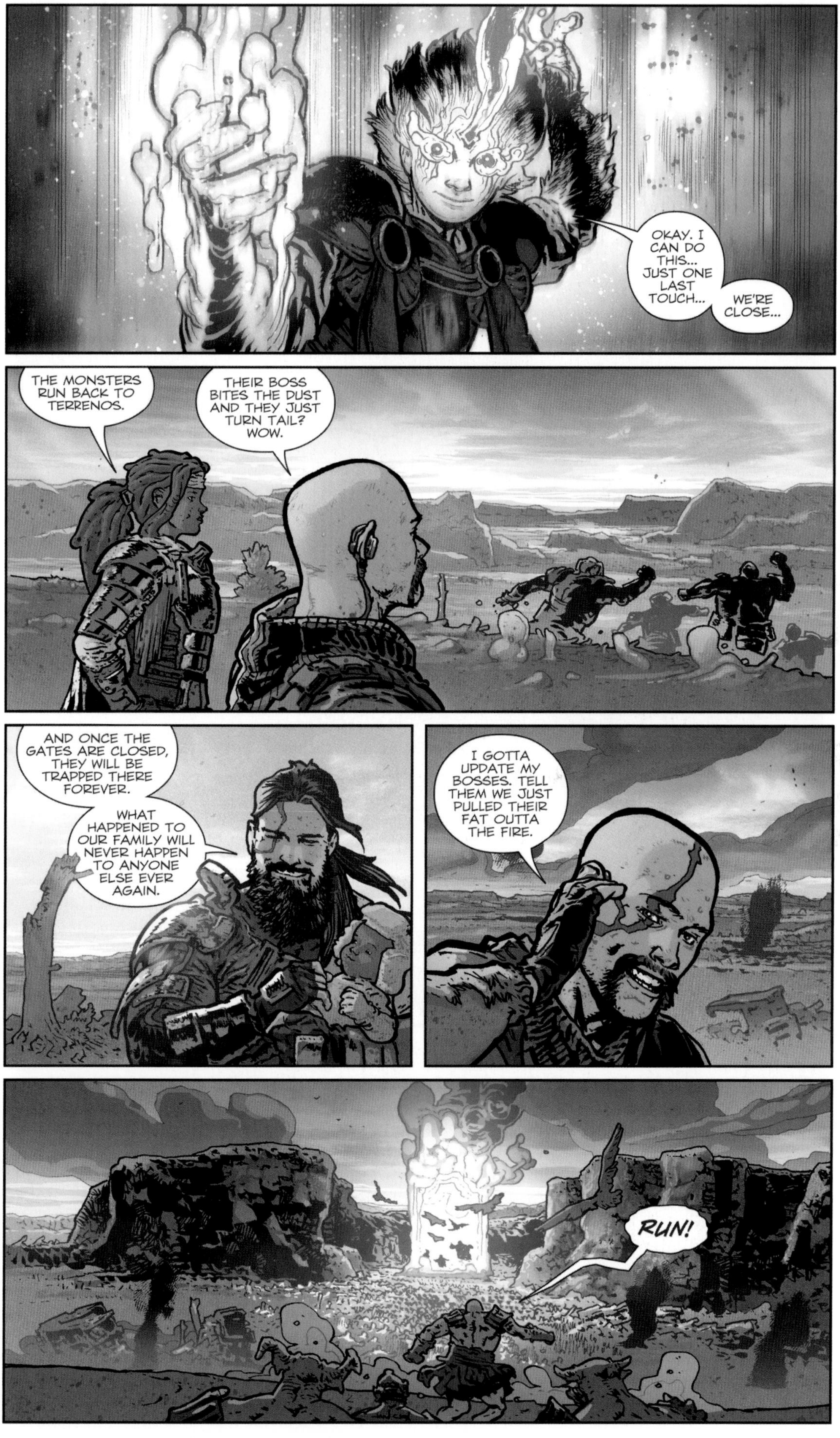
OKAY. I CAN DO THIS... JUST ONE LAST TOUCH...
WE'RE CLOSE...
THE MONSTERS RUN BACK TO TERRENOS.
THEIR BOSS BITES THE DUST AND THEY JUST TURN TAIL? WOW.
AND ONCE THE GATES ARE CLOSED, THEY WILL BE TRAPPED THERE FOREVER.
WHAT HAPPENED TO OUR FAMILY WILL NEVER HAPPEN TO ANYONE ELSE EVER AGAIN.
I GOTTA UPDATE MY BOSSES. TELL THEM WE JUST PULLED THEIR FAT OUTTA THE FIRE.
RUN!

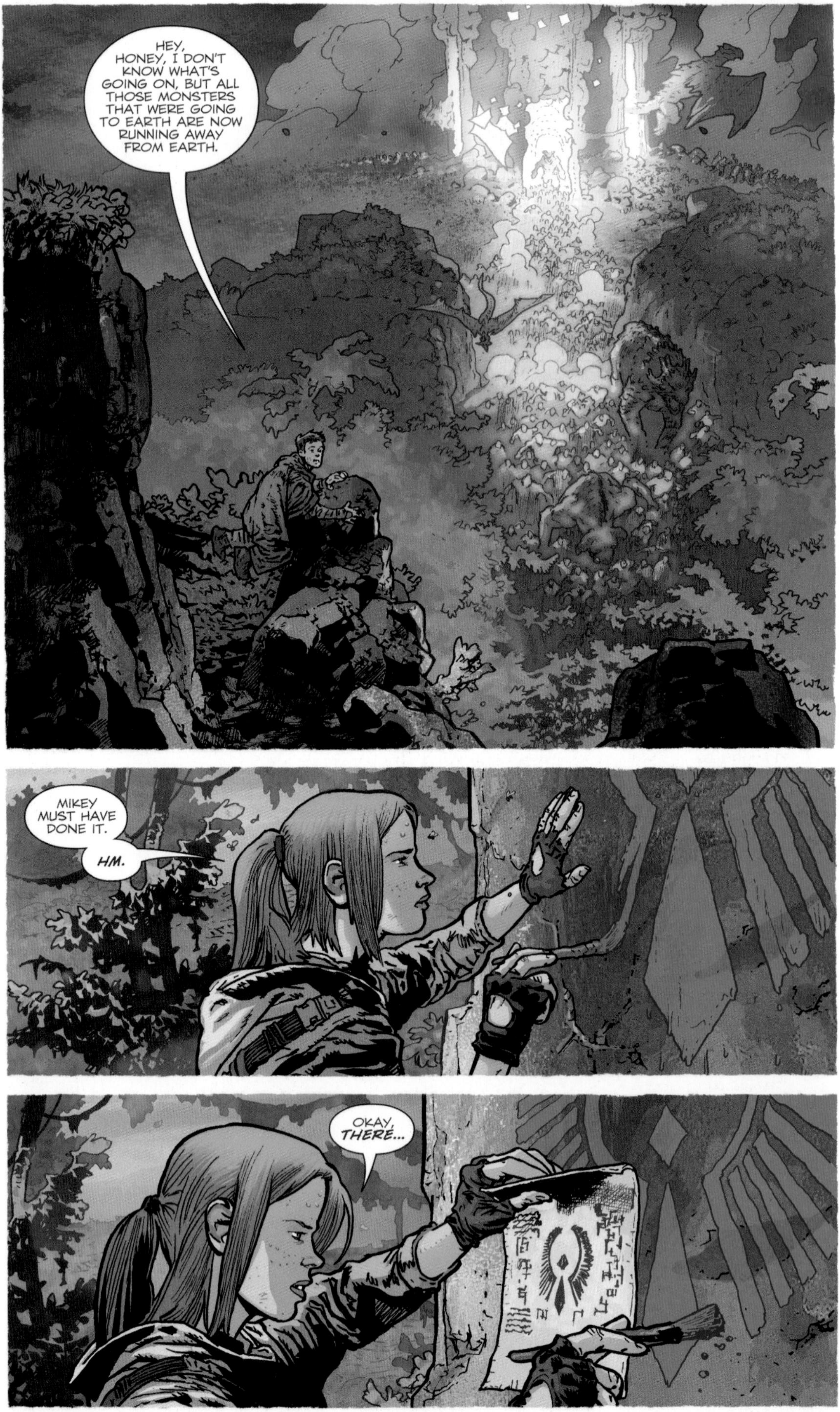
HEY, HONEY, I DON'T KNOW WHAT'S GOING ON, BUT ALL THOSE MONSTERS THAT WERE GOING TO EARTH ARE NOW RUNNING AWAY FROM EARTH.
MIKEY MUST HAVE DONE IT.
HM.
OKAY, *THERE...*

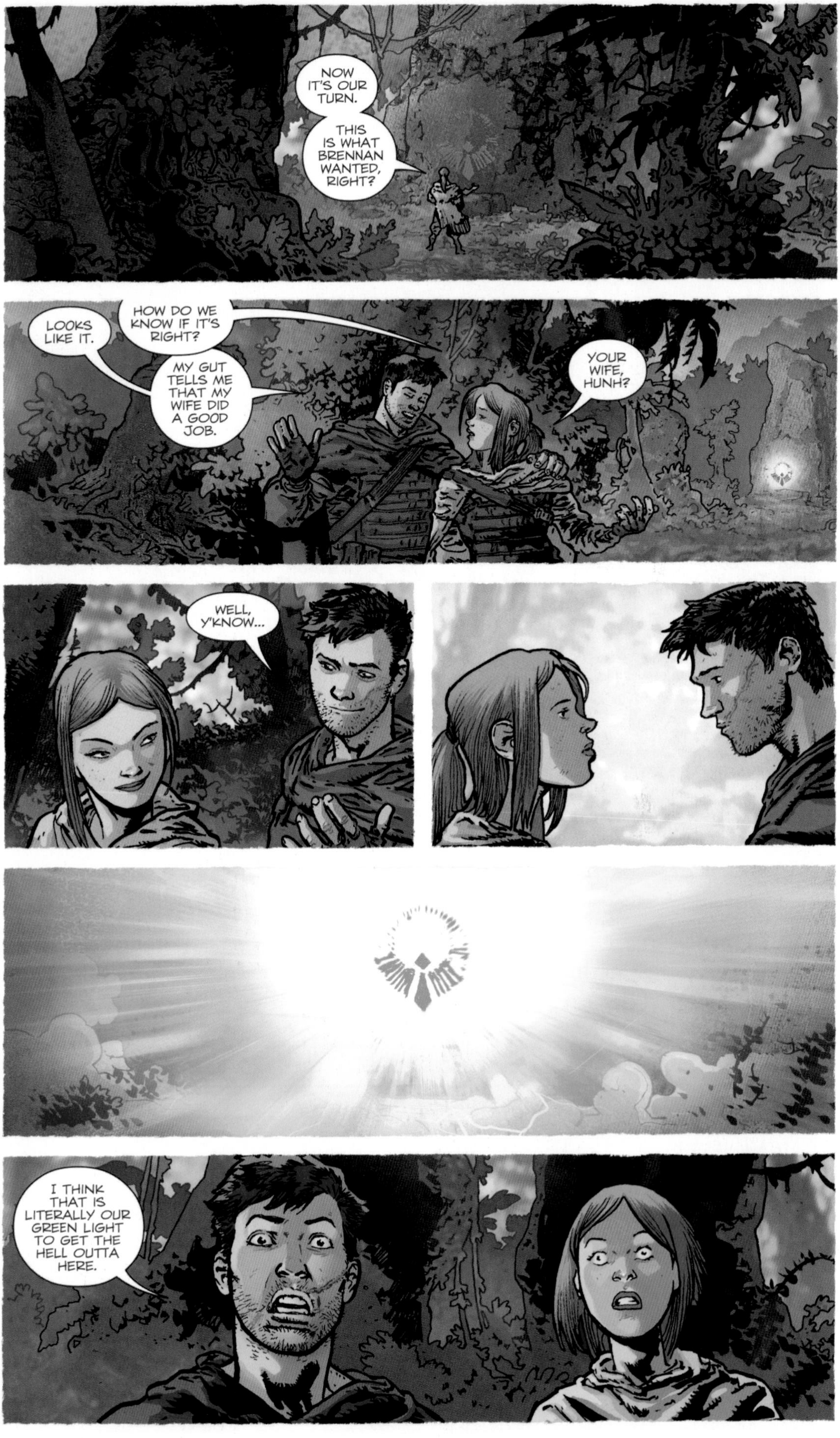
NOW IT'S OUR TURN.
THIS IS WHAT BRENNAN WANTED, RIGHT?
LOOKS LIKE IT.
HOW DO WE KNOW IF IT'S RIGHT?
MY GUT TELLS ME THAT MY WIFE DID A GOOD JOB.
YOUR WIFE, HUNH?
WELL, Y'KNOW...
I THINK THAT IS LITERALLY OUR GREEN LIGHT TO GET THE HELL OUTTA HERE.

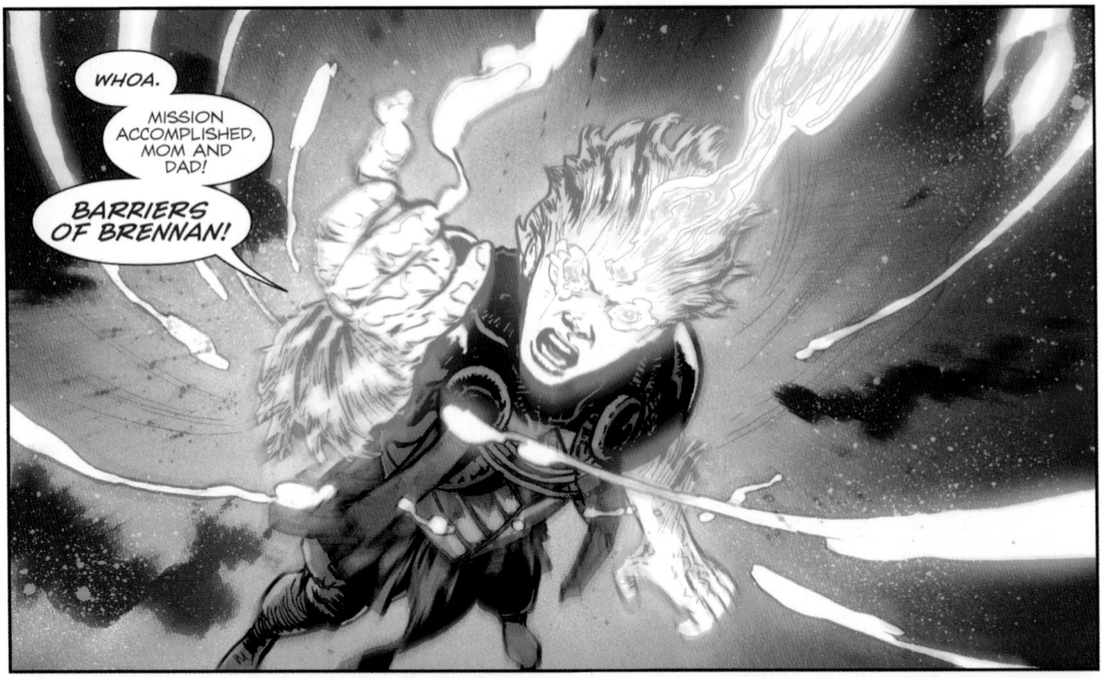
WHOA.
MISSION ACCOMPLISHED, MOM AND DAD!
BARRIERS OF BRENNAN!
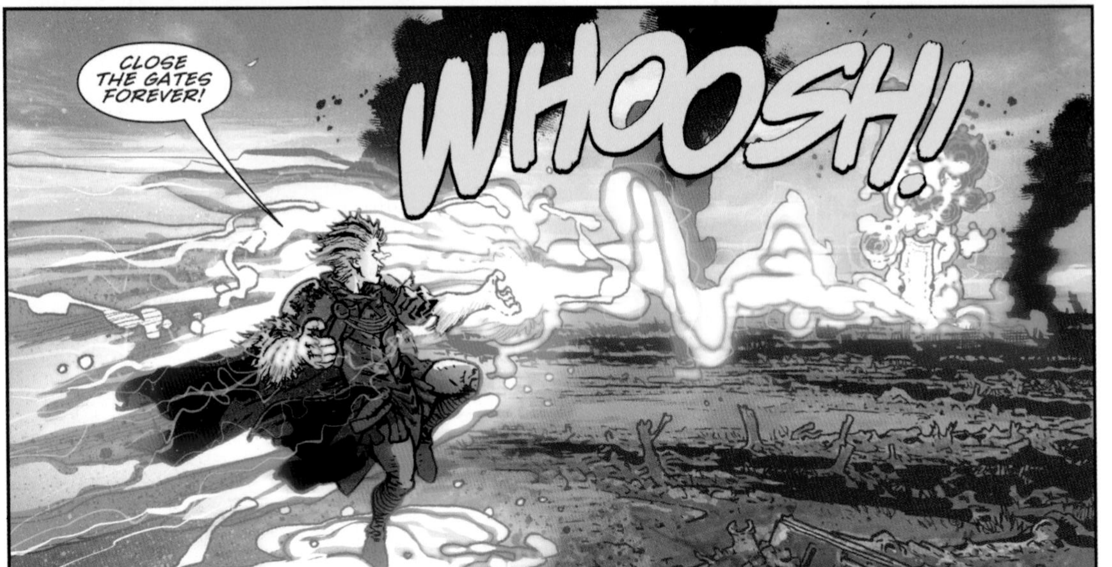
CLOSE THE GATES FOREVER!
WHOOSH!
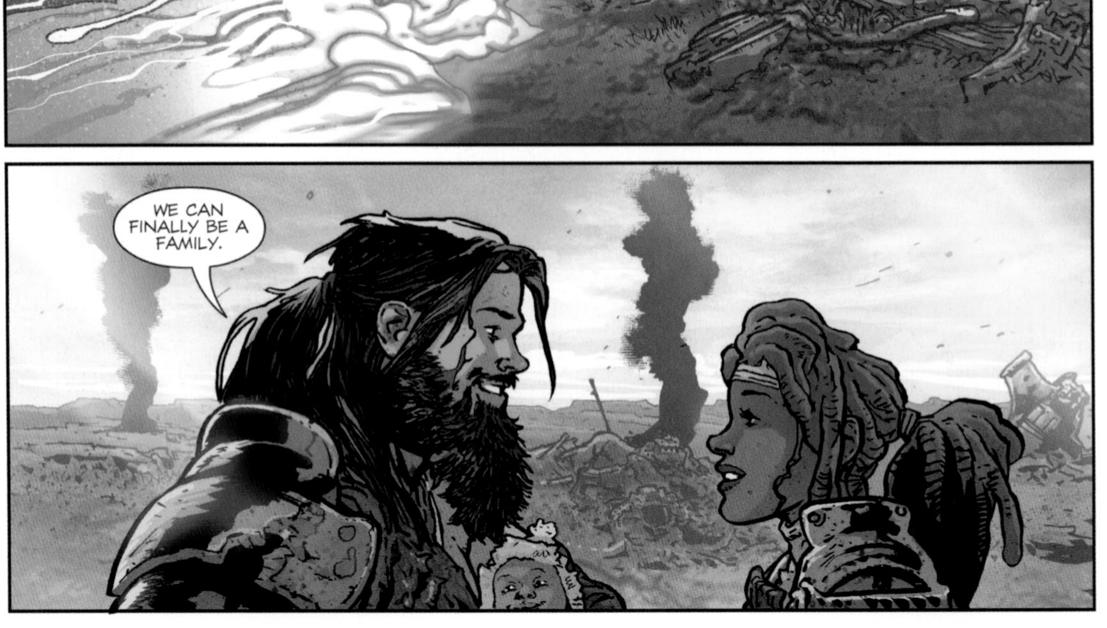
WE CAN FINALLY BE A FAMILY.

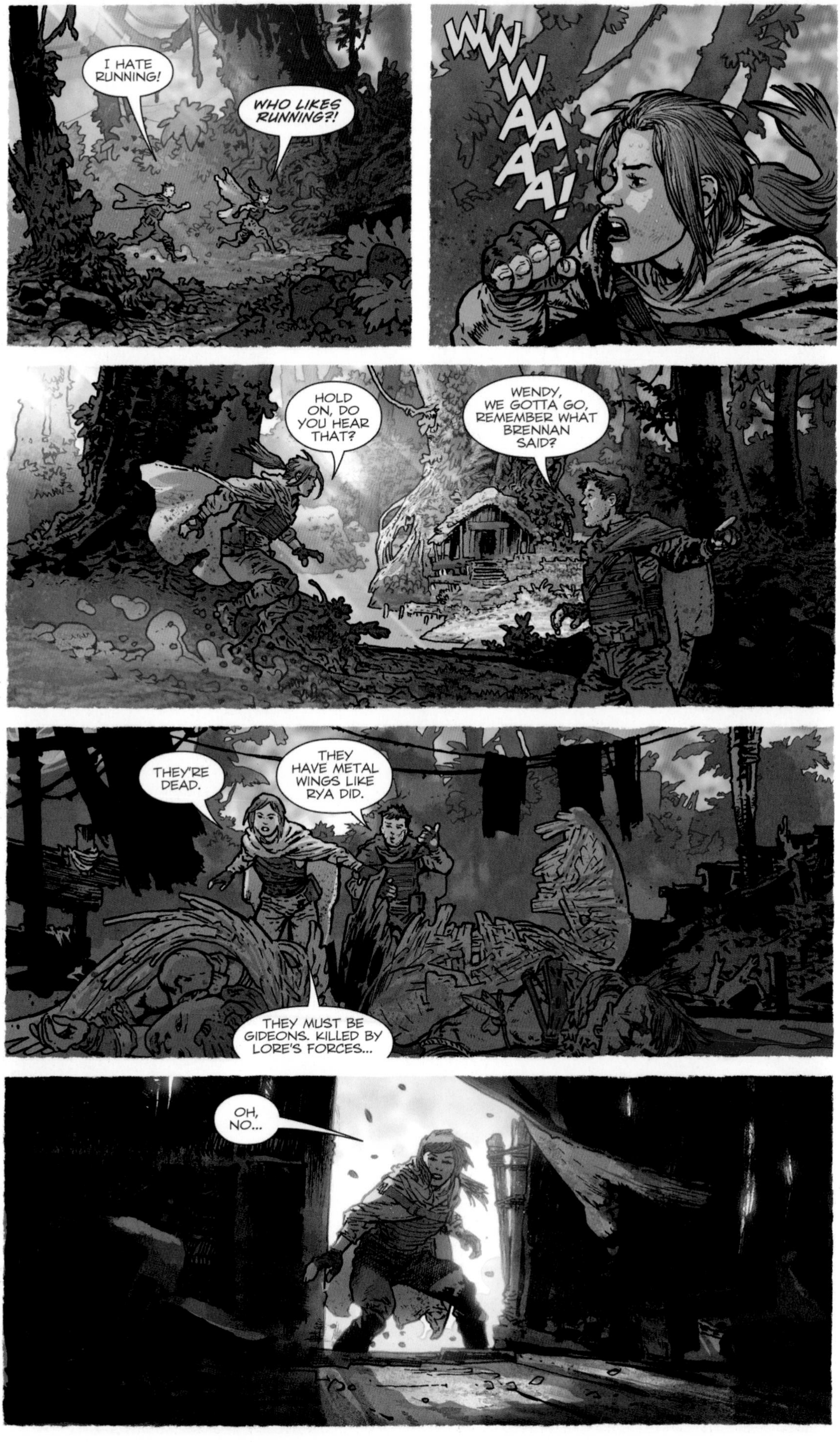
I HATE RUNNING!
WHO LIKES RUNNING?!
WWWAAAA!
HOLD ON, DO YOU HEAR THAT?
WENDY, WE GOTTA GO, REMEMBER WHAT BRENNAN SAID?
THEY'RE DEAD.
THEY HAVE METAL WINGS LIKE RYA DID.
THEY MUST BE GIDEONS. KILLED BY LORE'S FORCES...
OH, NO...

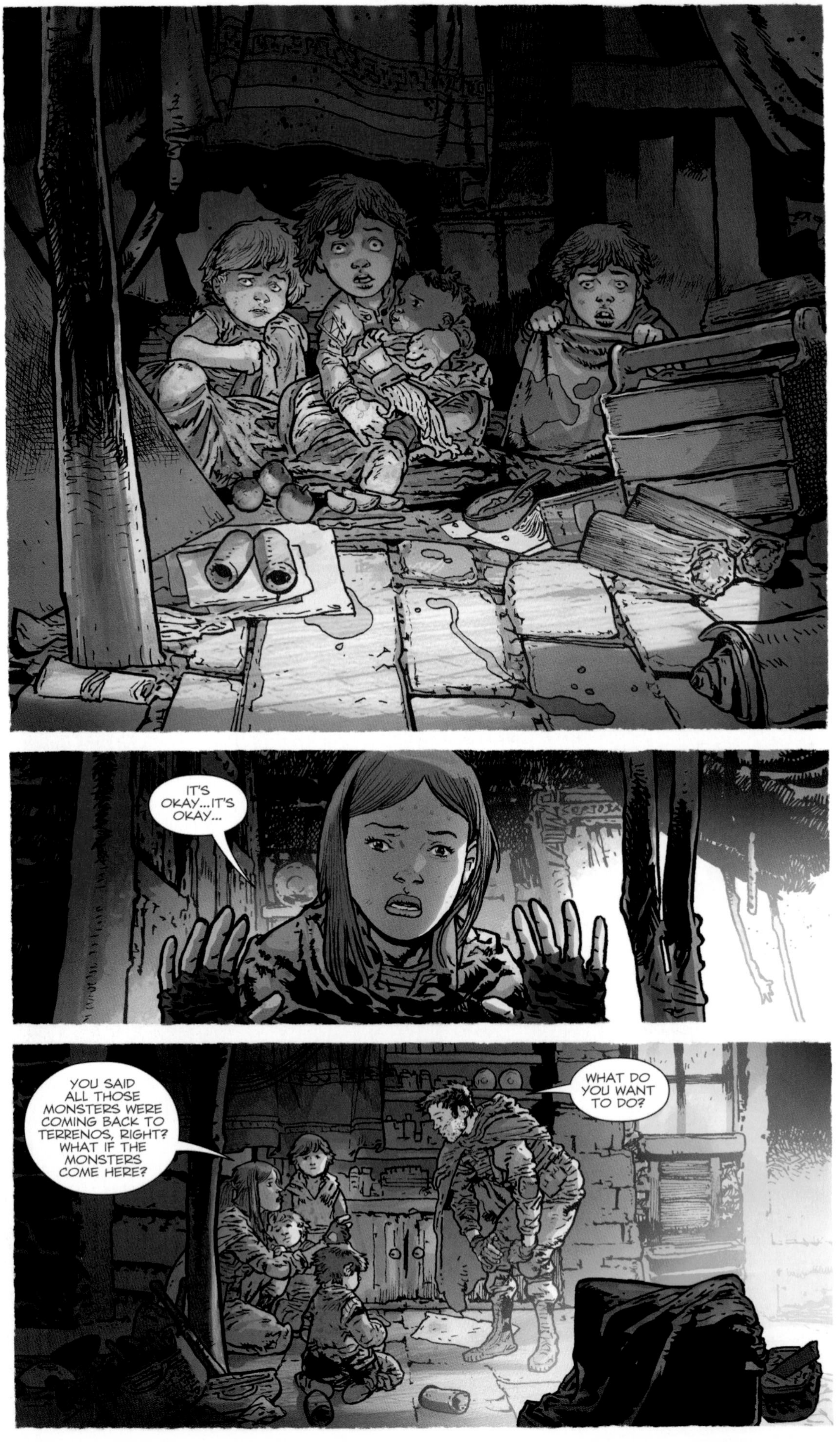
IT'S OKAY...IT'S OKAY...
YOU SAID ALL THOSE MONSTERS WERE COMING BACK TO TERRENOS, RIGHT? WHAT IF THE MONSTERS COME HERE?
WHAT DO YOU WANT TO DO?

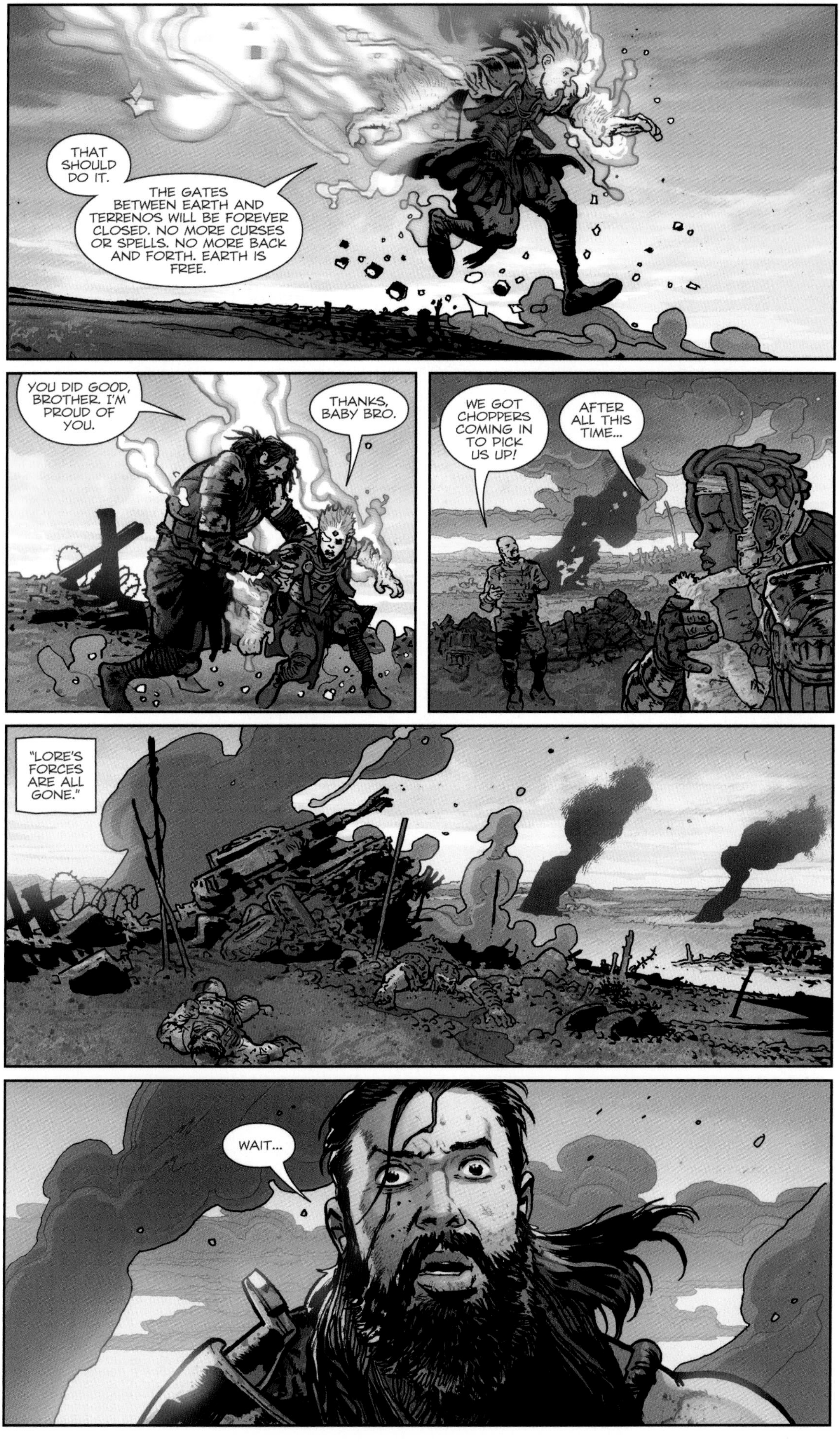
THAT SHOULD DO IT.
THE GATES BETWEEN EARTH AND TERRENOS WILL BE FOREVER CLOSED. NO MORE CURSES OR SPELLS. NO MORE BACK AND FORTH. EARTH IS FREE.
YOU DID GOOD, BROTHER. I'M PROUD OF YOU.
THANKS, BABY BRO.
WE GOT CHOPPERS COMING IN TO PICK US UP!
AFTER ALL THIS TIME...
"LORE'S FORCES ARE ALL GONE."
WAIT...

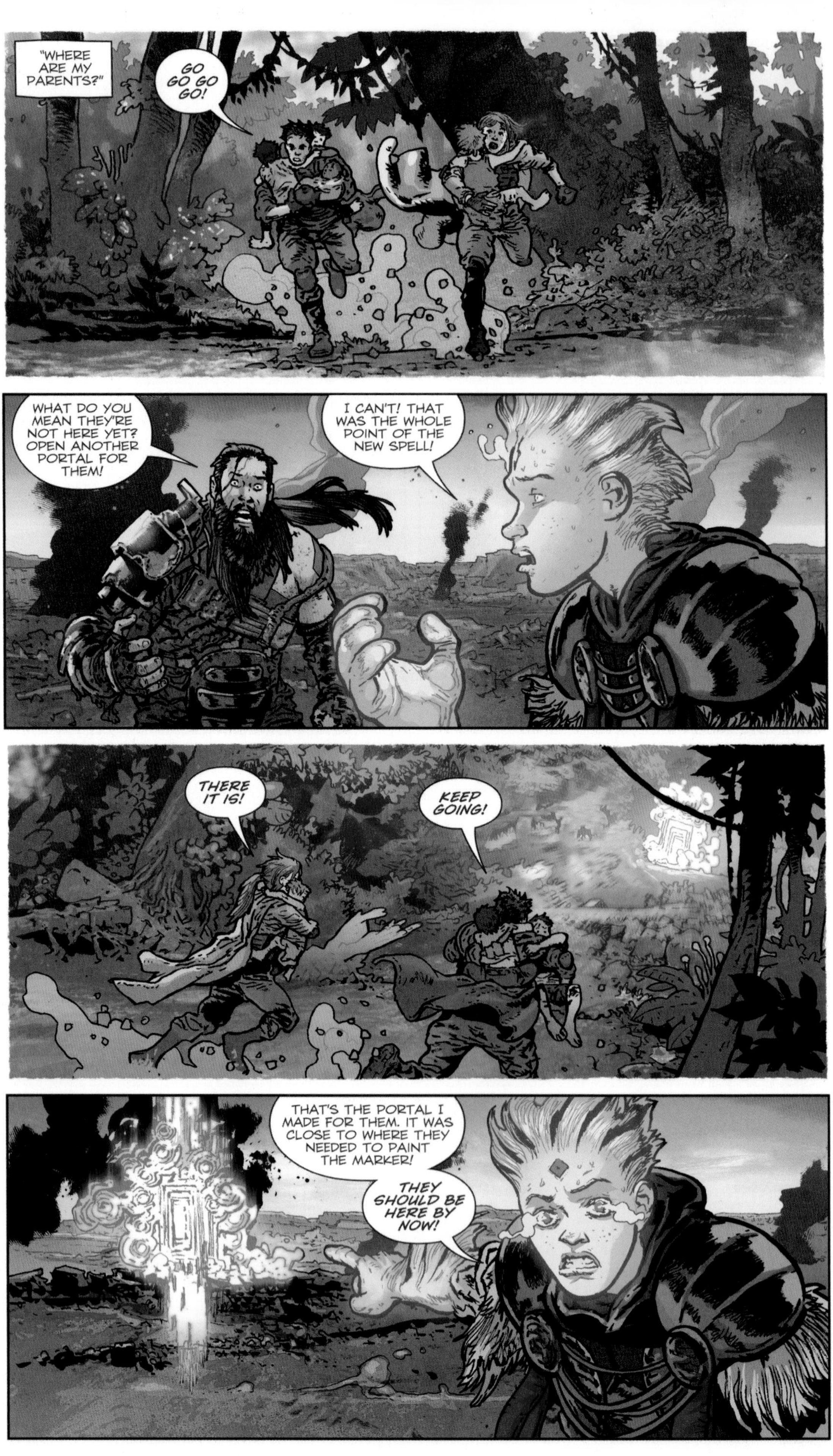
"WHERE ARE MY PARENTS?"
GO GO GO GO!
WHAT DO YOU MEAN THEY'RE NOT HERE YET? OPEN ANOTHER PORTAL FOR THEM!
I CAN'T! THAT WAS THE WHOLE POINT OF THE NEW SPELL!
THERE IT IS!
KEEP GOING!
THAT'S THE PORTAL I MADE FOR THEM. IT WAS CLOSE TO WHERE THEY NEEDED TO PAINT THE MARKER!
THEY SHOULD BE HERE BY NOW!

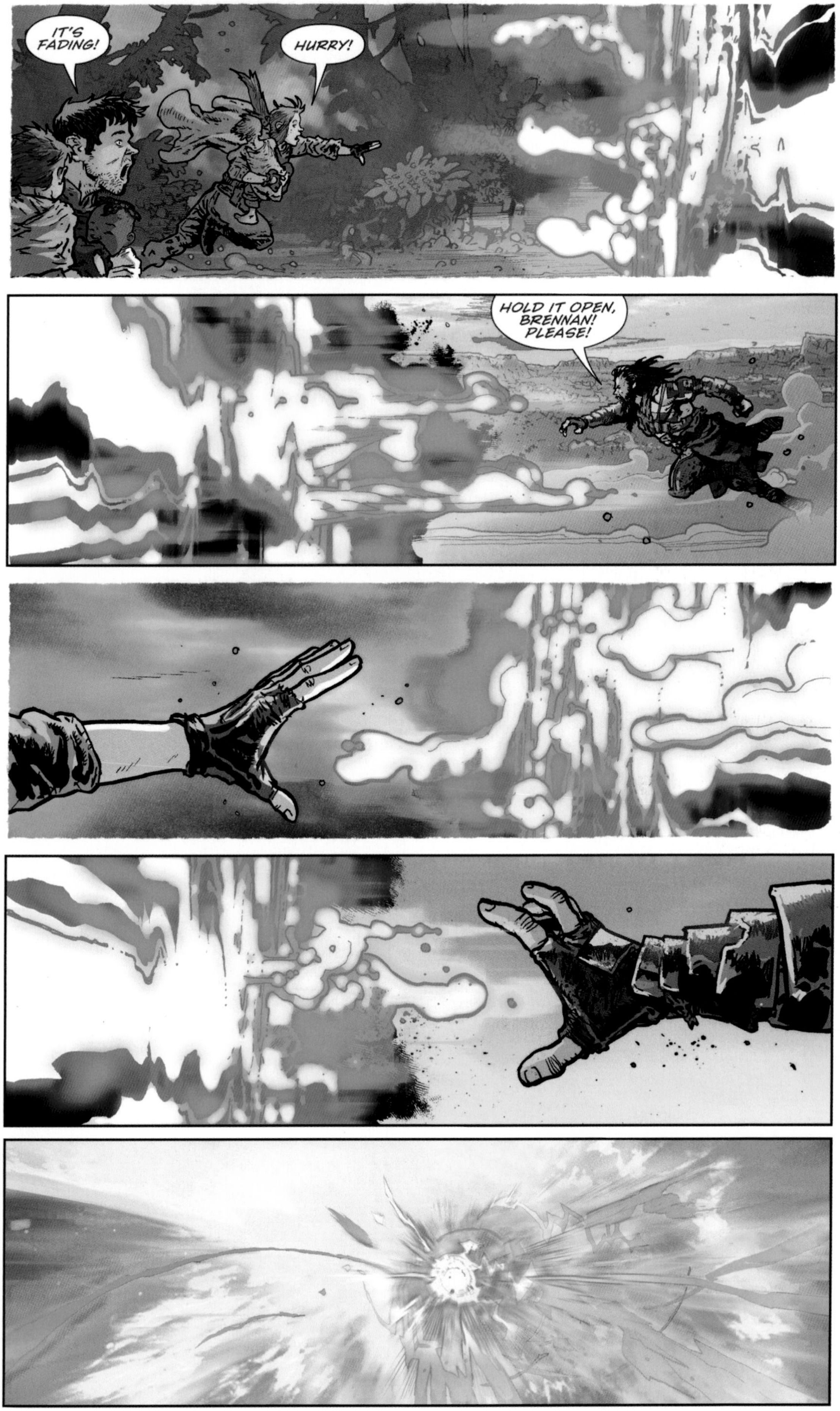
IT'S FADING!
HURRY!
HOLD IT OPEN, BRENNAN! PLEASE!

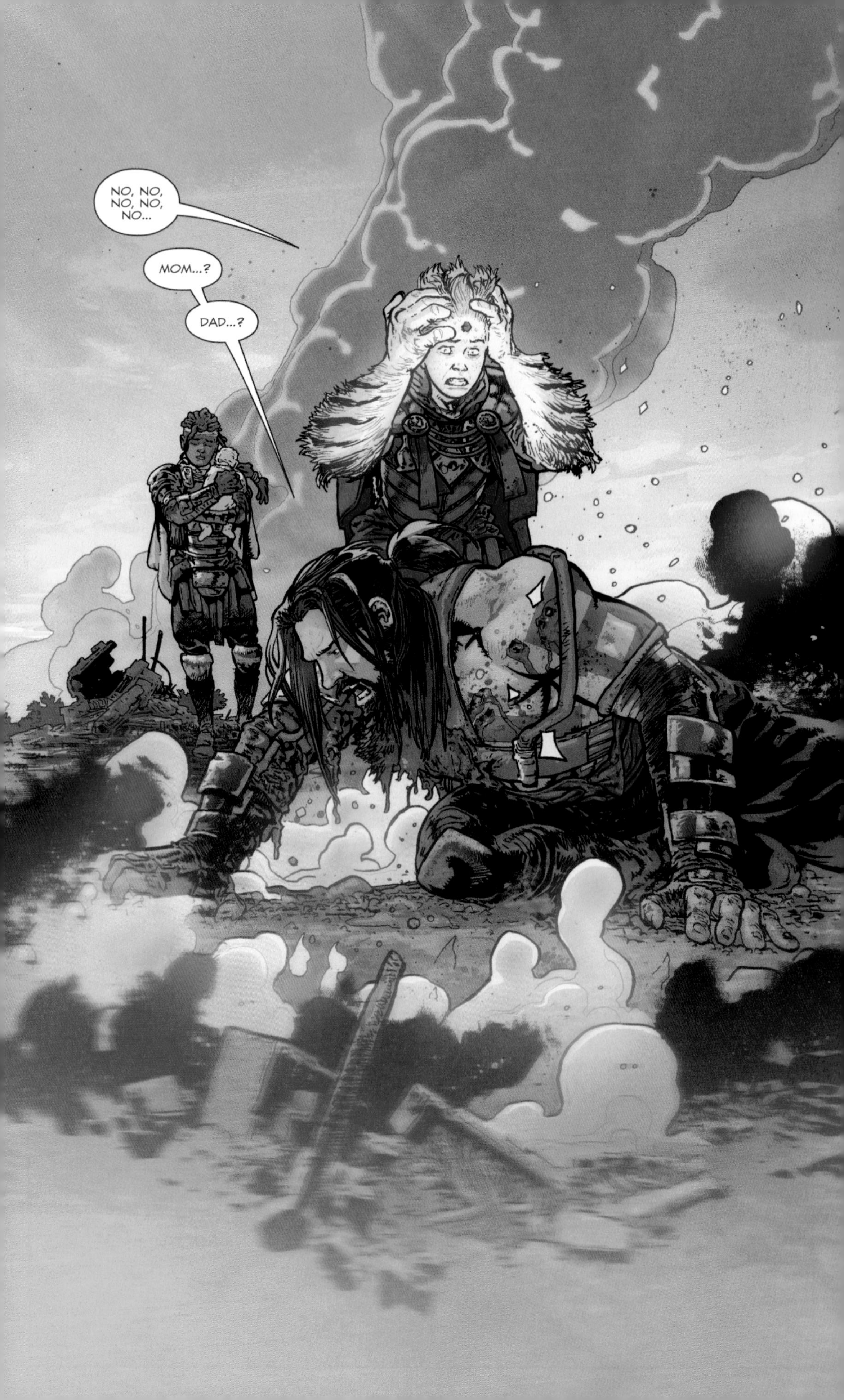
NO, NO, NO, NO, NO...
MOM...?
DAD...?

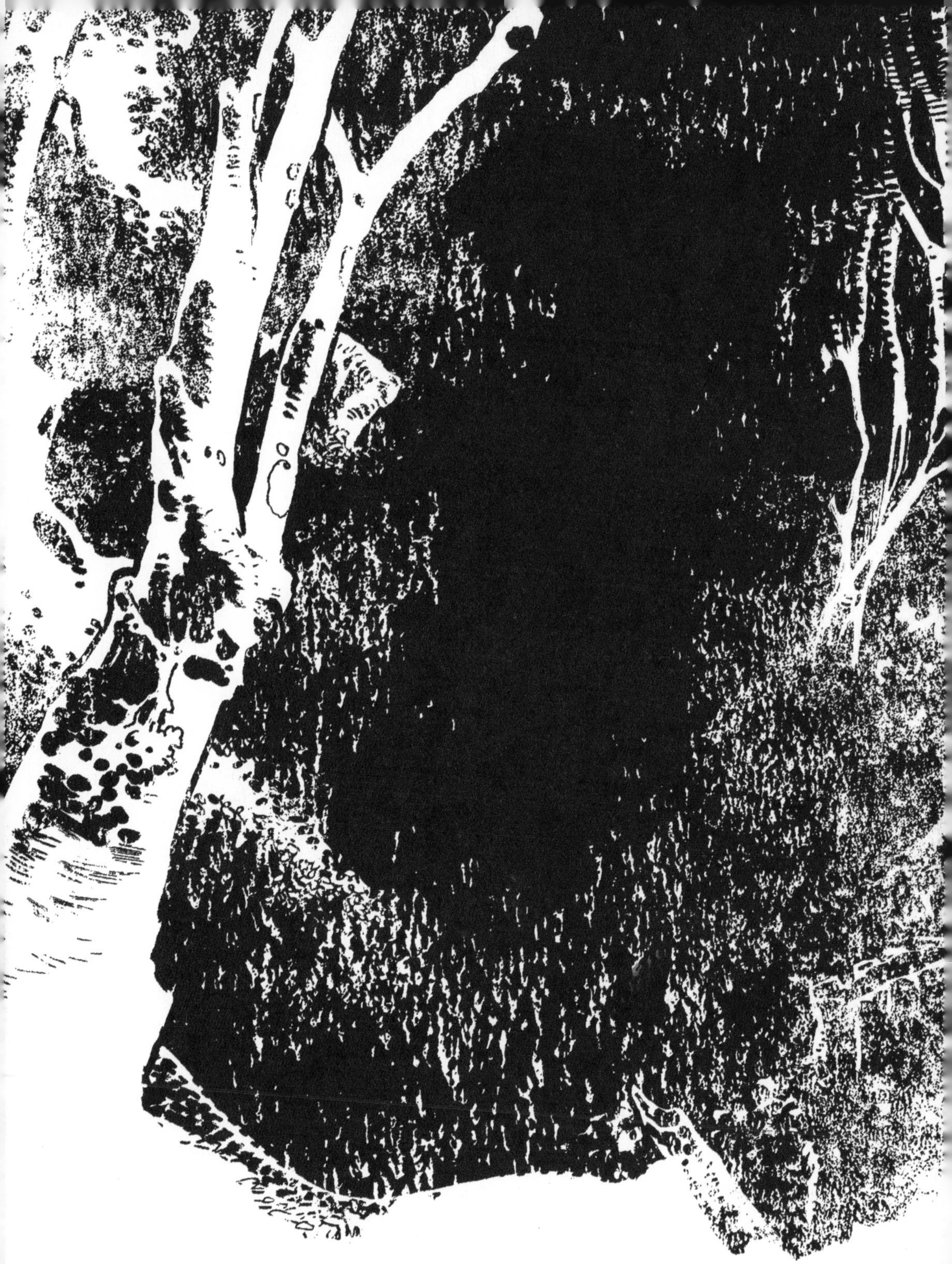

To be continued...

*"I killed in the name of peace.
Built the legend that would be sung.*

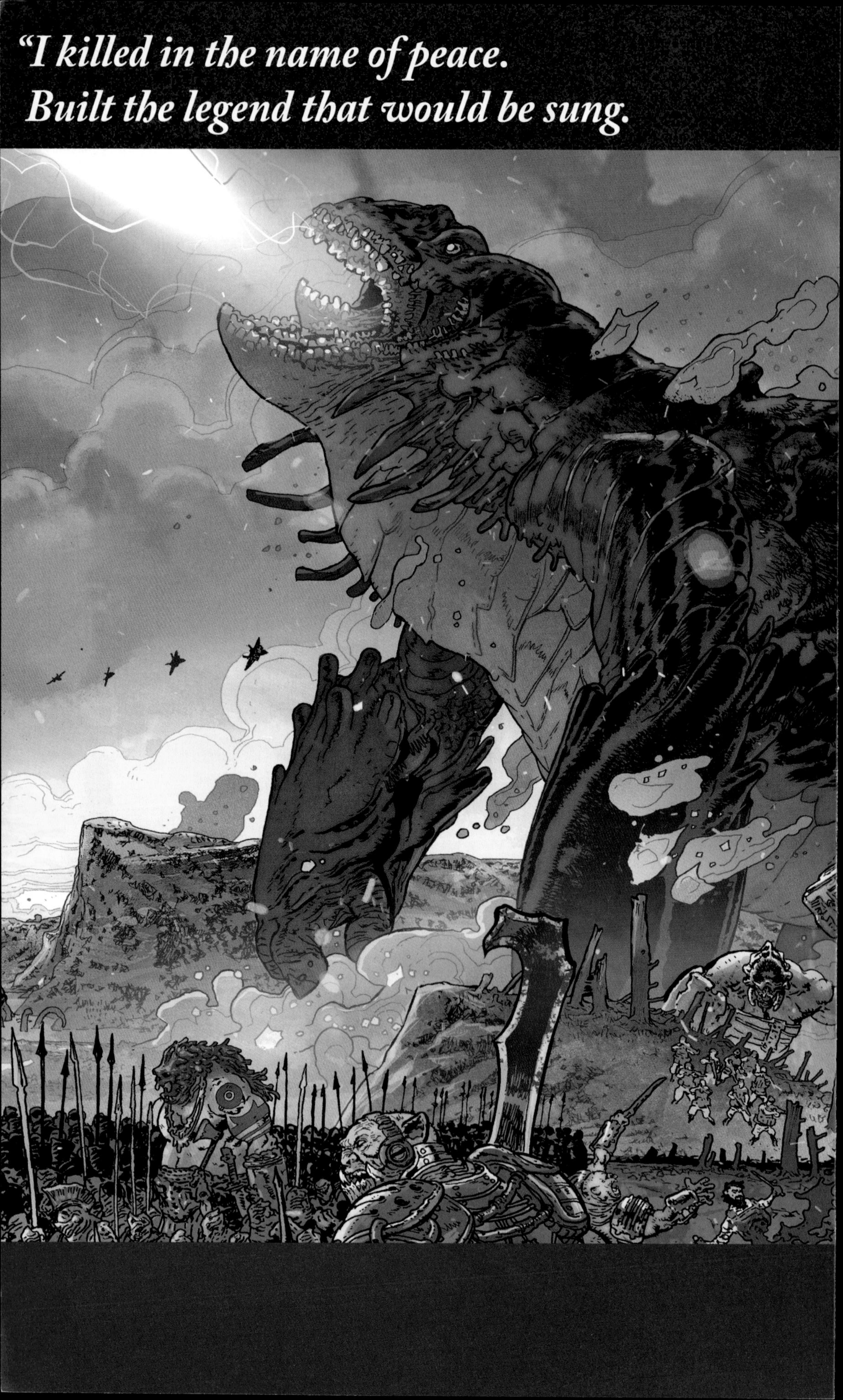

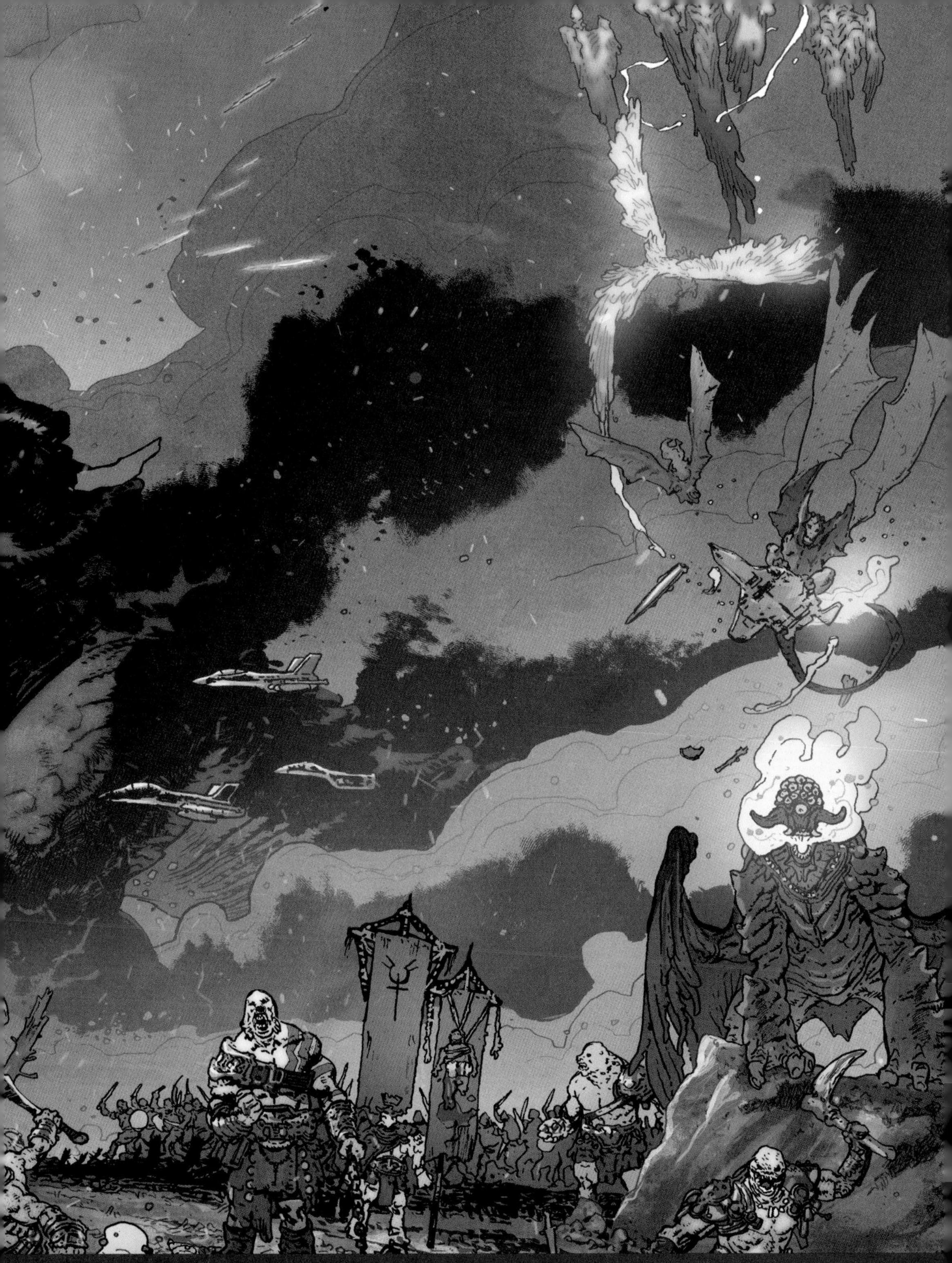

But it was not enough.”

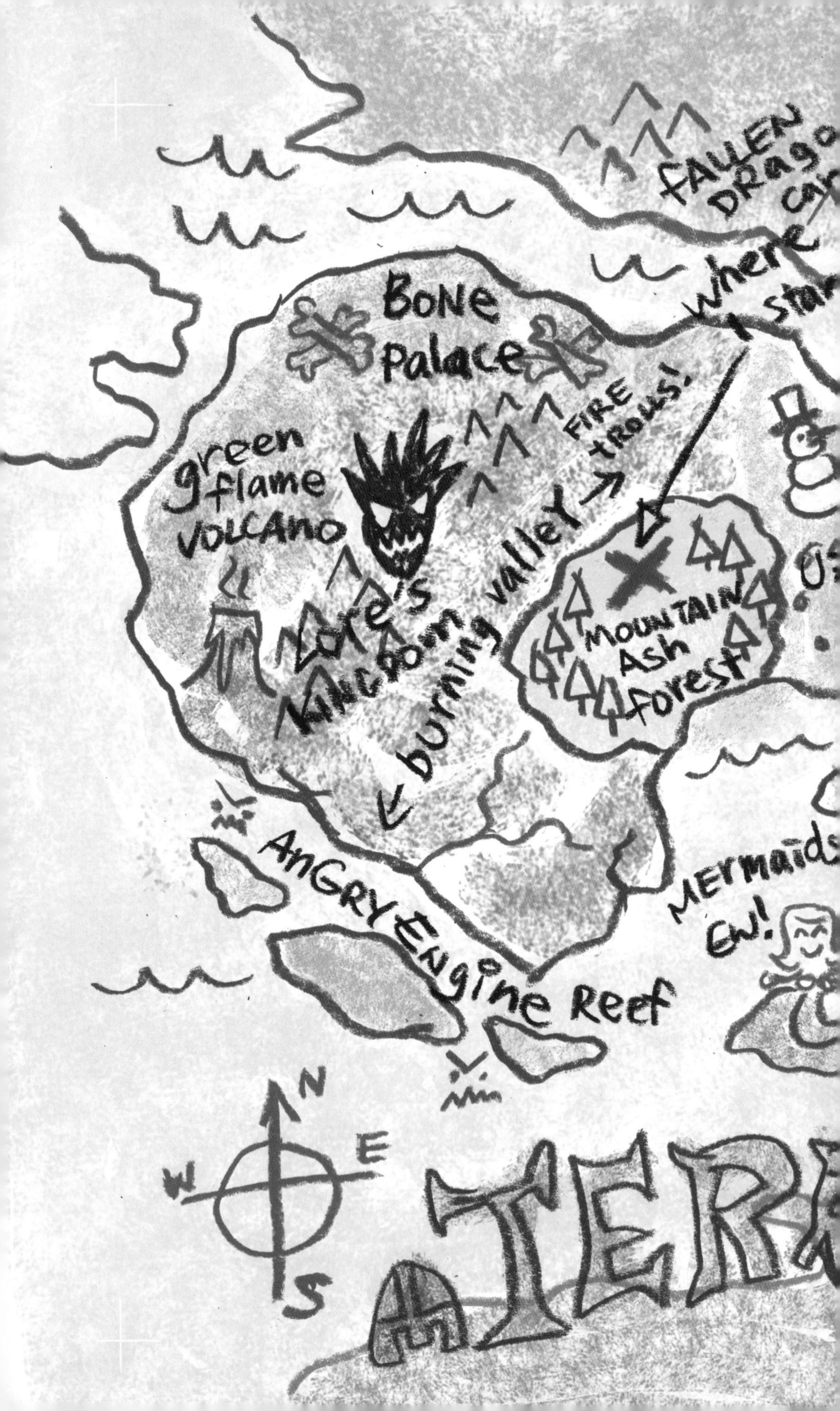
FALLEN
DRAGO
where
I star
Bone
Palace
FIRE
TROLLS!
green
flame
VOLCANO
Lore's
Kingdom
burning valley
MOUNTAIN
Ash
forest
ANGRY Engine Reef
MERMAIDS
EW!
N
E
W
S
TER

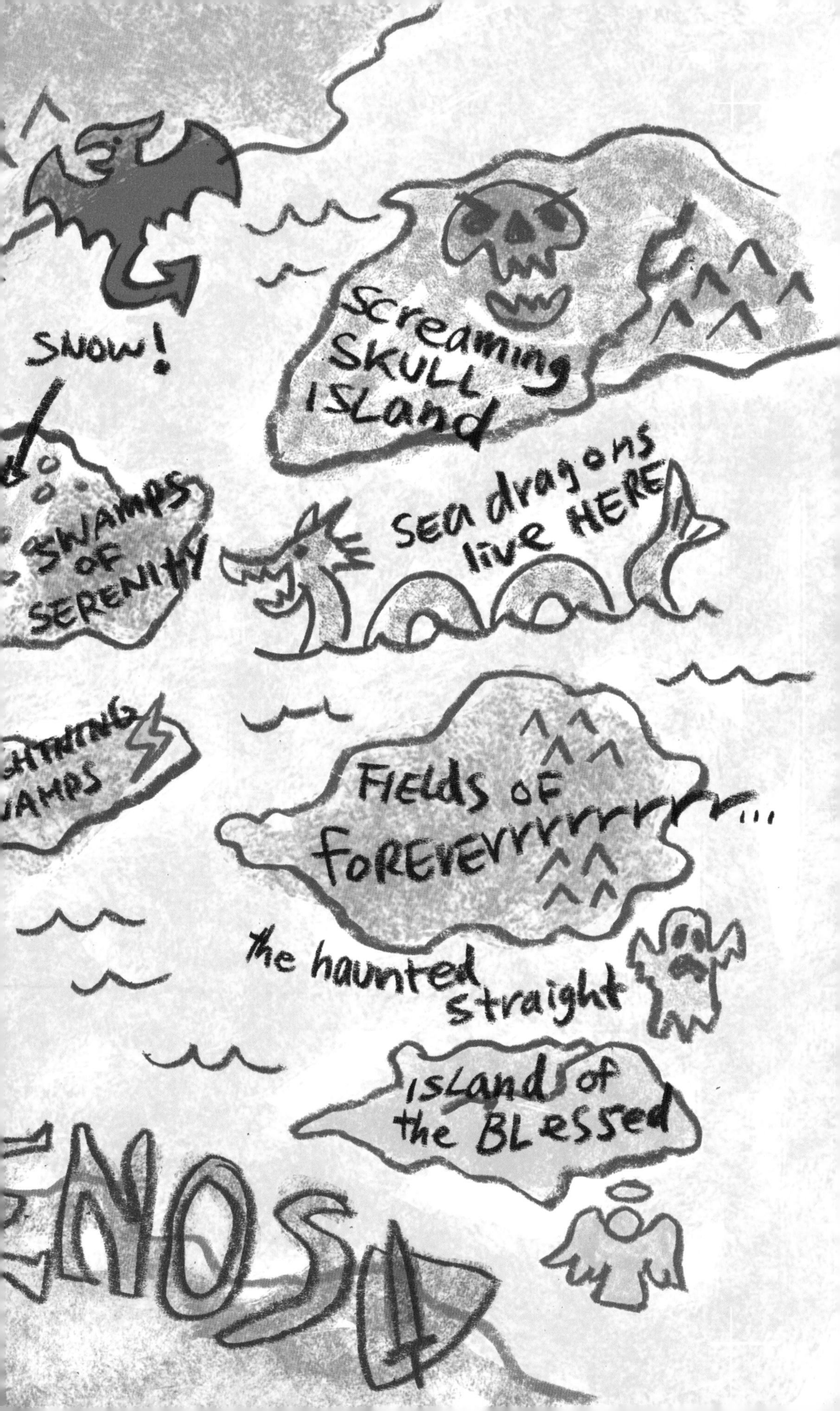
SNOW!
Screaming SKULL ISLand
SWAMPS OF SERENITY
SEA dragons live HERE
GHTNING
WAMPS
FIELDS OF
foREVErrrrrrrr...
the haunted straight
ISLand of the BLessed

FOR MORE OF INVINCIBLE

TRADEPAPERBACKS

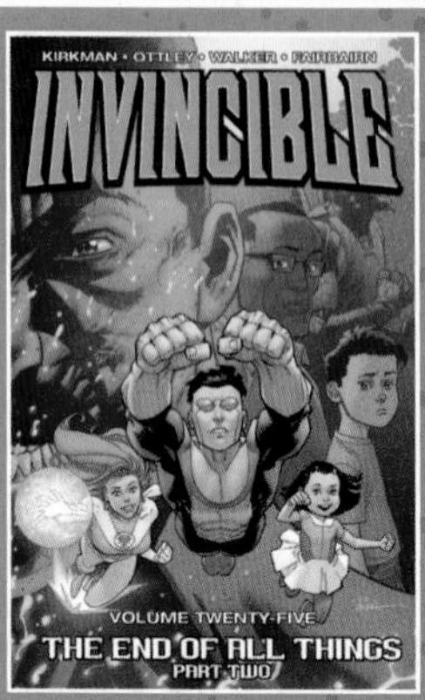
KIRKMAN • OTTLEY • WALKER • FAIRBAIRN
INVINCIBLE
VOLUME TWENTY-FIVE
THE END OF ALL THINGS
PART TWO

VOL. 1: FAMILY MATTERS TP
ISBN: 978-1-58240-711-1
$12.99
VOL. 2: EIGHT IS ENOUGH TP
ISBN: 978-1-58240-347-2
$12.99
VOL. 3: PERFECT STRANGERS TP
ISBN: 978-1-58240-793-7
$12.99
VOL. 4: HEAD OF THE CLASS TP
ISBN: 978-1-58240-778-4
$14.99
VOL. 5: THE FACTS OF LIFE TP
ISBN: 978-1-58240-554-4
$14.99
VOL. 6: A DIFFERENT WORLD TP
ISBN: 978-1-58240-579-7
$14.99
VOL. 7: THREE'S COMPANY TP
ISBN: 978-1-58240-656-5
$14.99

VOL. 8: MY FAVORITE MARTIAN TP
ISBN: 978-1-58240-683-1
$16.99
VOL. 9: OUT OF THIS WORLD TP
ISBN: 978-1-58240-827-9
$14.99
VOL. 10: WHO'S THE BOSS TP
ISBN: 978-1-60706-013-0
$16.99
VOL. 11: HAPPY DAYS TP
ISBN: 978-1-60706-062-8
$16.99
VOL. 12: STILL STANDING TP
ISBN: 978-1-60706-166-3
$16.99
VOL. 13: GROWING PAINS TP
ISBN: 978-1-60706-251-6
$16.99
VOL. 14: THE VILTRUMITE WAR TP
ISBN: 978-1-60706-367-4
$19.99

VOL. 15: GET SMART TP
ISBN: 978-1-60706-498-5
$16.99
VOL. 16: FAMILY TIES TP
ISBN: 978-1-60706-579-1
$16.99
VOL. 17: WHAT'S HAPPENING TP
ISBN: 978-1-60706-662-0
$16.99
VOL. 18: DEATH OF EVERYONE TP
ISBN: 978-1-60706-762-7
$16.99
VOL. 19: THE WAR AT HOME TP
ISBN: 978-1-60706-856-3
$16.99
VOL. 20: FRIENDS TP
ISBN: 978-1-63215-043-1
$16.99
VOL. 21: MODERN FAMILY TP
ISBN: 978-1-63215-318-0
$16.99

VOL. 22: REBOOT? TP
ISBN: 978-1-63215-626
$16.99
VOL. 23: FULL HOUSE TP
ISBN: 978-1-63215-888
$16.99
VOL. 24: THE END OF ALL THIN
PART ONE TP
ISBN: 978-1-5343-0322
$16.99
VOL. 25: THE END OF ALL THIN
PART TWO TP
ISBN: 978-1-5343-0503
$16.99
THE OFFICIAL HANDBOOK OF
THE INVINCIBLE UNIVERSE TP
ISBN: 978-1-58240-831
$12.99
INVINCIBLE PRESENTS, VOL. 1
ATOM EVE & REX SPLODE TP
ISBN: 978-1-60706-255
$14.99

COMPENDIUMS

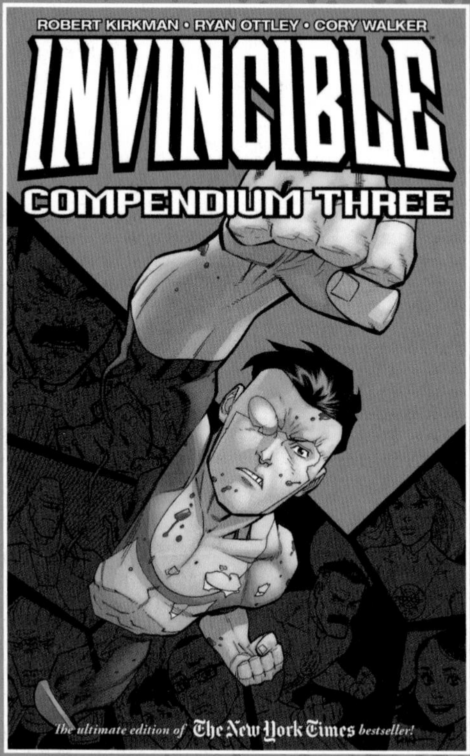
ROBERT KIRKMAN • RYAN OTTLEY • CORY WALKER
INVINCIBLE
COMPENDIUM THREE
The ultimate edition of The New York Times bestseller!

COMPENDIUM VOL. 1
ISBN: 978-1-60706-411-4
$64.99
COMPENDIUM VOL. 2
ISBN: 978-1-60706-772-6
$64.99
COMPENDIUM VOL. 3
ISBN: 978-1-5343-0686-8
$64.99

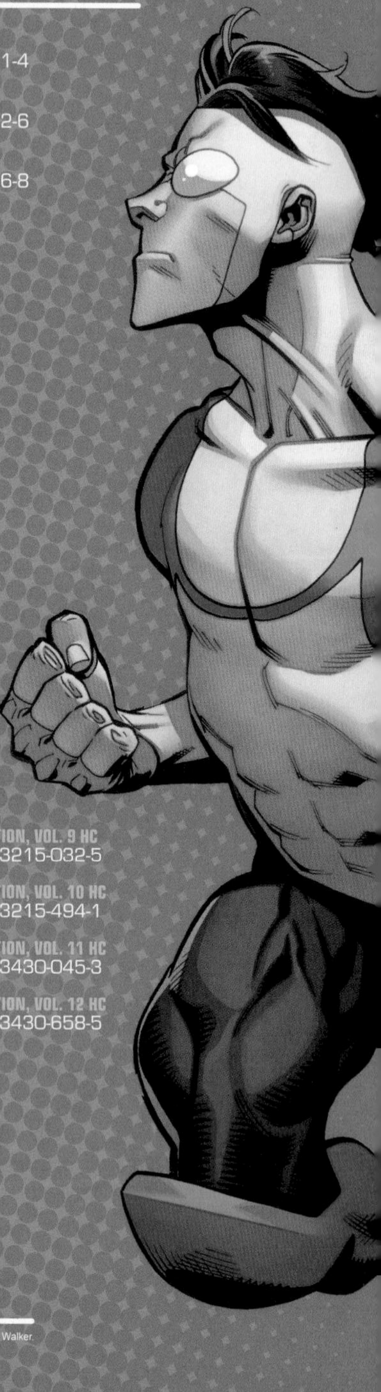

ULTIMATE COLLECTIONS

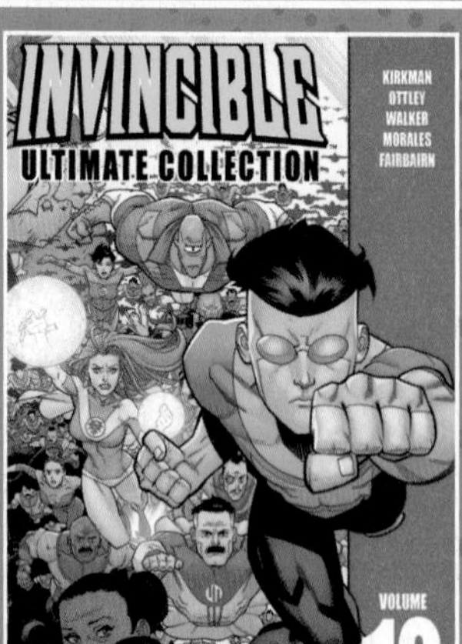
INVINCIBLE
ULTIMATE COLLECTION
KIRKMAN
OTTLEY
WALKER
MORALES
FAIRBAIRN
VOLUME
12

ULTIMATE COLLECTION, VOL. 1 HC
ISBN 978-1-58240-500-1
$34.99
ULTIMATE COLLECTION, VOL. 2 HC
ISBN: 978-1-58240-594-0
$34.99
ULTIMATE COLLECTION, VOL. 3 HC
ISBN: 978-1-58240-763-0
$34.99
ULTIMATE COLLECTION, VOL. 4 HC
ISBN: 978-1-58240-989-4
$34.99
ULTIMATE COLLECTION, VOL. 5 HC
ISBN: 978-1-60706-116-8
$34.99
ULTIMATE COLLECTION, VOL. 6 HC
ISBN: 978-1-60706-360-5
$34.99
ULTIMATE COLLECTION, VOL. 7 HC
ISBN: 978-1-60706-509-8
$39.99
ULTIMATE COLLECTION, VOL. 8 HC
ISBN: 978-1-60706-680-4
$39.99

ULTIMATE COLLECTION, VOL. 9 HC
ISBN: 978-1-63215-032-5
$39.99
ULTIMATE COLLECTION, VOL. 10 HC
ISBN: 978-1-63215-494-1
$39.99
ULTIMATE COLLECTION, VOL. 11 HC
ISBN: 978-1-53430-045-3
$39.99
ULTIMATE COLLECTION, VOL. 12 HC
ISBN: 978-1-53430-658-5
$39.99

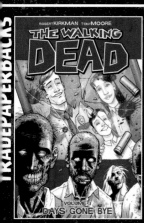
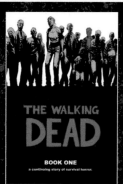

For more tales from ROBERT KIRKMAN and SKYBOUND

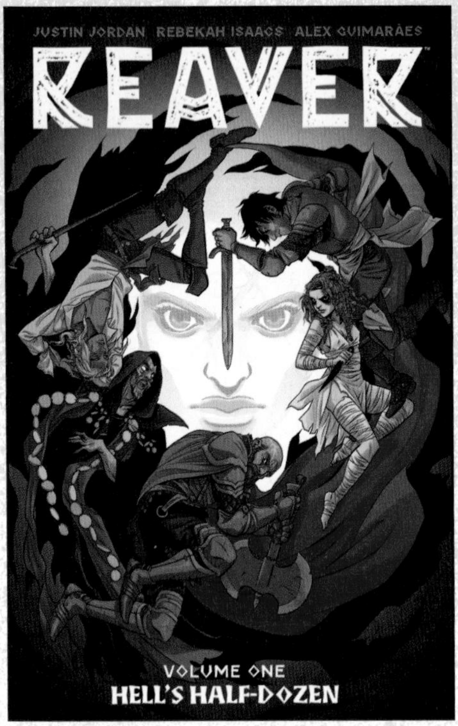

JUSTIN JORDAN REBEKAH ISAACS ALEX GUIMARÃES
REAVER
VOLUME ONE
HELL'S HALF-DOZEN

VOL. 1: HELL'S HALF-DOZEN
ISBN: 978-1-5343-1500-6
$16.99

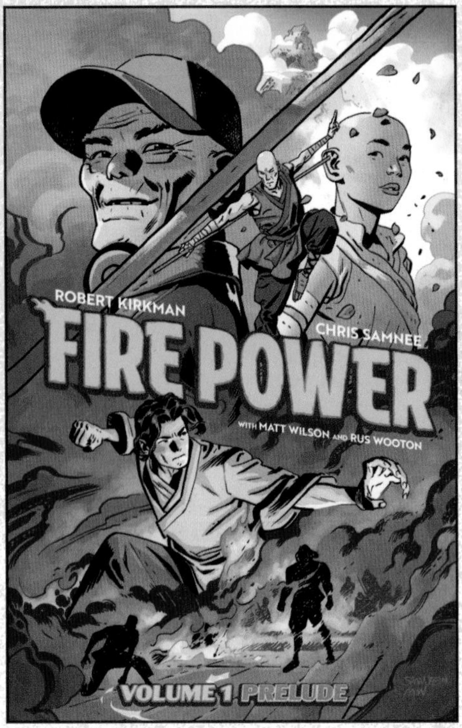

ROBERT KIRKMAN
CHRIS SAMNEE
FIRE POWER
WITH MATT WILSON AND RUS WOOTON
VOLUME 1 PRELUDE

VOL. 1: PRELUDE
ISBN: 978-1-5343-1655-3
$9.99

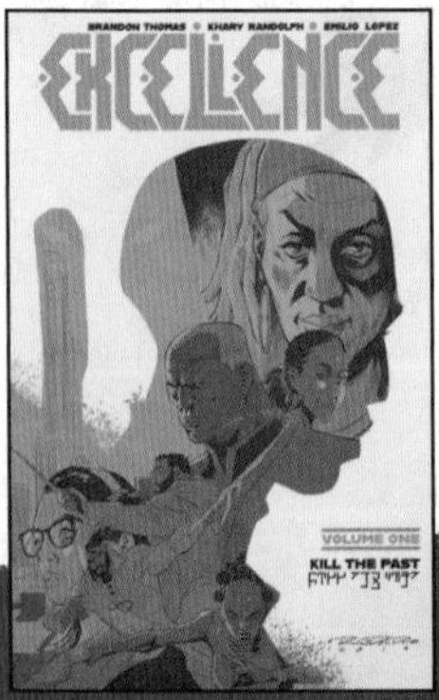

BRANDON THOMAS KHARY RANDOLPH EMILIO LOPEZ
EXCELLENCE
VOLUME ONE
KILL THE PAST

VOL. 1: KILL THE PAST TP
ISBN: 978-1-5343-1362-0
$16.99

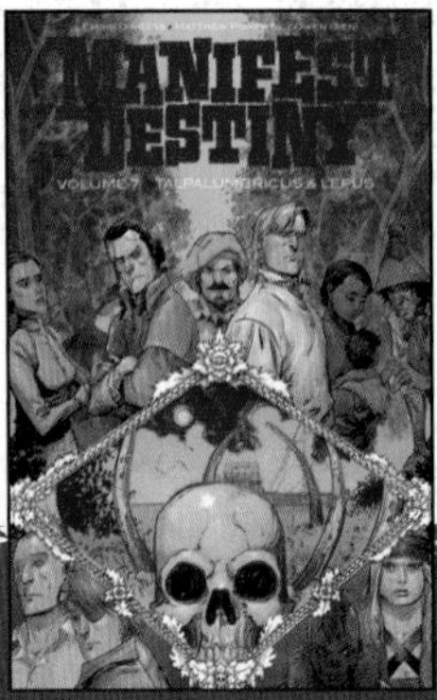

MANIFEST DESTINY

VOL. 1: FLORA & FAUNA TP
ISBN: 978-1-60706-982-9
$9.99

VOL. 2: AMPHIBIA & INSECTA TP
ISBN: 978-1-63215-052-3
$14.99

VOL. 3: CHIROPTERA & CARNIFORMAVES TP
ISBN: 978-1-63215-397-5
$14.99

VOL. 4: SASQUATCH TP
ISBN: 978-1-63215-890-1
$14.99

VOL. 5: MNEMOPHOBIA & CHRONOPHOBIA TP
ISBN: 978-1-5343-0230-3
$16.99

VOL. 6: FORTIS & INVISIBILIA TP
ISBN: 978-1-5343-0513-7
$16.99

VOL. 7: TALPA LUMBRICUS & LEPUS TP
ISBN: 978-1-5343-1589-1
$16.99

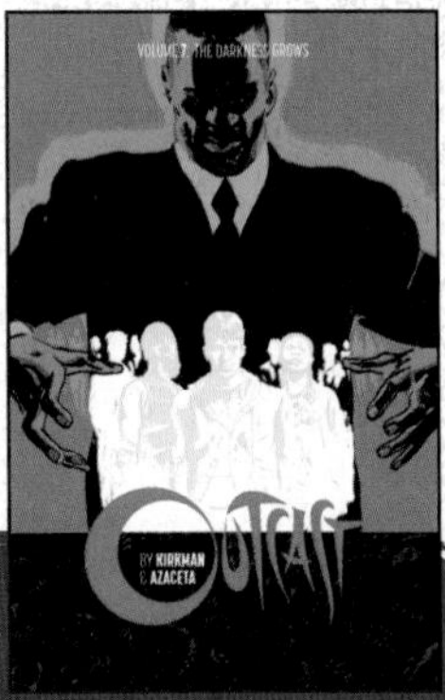

BY KIRKMAN & AZACETA
OUTCAST

VOL. 1: A DARKNESS SURROUNDS HIM TP
ISBN: 978-1-63215-053-0
$9.99

VOL. 2: A VAST AND UNENDING RUIN TP
ISBN: 978-1-63215-448-4
$14.99

VOL. 3: THIS LITTLE LIGHT TP
ISBN: 978-1-63215-693-8
$14.99

VOL. 4: UNDER DEVIL'S WING TP
ISBN: 978-1-5343-0050-7
$14.99

VOL. 5: THE NEW PATH TP
ISBN: 978-1-5343-0249-5
$16.99

VOL. 6: INVASION TP
ISBN: 978-1-5343-0751-3
$16.99

VOL. 7: THE DARKNESS GROWS TP
ISBN: 978-1-5343-1239-5
$16.99

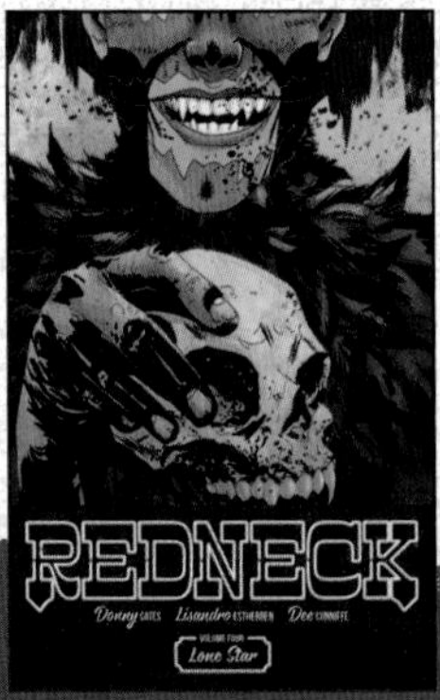

REDNECK
Lone Star

VOL. 1: DEEP IN THE HEART
ISBN: 978-1-5343-0331-7
$16.99

VOL. 2: EYES UPON YOU
ISBN: 978-1-5343-0665-3
$16.99

VOL. 3: LONGHORNS
ISBN: 978-1-5343-1050-6
$16.99

VOL. 4: LONE STAR
ISBN: 978-1-5343-1367-5
$16.99